GIANT DAYS

VOLUME EIGHT

BOOM! BOX™

GIANT DAYS Volume Eight, August 2018. Published by BOOM! Box, a division of Boom Entertainment, Inc. Giant Days is ™ &
© 2018 John Allison. Originally published in single magazine form as GIANT DAYS No. 29-32. ™ & © 2017 John Allison. All rights
reserved. BOOM! Box™ and the BOOM! Box logo are trademarks of Boom Entertainment, Inc., registered in various countries
and categories. All characters, events, and institutions depicted herein are fictional. Any similarity between any of the names,
characters, persons, events, and/or institutions in this publication to actual names, characters, and persons, whether living or dead,
events, and/or institutions is unintended and purely coincidental. BOOM! Box does not read or accept unsolicited submissions of
ideas, stories, or artwork.

For information regarding the CPSIA on this printed material, call: (203) 595-3636 and provide reference #RICH – 785217.

BOOM! Studios, 5670 Wilshire Boulevard, Suite 400, Los Angeles, CA 90036-5679. Printed in USA. First Printing.

ISBN: 978-1-68415-207-0, eISBN: 978-1-64144-022-6

GIANT DAYS

CREATED & WRITTEN BY
JOHN ALLISON

ILLUSTRATED BY
MAX SARIN

INKS BY
LIZ FLEMING

COLORS BY
WHITNEY COGAR

LETTERS BY
JIM CAMPBELL

COVER BY
LISSA TREIMAN

DESIGNER
KARA LEOPARD

ASSISTANT EDITOR
SOPHIE PHILIPS-ROBERTS

EDITOR
SHANNON WATTERS

SPECIAL THANKS TO JASMINE AMIRI

CHAPTER
TWENTY NINE

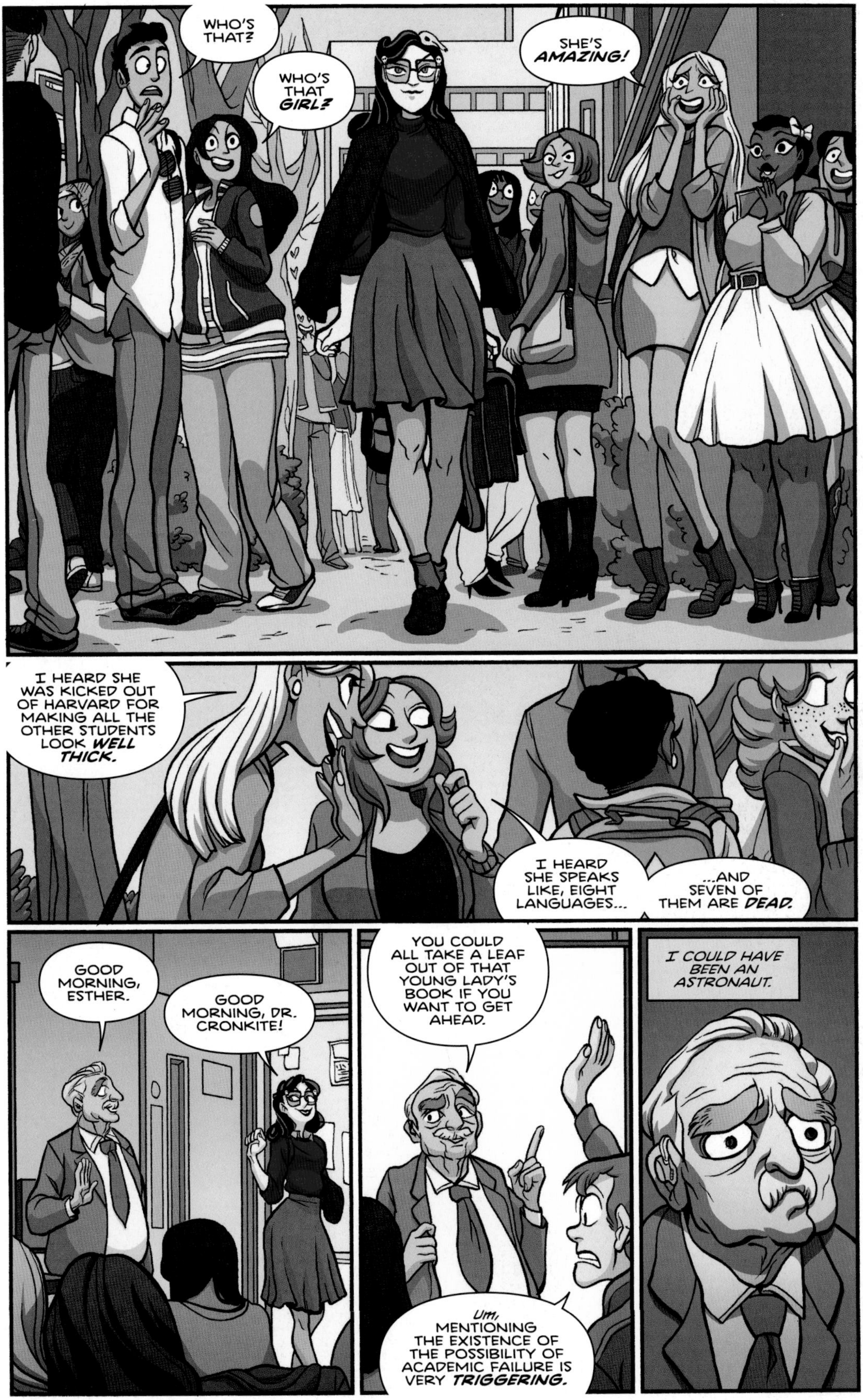
WHO'S THAT?
WHO'S THAT GIRL?
SHE'S AMAZING!
I HEARD SHE WAS KICKED OUT OF HARVARD FOR MAKING ALL THE OTHER STUDENTS LOOK WELL THICK.
I HEARD SHE SPEAKS LIKE, EIGHT LANGUAGES...
...AND SEVEN OF THEM ARE DEAD.
GOOD MORNING, ESTHER.
GOOD MORNING, DR. CRONKITE!
YOU COULD ALL TAKE A LEAF OUT OF THAT YOUNG LADY'S BOOK IF YOU WANT TO GET AHEAD.
Um, MENTIONING THE EXISTENCE OF THE POSSIBILITY OF ACADEMIC FAILURE IS VERY TRIGGERING.
I COULD HAVE BEEN AN ASTRONAUT.

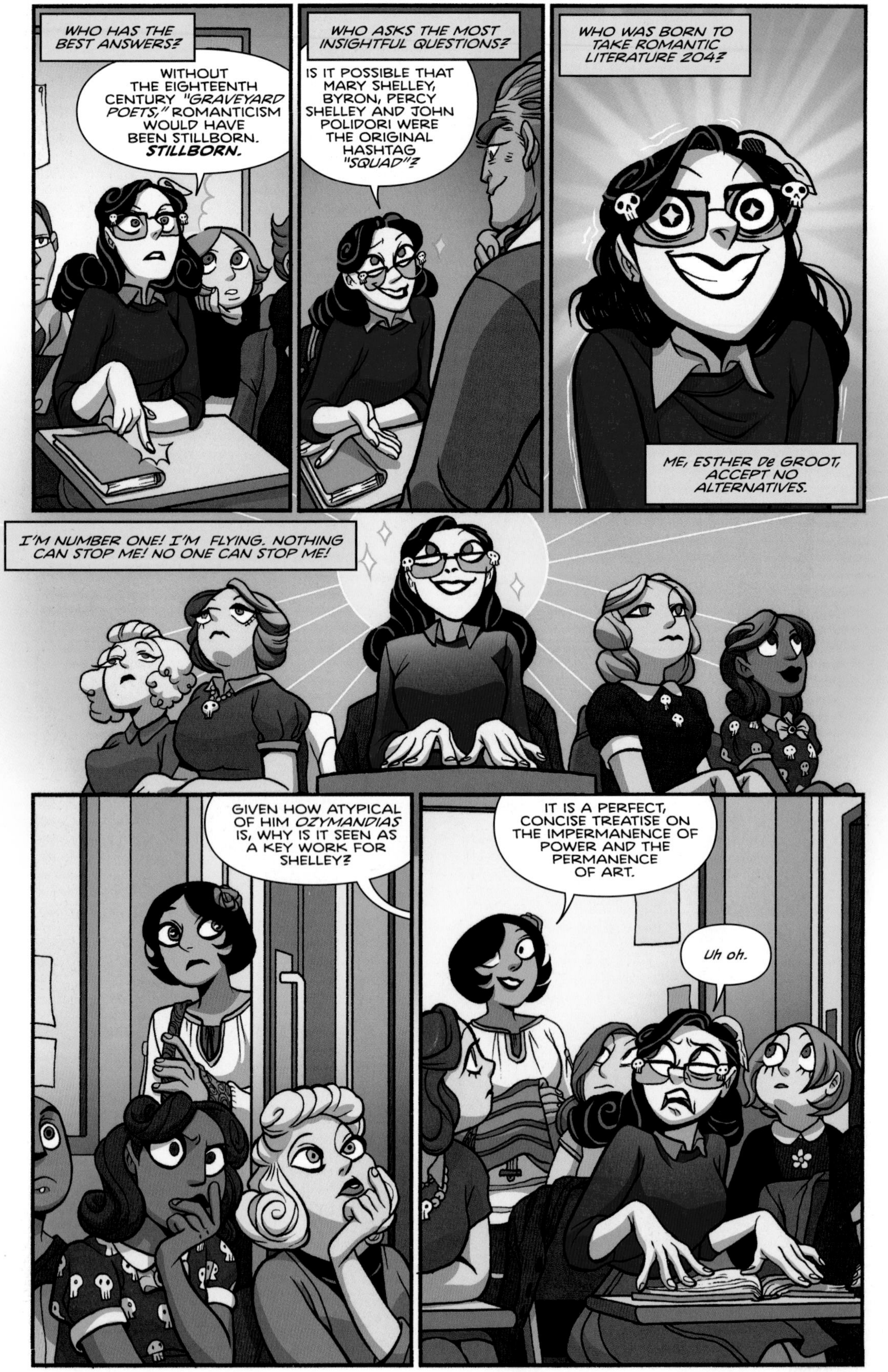

WHO HAS THE BEST ANSWERS?
WITHOUT THE EIGHTEENTH CENTURY "GRAVEYARD POETS," ROMANTICISM WOULD HAVE BEEN STILLBORN. STILLBORN.
WHO ASKS THE MOST INSIGHTFUL QUESTIONS?
IS IT POSSIBLE THAT MARY SHELLEY, BYRON, PERCY SHELLEY AND JOHN POLIDORI WERE THE ORIGINAL HASHTAG "SQUAD"?
WHO WAS BORN TO TAKE ROMANTIC LITERATURE 204?
ME, ESTHER De GROOT, ACCEPT NO ALTERNATIVES.
I'M NUMBER ONE! I'M FLYING. NOTHING CAN STOP ME! NO ONE CAN STOP ME!
GIVEN HOW ATYPICAL OF HIM OZYMANDIAS IS, WHY IS IT SEEN AS A KEY WORK FOR SHELLEY?
IT IS A PERFECT, CONCISE TREATISE ON THE IMPERMANENCE OF POWER AND THE PERMANENCE OF ART.
Uh oh.

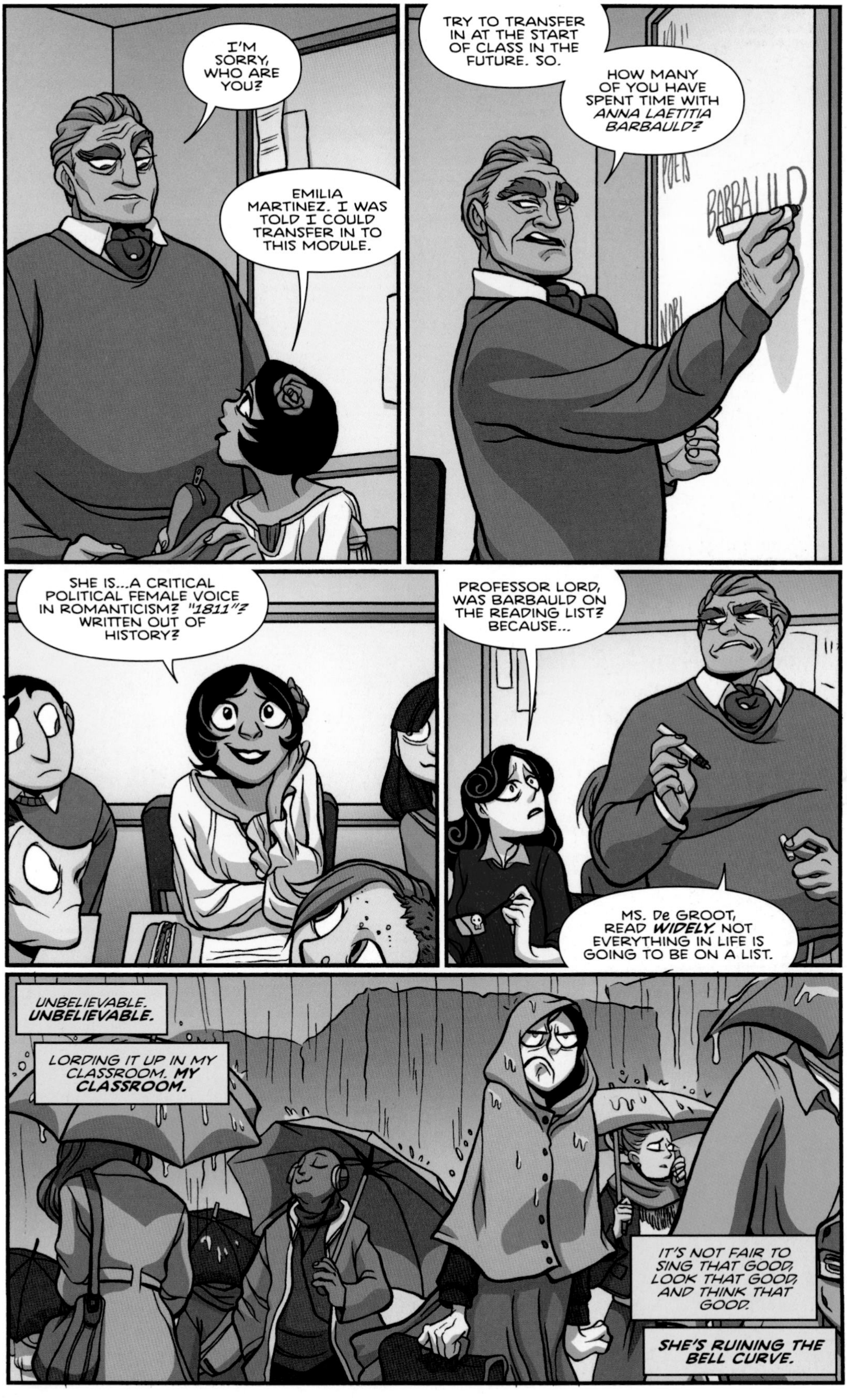
I'M SORRY, WHO ARE YOU?
EMILIA MARTINEZ. I WAS TOLD I COULD TRANSFER IN TO THIS MODULE.
TRY TO TRANSFER IN AT THE START OF CLASS IN THE FUTURE. SO.
HOW MANY OF YOU HAVE SPENT TIME WITH *ANNA LAETITIA BARBAULD?*
BARBAULD
SHE IS...A CRITICAL POLITICAL FEMALE VOICE IN ROMANTICISM? *"1811"?* WRITTEN OUT OF HISTORY?
PROFESSOR LORD, WAS BARBAULD ON THE READING LIST? BECAUSE...
MS. De GROOT, READ ***WIDELY.*** NOT EVERYTHING IN LIFE IS GOING TO BE ON A LIST.
UNBELIEVABLE. ***UNBELIEVABLE.***
LORDING IT UP IN MY CLASSROOM. ***MY CLASSROOM.***
IT'S NOT FAIR TO SING THAT GOOD, LOOK THAT GOOD, AND THINK THAT GOOD.
SHE'S RUINING THE BELL CURVE.

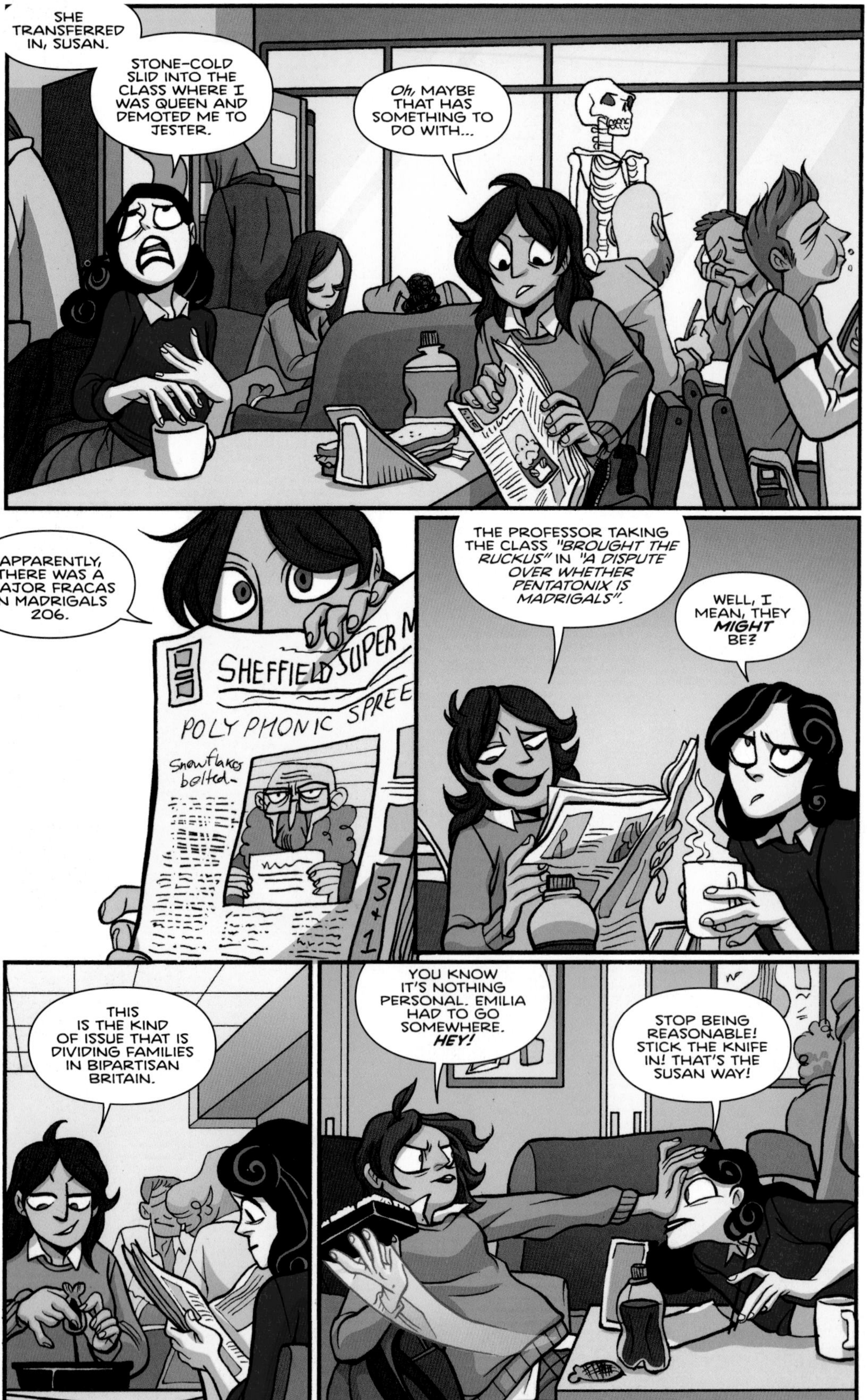
SHE TRANSFERRED IN, SUSAN.
STONE-COLD SLID INTO THE CLASS WHERE I WAS QUEEN AND DEMOTED ME TO JESTER.
Oh, MAYBE THAT HAS SOMETHING TO DO WITH...
APPARENTLY, THERE WAS A MAJOR FRACAS IN MADRIGALS 206.
SHEFFIELD SUPER M
POLYPHONIC SPREE
Snowflakes belted
THE PROFESSOR TAKING THE CLASS *"BROUGHT THE RUCKUS"* IN *"A DISPUTE OVER WHETHER PENTATONIX IS MADRIGALS".*
WELL, I MEAN, THEY ***MIGHT*** BE?
THIS IS THE KIND OF ISSUE THAT IS DIVIDING FAMILIES IN BIPARTISAN BRITAIN.
YOU KNOW IT'S NOTHING PERSONAL. EMILIA HAD TO GO SOMEWHERE. ***HEY!***
STOP BEING REASONABLE! STICK THE KNIFE IN! THAT'S THE SUSAN WAY!

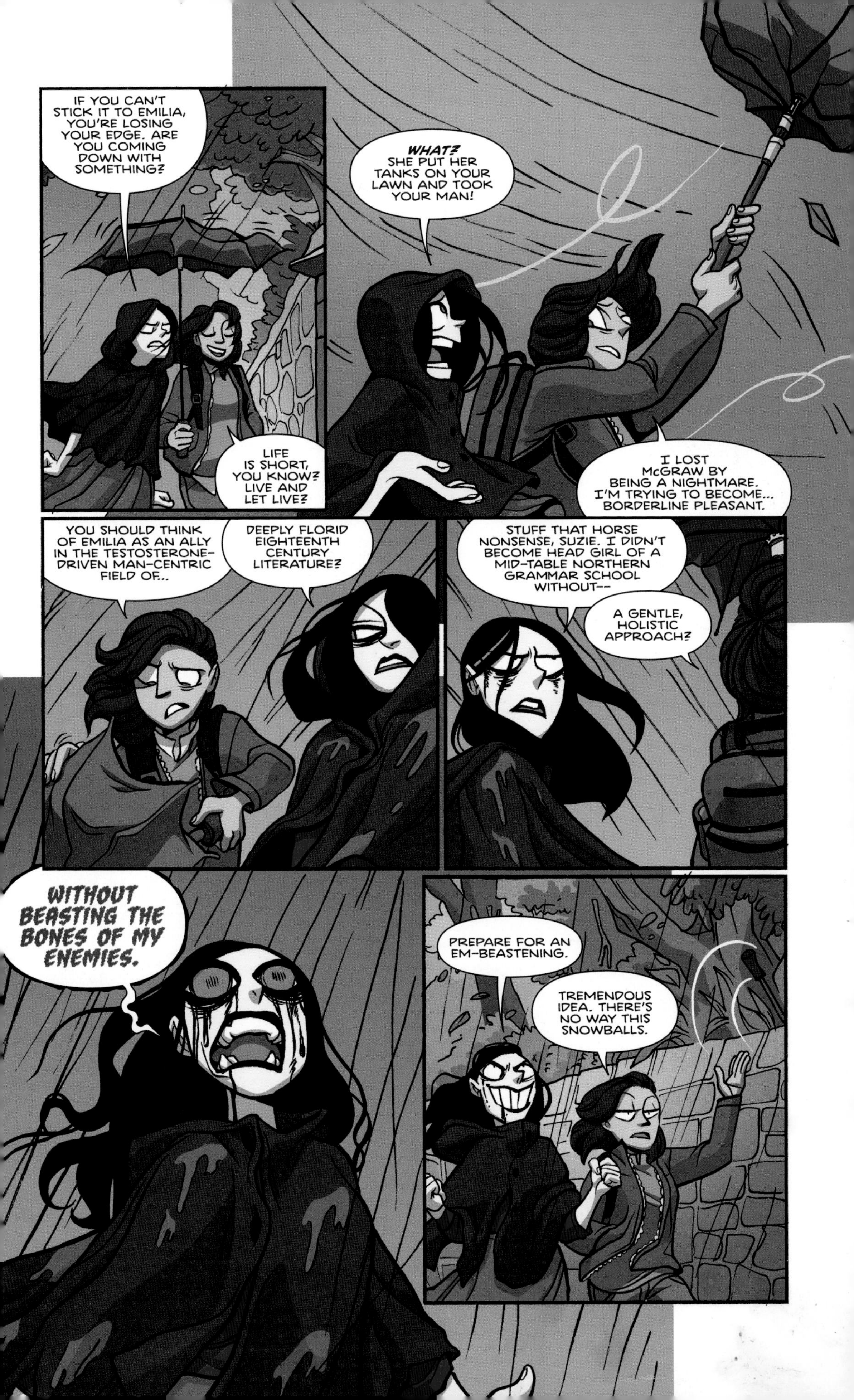
IF YOU CAN'T STICK IT TO EMILIA, YOU'RE LOSING YOUR EDGE. ARE YOU COMING DOWN WITH SOMETHING?
LIFE IS SHORT, YOU KNOW? LIVE AND LET LIVE?
WHAT? SHE PUT HER TANKS ON YOUR LAWN AND TOOK YOUR MAN!
I LOST McGRAW BY BEING A NIGHTMARE. I'M TRYING TO BECOME... BORDERLINE PLEASANT.
YOU SHOULD THINK OF EMILIA AS AN ALLY IN THE TESTOSTERONE-DRIVEN MAN-CENTRIC FIELD OF...
DEEPLY FLORID EIGHTEENTH CENTURY LITERATURE?
STUFF THAT HORSE NONSENSE, SUZIE. I DIDN'T BECOME HEAD GIRL OF A MID-TABLE NORTHERN GRAMMAR SCHOOL WITHOUT--
A GENTLE, HOLISTIC APPROACH?
WITHOUT BEASTING THE BONES OF MY ENEMIES.
PREPARE FOR AN EM-BEASTENING.
TREMENDOUS IDEA. THERE'S NO WAY THIS SNOWBALLS.

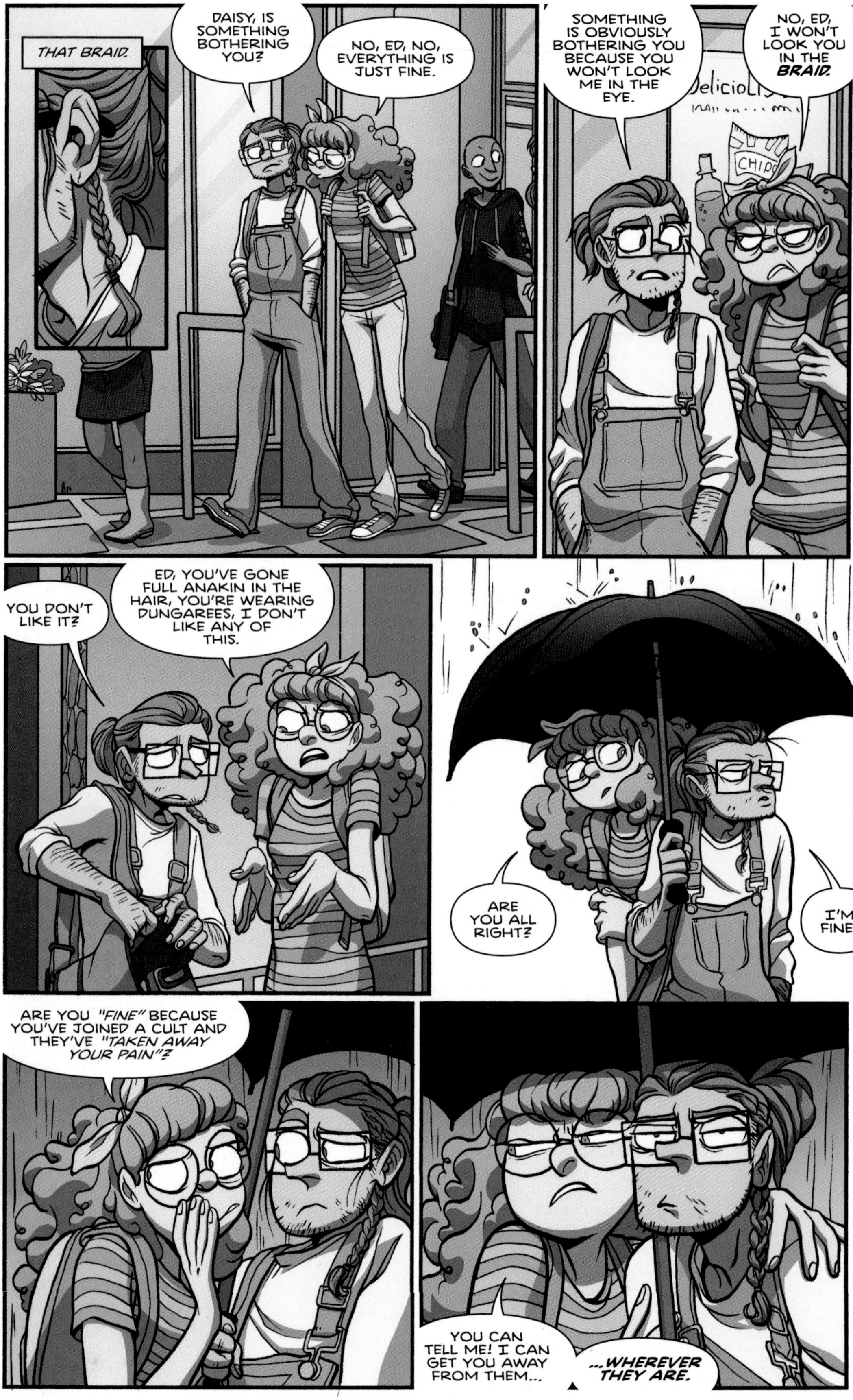
THAT BRAID.
DAISY, IS SOMETHING BOTHERING YOU?
NO, ED, NO, EVERYTHING IS JUST FINE.
SOMETHING IS OBVIOUSLY BOTHERING YOU BECAUSE YOU WON'T LOOK ME IN THE EYE.
NO, ED, I WON'T LOOK YOU IN THE *BRAID.*
CHIPS
YOU DON'T LIKE IT?
ED, YOU'VE GONE FULL ANAKIN IN THE HAIR, YOU'RE WEARING DUNGAREES, I DON'T LIKE ANY OF THIS.
ARE YOU ALL RIGHT?
I'M FINE.
ARE YOU *"FINE"* BECAUSE YOU'VE JOINED A CULT AND THEY'VE *"TAKEN AWAY YOUR PAIN"*?
YOU CAN TELL ME! I CAN GET YOU AWAY FROM THEM...
...WHEREVER THEY ARE.

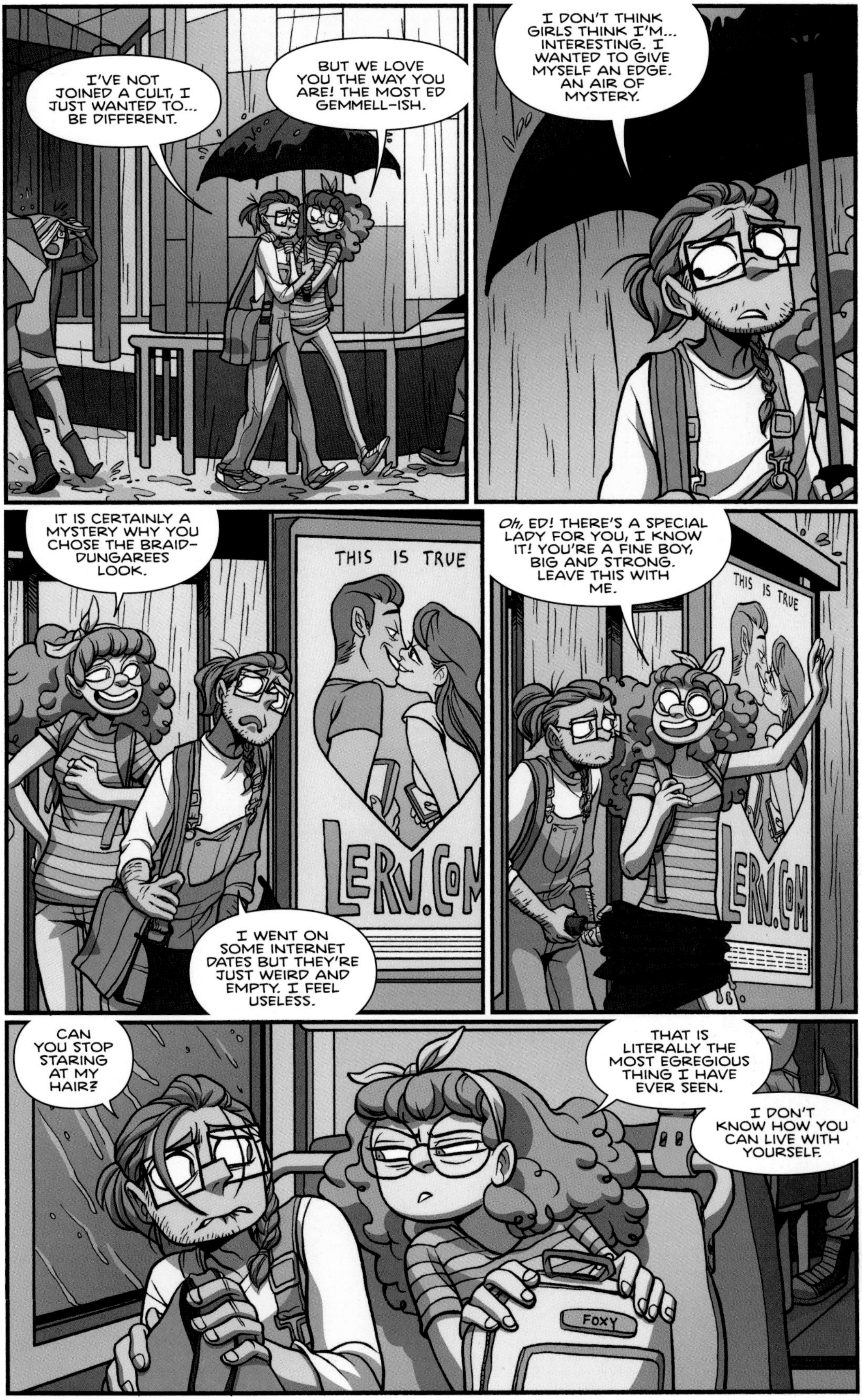
I'VE NOT JOINED A CULT, I JUST WANTED TO... BE DIFFERENT.
BUT WE LOVE YOU THE WAY YOU ARE! THE MOST ED GEMMELL-ISH.
I DON'T THINK GIRLS THINK I'M... INTERESTING. I WANTED TO GIVE MYSELF AN EDGE. AN AIR OF MYSTERY.
IT IS CERTAINLY A MYSTERY WHY YOU CHOSE THE BRAID-DUNGAREES LOOK.
THIS IS TRUE
LERV.COM
I WENT ON SOME INTERNET DATES BUT THEY'RE JUST WEIRD AND EMPTY. I FEEL USELESS.
Oh, ED! THERE'S A SPECIAL LADY FOR YOU, I KNOW IT! YOU'RE A FINE BOY, BIG AND STRONG. LEAVE THIS WITH ME.
THIS IS TRUE
LERV.COM
CAN YOU STOP STARING AT MY HAIR?
THAT IS LITERALLY THE MOST EGREGIOUS THING I HAVE EVER SEEN.
I DON'T KNOW HOW YOU CAN LIVE WITH YOURSELF.
FOXY

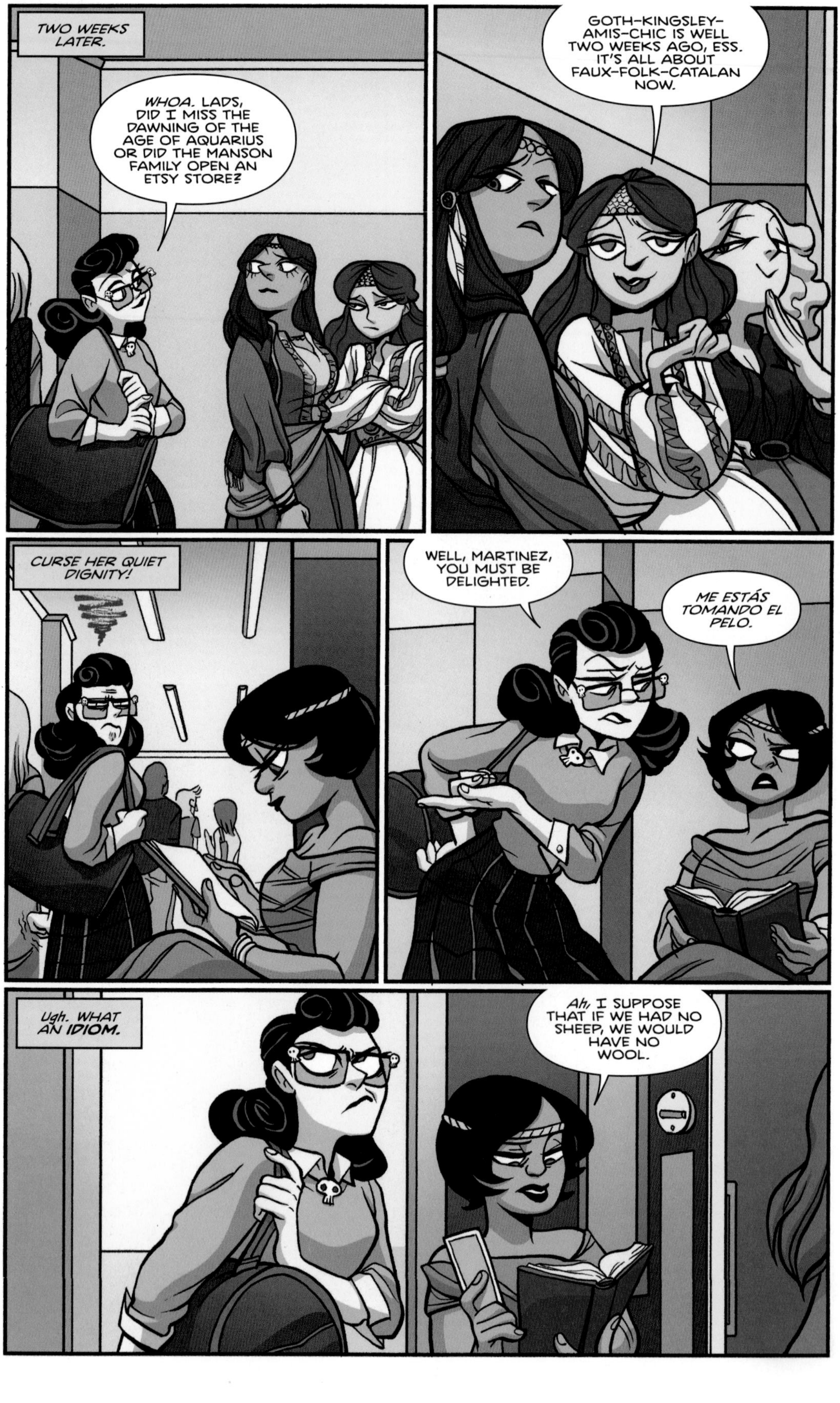
TWO WEEKS LATER.
WHOA. LADS, DID I MISS THE DAWNING OF THE AGE OF AQUARIUS OR DID THE MANSON FAMILY OPEN AN ETSY STORE?
GOTH-KINGSLEY-AMIS-CHIC IS WELL TWO WEEKS AGO, ESS. IT'S ALL ABOUT FAUX-FOLK-CATALAN NOW.
CURSE HER QUIET DIGNITY!
WELL, MARTINEZ, YOU MUST BE DELIGHTED.
ME ESTÁS TOMANDO EL PELO.
Ugh. WHAT AN IDIOM.
Ah, I SUPPOSE THAT IF WE HAD NO SHEEP, WE WOULD HAVE NO WOOL.

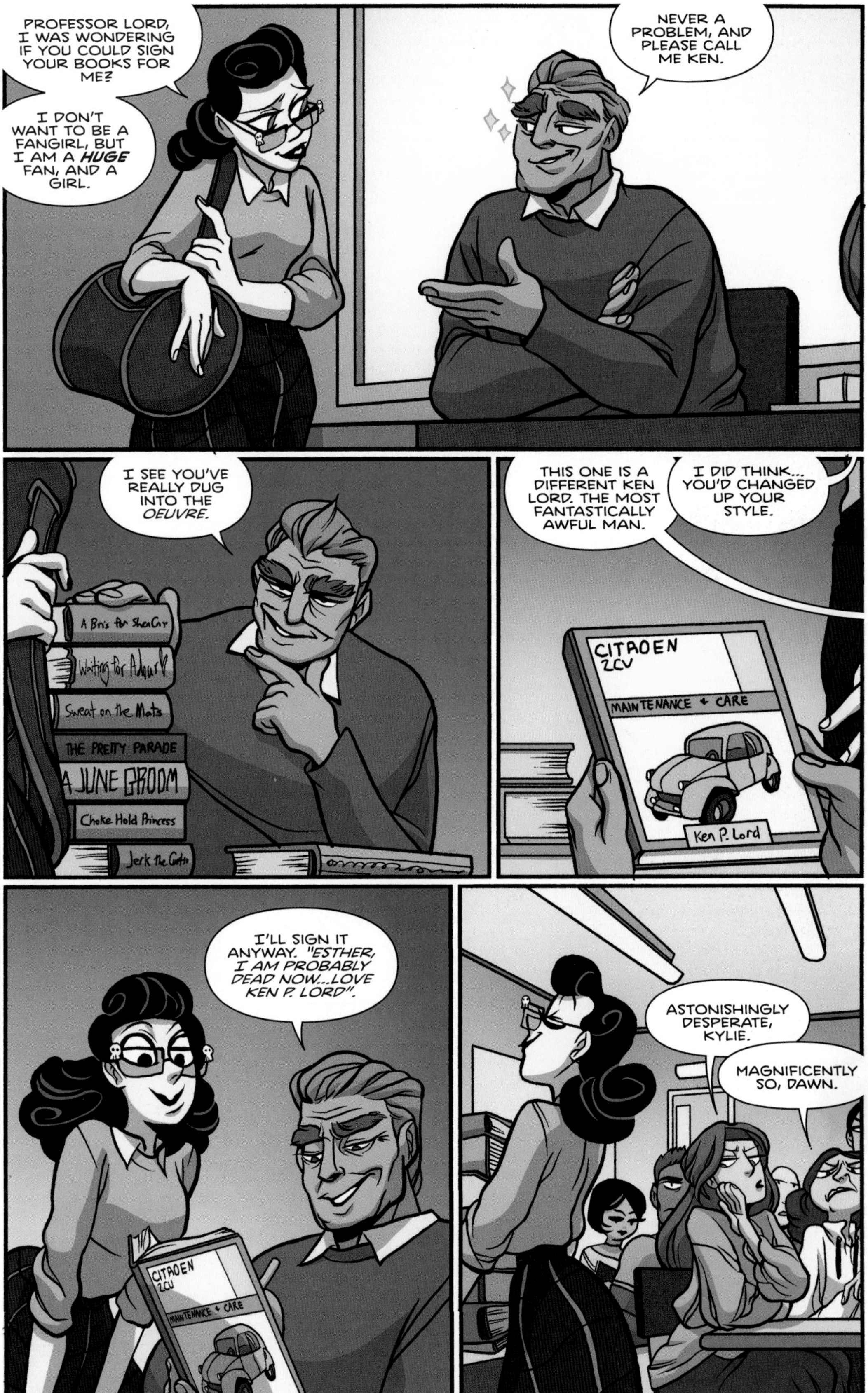
PROFESSOR LORD, I WAS WONDERING IF YOU COULD SIGN YOUR BOOKS FOR ME?
I DON'T WANT TO BE A FANGIRL, BUT I AM A ***HUGE*** FAN, AND A GIRL.
NEVER A PROBLEM, AND PLEASE CALL ME KEN.
I SEE YOU'VE REALLY DUG INTO THE *OEUVRE.*
A Bris for Shea Cur
Waiting for Adaur
Sweat on the Mats
THE PRETTY PARADE
A JUNE GROOM
Choke Hold Princess
Jerk the Gutn
THIS ONE IS A DIFFERENT KEN LORD. THE MOST FANTASTICALLY AWFUL MAN.
I DID THINK... YOU'D CHANGED UP YOUR STYLE.
CITROEN 2CV
MAINTENANCE + CARE
Ken P. Lord
I'LL SIGN IT ANYWAY. *"ESTHER, I AM PROBABLY DEAD NOW...LOVE KEN P. LORD".*
CITROEN 2CV
MAINTENANCE + CARE
ASTONISHINGLY DESPERATE, KYLIE.
MAGNIFICENTLY SO, DAWN.

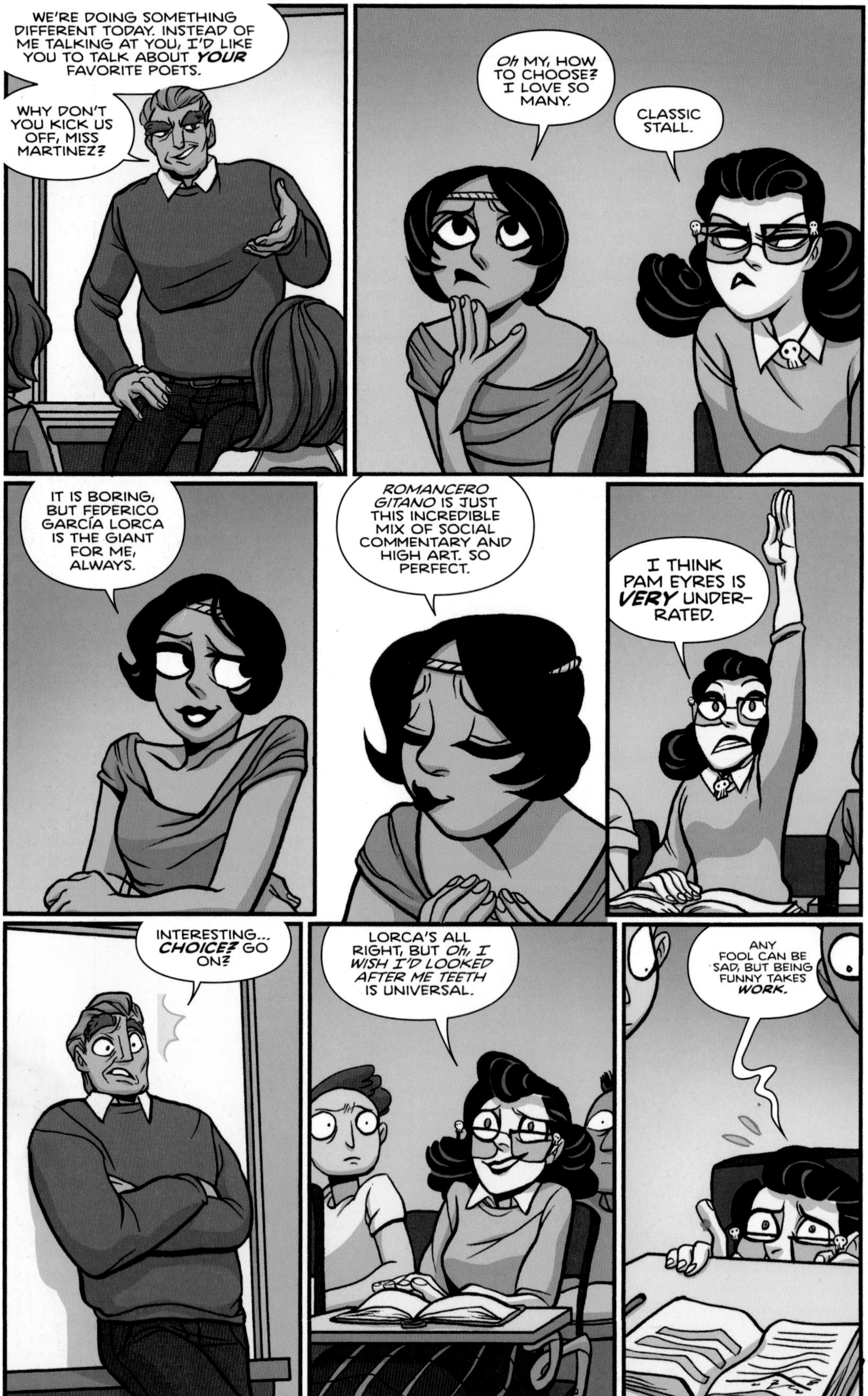
WE'RE DOING SOMETHING DIFFERENT TODAY. INSTEAD OF ME TALKING AT YOU, I'D LIKE YOU TO TALK ABOUT ***YOUR*** FAVORITE POETS.
WHY DON'T YOU KICK US OFF, MISS MARTINEZ?
Oh MY, HOW TO CHOOSE? I LOVE SO MANY.
CLASSIC STALL.
IT IS BORING, BUT FEDERICO GARCÍA LORCA IS THE GIANT FOR ME, ALWAYS.
ROMANCERO GITANO IS JUST THIS INCREDIBLE MIX OF SOCIAL COMMENTARY AND HIGH ART. SO PERFECT.
I THINK PAM EYRES IS ***VERY*** UNDER-RATED.
INTERESTING... ***CHOICE?*** GO ON?
LORCA'S ALL RIGHT, BUT *Oh, I WISH I'D LOOKED AFTER ME TEETH* IS UNIVERSAL.
ANY FOOL CAN BE SAD, BUT BEING FUNNY TAKES ***WORK.***

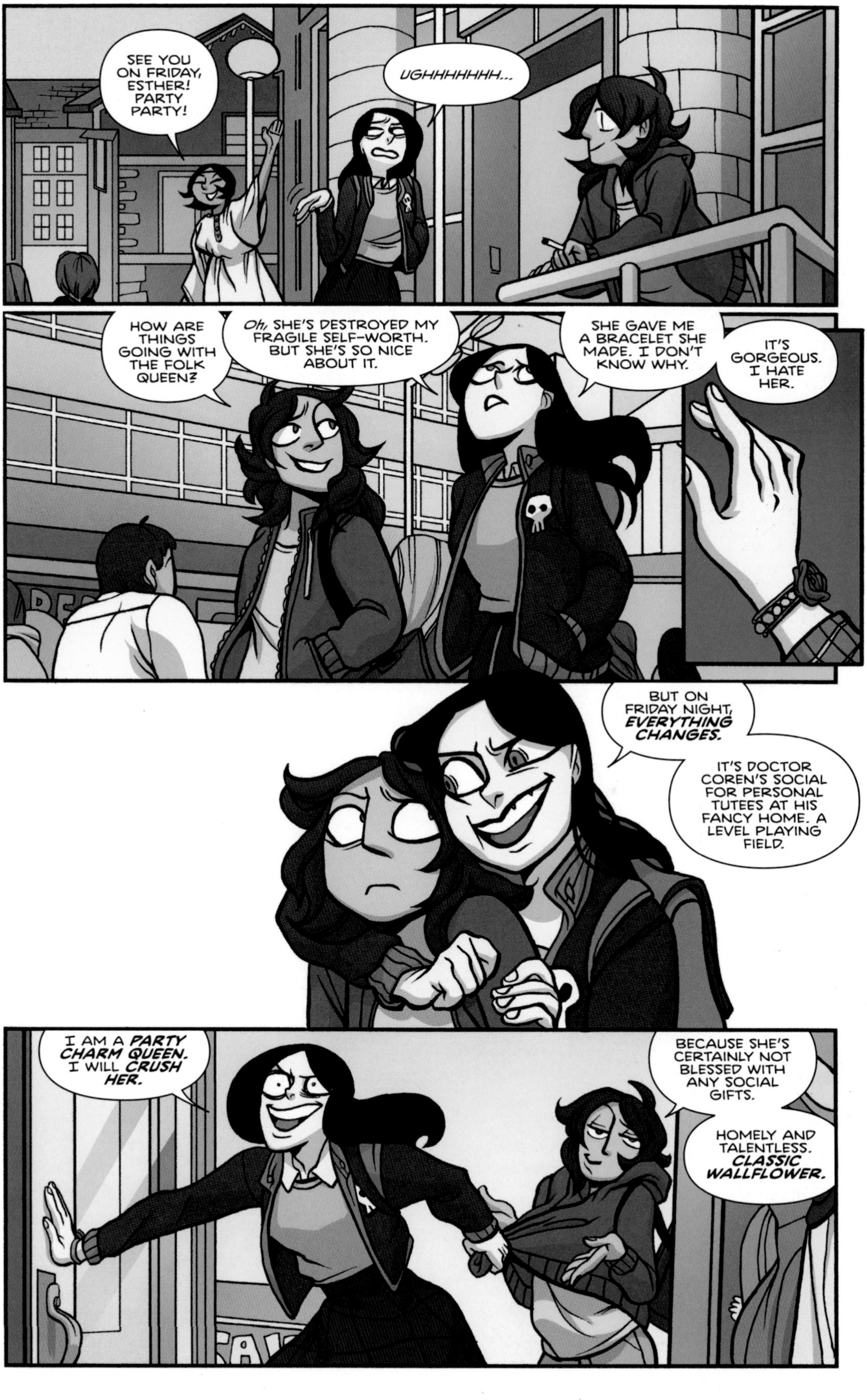
SEE YOU ON FRIDAY, ESTHER! PARTY PARTY!
UGHHHHHHH...
HOW ARE THINGS GOING WITH THE FOLK QUEEN?
Oh, SHE'S DESTROYED MY FRAGILE SELF-WORTH. BUT SHE'S SO NICE ABOUT IT.
SHE GAVE ME A BRACELET SHE MADE. I DON'T KNOW WHY.
IT'S GORGEOUS. I HATE HER.
BUT ON FRIDAY NIGHT, EVERYTHING CHANGES.
IT'S DOCTOR COREN'S SOCIAL FOR PERSONAL TUTEES AT HIS FANCY HOME. A LEVEL PLAYING FIELD.
I AM A PARTY CHARM QUEEN. I WILL CRUSH HER.
BECAUSE SHE'S CERTAINLY NOT BLESSED WITH ANY SOCIAL GIFTS.
HOMELY AND TALENTLESS. CLASSIC WALLFLOWER.

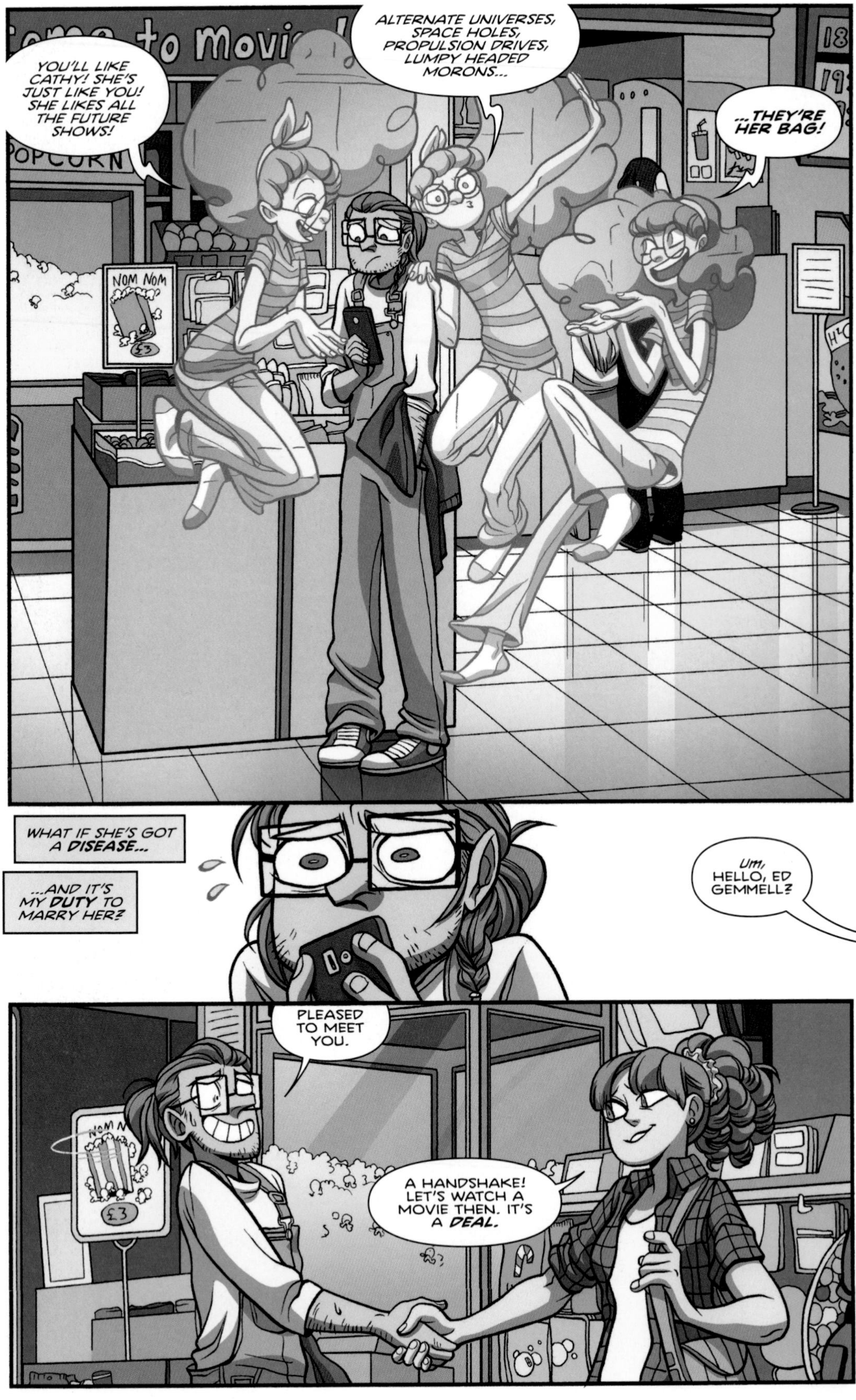
Come to Movie
POPCORN
NOM NOM
£3
YOU'LL LIKE CATHY! SHE'S JUST LIKE YOU! SHE LIKES ALL THE FUTURE SHOWS!
ALTERNATE UNIVERSES, SPACE HOLES, PROPULSION DRIVES, LUMPY HEADED MORONS...
...THEY'RE HER BAG!
WHAT IF SHE'S GOT A DISEASE...
...AND IT'S MY DUTY TO MARRY HER?
UM, HELLO, ED GEMMELL?
PLEASED TO MEET YOU.
A HANDSHAKE! LET'S WATCH A MOVIE THEN. IT'S A DEAL.
£3

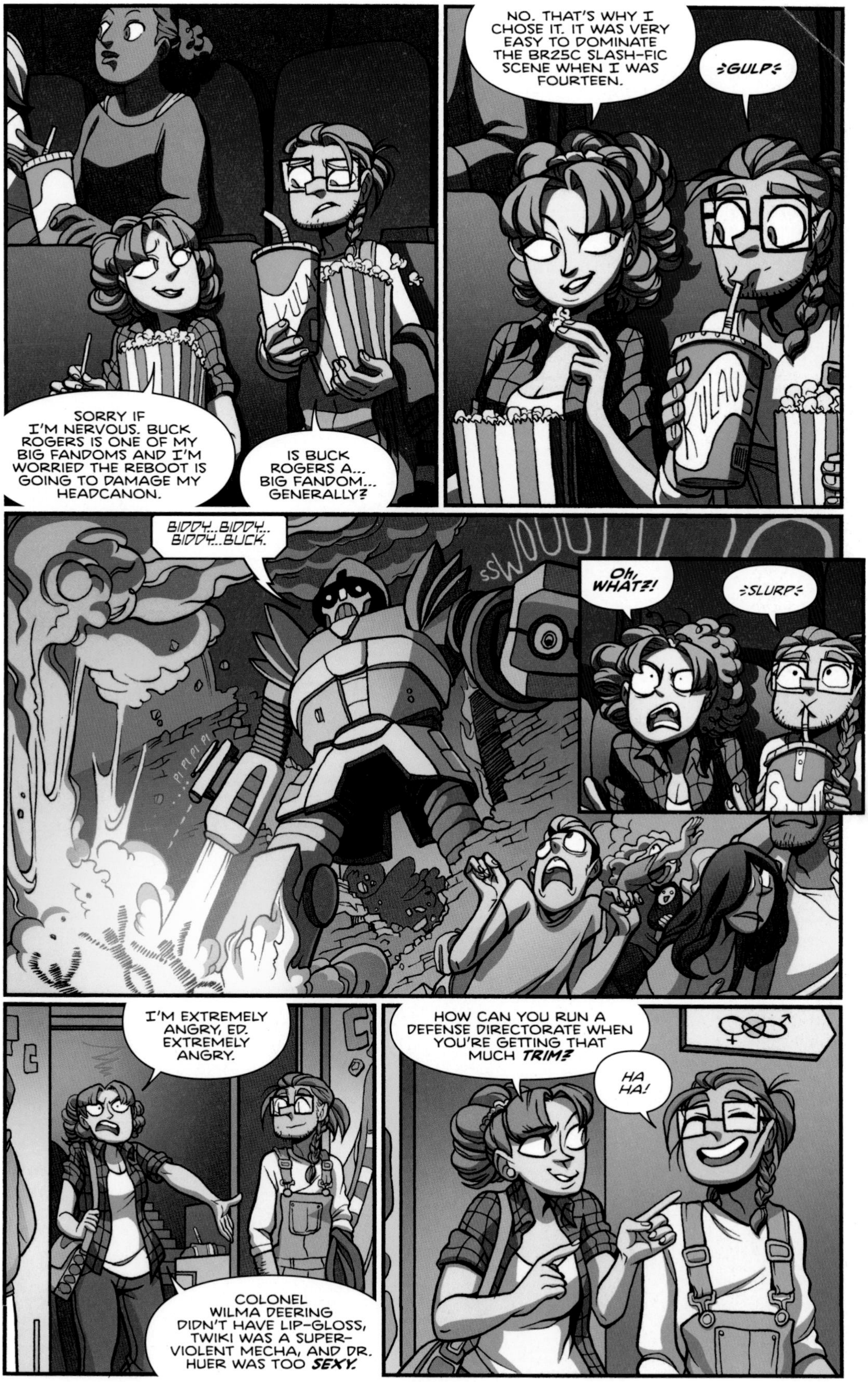

SORRY IF I'M NERVOUS. BUCK ROGERS IS ONE OF MY BIG FANDOMS AND I'M WORRIED THE REBOOT IS GOING TO DAMAGE MY HEADCANON.
IS BUCK ROGERS A... BIG FANDOM... GENERALLY?
NO. THAT'S WHY I CHOSE IT. IT WAS VERY EASY TO DOMINATE THE BR25C SLASH-FIC SCENE WHEN I WAS FOURTEEN.
GULP
BIDDY...BIDDY... BIDDY...BUCK.
Oh, WHAT?!
SLURP
I'M EXTREMELY ANGRY, ED. EXTREMELY ANGRY.
COLONEL WILMA DEERING DIDN'T HAVE LIP-GLOSS, TWIKI WAS A SUPER-VIOLENT MECHA, AND DR. HUER WAS TOO SEXY.
HOW CAN YOU RUN A DEFENSE DIRECTORATE WHEN YOU'RE GETTING THAT MUCH TRIM?
HA HA!

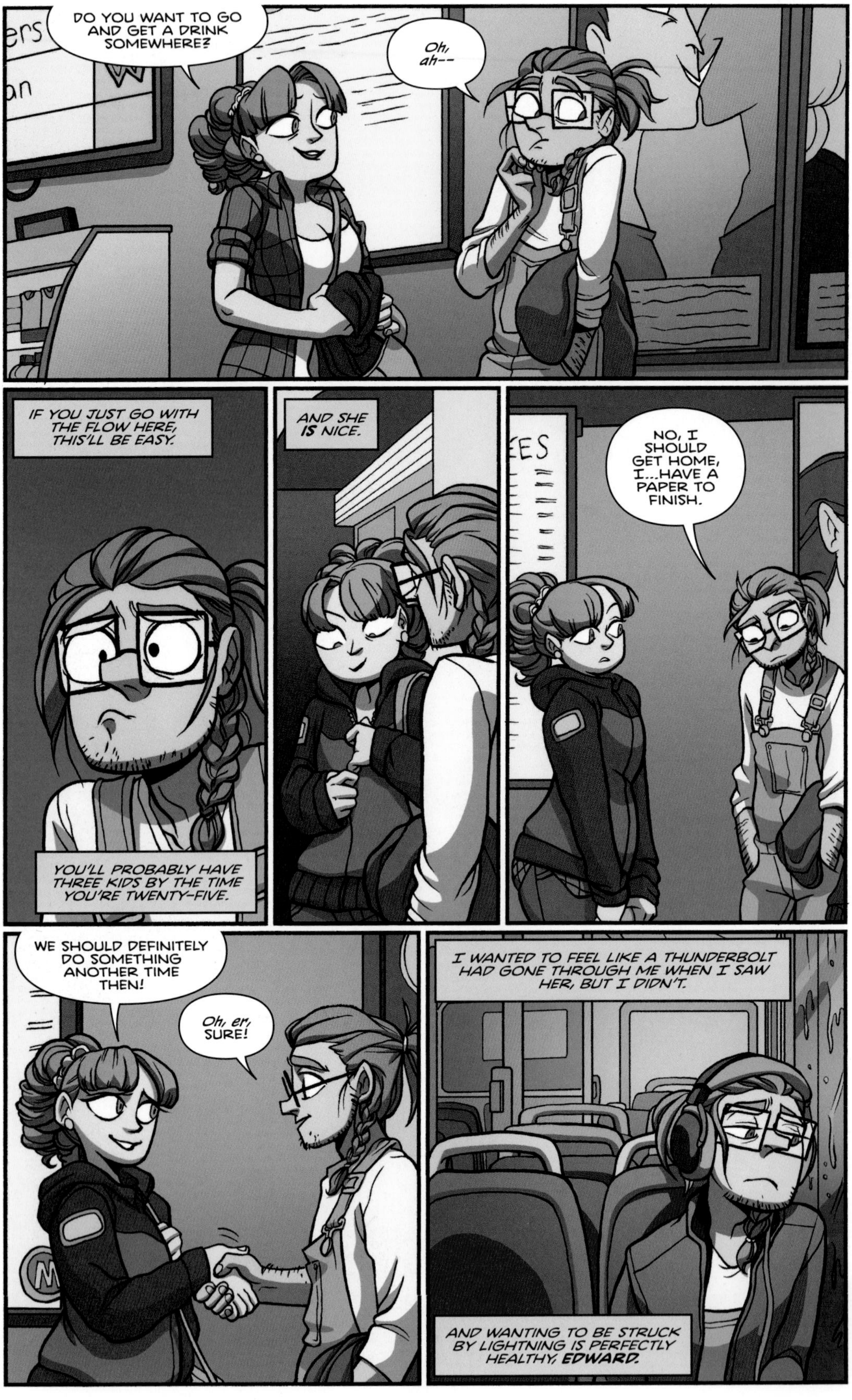
DO YOU WANT TO GO AND GET A DRINK SOMEWHERE?
Oh, ah--
IF YOU JUST GO WITH THE FLOW HERE, THIS'LL BE EASY.
YOU'LL PROBABLY HAVE THREE KIDS BY THE TIME YOU'RE TWENTY-FIVE.
AND SHE IS NICE.
NO, I SHOULD GET HOME, I...HAVE A PAPER TO FINISH.
WE SHOULD DEFINITELY DO SOMETHING ANOTHER TIME THEN!
Oh, er, SURE!
I WANTED TO FEEL LIKE A THUNDERBOLT HAD GONE THROUGH ME WHEN I SAW HER, BUT I DIDN'T.
AND WANTING TO BE STRUCK BY LIGHTNING IS PERFECTLY HEALTHY, EDWARD.

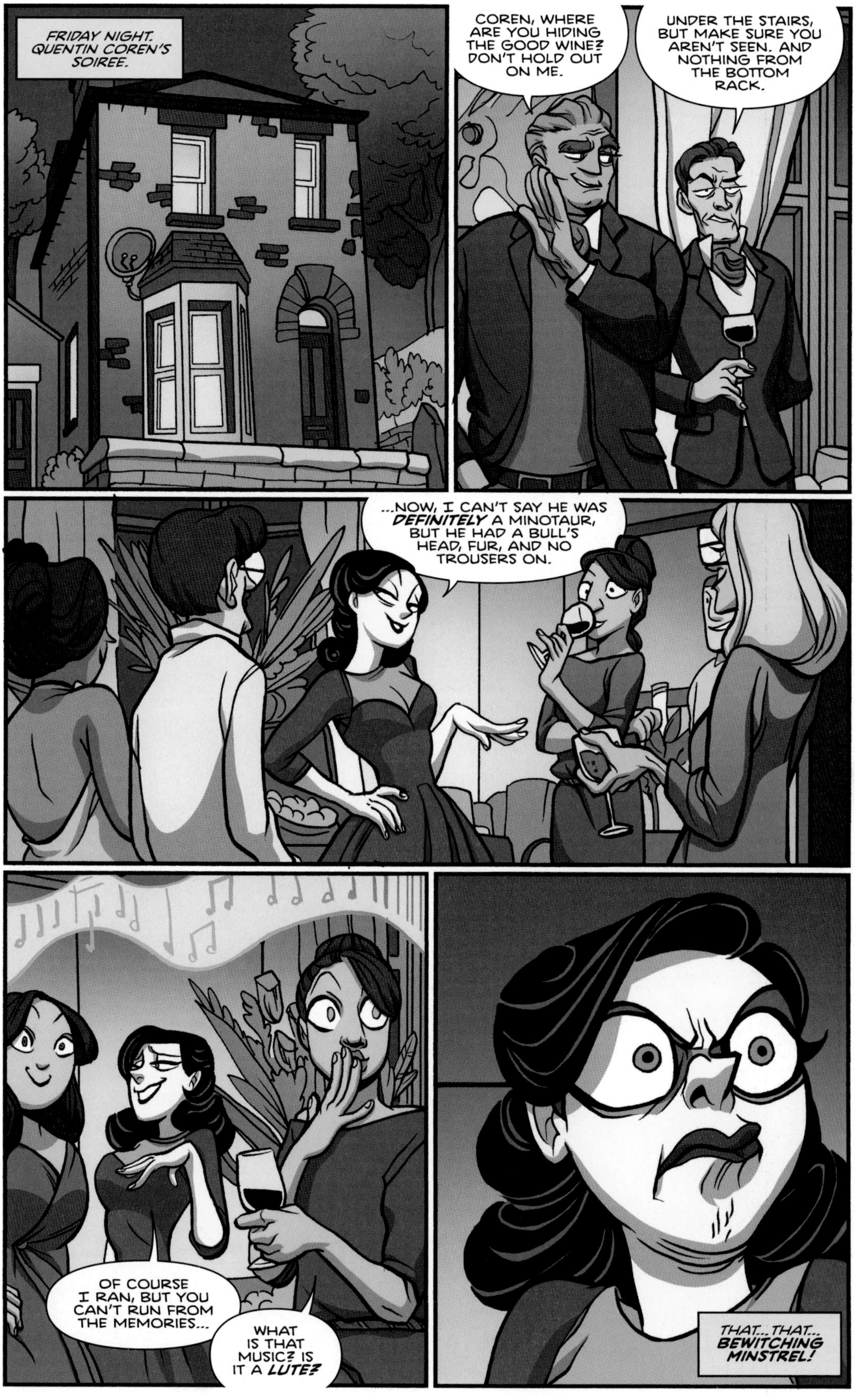
FRIDAY NIGHT. QUENTIN COREN'S SOIREE.
COREN, WHERE ARE YOU HIDING THE GOOD WINE? DON'T HOLD OUT ON ME.
UNDER THE STAIRS, BUT MAKE SURE YOU AREN'T SEEN. AND NOTHING FROM THE BOTTOM RACK.
...NOW, I CAN'T SAY HE WAS DEFINITELY A MINOTAUR, BUT HE HAD A BULL'S HEAD, FUR, AND NO TROUSERS ON.
OF COURSE I RAN, BUT YOU CAN'T RUN FROM THE MEMORIES...
WHAT IS THAT MUSIC? IS IT A LUTE?
THAT... THAT... BEWITCHING MINSTREL!

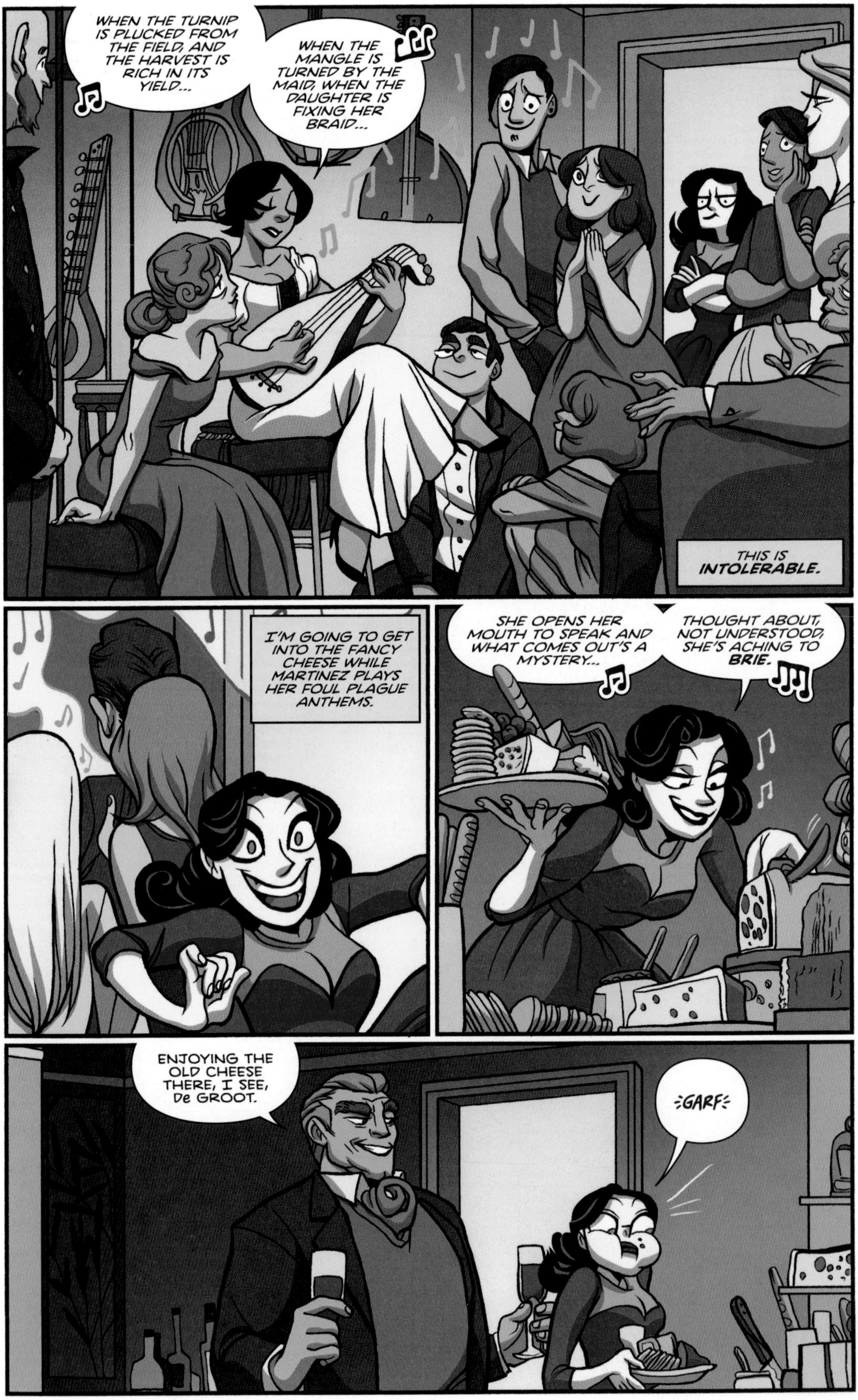
WHEN THE TURNIP IS PLUCKED FROM THE FIELD, AND THE HARVEST IS RICH IN ITS YIELD...
WHEN THE MANGLE IS TURNED BY THE MAID, WHEN THE DAUGHTER IS FIXING HER BRAID...
THIS IS INTOLERABLE.
I'M GOING TO GET INTO THE FANCY CHEESE WHILE MARTINEZ PLAYS HER FOUL PLAGUE ANTHEMS.
SHE OPENS HER MOUTH TO SPEAK AND WHAT COMES OUT'S A MYSTERY...
THOUGHT ABOUT, NOT UNDERSTOOD, SHE'S ACHING TO BRIE.
ENJOYING THE OLD CHEESE THERE, I SEE, De GROOT.
GARF

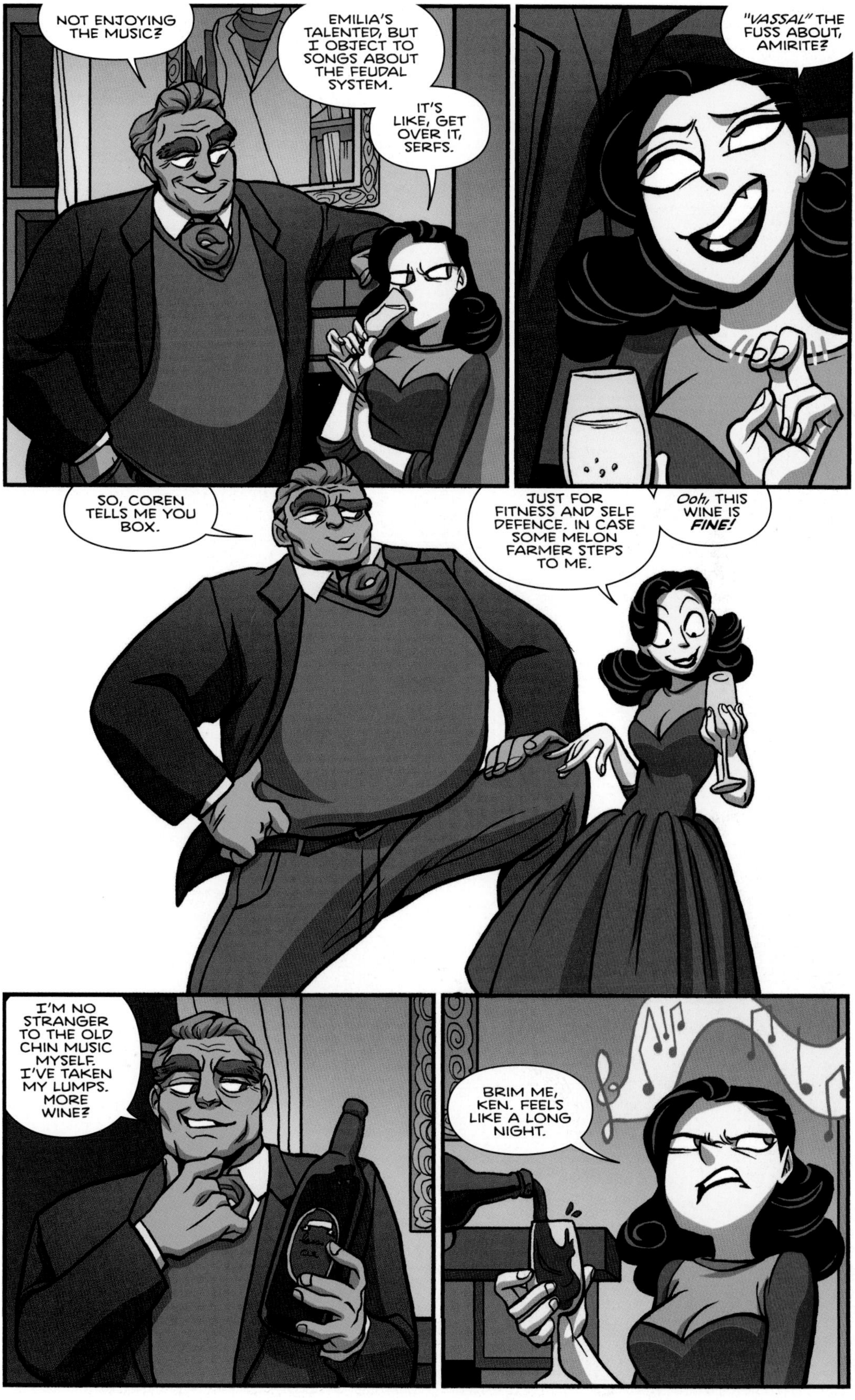
NOT ENJOYING THE MUSIC?
EMILIA'S TALENTED, BUT I OBJECT TO SONGS ABOUT THE FEUDAL SYSTEM.
IT'S LIKE, GET OVER IT, SERFS.
"VASSAL" THE FUSS ABOUT, AMIRITE?
SO, COREN TELLS ME YOU BOX.
JUST FOR FITNESS AND SELF DEFENCE. IN CASE SOME MELON FARMER STEPS TO ME.
Ooh, THIS WINE IS FINE!
I'M NO STRANGER TO THE OLD CHIN MUSIC MYSELF. I'VE TAKEN MY LUMPS. MORE WINE?
BRIM ME, KEN. FEELS LIKE A LONG NIGHT.

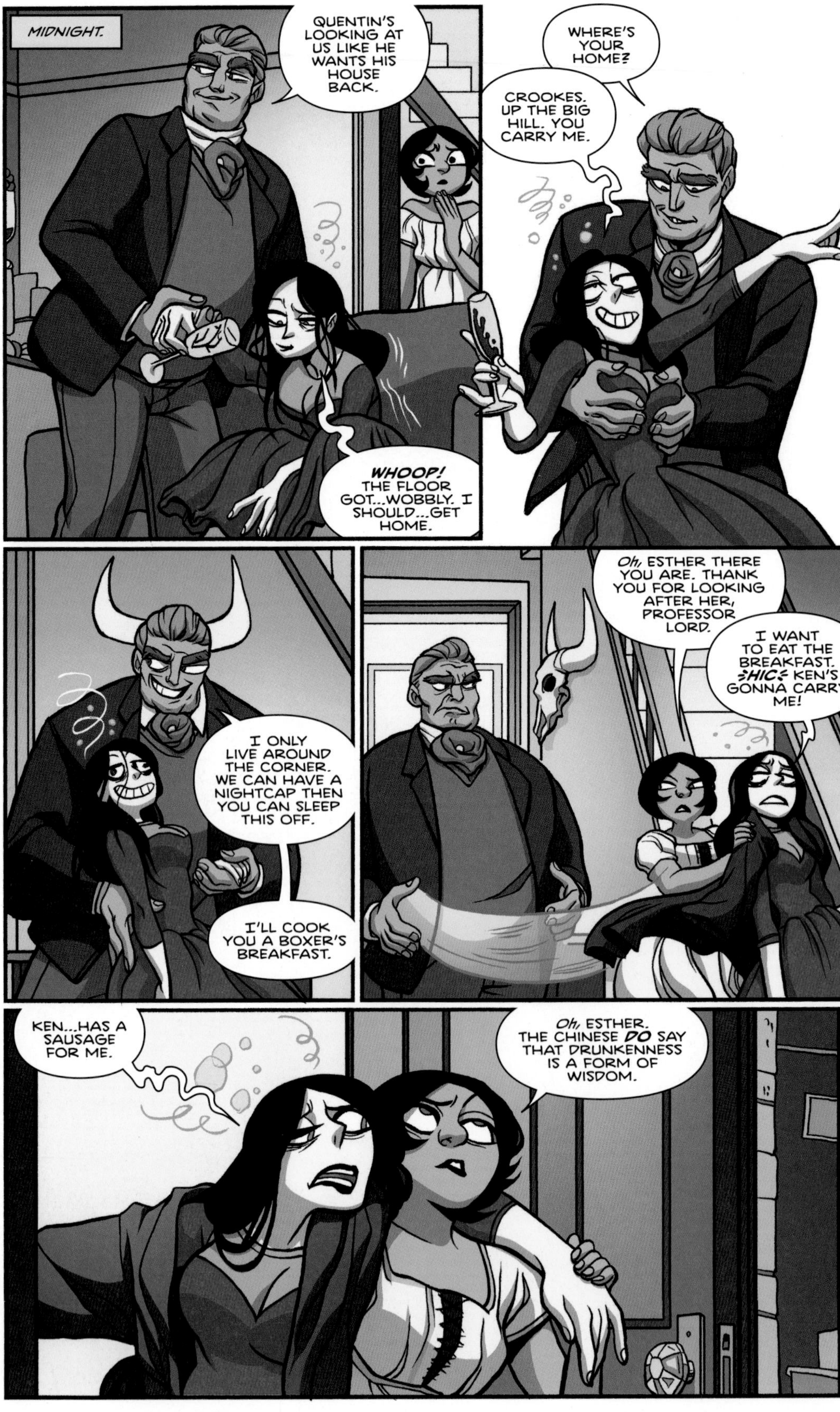
MIDNIGHT.
QUENTIN'S LOOKING AT US LIKE HE WANTS HIS HOUSE BACK.
WHOOP! THE FLOOR GOT...WOBBLY. I SHOULD...GET HOME.
WHERE'S YOUR HOME?
CROOKES. UP THE BIG HILL. YOU CARRY ME.
I ONLY LIVE AROUND THE CORNER. WE CAN HAVE A NIGHTCAP THEN YOU CAN SLEEP THIS OFF.
I'LL COOK YOU A BOXER'S BREAKFAST.
Oh, ESTHER THERE YOU ARE. THANK YOU FOR LOOKING AFTER HER, PROFESSOR LORD.
I WANT TO EAT THE BREAKFAST. *HIC* KEN'S GONNA CARRY ME!
KEN...HAS A SAUSAGE FOR ME.
Oh, ESTHER. THE CHINESE ***DO*** SAY THAT DRUNKENNESS IS A FORM OF WISDOM.

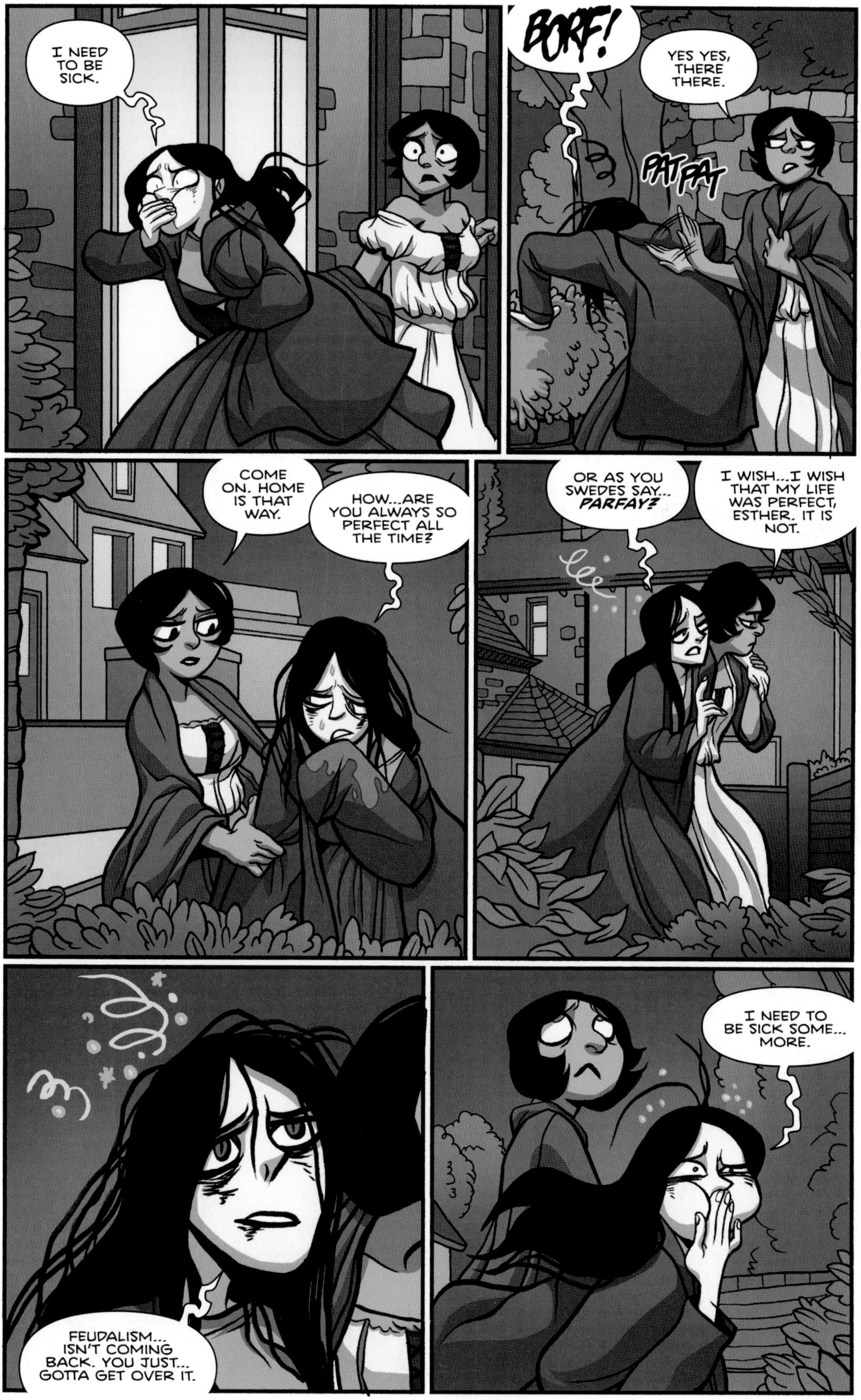
I NEED TO BE SICK.
BORF!
YES YES, THERE THERE.
PAT PAT
COME ON. HOME IS THAT WAY.
HOW...ARE YOU ALWAYS SO PERFECT ALL THE TIME?
OR AS YOU SWEDES SAY... PARFAY?
I WISH...I WISH THAT MY LIFE WAS PERFECT, ESTHER. IT IS NOT.
FEUDALISM... ISN'T COMING BACK. YOU JUST... GOTTA GET OVER IT.
I NEED TO BE SICK SOME... MORE.

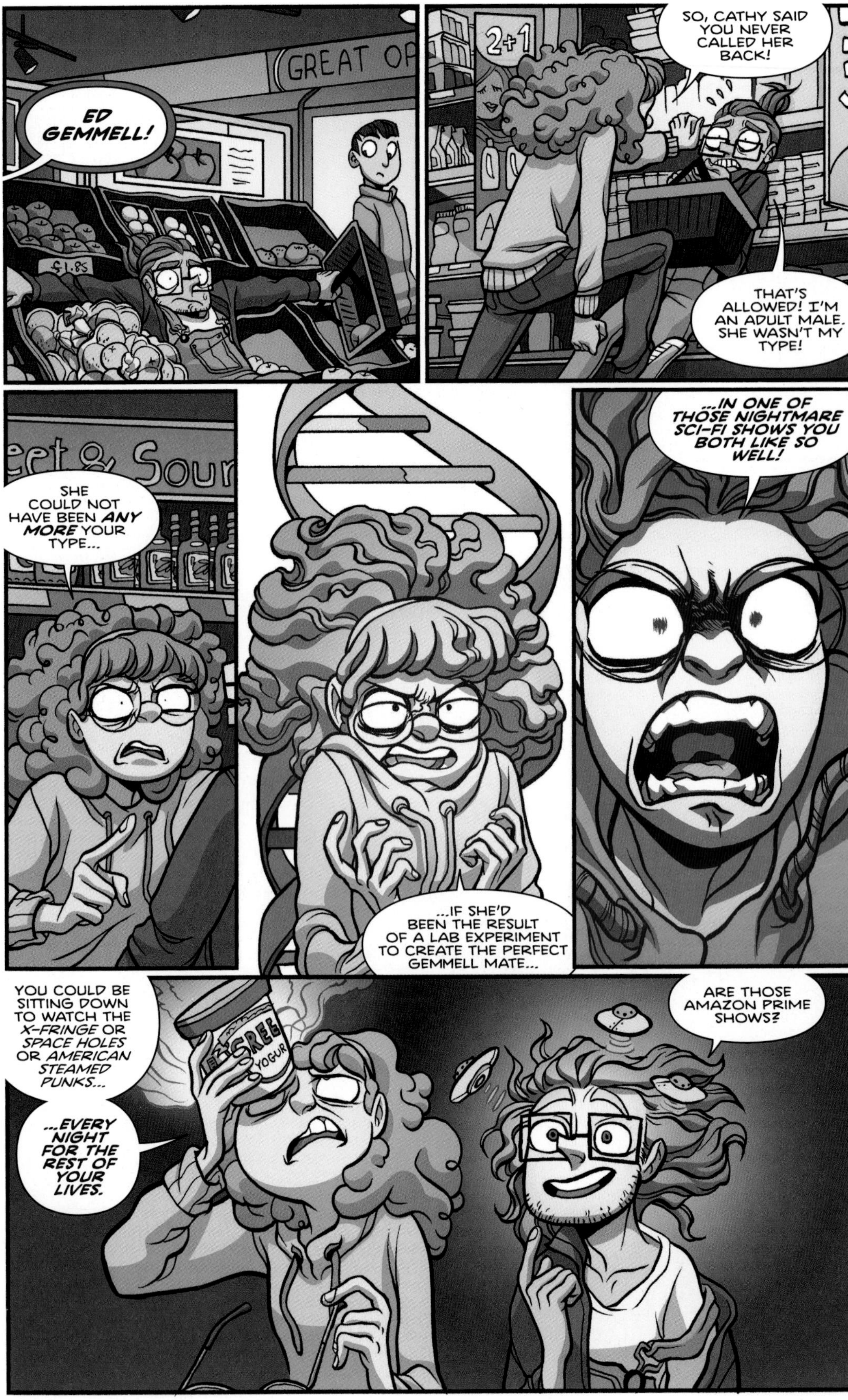
ED GEMMELL!
£1.85
2+1
SO, CATHY SAID YOU NEVER CALLED HER BACK!
THAT'S ALLOWED! I'M AN ADULT MALE. SHE WASN'T MY TYPE!
SHE COULD NOT HAVE BEEN *ANY MORE* YOUR TYPE...
...IF SHE'D BEEN THE RESULT OF A LAB EXPERIMENT TO CREATE THE PERFECT GEMMELL MATE...
...IN ONE OF THOSE NIGHTMARE SCI-FI SHOWS YOU BOTH LIKE SO WELL!
YOU COULD BE SITTING DOWN TO WATCH THE *X-FRINGE* OR *SPACE HOLES* OR *AMERICAN STEAMED PUNKS*...
...EVERY NIGHT FOR THE REST OF YOUR LIVES.
ARE THOSE AMAZON PRIME SHOWS?

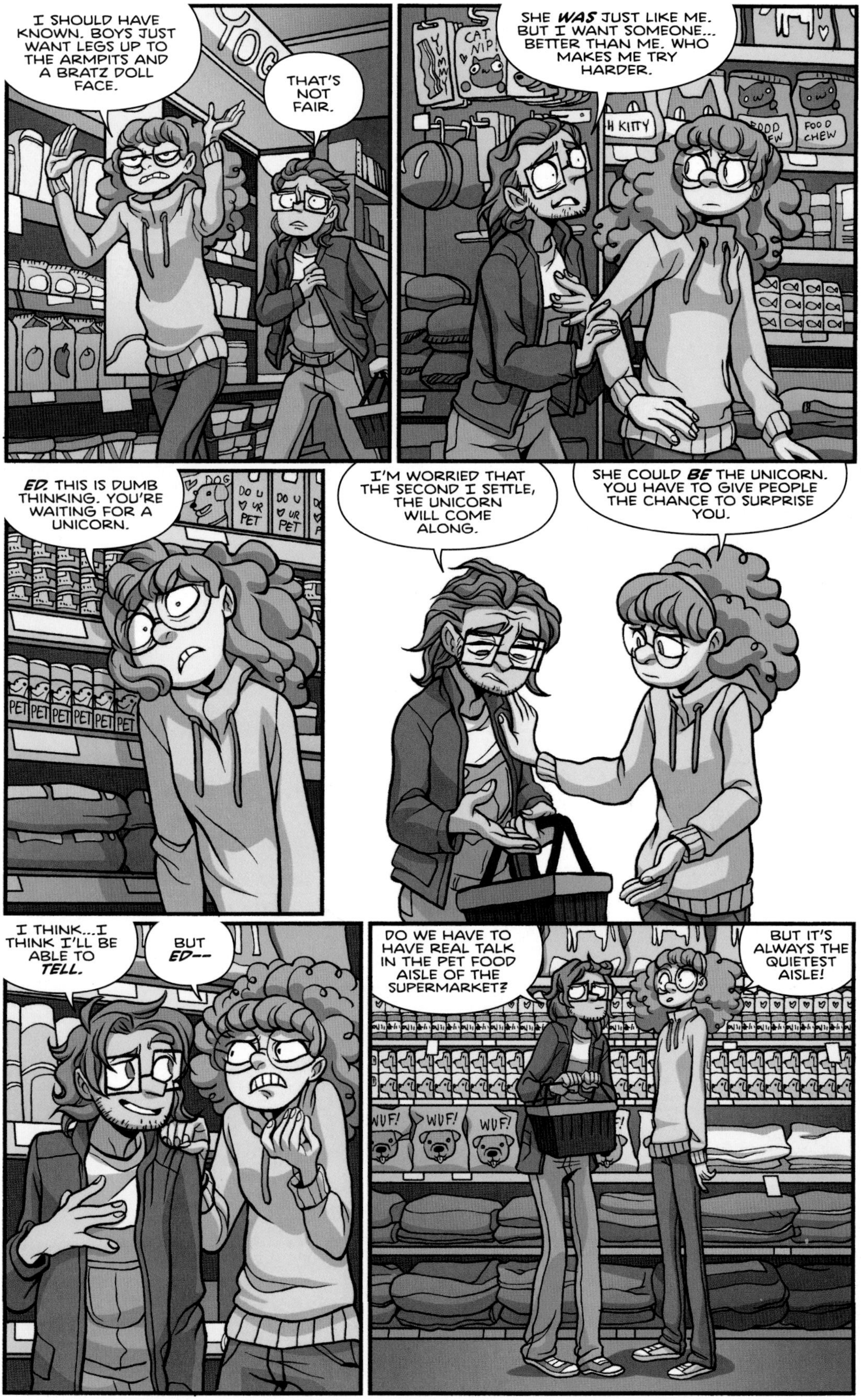

I SHOULD HAVE KNOWN. BOYS JUST WANT LEGS UP TO THE ARMPITS AND A BRATZ DOLL FACE.
THAT'S NOT FAIR.
YOG
CAT NIP!
YUMMY
SHE *WAS* JUST LIKE ME. BUT I WANT SOMEONE... BETTER THAN ME. WHO MAKES ME TRY HARDER.
H KITTY
FOOD CHEW
FOOD CHEW
ED. THIS IS DUMB THINKING. YOU'RE WAITING FOR A UNICORN.
DOG
DO U ♡ UR PET
DO U ♡ UR PET
PET PET PET PET PET PET
I'M WORRIED THAT THE SECOND I SETTLE, THE UNICORN WILL COME ALONG.
SHE COULD *BE* THE UNICORN. YOU HAVE TO GIVE PEOPLE THE CHANCE TO SURPRISE YOU.
I THINK...I THINK I'LL BE ABLE TO *TELL.*
BUT *ED--*
DO WE HAVE TO HAVE REAL TALK IN THE PET FOOD AISLE OF THE SUPERMARKET?
BUT IT'S ALWAYS THE QUIETEST AISLE!
WUF!
WUF!
WUF!

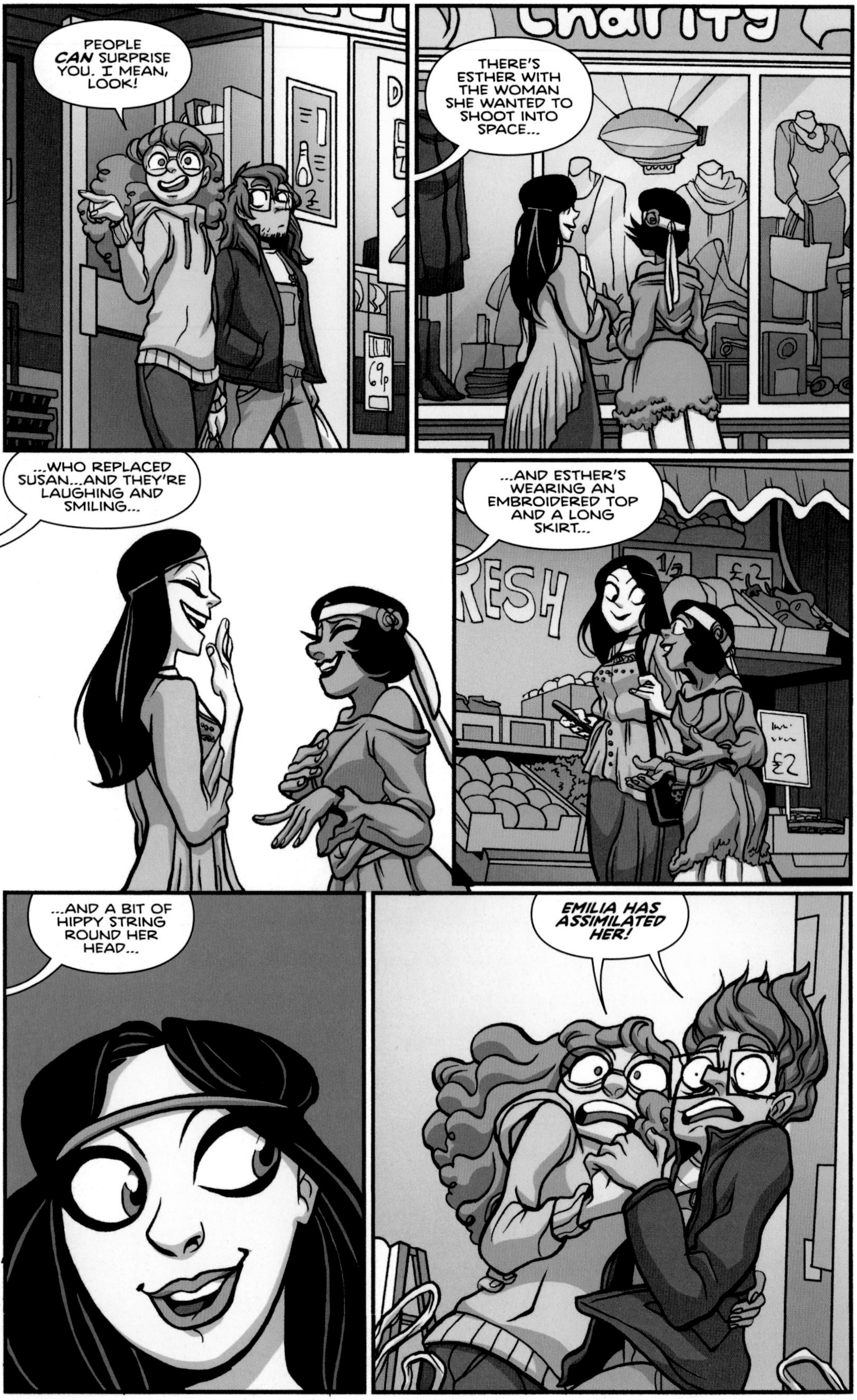
PEOPLE CAN SURPRISE YOU. I MEAN, LOOK!
Charity
THERE'S ESTHER WITH THE WOMAN SHE WANTED TO SHOOT INTO SPACE...
69p
...WHO REPLACED SUSAN...AND THEY'RE LAUGHING AND SMILING...
...AND ESTHER'S WEARING AN EMBROIDERED TOP AND A LONG SKIRT...
RESH
£2
£2
...AND A BIT OF HIPPY STRING ROUND HER HEAD...
EMILIA HAS ASSIMILATED HER!

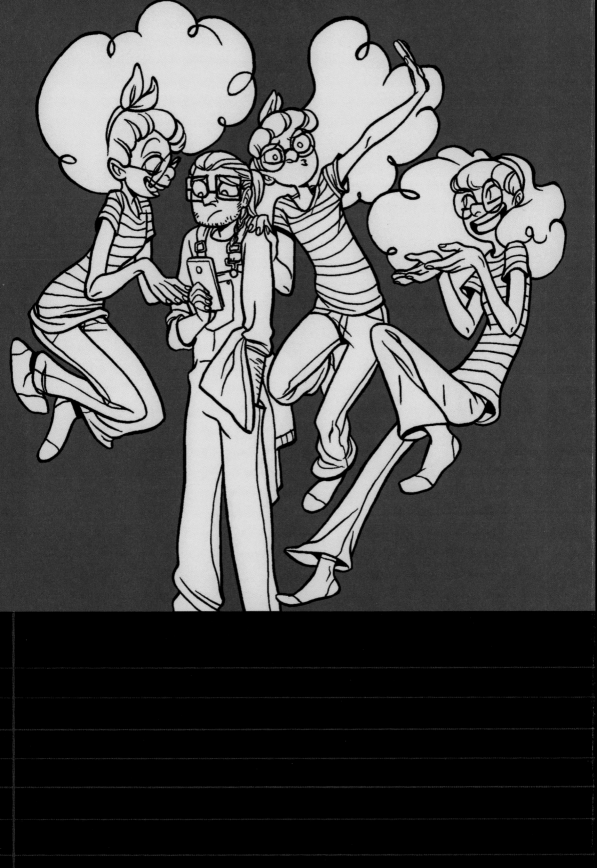

CHAPTER
THIRTY

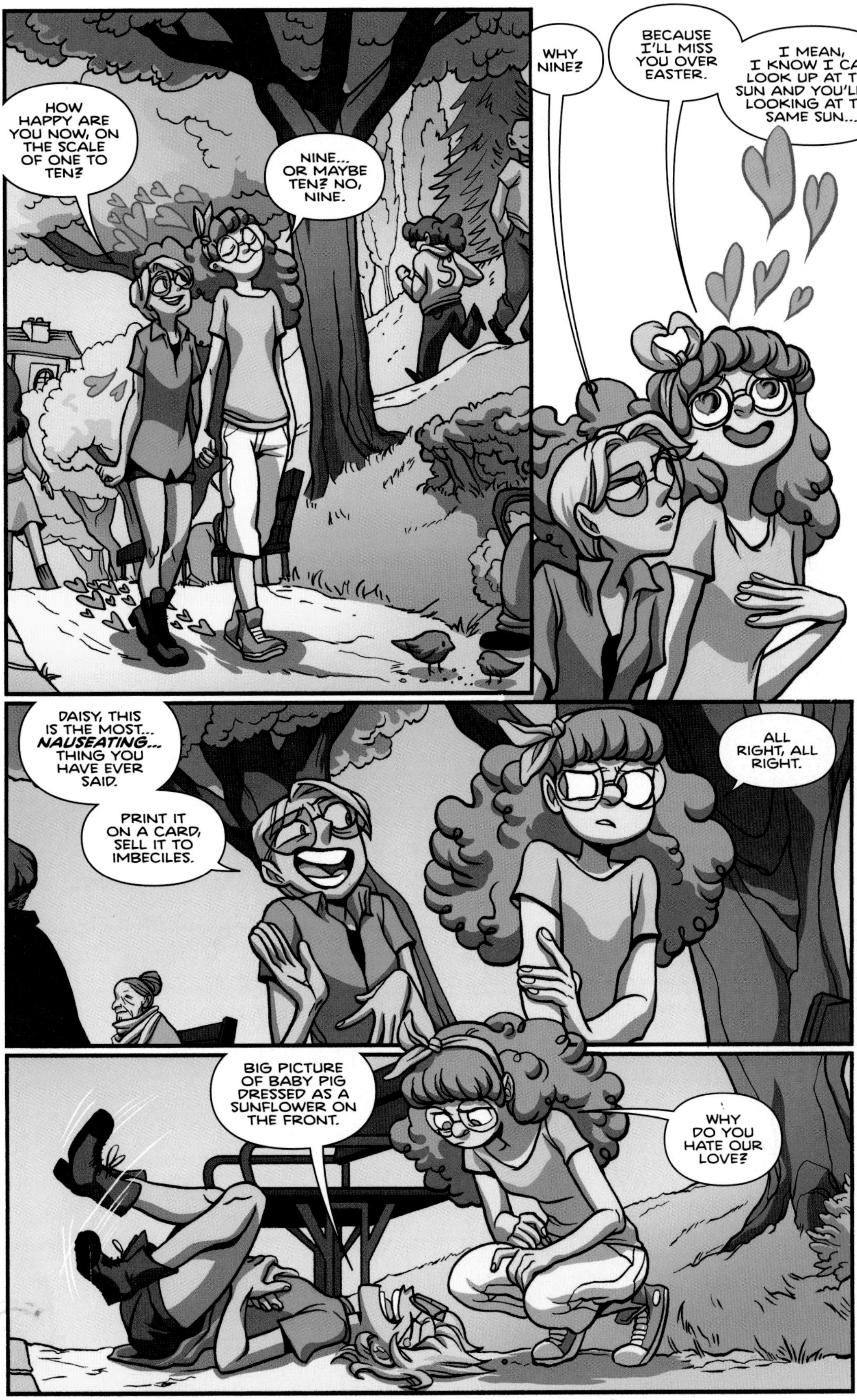
HOW HAPPY ARE YOU NOW, ON THE SCALE OF ONE TO TEN?
NINE... OR MAYBE TEN? NO, NINE.
WHY NINE?
BECAUSE I'LL MISS YOU OVER EASTER.
I MEAN, I KNOW I CAN LOOK UP AT THE SUN AND YOU'LL BE LOOKING AT THE SAME SUN...
DAISY, THIS IS THE MOST... NAUSEATING... THING YOU HAVE EVER SAID.
PRINT IT ON A CARD, SELL IT TO IMBECILES.
ALL RIGHT, ALL RIGHT.
BIG PICTURE OF BABY PIG DRESSED AS A SUNFLOWER ON THE FRONT.
WHY DO YOU HATE OUR LOVE?

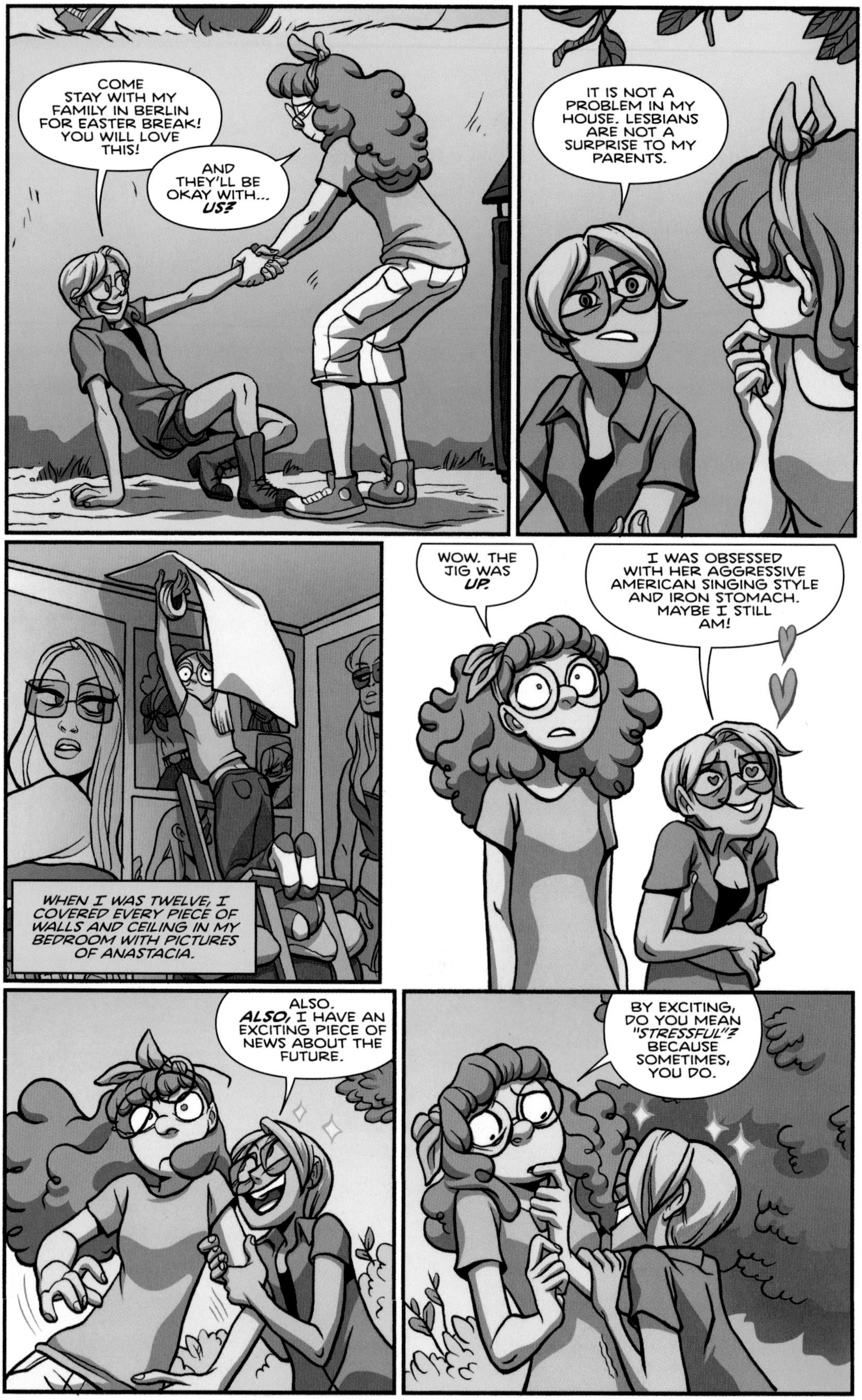
COME STAY WITH MY FAMILY IN BERLIN FOR EASTER BREAK! YOU WILL LOVE THIS!
AND THEY'LL BE OKAY WITH... US?
IT IS NOT A PROBLEM IN MY HOUSE. LESBIANS ARE NOT A SURPRISE TO MY PARENTS.
WHEN I WAS TWELVE, I COVERED EVERY PIECE OF WALLS AND CEILING IN MY BEDROOM WITH PICTURES OF ANASTACIA.
WOW. THE JIG WAS UP.
I WAS OBSESSED WITH HER AGGRESSIVE AMERICAN SINGING STYLE AND IRON STOMACH. MAYBE I STILL AM!
ALSO. ALSO, I HAVE AN EXCITING PIECE OF NEWS ABOUT THE FUTURE.
BY EXCITING, DO YOU MEAN "STRESSFUL"? BECAUSE SOMETIMES, YOU DO.

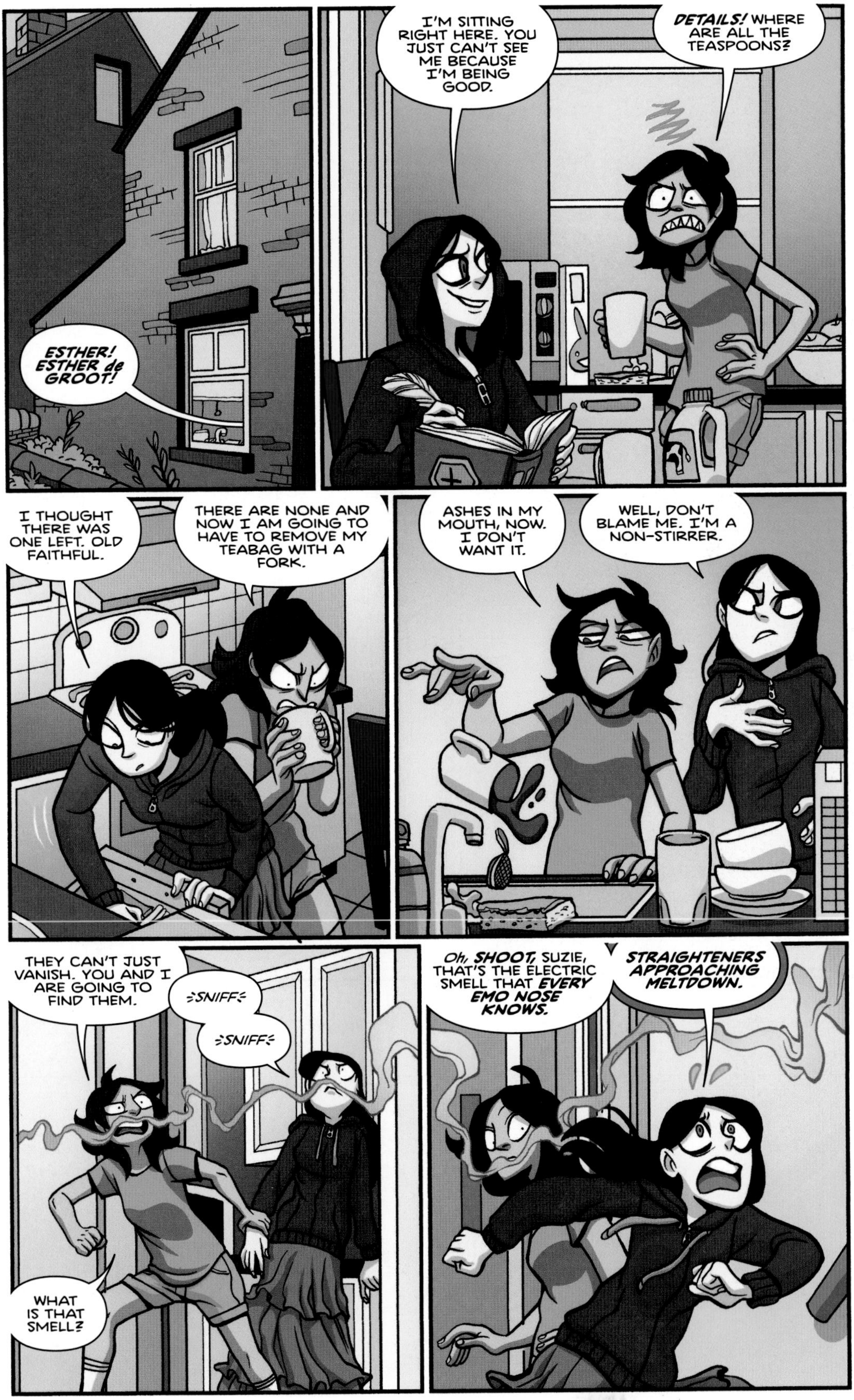
ESTHER! ESTHER de GROOT!
I'M SITTING RIGHT HERE. YOU JUST CAN'T SEE ME BECAUSE I'M BEING GOOD.
DETAILS! WHERE ARE ALL THE TEASPOONS?
I THOUGHT THERE WAS ONE LEFT. OLD FAITHFUL.
THERE ARE NONE AND NOW I AM GOING TO HAVE TO REMOVE MY TEABAG WITH A FORK.
ASHES IN MY MOUTH, NOW. I DON'T WANT IT.
WELL, DON'T BLAME ME. I'M A NON-STIRRER.
THEY CAN'T JUST VANISH. YOU AND I ARE GOING TO FIND THEM.
SNIFF
SNIFF
WHAT IS THAT SMELL?
Oh, SHOOT, SUZIE, THAT'S THE ELECTRIC SMELL THAT EVERY EMO NOSE KNOWS.
STRAIGHTENERS APPROACHING MELTDOWN.

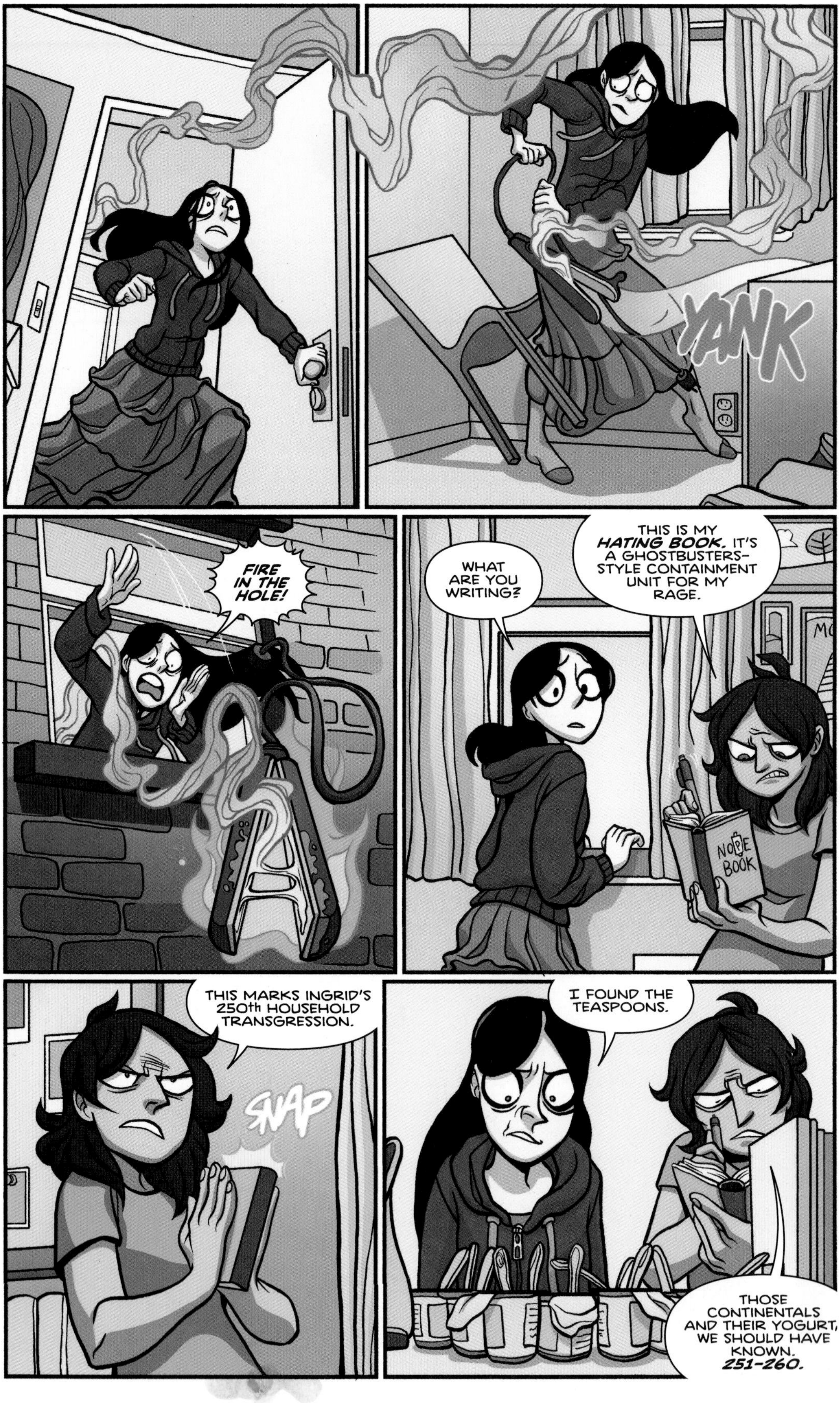
YANK
FIRE IN THE HOLE!
WHAT ARE YOU WRITING?
THIS IS MY HATING BOOK. IT'S A GHOSTBUSTERS-STYLE CONTAINMENT UNIT FOR MY RAGE.
NOPE BOOK
THIS MARKS INGRID'S 250th HOUSEHOLD TRANSGRESSION.
SNAP
I FOUND THE TEASPOONS.
THOSE CONTINENTALS AND THEIR YOGURT, WE SHOULD HAVE KNOWN. 251-260.

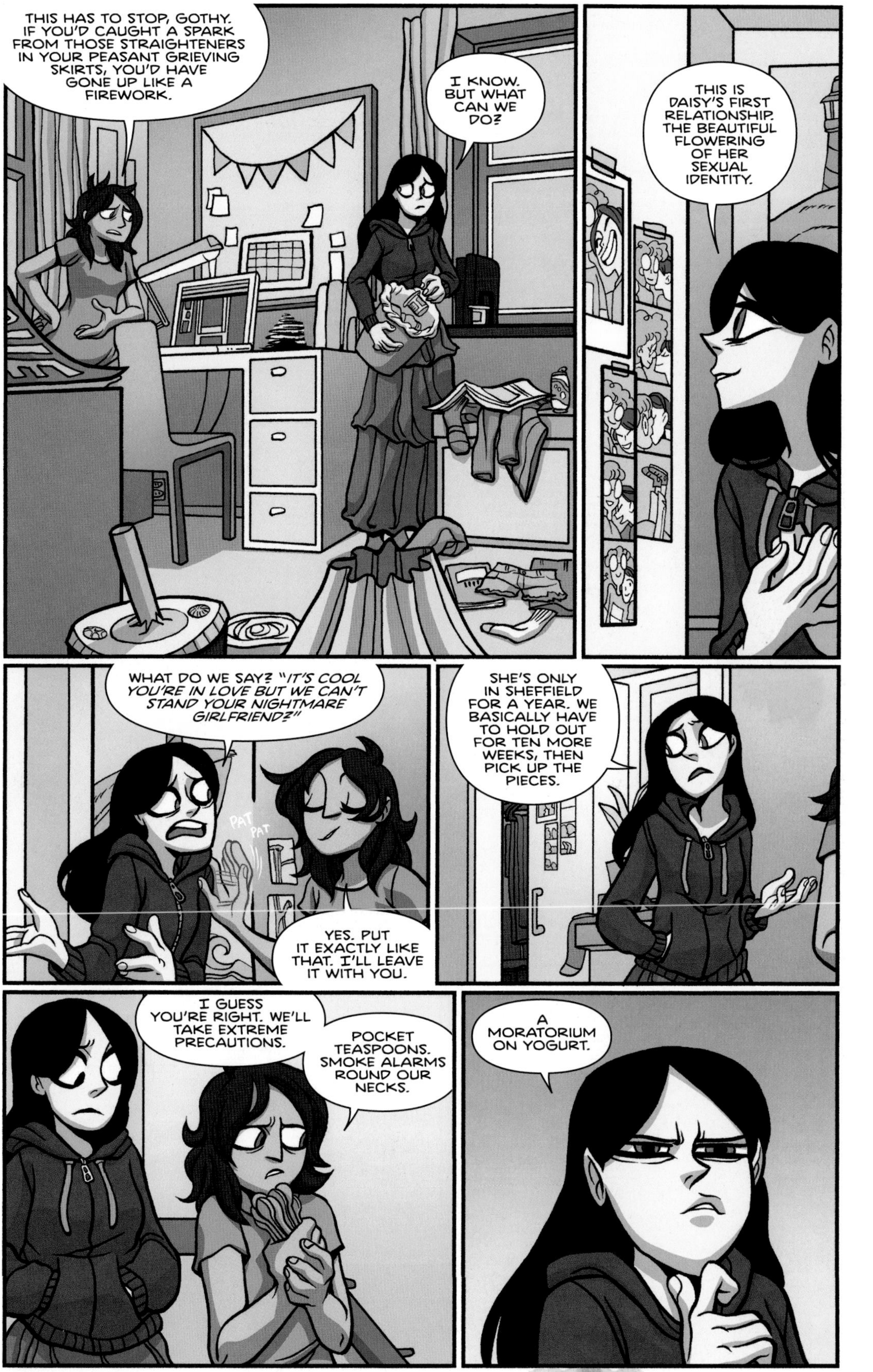
THIS HAS TO STOP, GOTHY. IF YOU'D CAUGHT A SPARK FROM THOSE STRAIGHTENERS IN YOUR PEASANT GRIEVING SKIRTS, YOU'D HAVE GONE UP LIKE A FIREWORK.
I KNOW. BUT WHAT CAN WE DO?
THIS IS DAISY'S FIRST RELATIONSHIP. THE BEAUTIFUL FLOWERING OF HER SEXUAL IDENTITY.
WHAT DO WE SAY? "IT'S COOL YOU'RE IN LOVE BUT WE CAN'T STAND YOUR NIGHTMARE GIRLFRIEND?"
PAT PAT
YES. PUT IT EXACTLY LIKE THAT. I'LL LEAVE IT WITH YOU.
SHE'S ONLY IN SHEFFIELD FOR A YEAR. WE BASICALLY HAVE TO HOLD OUT FOR TEN MORE WEEKS, THEN PICK UP THE PIECES.
I GUESS YOU'RE RIGHT. WE'LL TAKE EXTREME PRECAUTIONS.
POCKET TEASPOONS. SMOKE ALARMS ROUND OUR NECKS.
A MORATORIUM ON YOGURT.

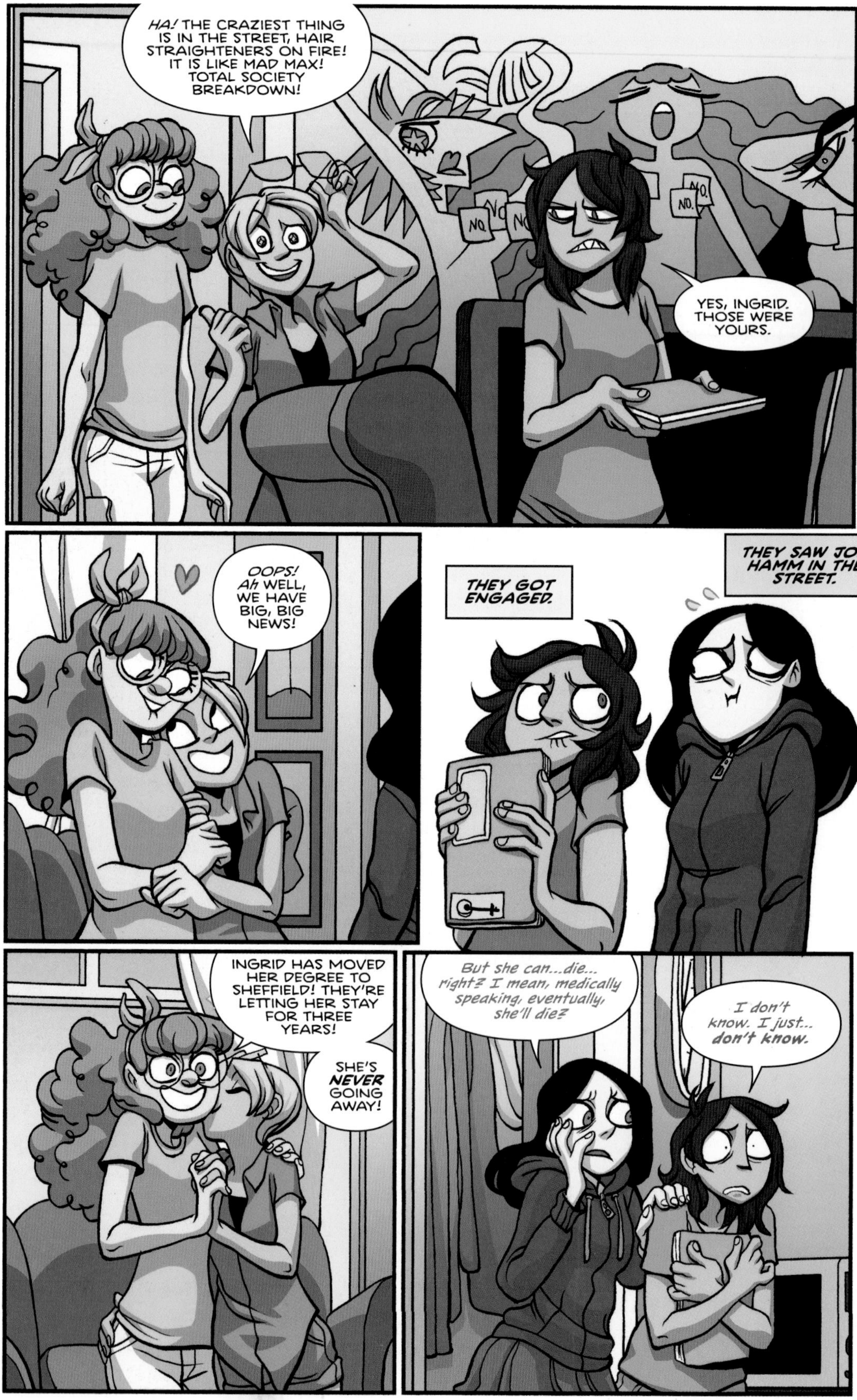
HA! THE CRAZIEST THING IS IN THE STREET, HAIR STRAIGHTENERS ON FIRE! IT IS LIKE MAD MAX! TOTAL SOCIETY BREAKDOWN!
NO.
YES, INGRID. THOSE WERE YOURS.
OOPS! Ah WELL, WE HAVE BIG, BIG NEWS!
THEY GOT ENGAGED.
THEY SAW JON HAMM IN THE STREET.
INGRID HAS MOVED HER DEGREE TO SHEFFIELD! THEY'RE LETTING HER STAY FOR THREE YEARS!
SHE'S NEVER GOING AWAY!
But she can...die... right? I mean, medically speaking, eventually, she'll die?
I don't know. I just... don't know.

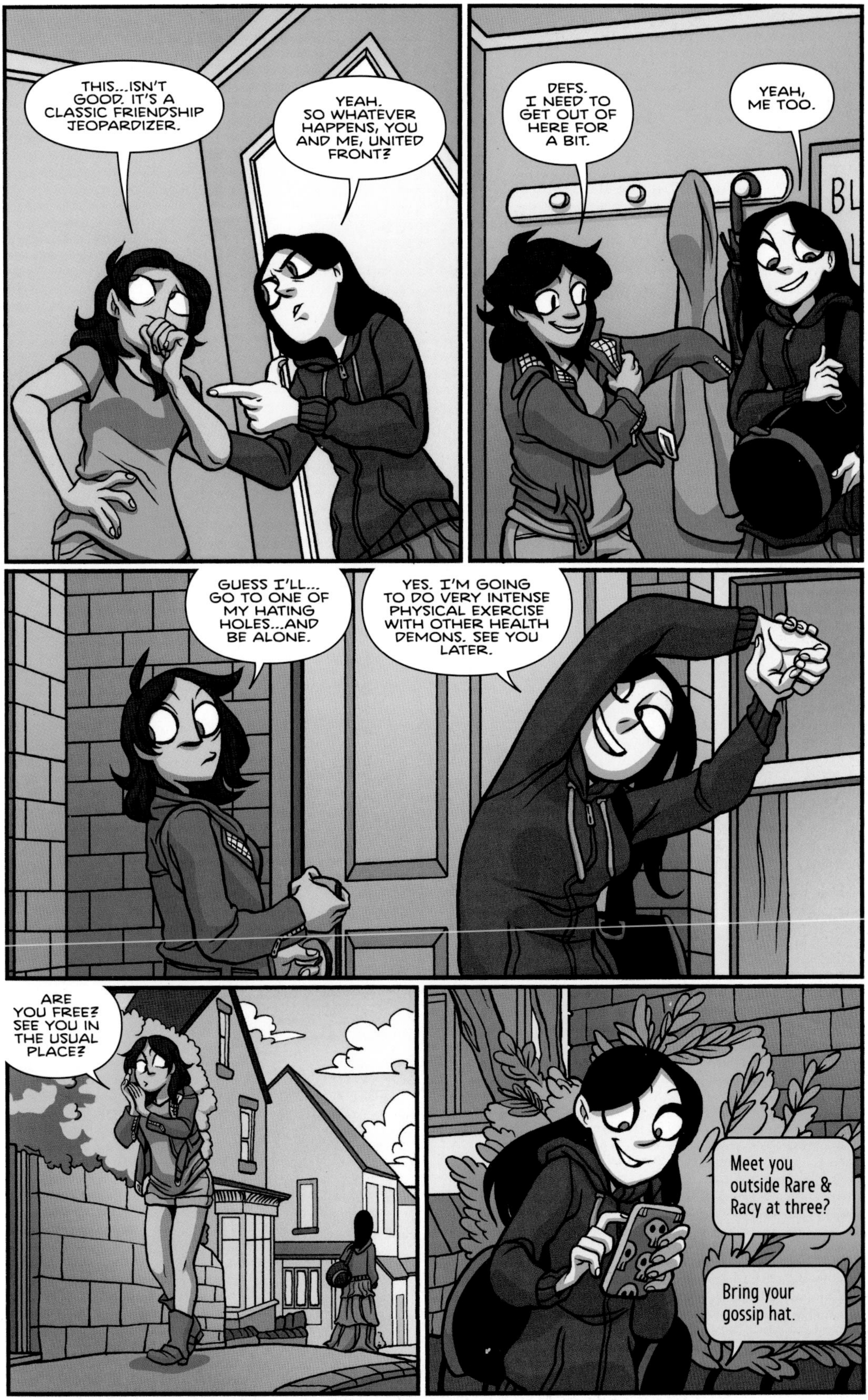
THIS...ISN'T GOOD. IT'S A CLASSIC FRIENDSHIP JEOPARDIZER.
YEAH. SO WHATEVER HAPPENS, YOU AND ME, UNITED FRONT?
DEFS. I NEED TO GET OUT OF HERE FOR A BIT.
YEAH, ME TOO.
GUESS I'LL... GO TO ONE OF MY HATING HOLES...AND BE ALONE.
YES. I'M GOING TO DO VERY INTENSE PHYSICAL EXERCISE WITH OTHER HEALTH DEMONS. SEE YOU LATER.
ARE YOU FREE? SEE YOU IN THE USUAL PLACE?
Meet you outside Rare & Racy at three?
Bring your gossip hat.

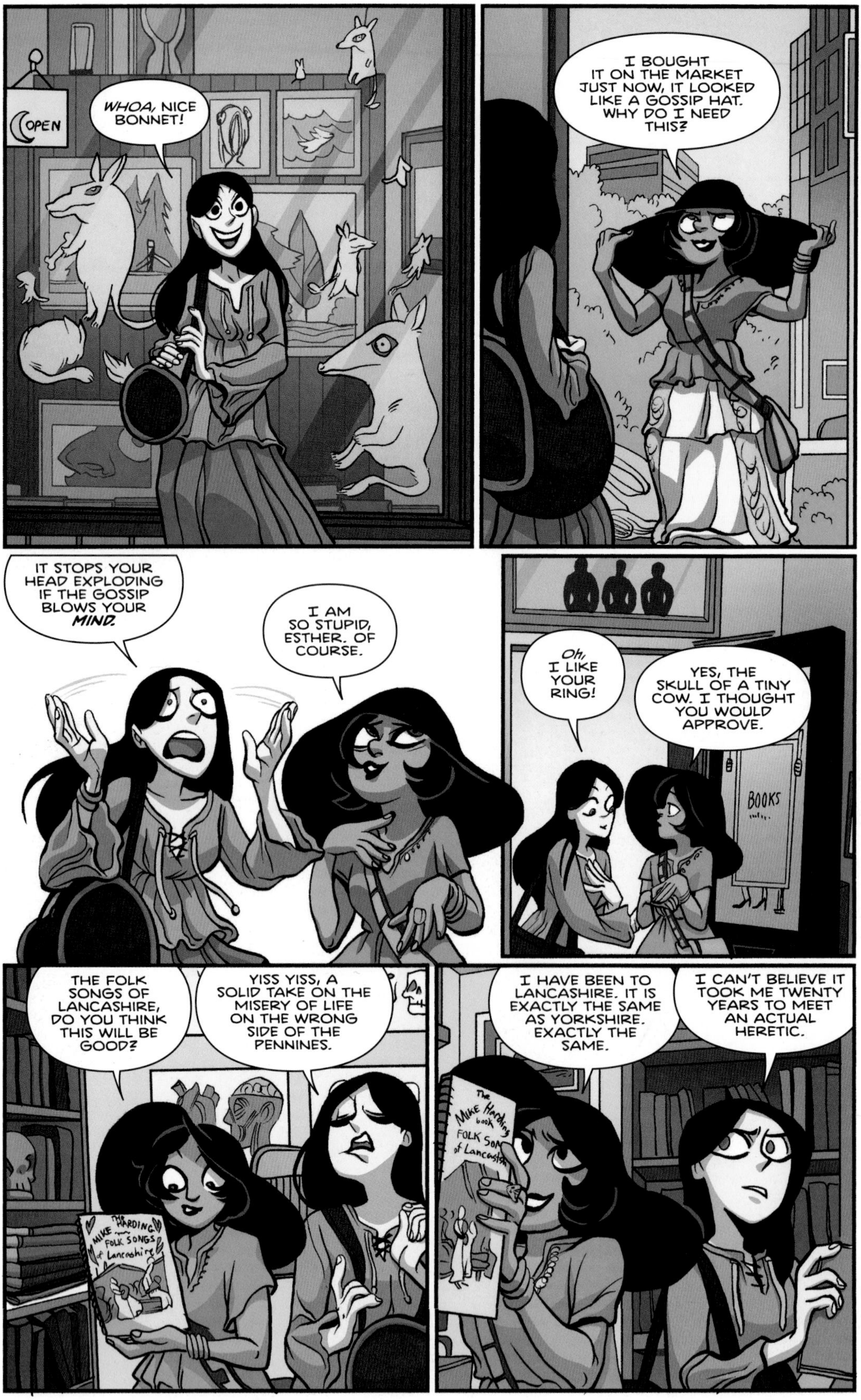
OPEN
WHOA, NICE BONNET!
I BOUGHT IT ON THE MARKET JUST NOW, IT LOOKED LIKE A GOSSIP HAT. WHY DO I NEED THIS?
IT STOPS YOUR HEAD EXPLODING IF THE GOSSIP BLOWS YOUR MIND.
I AM SO STUPID, ESTHER. OF COURSE.
Oh, I LIKE YOUR RING!
YES, THE SKULL OF A TINY COW. I THOUGHT YOU WOULD APPROVE.
BOOKS
THE FOLK SONGS OF LANCASHIRE, DO YOU THINK THIS WILL BE GOOD?
YISS YISS, A SOLID TAKE ON THE MISERY OF LIFE ON THE WRONG SIDE OF THE PENNINES.
The MIKE HARDING FOLK SONGS of Lancashire
I HAVE BEEN TO LANCASHIRE. IT IS EXACTLY THE SAME AS YORKSHIRE. EXACTLY THE SAME.
I CAN'T BELIEVE IT TOOK ME TWENTY YEARS TO MEET AN ACTUAL HERETIC.

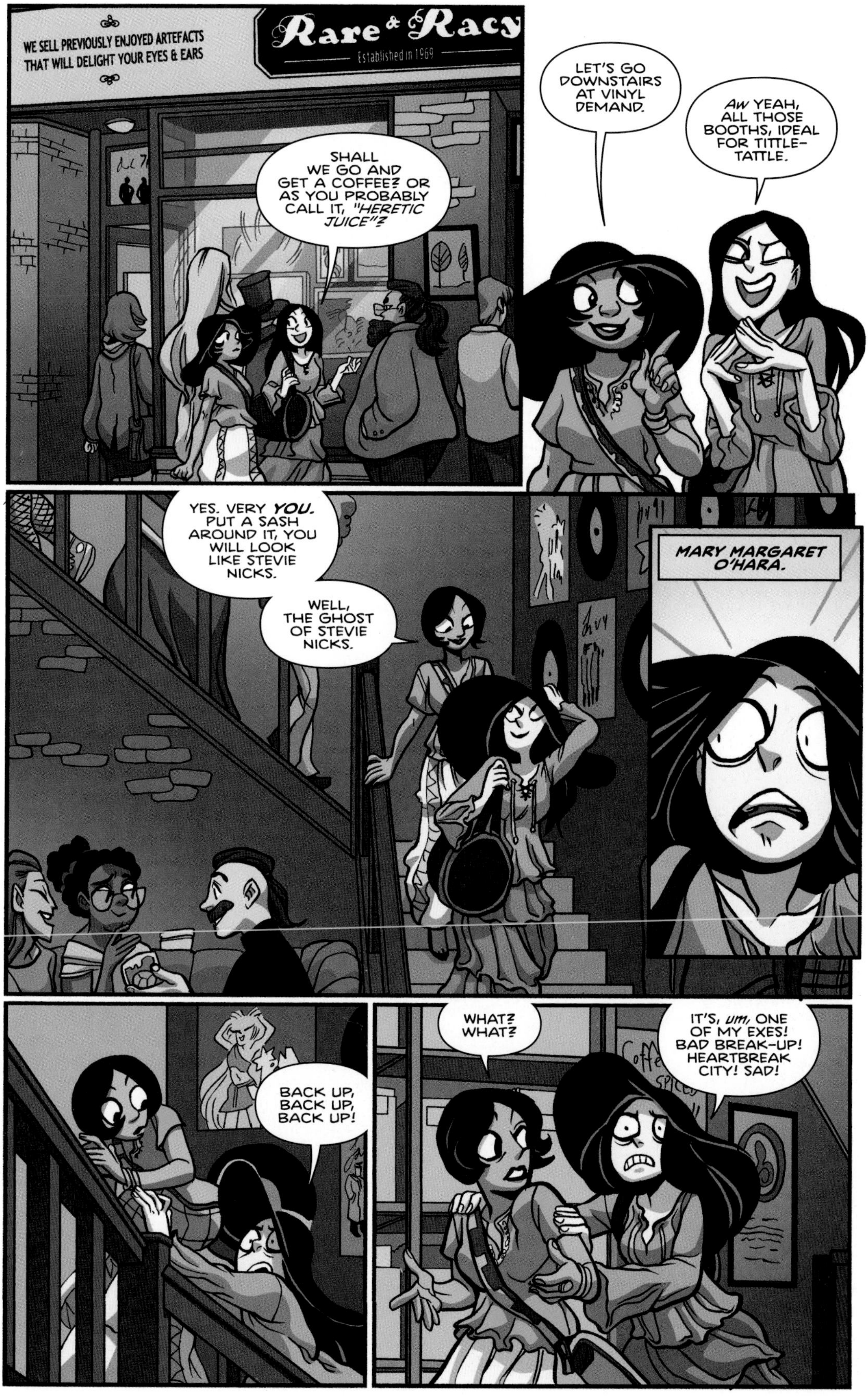

WE SELL PREVIOUSLY ENJOYED ARTEFACTS THAT WILL DELIGHT YOUR EYES & EARS
Rare & Racy
Established in 1969
SHALL WE GO AND GET A COFFEE? OR AS YOU PROBABLY CALL IT, "HERETIC JUICE"?
LET'S GO DOWNSTAIRS AT VINYL DEMAND.
AW YEAH, ALL THOSE BOOTHS, IDEAL FOR TITTLE-TATTLE.
YES. VERY YOU. PUT A SASH AROUND IT, YOU WILL LOOK LIKE STEVIE NICKS.
WELL, THE GHOST OF STEVIE NICKS.
MARY MARGARET O'HARA.
BACK UP, BACK UP, BACK UP!
WHAT? WHAT?
IT'S, UM, ONE OF MY EXES! BAD BREAK-UP! HEARTBREAK CITY! SAD!

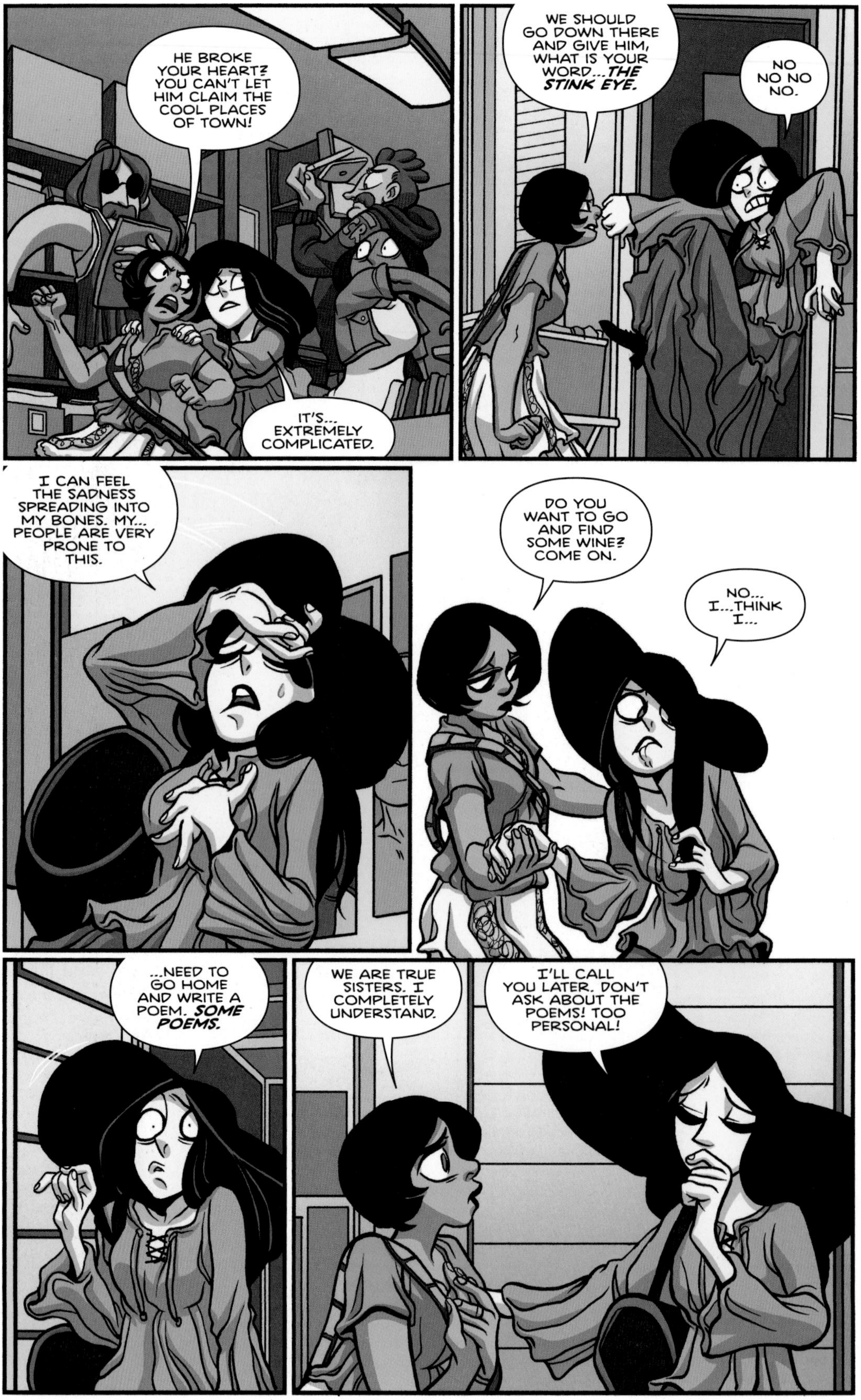
HE BROKE YOUR HEART? YOU CAN'T LET HIM CLAIM THE COOL PLACES OF TOWN!
IT'S... EXTREMELY COMPLICATED.
WE SHOULD GO DOWN THERE AND GIVE HIM, WHAT IS YOUR WORD... *THE STINK EYE.*
NO NO NO NO.
I CAN FEEL THE SADNESS SPREADING INTO MY BONES. MY... PEOPLE ARE VERY PRONE TO THIS.
DO YOU WANT TO GO AND FIND SOME WINE? COME ON.
NO... I...THINK I...
...NEED TO GO HOME AND WRITE A POEM. *SOME POEMS.*
WE ARE TRUE SISTERS. I COMPLETELY UNDERSTAND.
I'LL CALL YOU LATER. DON'T ASK ABOUT THE POEMS! TOO PERSONAL!

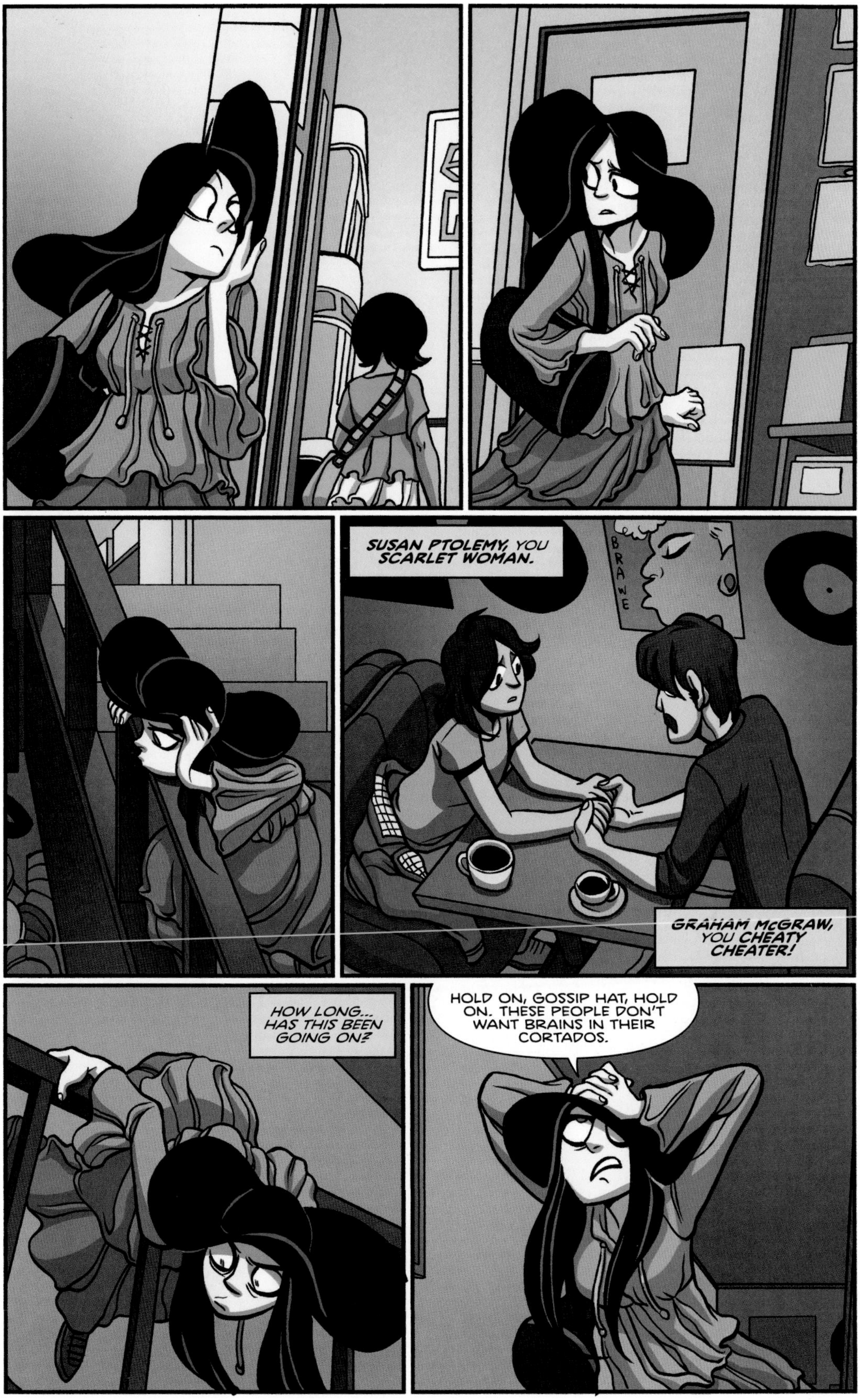
SUSAN PTOLEMY, YOU SCARLET WOMAN.
BRAWE
GRAHAM McGRAW, YOU CHEATY CHEATER!
HOW LONG... HAS THIS BEEN GOING ON?
HOLD ON, GOSSIP HAT, HOLD ON. THESE PEOPLE DON'T WANT BRAINS IN THEIR CORTADOS.

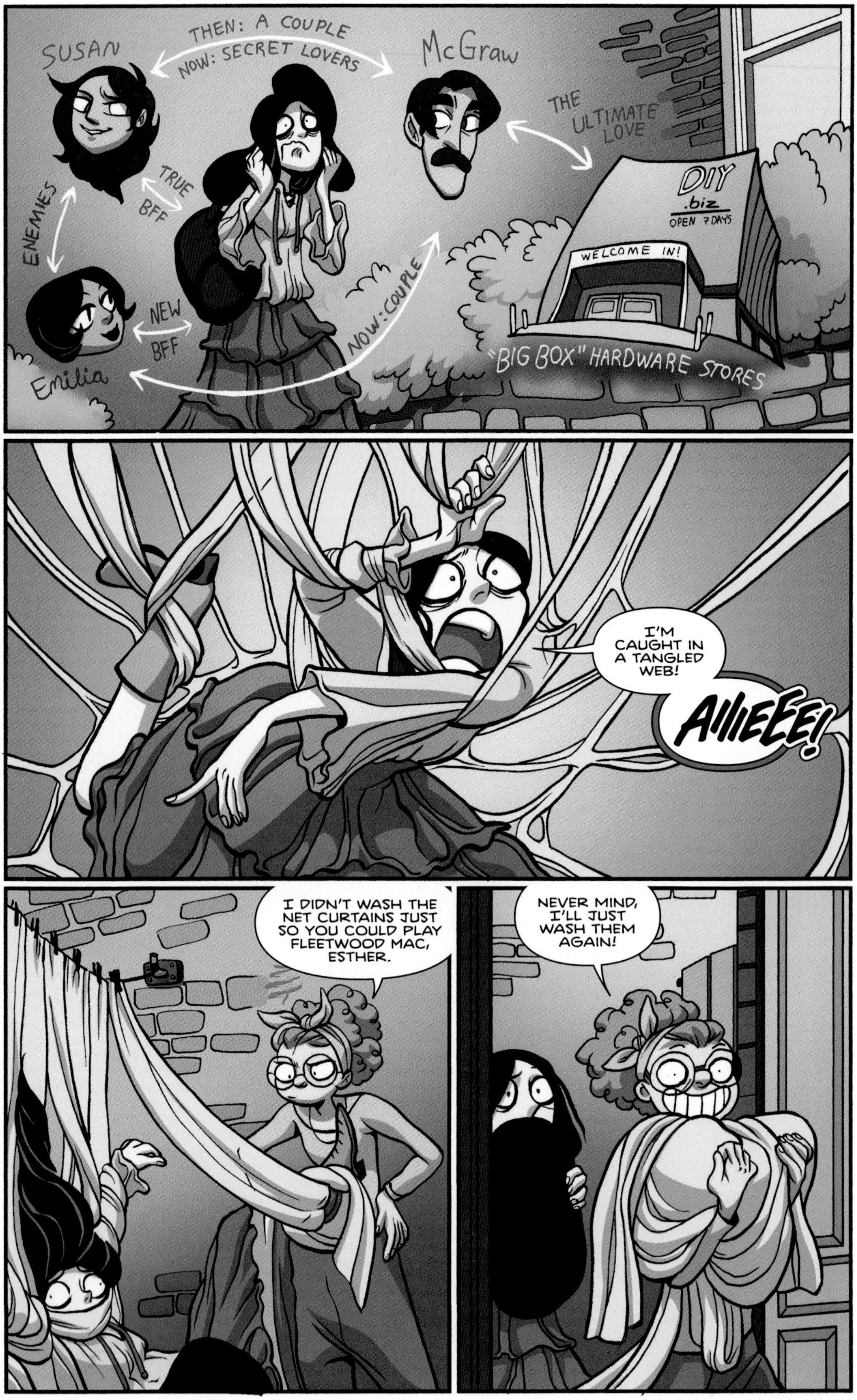
SUSAN
THEN: A COUPLE
NOW: SECRET LOVERS
McGraw
THE ULTIMATE LOVE
TRUE BFF
ENEMIES
NEW BFF
Emilia
NOW: COUPLE
DIY .biz
OPEN 7 DAYS
WELCOME IN!
"BIG BOX" HARDWARE STORES
I'M CAUGHT IN A TANGLED WEB!
AIIIEEE!
I DIDN'T WASH THE NET CURTAINS JUST SO YOU COULD PLAY FLEETWOOD MAC, ESTHER.
NEVER MIND, I'LL JUST WASH THEM AGAIN!

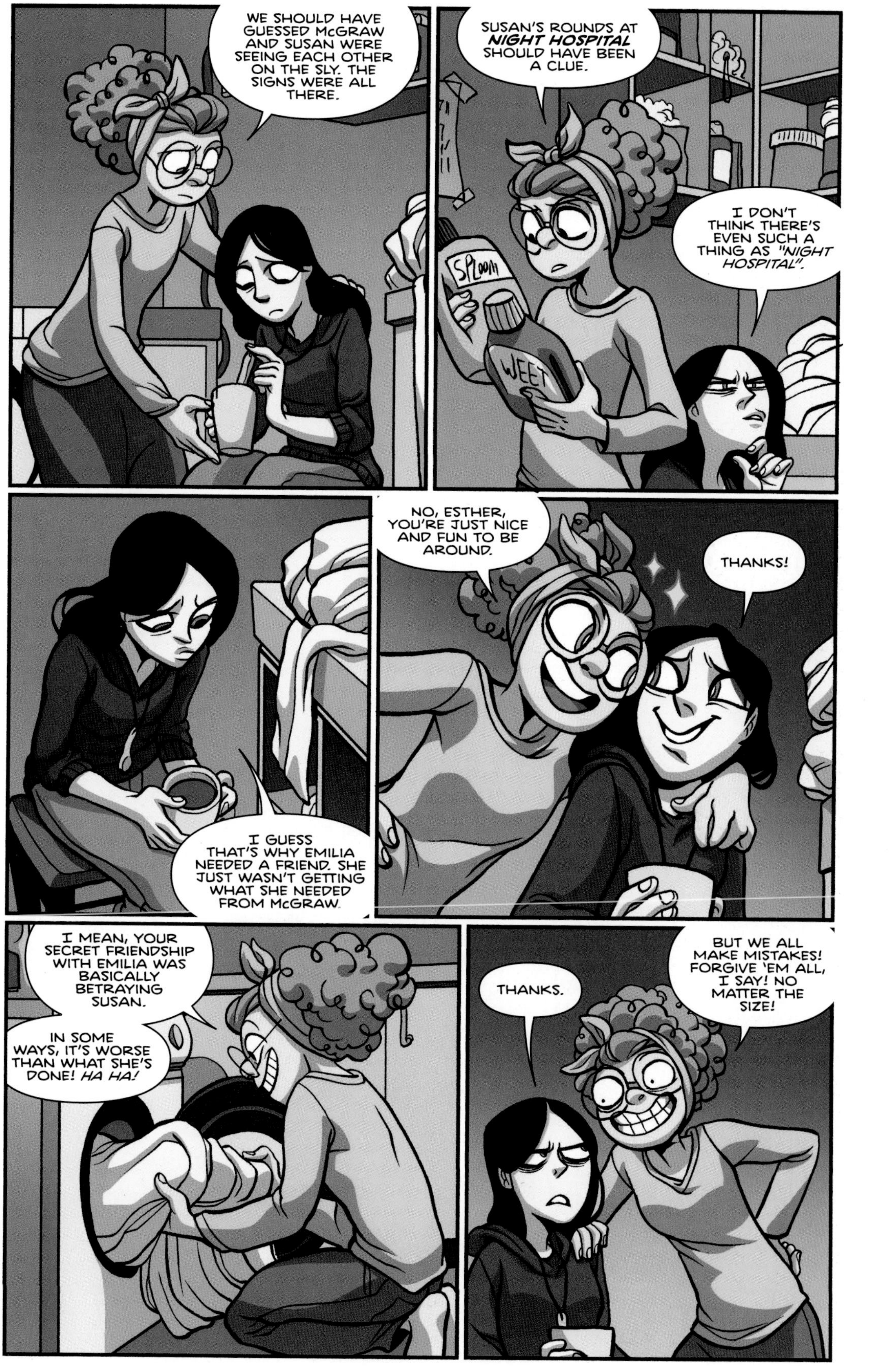
WE SHOULD HAVE GUESSED McGRAW AND SUSAN WERE SEEING EACH OTHER ON THE SLY. THE SIGNS WERE ALL THERE.
SUSAN'S ROUNDS AT *NIGHT HOSPITAL* SHOULD HAVE BEEN A CLUE.
SPLOOM
WEET
I DON'T THINK THERE'S EVEN SUCH A THING AS *"NIGHT HOSPITAL"*.
I GUESS THAT'S WHY EMILIA NEEDED A FRIEND. SHE JUST WASN'T GETTING WHAT SHE NEEDED FROM McGRAW.
NO, ESTHER, YOU'RE JUST NICE AND FUN TO BE AROUND.
THANKS!
I MEAN, YOUR SECRET FRIENDSHIP WITH EMILIA WAS BASICALLY BETRAYING SUSAN.
IN SOME WAYS, IT'S WORSE THAN WHAT SHE'S DONE! *HA HA!*
THANKS.
BUT WE ALL MAKE MISTAKES! FORGIVE 'EM ALL, I SAY! NO MATTER THE SIZE!

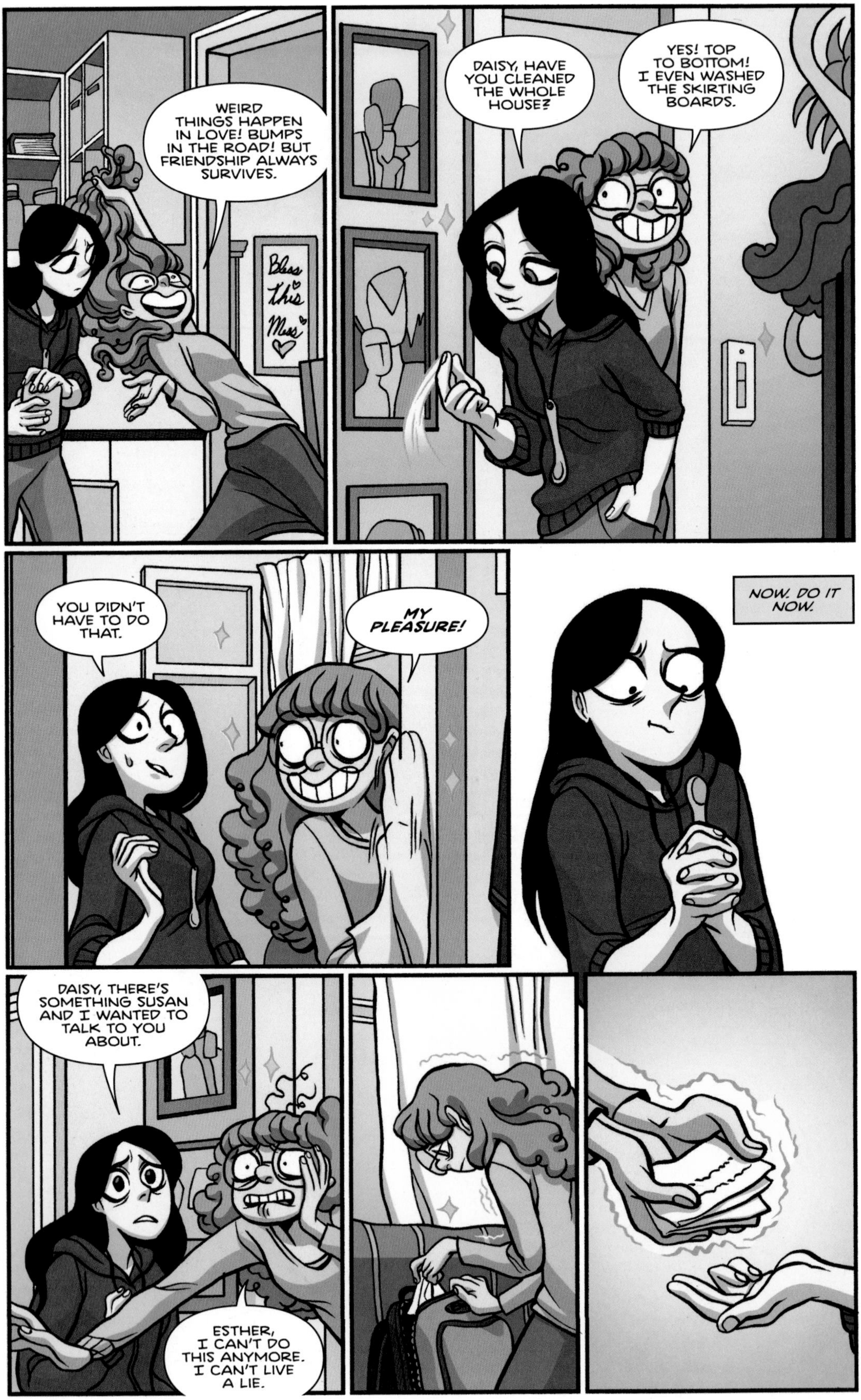
WEIRD THINGS HAPPEN IN LOVE! BUMPS IN THE ROAD! BUT FRIENDSHIP ALWAYS SURVIVES.
Bless This Mess
DAISY, HAVE YOU CLEANED THE WHOLE HOUSE?
YES! TOP TO BOTTOM! I EVEN WASHED THE SKIRTING BOARDS.
YOU DIDN'T HAVE TO DO THAT.
MY PLEASURE!
NOW. DO IT NOW.
DAISY, THERE'S SOMETHING SUSAN AND I WANTED TO TALK TO YOU ABOUT.
ESTHER, I CAN'T DO THIS ANYMORE. I CAN'T LIVE A LIE.

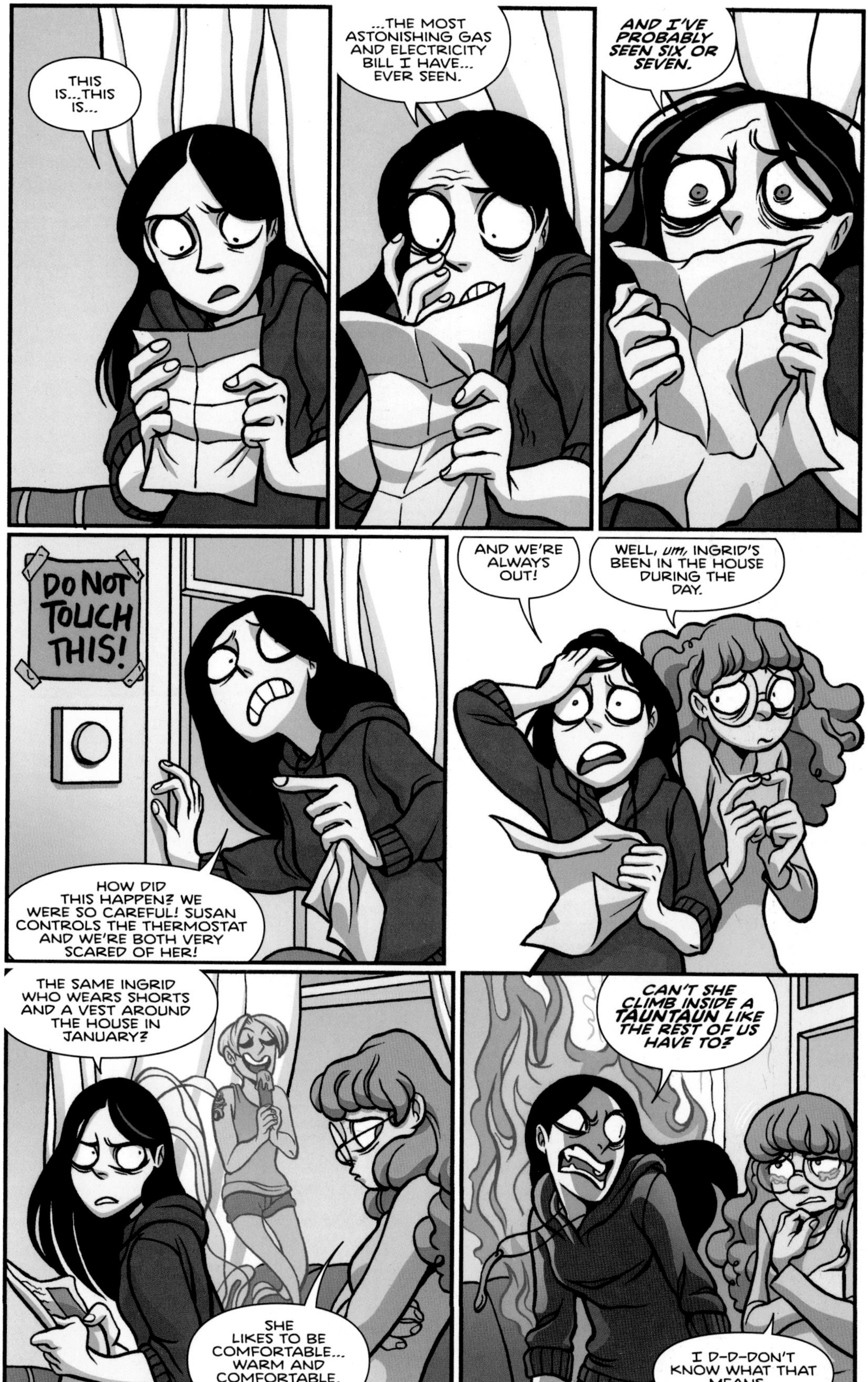
THIS IS... THIS IS...
...THE MOST ASTONISHING GAS AND ELECTRICITY BILL I HAVE... EVER SEEN.
AND I'VE PROBABLY SEEN SIX OR SEVEN.
DO NOT TOUCH THIS!
HOW DID THIS HAPPEN? WE WERE SO CAREFUL! SUSAN CONTROLS THE THERMOSTAT AND WE'RE BOTH VERY SCARED OF HER!
AND WE'RE ALWAYS OUT!
WELL, UM, INGRID'S BEEN IN THE HOUSE DURING THE DAY.
THE SAME INGRID WHO WEARS SHORTS AND A VEST AROUND THE HOUSE IN JANUARY?
SHE LIKES TO BE COMFORTABLE... WARM AND COMFORTABLE.
CAN'T SHE CLIMB INSIDE A TAUNTAUN LIKE THE REST OF US HAVE TO?
I D-D-DON'T KNOW WHAT THAT MEANS...

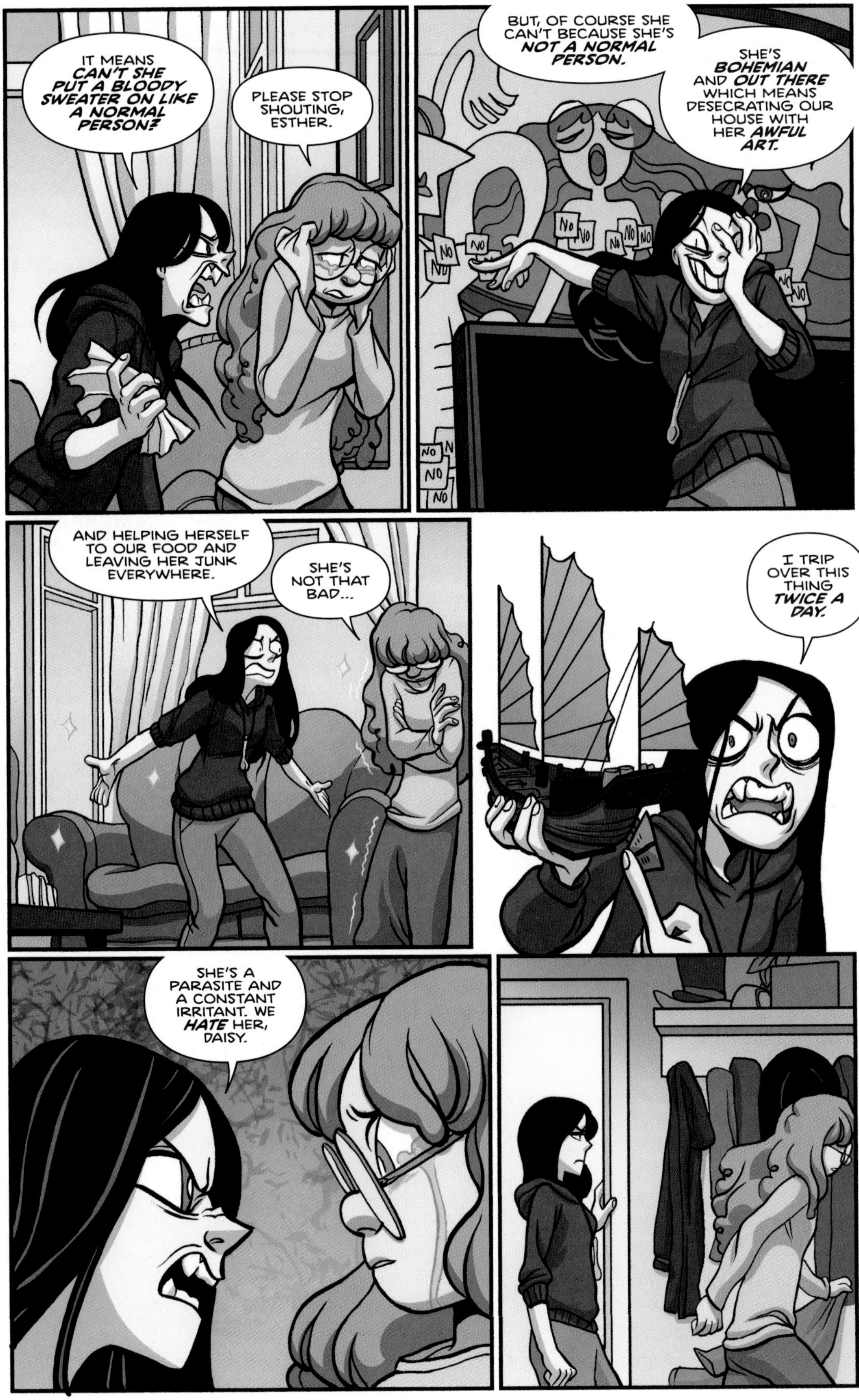

IT MEANS CAN'T SHE PUT A BLOODY SWEATER ON LIKE A NORMAL PERSON?
PLEASE STOP SHOUTING, ESTHER.
BUT, OF COURSE SHE CAN'T BECAUSE SHE'S NOT A NORMAL PERSON.
SHE'S BOHEMIAN AND OUT THERE WHICH MEANS DESECRATING OUR HOUSE WITH HER AWFUL ART.
NO
AND HELPING HERSELF TO OUR FOOD AND LEAVING HER JUNK EVERYWHERE.
SHE'S NOT THAT BAD...
I TRIP OVER THIS THING TWICE A DAY.
SHE'S A PARASITE AND A CONSTANT IRRITANT. WE HATE HER, DAISY.

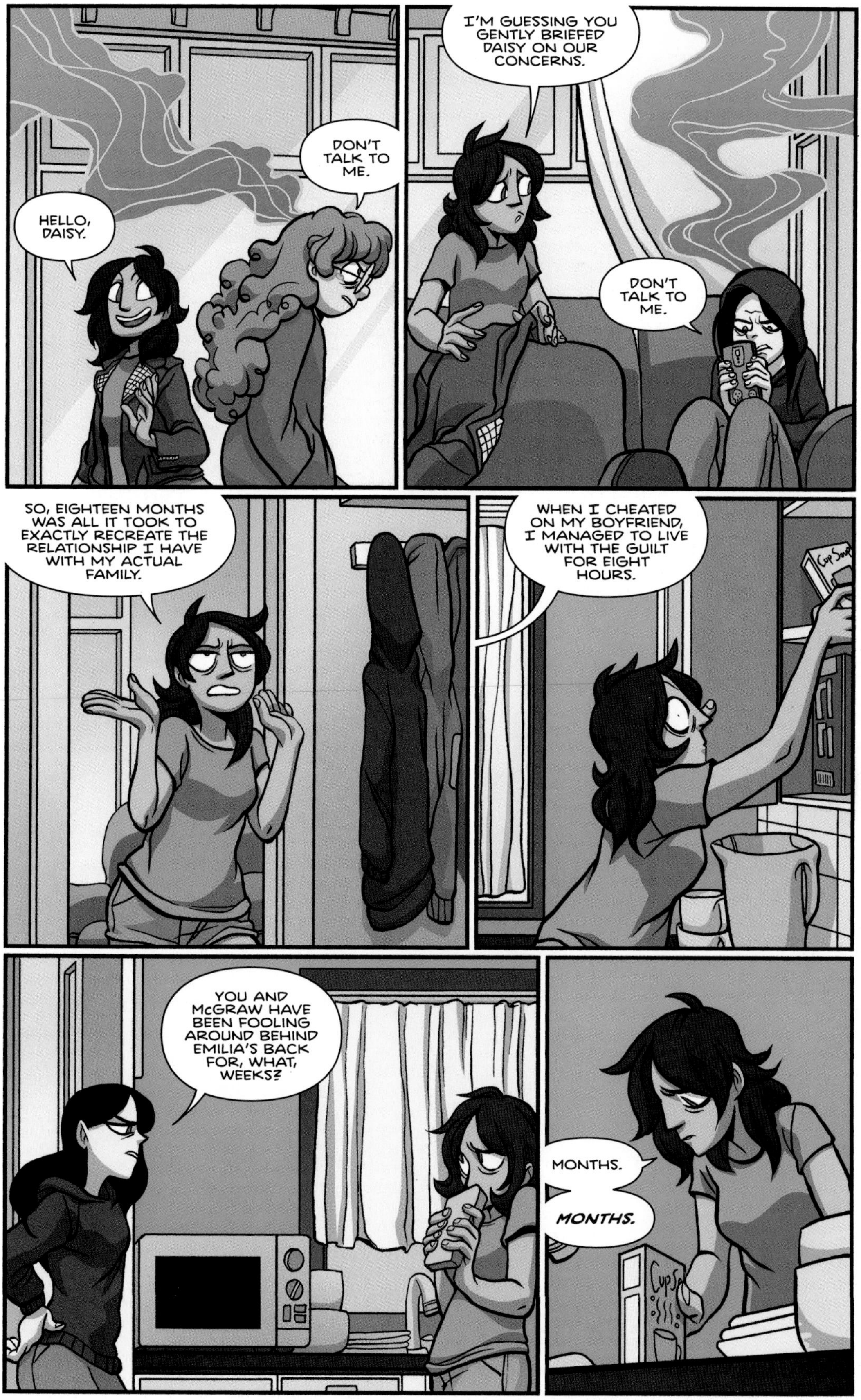
HELLO, DAISY.
DON'T TALK TO ME.
I'M GUESSING YOU GENTLY BRIEFED DAISY ON OUR CONCERNS.
DON'T TALK TO ME.
SO, EIGHTEEN MONTHS WAS ALL IT TOOK TO EXACTLY RECREATE THE RELATIONSHIP I HAVE WITH MY ACTUAL FAMILY.
WHEN I CHEATED ON MY BOYFRIEND, I MANAGED TO LIVE WITH THE GUILT FOR EIGHT HOURS.
YOU AND McGRAW HAVE BEEN FOOLING AROUND BEHIND EMILIA'S BACK FOR, WHAT, WEEKS?
MONTHS.
MONTHS.

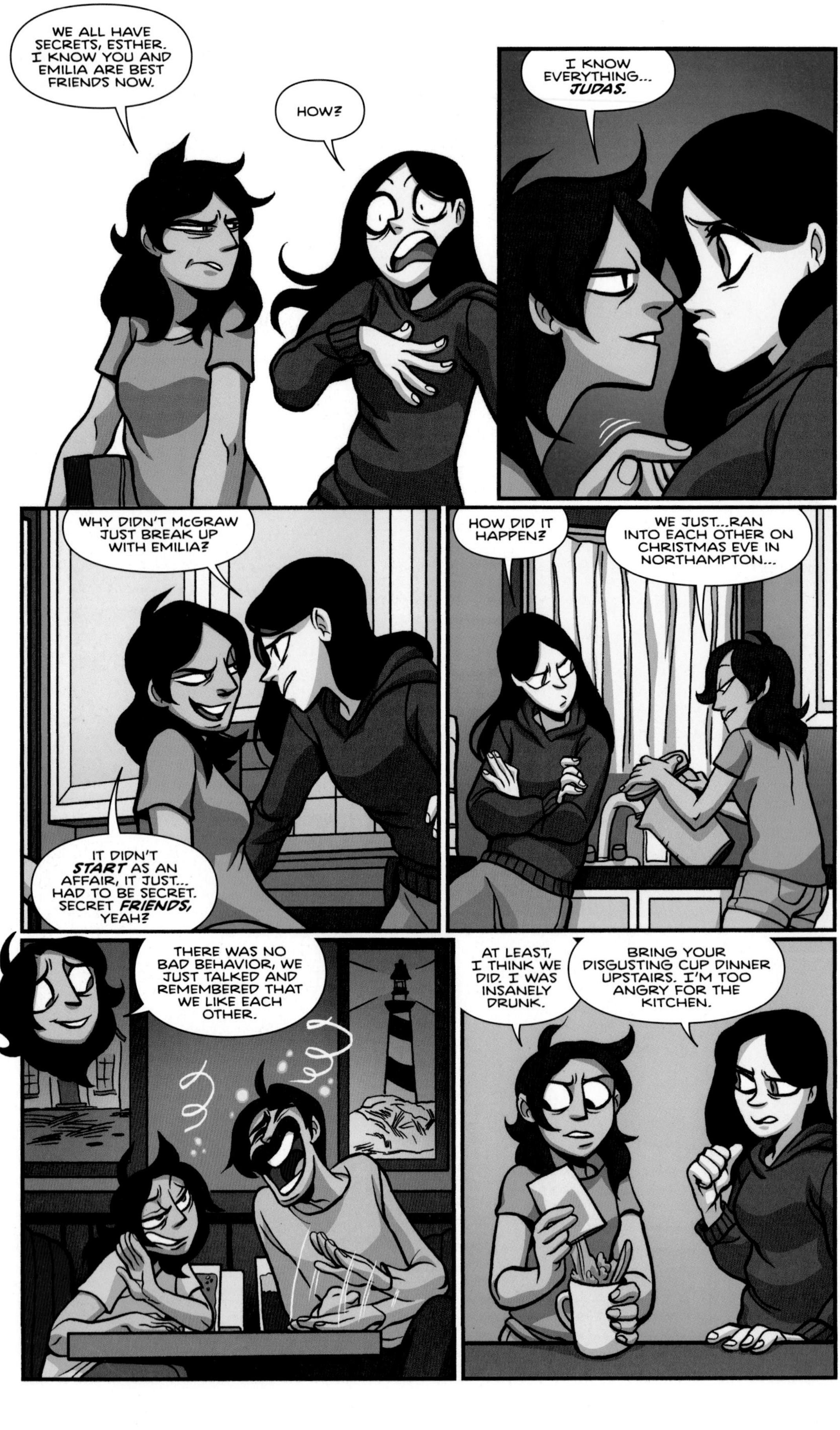
WE ALL HAVE SECRETS, ESTHER. I KNOW YOU AND EMILIA ARE BEST FRIENDS NOW.
HOW?
I KNOW EVERYTHING... JUDAS.
WHY DIDN'T McGRAW JUST BREAK UP WITH EMILIA?
IT DIDN'T START AS AN AFFAIR, IT JUST... HAD TO BE SECRET. SECRET FRIENDS, YEAH?
HOW DID IT HAPPEN?
WE JUST...RAN INTO EACH OTHER ON CHRISTMAS EVE IN NORTHAMPTON...
THERE WAS NO BAD BEHAVIOR, WE JUST TALKED AND REMEMBERED THAT WE LIKE EACH OTHER.
AT LEAST, I THINK WE DID. I WAS INSANELY DRUNK.
BRING YOUR DISGUSTING CUP DINNER UPSTAIRS. I'M TOO ANGRY FOR THE KITCHEN.

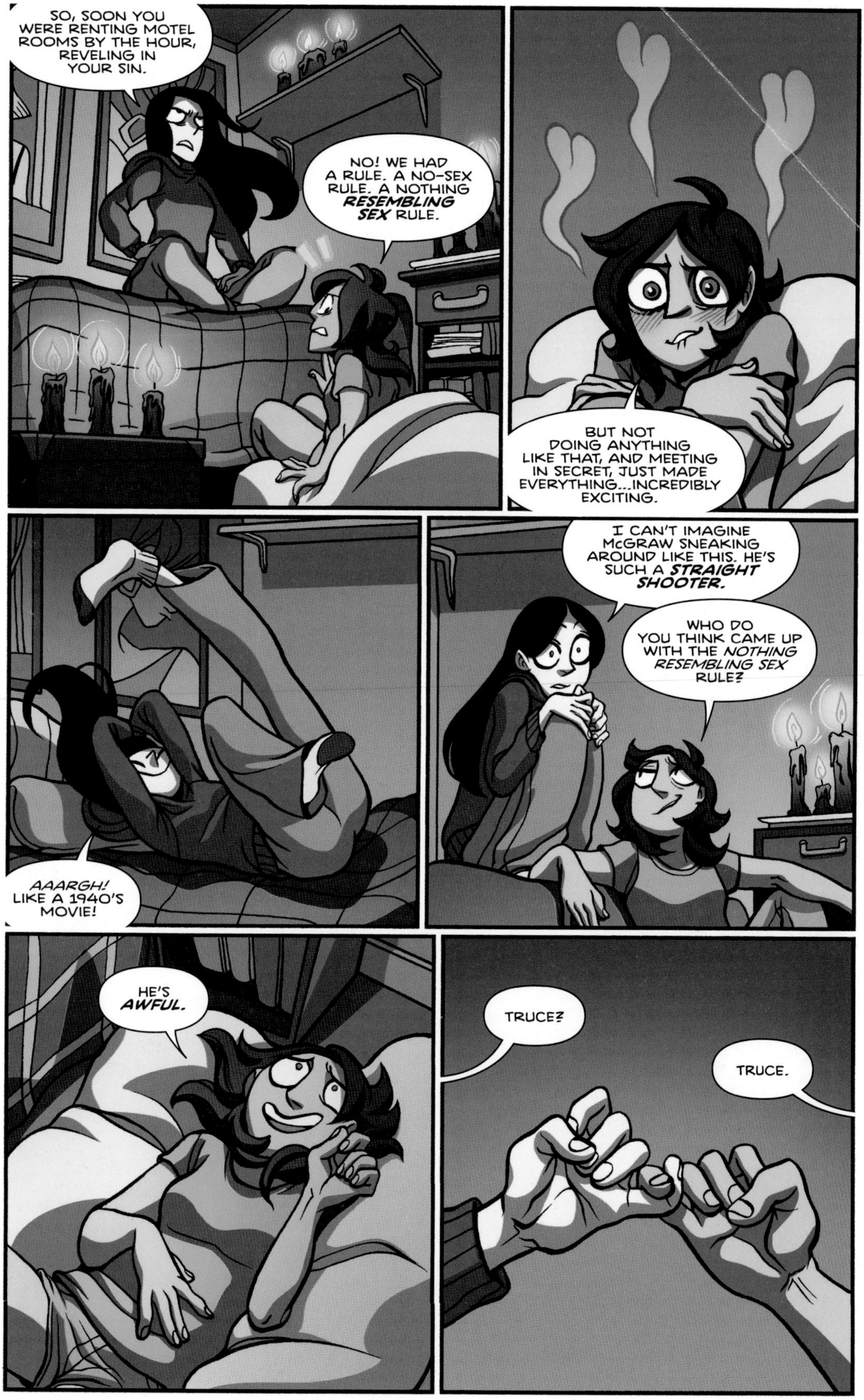
SO, SOON YOU WERE RENTING MOTEL ROOMS BY THE HOUR, REVELING IN YOUR SIN.
NO! WE HAD A RULE. A NO-SEX RULE. A NOTHING ***RESEMBLING SEX*** RULE.
BUT NOT DOING ANYTHING LIKE THAT, AND MEETING IN SECRET, JUST MADE EVERYTHING...INCREDIBLY EXCITING.
AAARGH! LIKE A 1940'S MOVIE!
I CAN'T IMAGINE McGRAW SNEAKING AROUND LIKE THIS. HE'S SUCH A ***STRAIGHT SHOOTER.***
WHO DO YOU THINK CAME UP WITH THE *NOTHING RESEMBLING SEX* RULE?
HE'S ***AWFUL.***
TRUCE?
TRUCE.

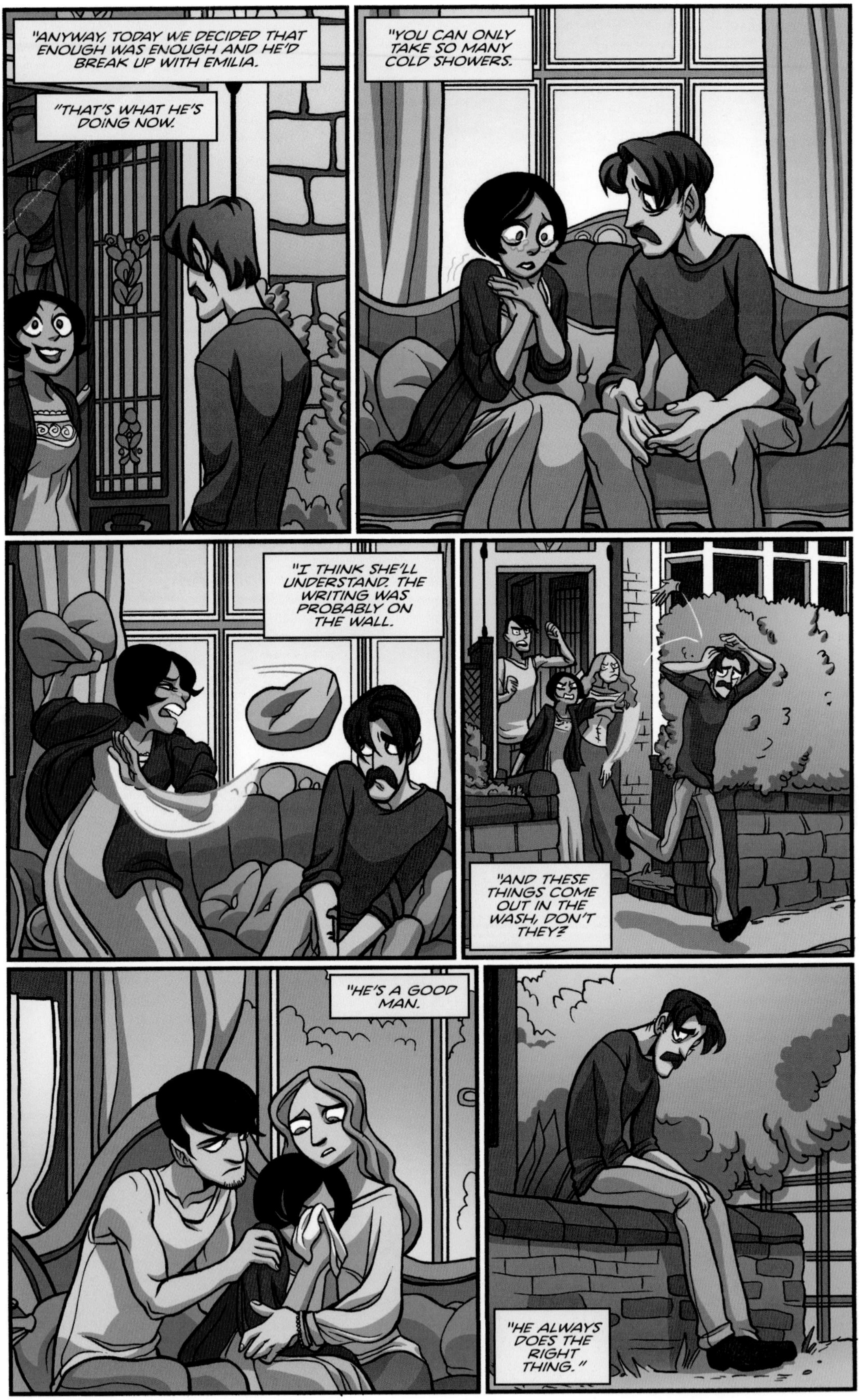
"ANYWAY, TODAY WE DECIDED THAT ENOUGH WAS ENOUGH AND HE'D BREAK UP WITH EMILIA.
"THAT'S WHAT HE'S DOING NOW.
"YOU CAN ONLY TAKE SO MANY COLD SHOWERS.
"I THINK SHE'LL UNDERSTAND. THE WRITING WAS PROBABLY ON THE WALL.
"AND THESE THINGS COME OUT IN THE WASH, DON'T THEY?
"HE'S A GOOD MAN.
"HE ALWAYS DOES THE RIGHT THING."

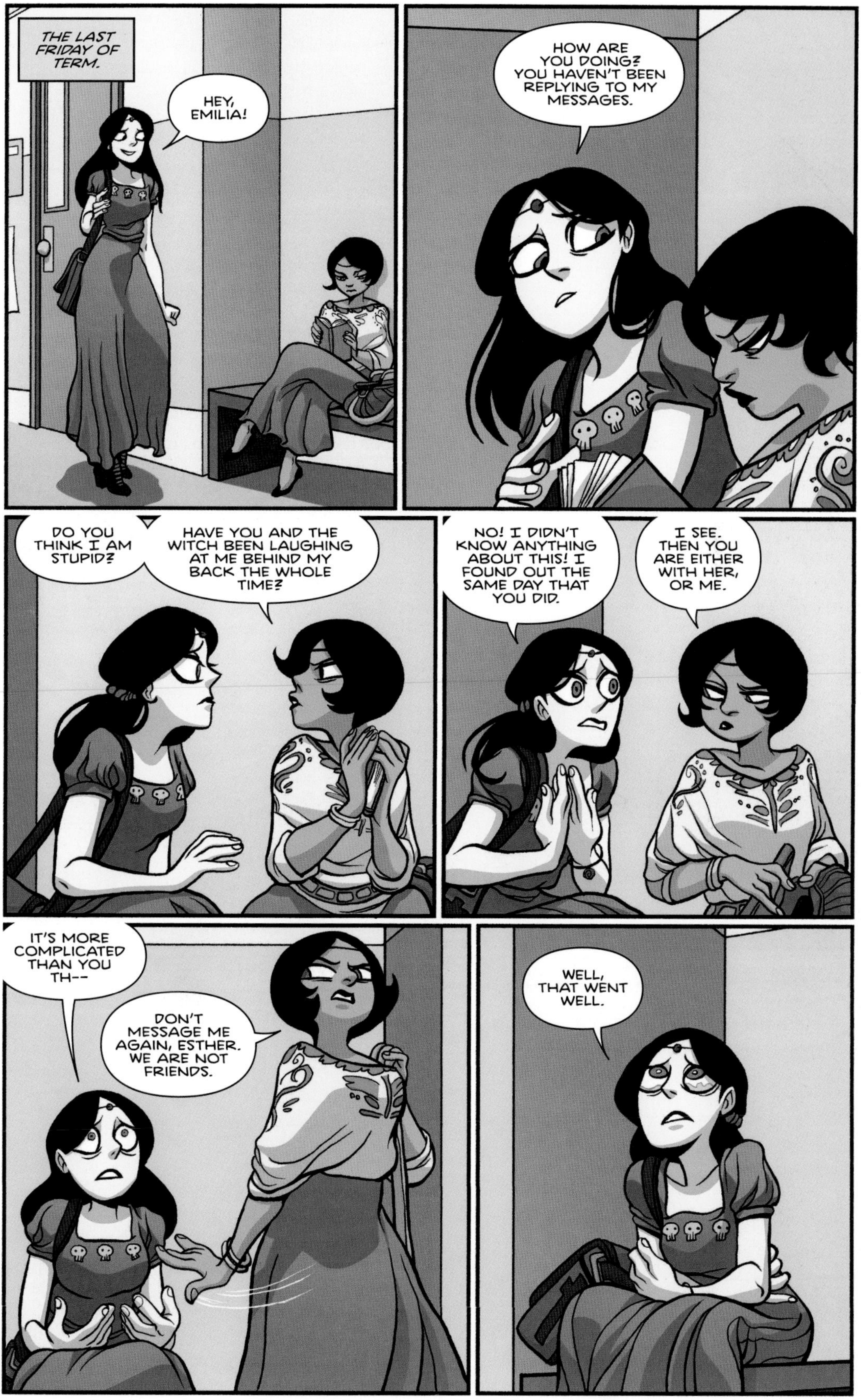
THE LAST FRIDAY OF TERM.
HEY, EMILIA!
HOW ARE YOU DOING? YOU HAVEN'T BEEN REPLYING TO MY MESSAGES.
DO YOU THINK I AM STUPID?
HAVE YOU AND THE WITCH BEEN LAUGHING AT ME BEHIND MY BACK THE WHOLE TIME?
NO! I DIDN'T KNOW ANYTHING ABOUT THIS! I FOUND OUT THE SAME DAY THAT YOU DID.
I SEE. THEN YOU ARE EITHER WITH HER, OR ME.
IT'S MORE COMPLICATED THAN YOU TH--
DON'T MESSAGE ME AGAIN, ESTHER. WE ARE NOT FRIENDS.
WELL, THAT WENT WELL.

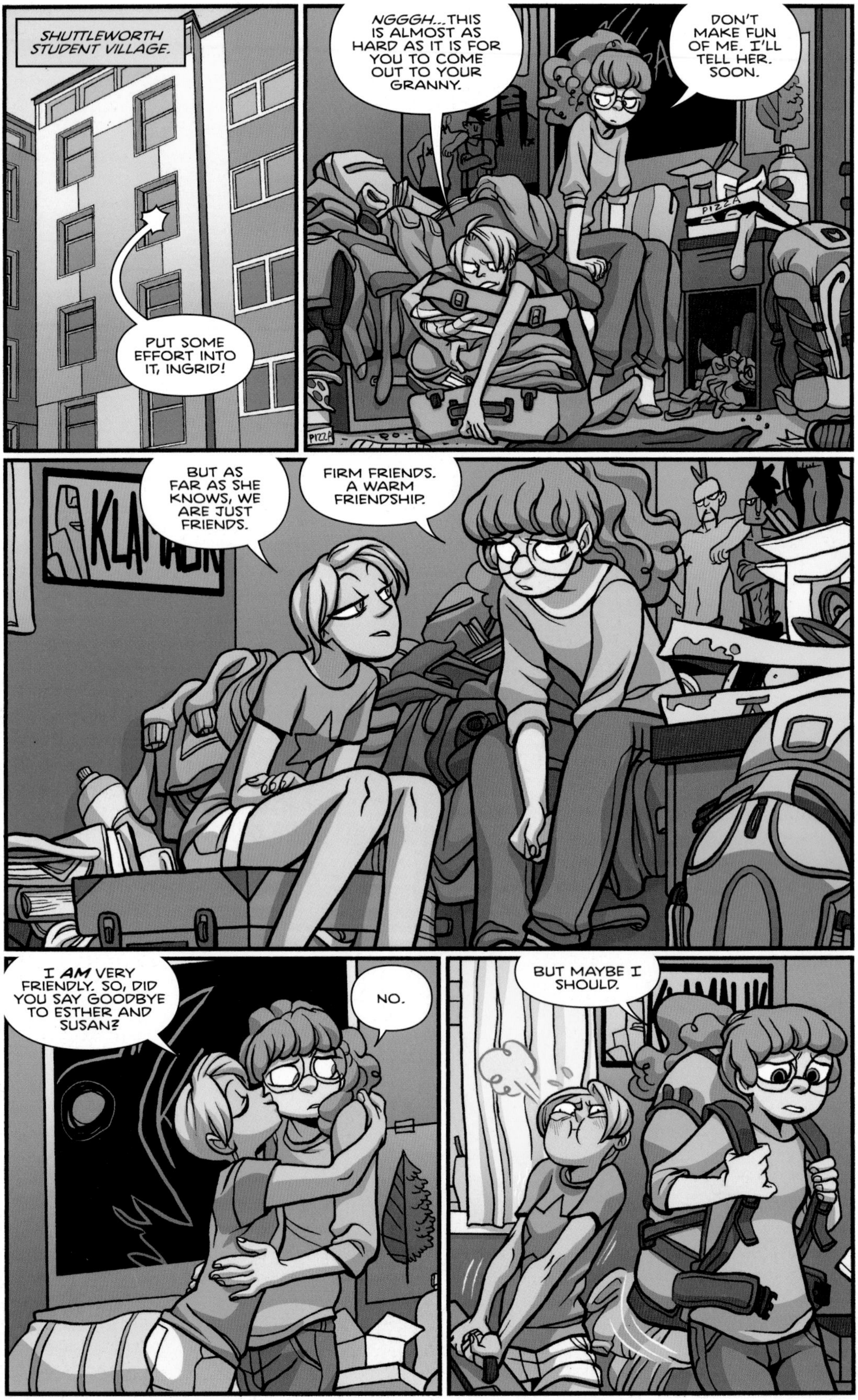
SHUTTLEWORTH STUDENT VILLAGE.
PUT SOME EFFORT INTO IT, INGRID!
NGGGH... THIS IS ALMOST AS HARD AS IT IS FOR YOU TO COME OUT TO YOUR GRANNY.
DON'T MAKE FUN OF ME. I'LL TELL HER. SOON.
PIZZA
BUT AS FAR AS SHE KNOWS, WE ARE JUST FRIENDS.
FIRM FRIENDS. A WARM FRIENDSHIP.
I AM VERY FRIENDLY. SO, DID YOU SAY GOODBYE TO ESTHER AND SUSAN?
NO.
BUT MAYBE I SHOULD.

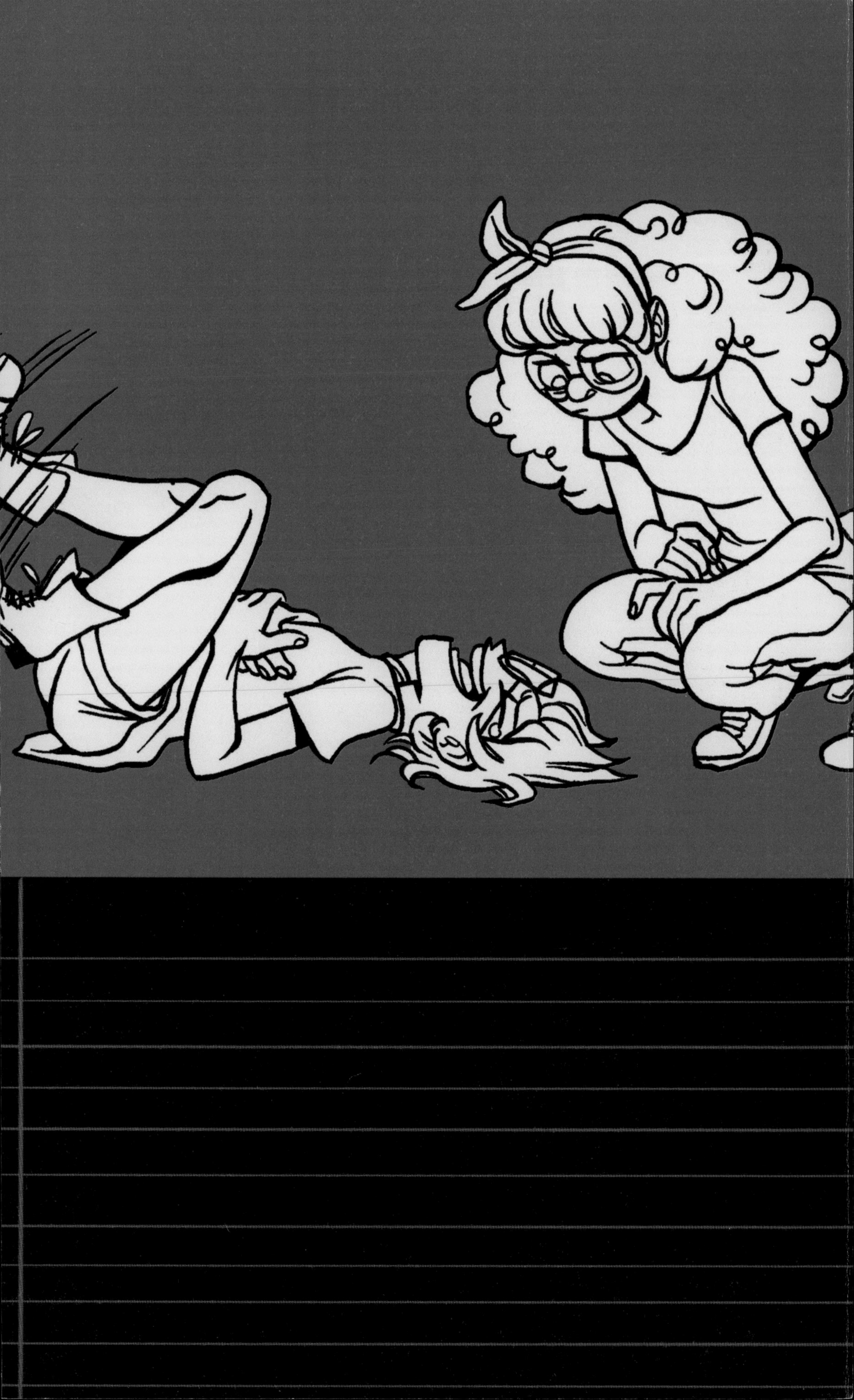

CHAPTER
THIRTY-ONE

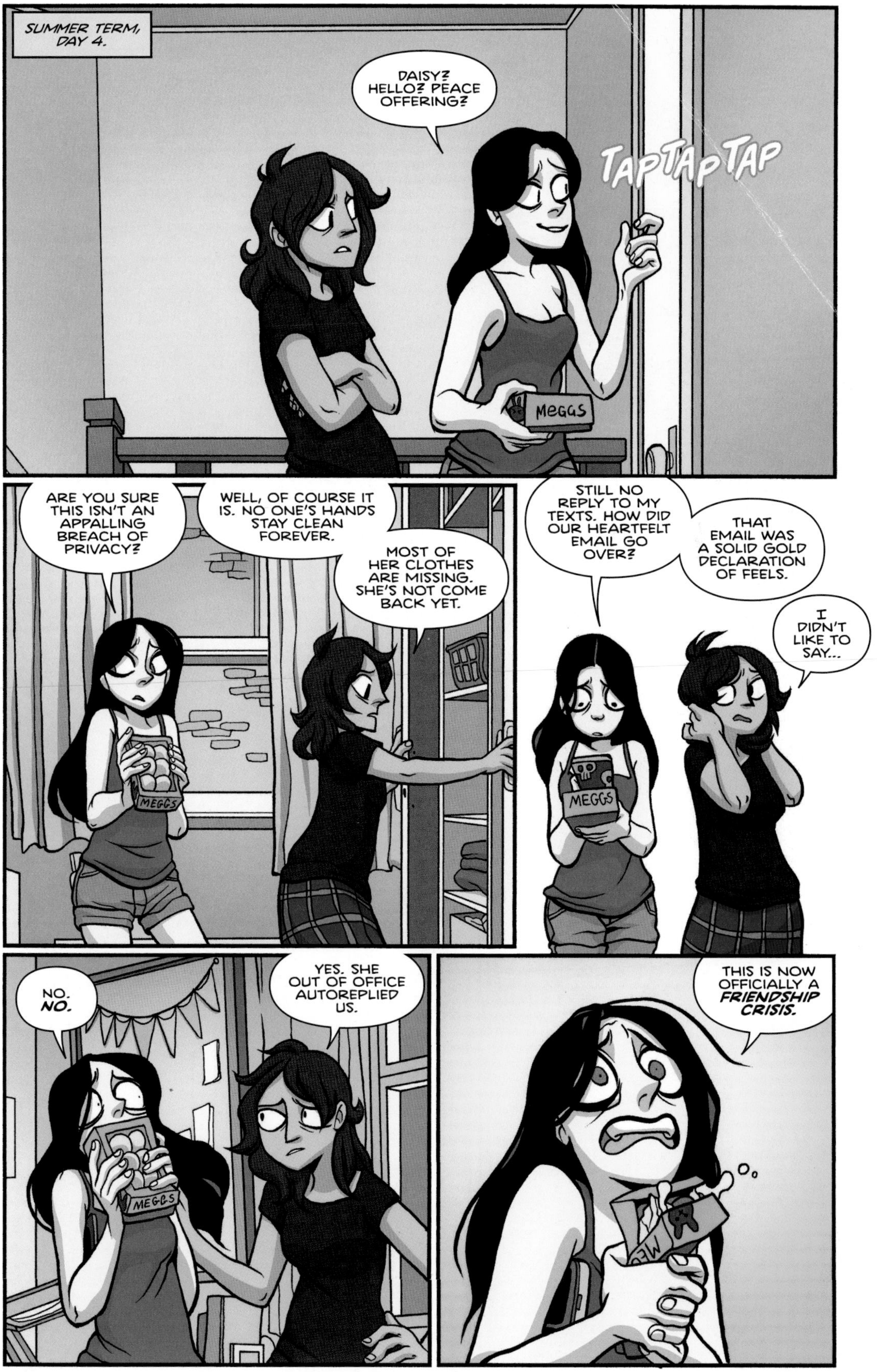
SUMMER TERM, DAY 4.
DAISY? HELLO? PEACE OFFERING?
TAPTAPTAP
MEGGS
ARE YOU SURE THIS ISN'T AN APPALLING BREACH OF PRIVACY?
WELL, OF COURSE IT IS. NO ONE'S HANDS STAY CLEAN FOREVER.
MOST OF HER CLOTHES ARE MISSING. SHE'S NOT COME BACK YET.
MEGGS
STILL NO REPLY TO MY TEXTS. HOW DID OUR HEARTFELT EMAIL GO OVER?
THAT EMAIL WAS A SOLID GOLD DECLARATION OF FEELS.
I DIDN'T LIKE TO SAY...
MEGGS
NO. NO.
YES. SHE OUT OF OFFICE AUTOREPLIED US.
MEGGS
THIS IS NOW OFFICIALLY A FRIENDSHIP CRISIS.

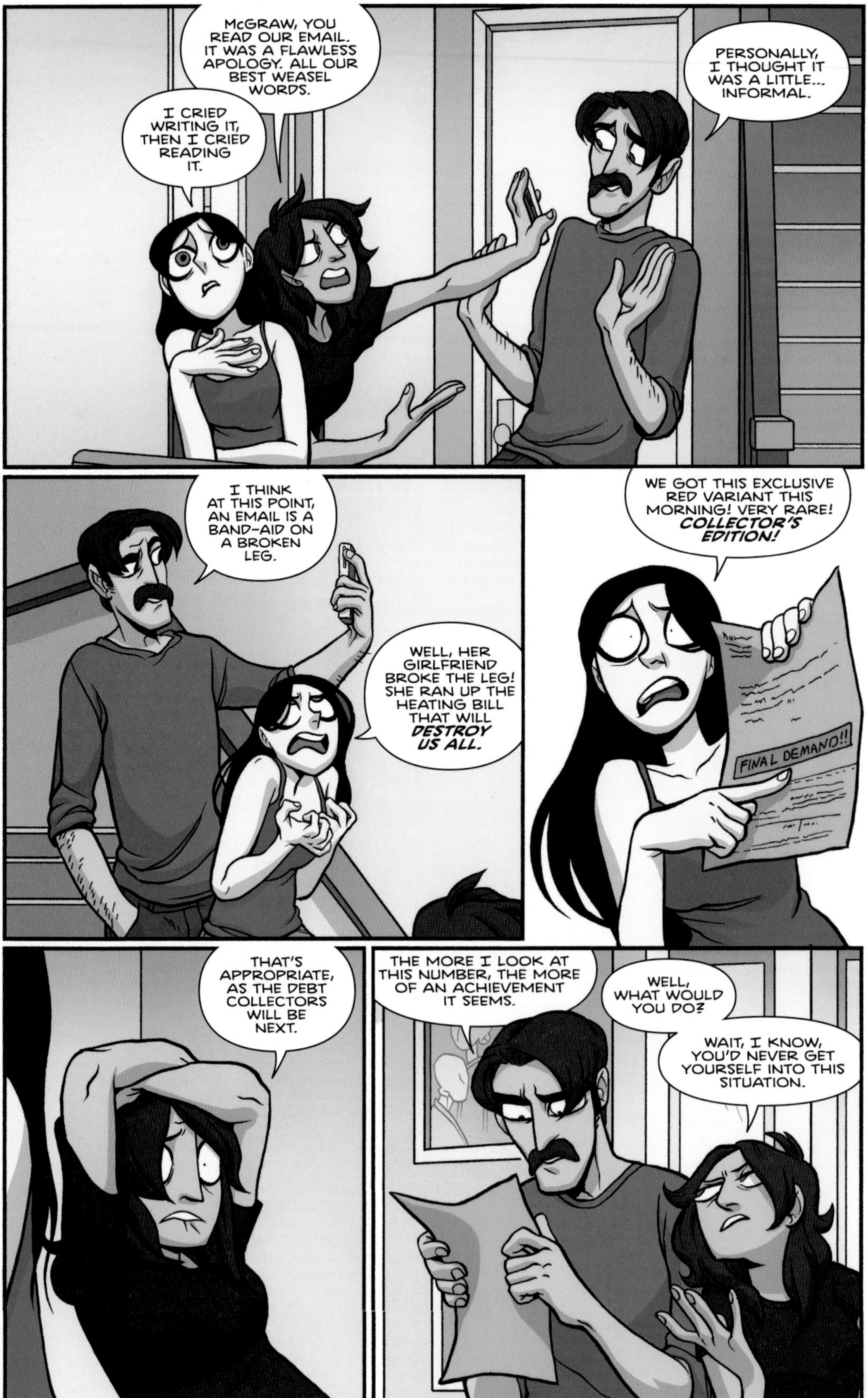
McGRAW, YOU READ OUR EMAIL. IT WAS A FLAWLESS APOLOGY. ALL OUR BEST WEASEL WORDS.
I CRIED WRITING IT, THEN I CRIED READING IT.
PERSONALLY, I THOUGHT IT WAS A LITTLE... INFORMAL.
I THINK AT THIS POINT, AN EMAIL IS A BAND-AID ON A BROKEN LEG.
WELL, HER GIRLFRIEND BROKE THE LEG! SHE RAN UP THE HEATING BILL THAT WILL DESTROY US ALL.
WE GOT THIS EXCLUSIVE RED VARIANT THIS MORNING! VERY RARE! COLLECTOR'S EDITION!
FINAL DEMAND!!
THAT'S APPROPRIATE, AS THE DEBT COLLECTORS WILL BE NEXT.
THE MORE I LOOK AT THIS NUMBER, THE MORE OF AN ACHIEVEMENT IT SEEMS.
WELL, WHAT WOULD YOU DO?
WAIT, I KNOW, YOU'D NEVER GET YOURSELF INTO THIS SITUATION.

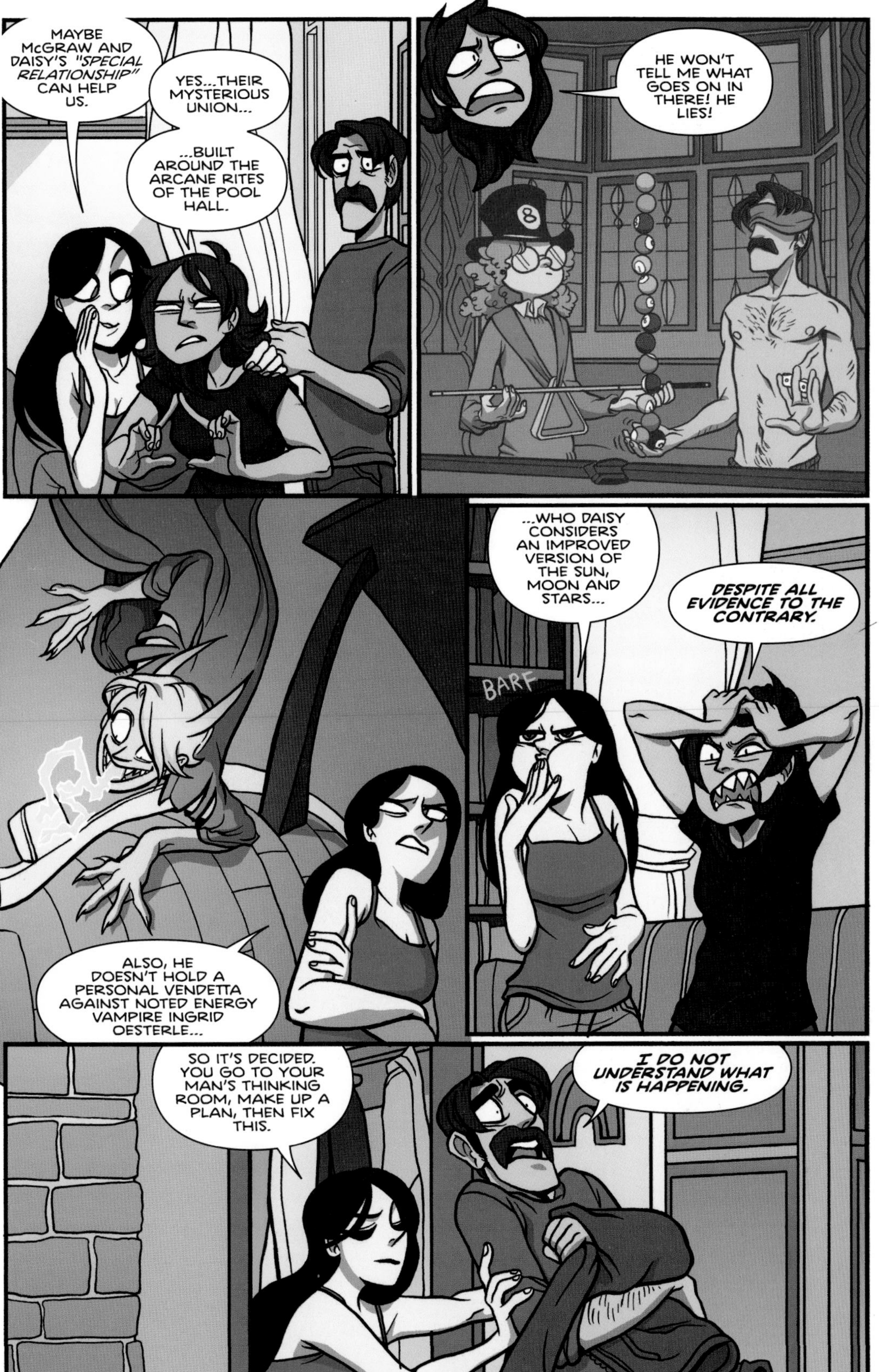

MAYBE McGRAW AND DAISY'S "SPECIAL RELATIONSHIP" CAN HELP US.
YES...THEIR MYSTERIOUS UNION...
...BUILT AROUND THE ARCANE RITES OF THE POOL HALL.
HE WON'T TELL ME WHAT GOES ON IN THERE! HE LIES!
ALSO, HE DOESN'T HOLD A PERSONAL VENDETTA AGAINST NOTED ENERGY VAMPIRE INGRID OESTERLE...
...WHO DAISY CONSIDERS AN IMPROVED VERSION OF THE SUN, MOON AND STARS...
DESPITE ALL EVIDENCE TO THE CONTRARY.
BARF
SO IT'S DECIDED. YOU GO TO YOUR MAN'S THINKING ROOM, MAKE UP A PLAN, THEN FIX THIS.
I DO NOT UNDERSTAND WHAT IS HAPPENING.

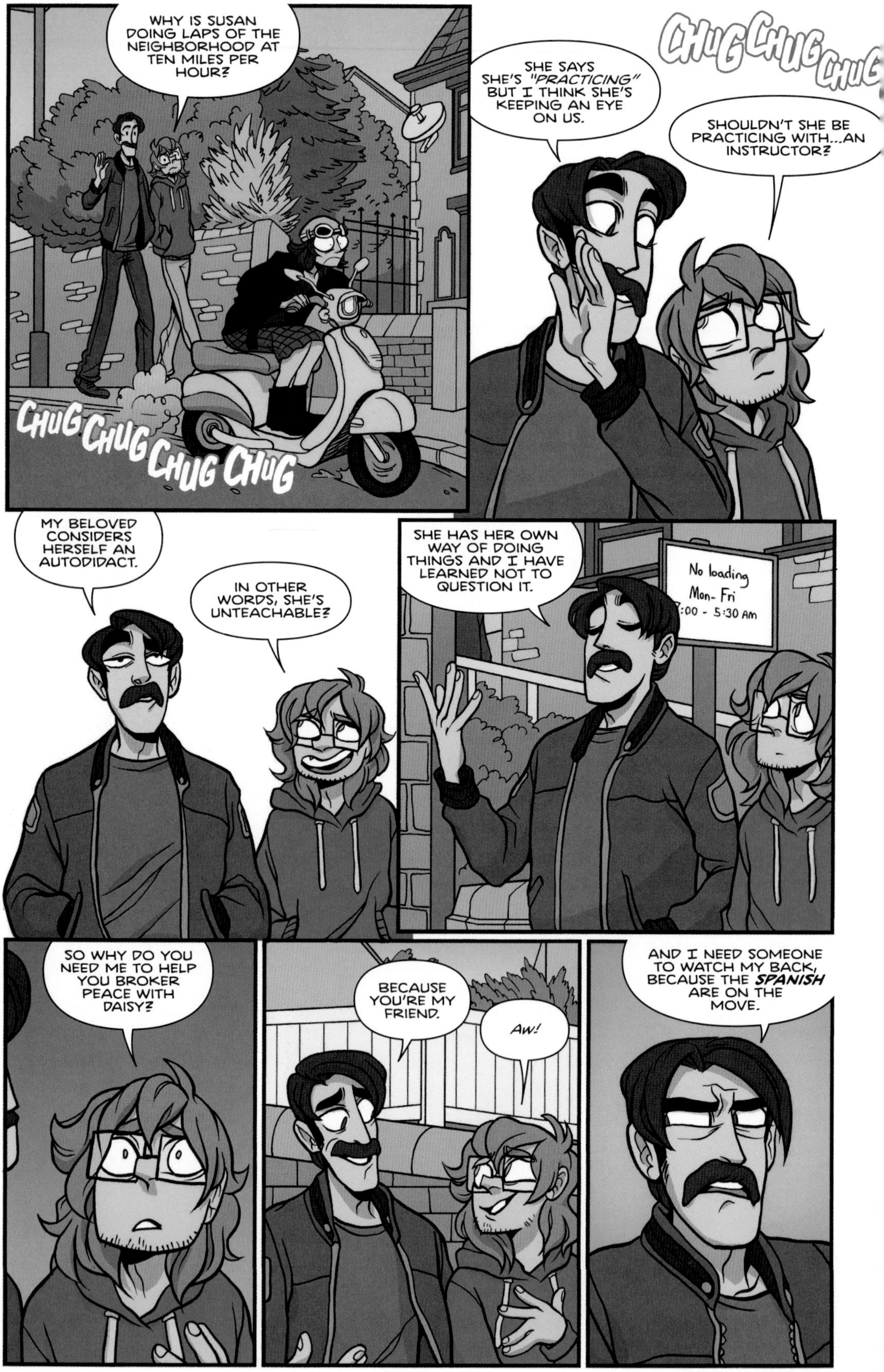
WHY IS SUSAN DOING LAPS OF THE NEIGHBORHOOD AT TEN MILES PER HOUR?
CHUG CHUG CHUG CHUG
CHUG CHUG CHUG
SHE SAYS SHE'S "PRACTICING" BUT I THINK SHE'S KEEPING AN EYE ON US.
SHOULDN'T SHE BE PRACTICING WITH...AN INSTRUCTOR?
MY BELOVED CONSIDERS HERSELF AN AUTODIDACT.
IN OTHER WORDS, SHE'S UNTEACHABLE?
SHE HAS HER OWN WAY OF DOING THINGS AND I HAVE LEARNED NOT TO QUESTION IT.
No loading
Mon- Fri
:00 - 5:30 Am
SO WHY DO YOU NEED ME TO HELP YOU BROKER PEACE WITH DAISY?
BECAUSE YOU'RE MY FRIEND.
AW!
AND I NEED SOMEONE TO WATCH MY BACK, BECAUSE THE SPANISH ARE ON THE MOVE.

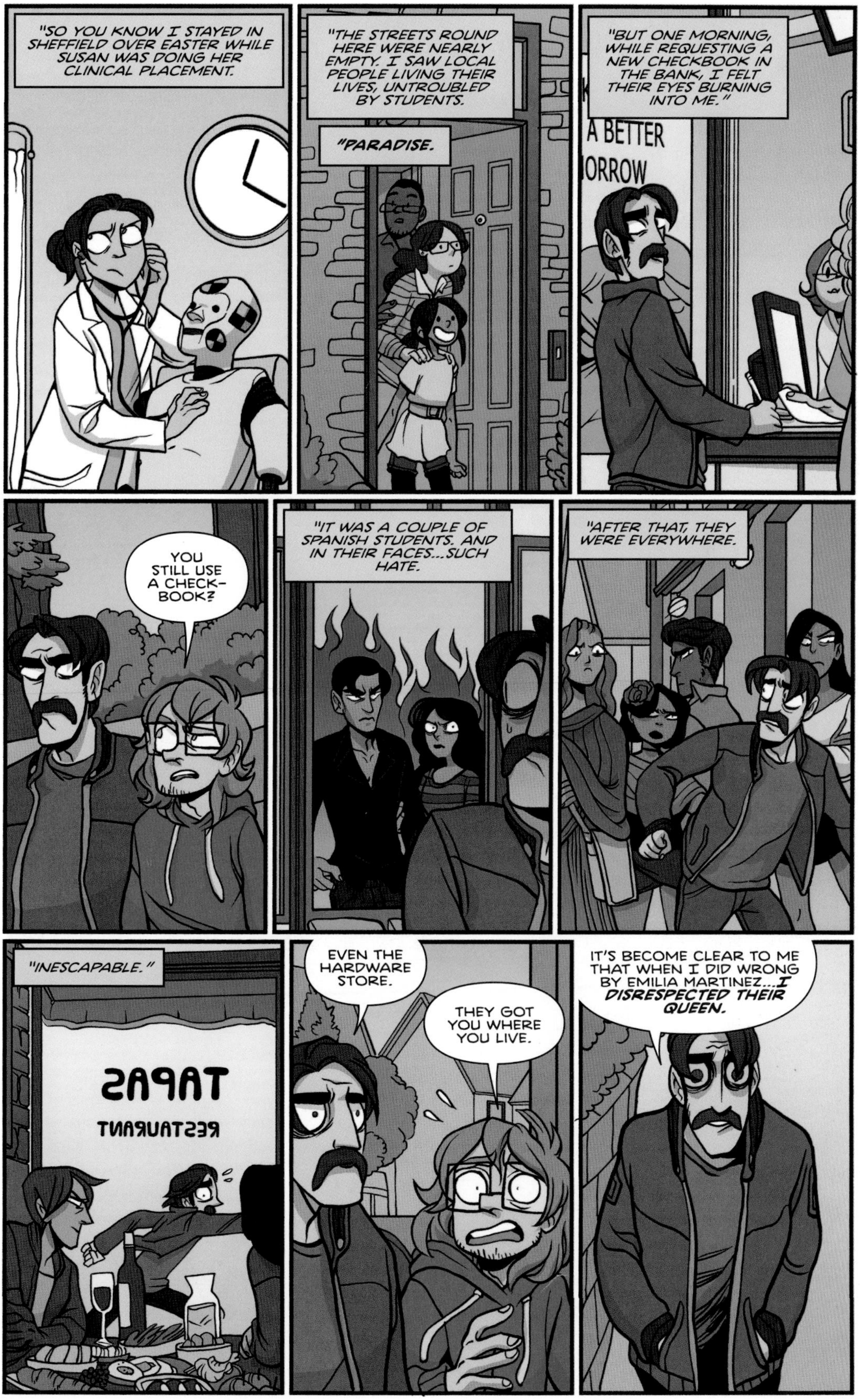
"SO YOU KNOW I STAYED IN SHEFFIELD OVER EASTER WHILE SUSAN WAS DOING HER CLINICAL PLACEMENT.
"THE STREETS ROUND HERE WERE NEARLY EMPTY. I SAW LOCAL PEOPLE LIVING THEIR LIVES, UNTROUBLED BY STUDENTS.
"PARADISE.
"BUT ONE MORNING, WHILE REQUESTING A NEW CHECKBOOK IN THE BANK, I FELT THEIR EYES BURNING INTO ME."
A BETTER
ORROW
YOU STILL USE A CHECK-BOOK?
"IT WAS A COUPLE OF SPANISH STUDENTS. AND IN THEIR FACES...SUCH HATE.
"AFTER THAT, THEY WERE EVERYWHERE.
"INESCAPABLE."
TAPAS
RESTAURANT
EVEN THE HARDWARE STORE.
THEY GOT YOU WHERE YOU LIVE.
IT'S BECOME CLEAR TO ME THAT WHEN I DID WRONG BY EMILIA MARTINEZ...I DISRESPECTED THEIR QUEEN.

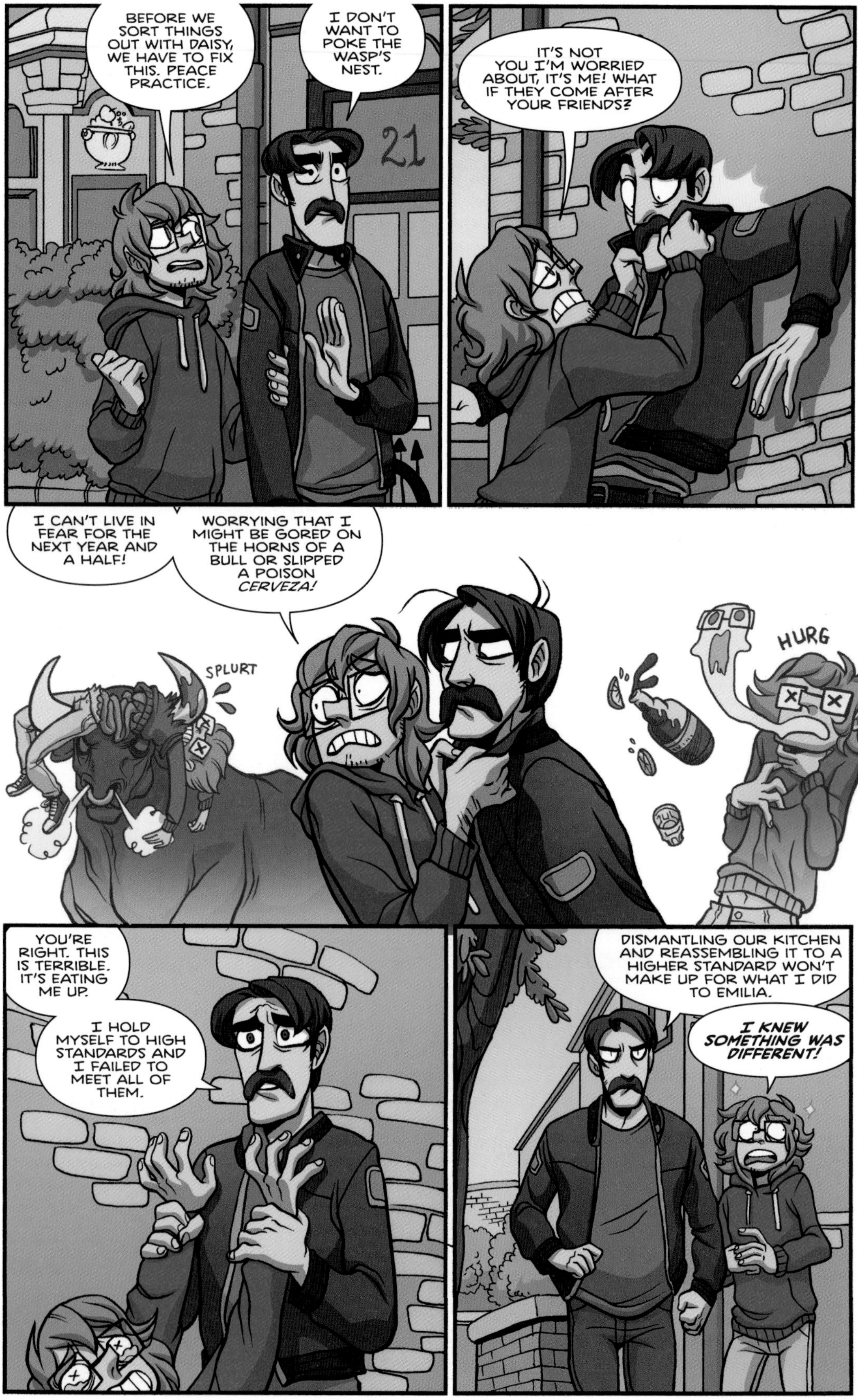
BEFORE WE SORT THINGS OUT WITH DAISY, WE HAVE TO FIX THIS. PEACE PRACTICE.
I DON'T WANT TO POKE THE WASP'S NEST.
21
IT'S NOT YOU I'M WORRIED ABOUT, IT'S ME! WHAT IF THEY COME AFTER YOUR FRIENDS?
I CAN'T LIVE IN FEAR FOR THE NEXT YEAR AND A HALF!
WORRYING THAT I MIGHT BE GORED ON THE HORNS OF A BULL OR SLIPPED A POISON *CERVEZA!*
SPLURT
HURG
YOU'RE RIGHT. THIS IS TERRIBLE. IT'S EATING ME UP.
I HOLD MYSELF TO HIGH STANDARDS AND I FAILED TO MEET ALL OF THEM.
DISMANTLING OUR KITCHEN AND REASSEMBLING IT TO A HIGHER STANDARD WON'T MAKE UP FOR WHAT I DID TO EMILIA.
I KNEW SOMETHING WAS DIFFERENT!

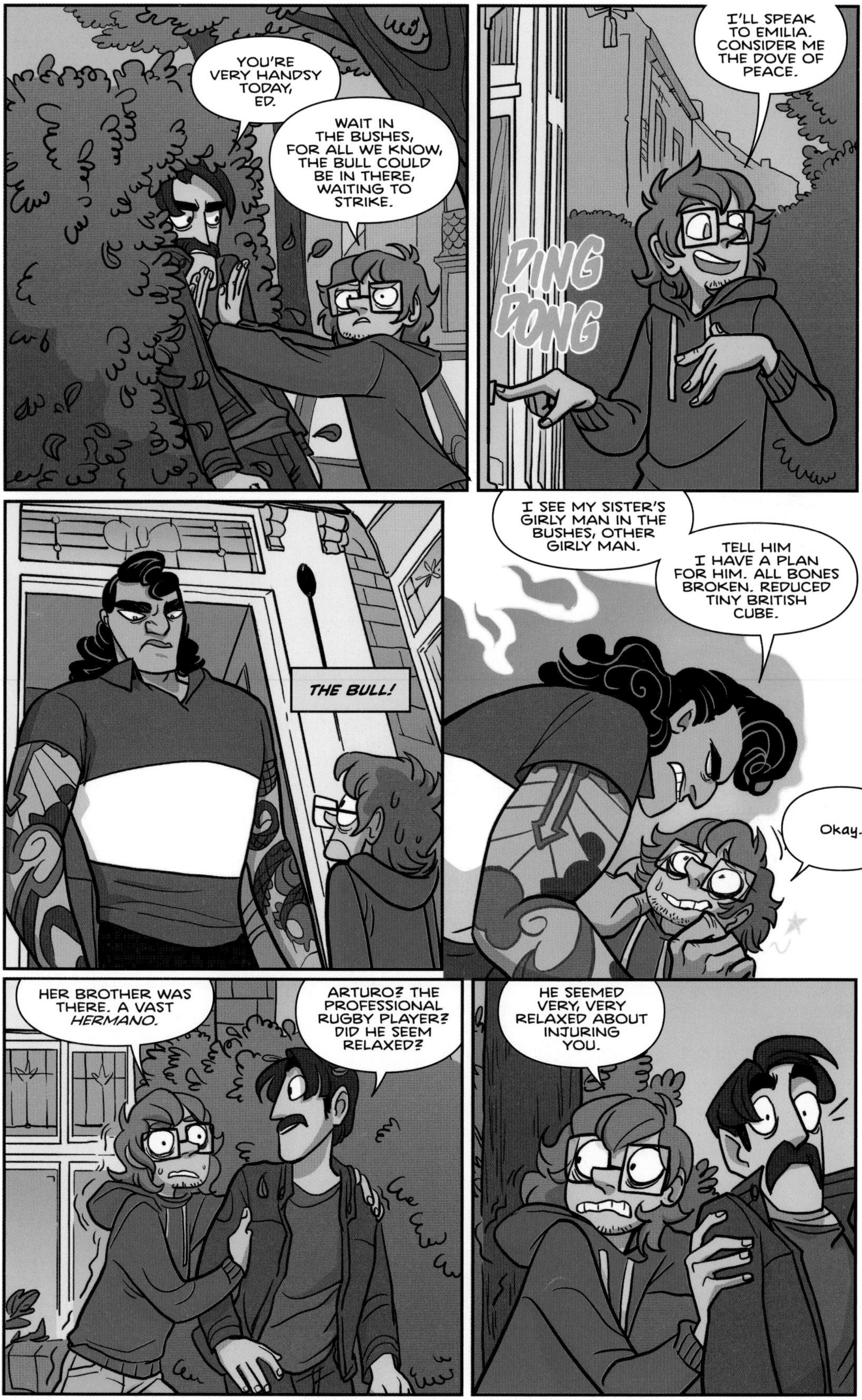
YOU'RE VERY HANDSY TODAY, ED.
WAIT IN THE BUSHES, FOR ALL WE KNOW, THE BULL COULD BE IN THERE, WAITING TO STRIKE.
I'LL SPEAK TO EMILIA. CONSIDER ME THE DOVE OF PEACE.
DING DONG
THE BULL!
I SEE MY SISTER'S GIRLY MAN IN THE BUSHES, OTHER GIRLY MAN.
TELL HIM I HAVE A PLAN FOR HIM. ALL BONES BROKEN. REDUCED TINY BRITISH CUBE.
Okay.
HER BROTHER WAS THERE. A VAST *HERMANO.*
ARTURO? THE PROFESSIONAL RUGBY PLAYER? DID HE SEEM RELAXED?
HE SEEMED VERY, VERY RELAXED ABOUT INJURING YOU.

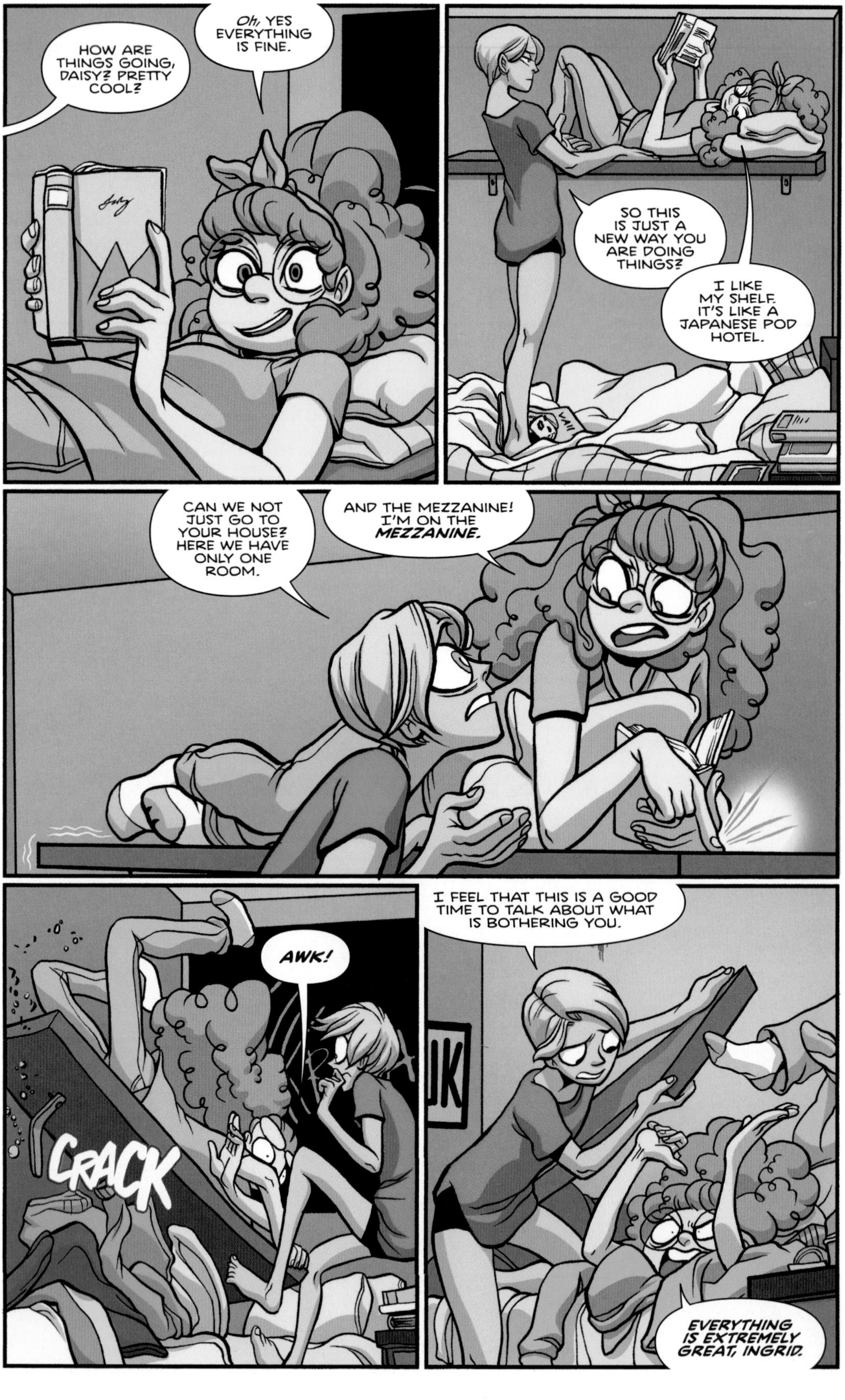
HOW ARE THINGS GOING, DAISY? PRETTY COOL?
Oh, YES EVERYTHING IS FINE.
SO THIS IS JUST A NEW WAY YOU ARE DOING THINGS?
I LIKE MY SHELF. IT'S LIKE A JAPANESE POD HOTEL.
CAN WE NOT JUST GO TO YOUR HOUSE? HERE WE HAVE ONLY ONE ROOM.
AND THE MEZZANINE! I'M ON THE *MEZZANINE.*
AWK!
CRACK
I FEEL THAT THIS IS A GOOD TIME TO TALK ABOUT WHAT IS BOTHERING YOU.
EVERYTHING IS EXTREMELY GREAT, INGRID.

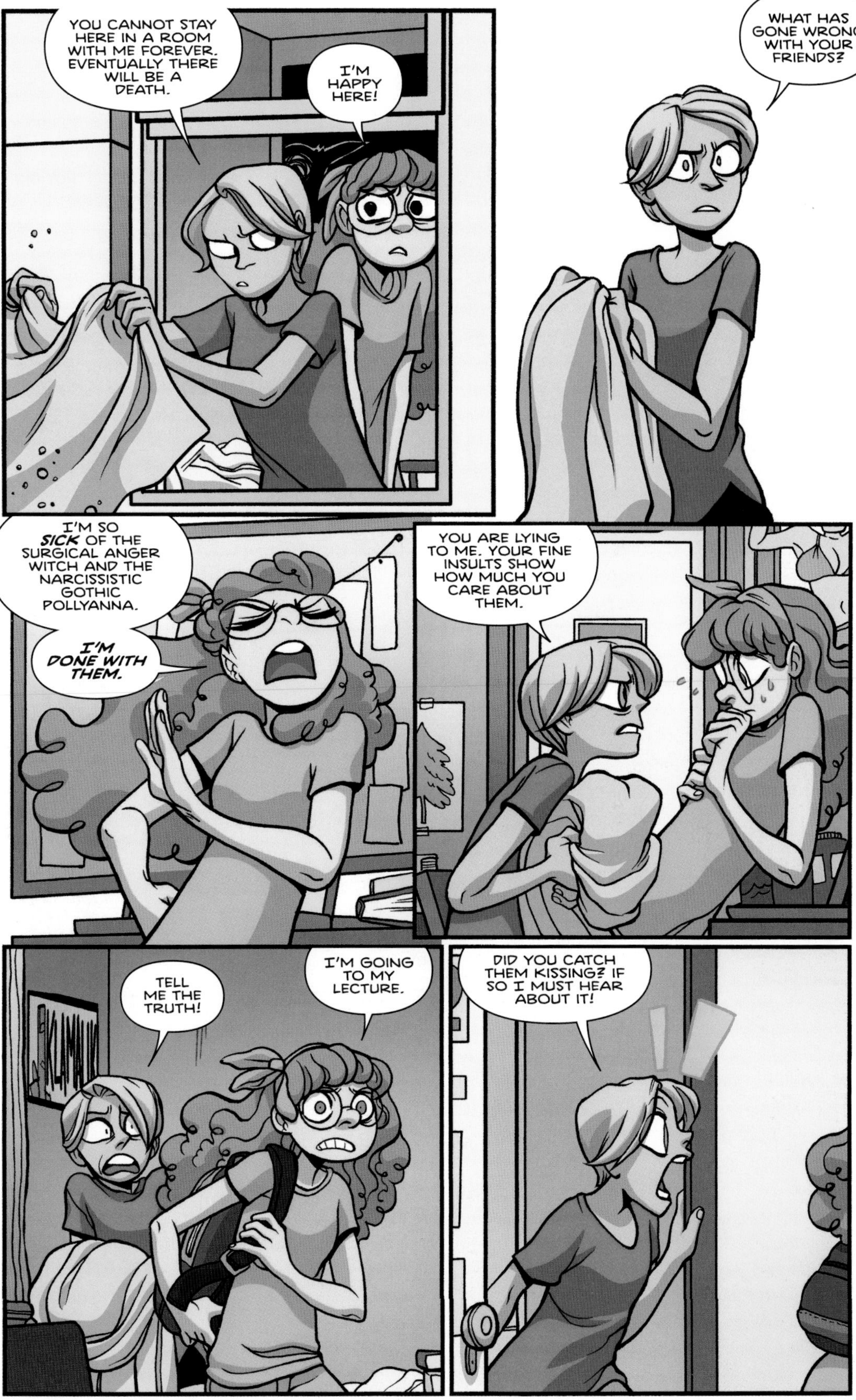
YOU CANNOT STAY HERE IN A ROOM WITH ME FOREVER. EVENTUALLY THERE WILL BE A DEATH.
I'M HAPPY HERE!
WHAT HAS GONE WRONG WITH YOUR FRIENDS?
I'M SO SICK OF THE SURGICAL ANGER WITCH AND THE NARCISSISTIC GOTHIC POLLYANNA.
I'M DONE WITH THEM.
YOU ARE LYING TO ME. YOUR FINE INSULTS SHOW HOW MUCH YOU CARE ABOUT THEM.
TELL ME THE TRUTH!
I'M GOING TO MY LECTURE.
DID YOU CATCH THEM KISSING? IF SO I MUST HEAR ABOUT IT!
!

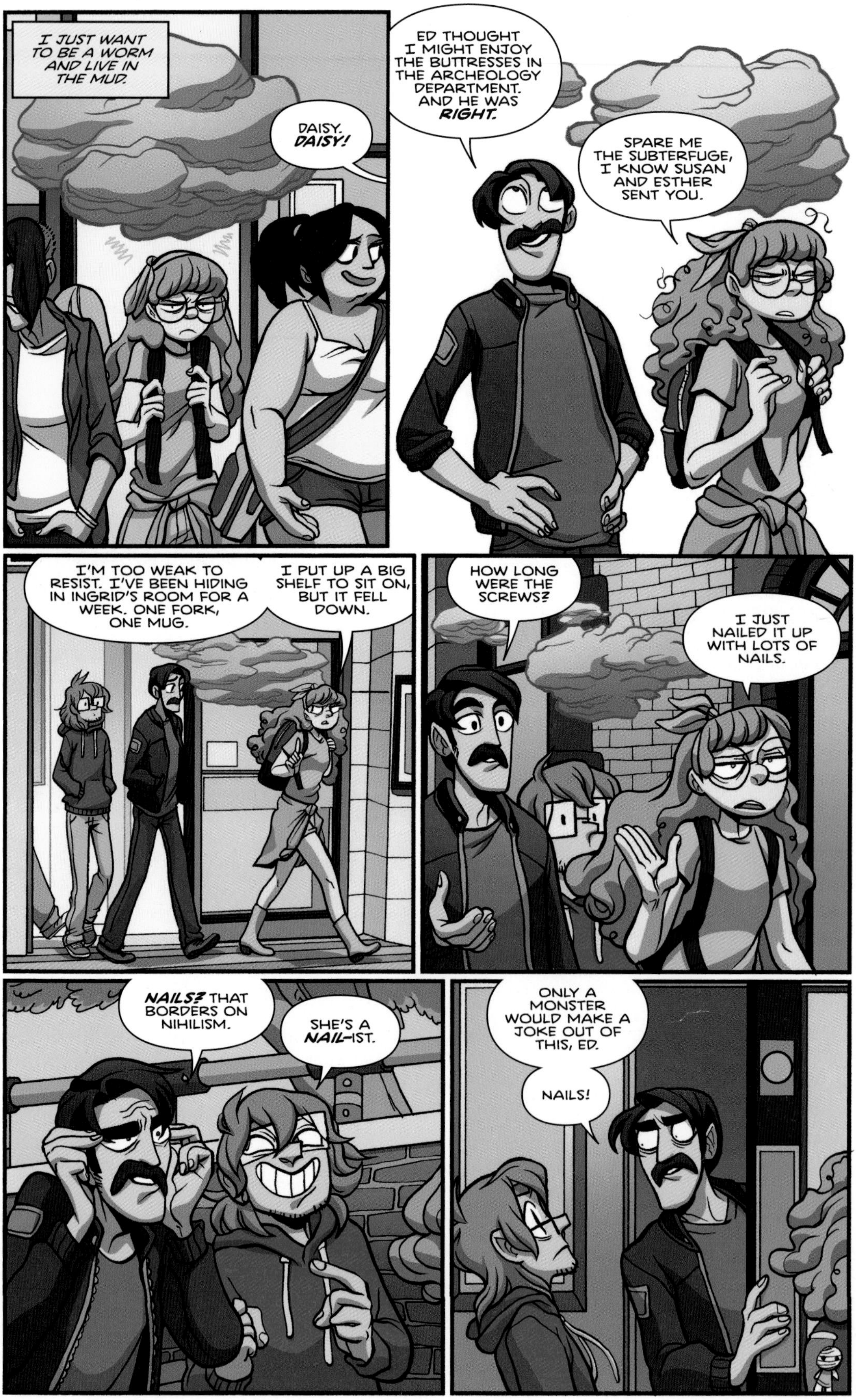
I JUST WANT TO BE A WORM AND LIVE IN THE MUD.
DAISY. DAISY!
ED THOUGHT I MIGHT ENJOY THE BUTTRESSES IN THE ARCHEOLOGY DEPARTMENT. AND HE WAS RIGHT.
SPARE ME THE SUBTERFUGE, I KNOW SUSAN AND ESTHER SENT YOU.
I'M TOO WEAK TO RESIST. I'VE BEEN HIDING IN INGRID'S ROOM FOR A WEEK. ONE FORK, ONE MUG.
I PUT UP A BIG SHELF TO SIT ON, BUT IT FELL DOWN.
HOW LONG WERE THE SCREWS?
I JUST NAILED IT UP WITH LOTS OF NAILS.
NAILS? THAT BORDERS ON NIHILISM.
SHE'S A NAIL-IST.
ONLY A MONSTER WOULD MAKE A JOKE OUT OF THIS, ED.
NAILS!

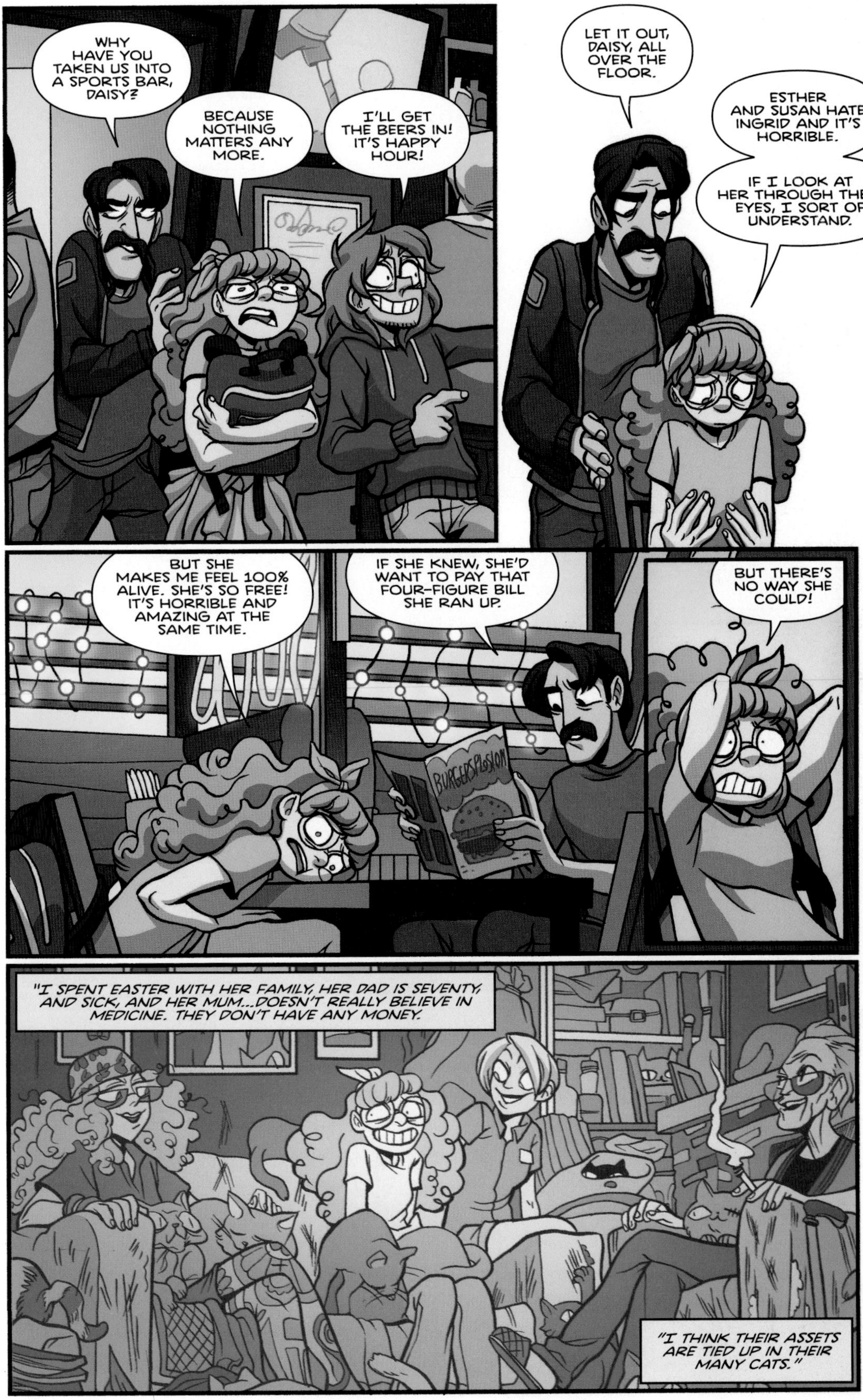
WHY HAVE YOU TAKEN US INTO A SPORTS BAR, DAISY?
BECAUSE NOTHING MATTERS ANY MORE.
I'LL GET THE BEERS IN! IT'S HAPPY HOUR!
LET IT OUT, DAISY, ALL OVER THE FLOOR.
ESTHER AND SUSAN HATE INGRID AND IT'S HORRIBLE.
IF I LOOK AT HER THROUGH THEIR EYES, I SORT OF UNDERSTAND.
BUT SHE MAKES ME FEEL 100% ALIVE. SHE'S SO FREE! IT'S HORRIBLE AND AMAZING AT THE SAME TIME.
IF SHE KNEW, SHE'D WANT TO PAY THAT FOUR-FIGURE BILL SHE RAN UP.
BURGERSPLOSION
BUT THERE'S NO WAY SHE COULD!
"I SPENT EASTER WITH HER FAMILY, HER DAD IS SEVENTY, AND SICK, AND HER MUM...DOESN'T REALLY BELIEVE IN MEDICINE. THEY DON'T HAVE ANY MONEY.
"I THINK THEIR ASSETS ARE TIED UP IN THEIR MANY CATS."

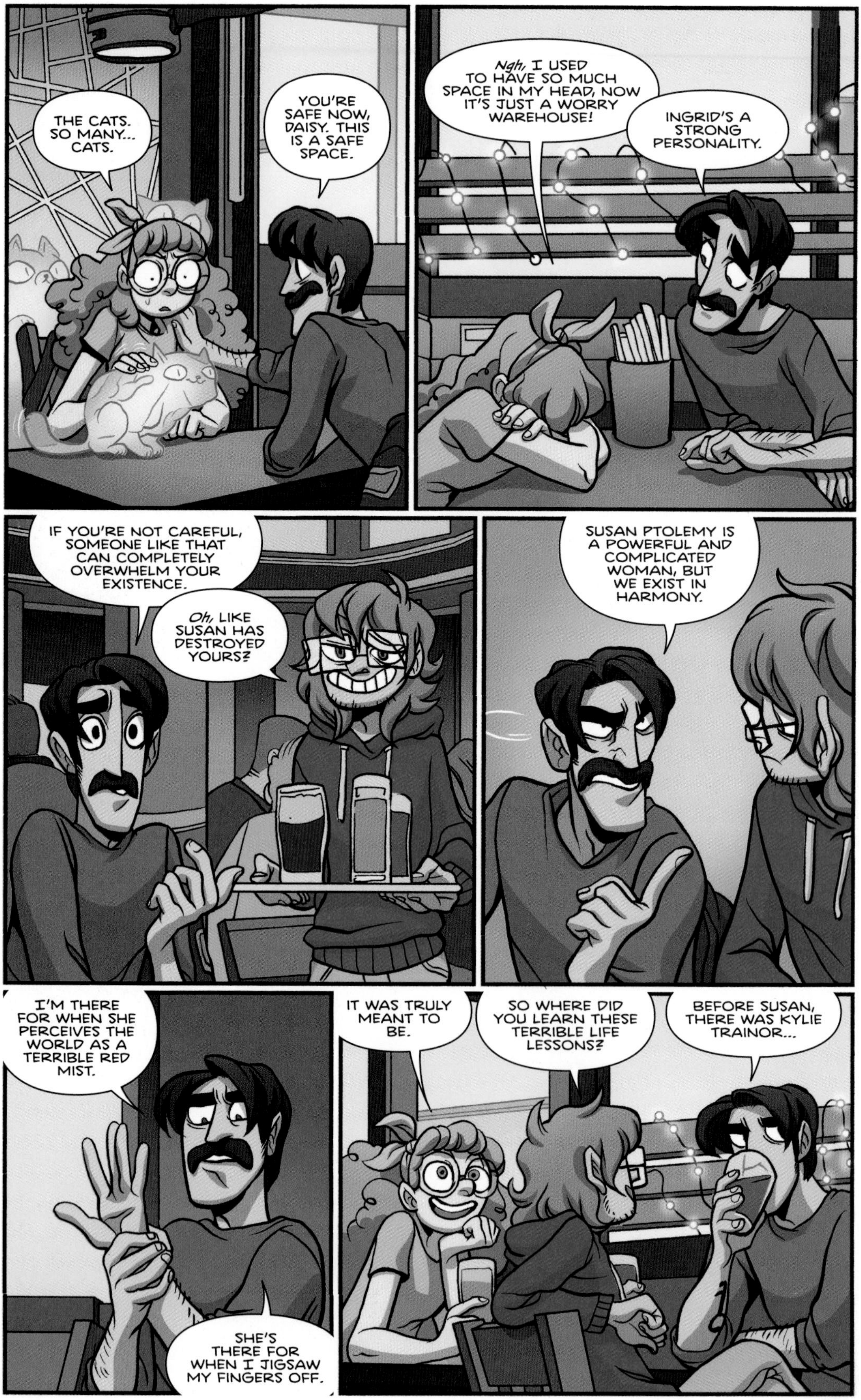
THE CATS. SO MANY... CATS.
YOU'RE SAFE NOW, DAISY. THIS IS A SAFE SPACE.
Ngh, I USED TO HAVE SO MUCH SPACE IN MY HEAD, NOW IT'S JUST A WORRY WAREHOUSE!
INGRID'S A STRONG PERSONALITY.
IF YOU'RE NOT CAREFUL, SOMEONE LIKE THAT CAN COMPLETELY OVERWHELM YOUR EXISTENCE.
Oh, LIKE SUSAN HAS DESTROYED YOURS?
SUSAN PTOLEMY IS A POWERFUL AND COMPLICATED WOMAN, BUT WE EXIST IN HARMONY.
I'M THERE FOR WHEN SHE PERCEIVES THE WORLD AS A TERRIBLE RED MIST.
SHE'S THERE FOR WHEN I JIGSAW MY FINGERS OFF.
IT WAS TRULY MEANT TO BE.
SO WHERE DID YOU LEARN THESE TERRIBLE LIFE LESSONS?
BEFORE SUSAN, THERE WAS KYLIE TRAINOR...

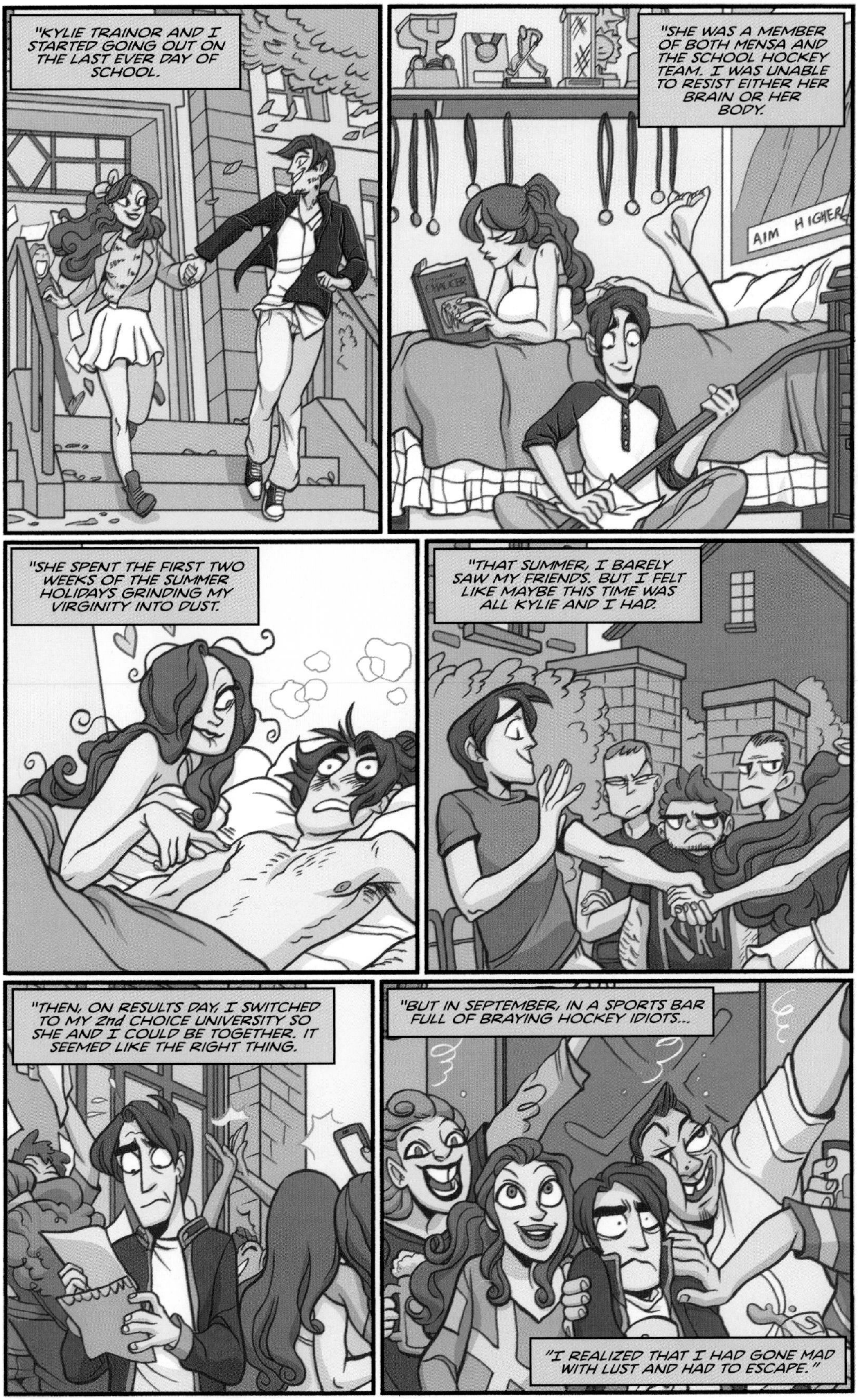
"KYLIE TRAINOR AND I STARTED GOING OUT ON THE LAST EVER DAY OF SCHOOL.
"SHE WAS A MEMBER OF BOTH MENSA AND THE SCHOOL HOCKEY TEAM. I WAS UNABLE TO RESIST EITHER HER BRAIN OR HER BODY.
CHAUCER
AIM HIGHER
"SHE SPENT THE FIRST TWO WEEKS OF THE SUMMER HOLIDAYS GRINDING MY VIRGINITY INTO DUST.
"THAT SUMMER, I BARELY SAW MY FRIENDS. BUT I FELT LIKE MAYBE THIS TIME WAS ALL KYLIE AND I HAD.
"THEN, ON RESULTS DAY, I SWITCHED TO MY 2nd CHOICE UNIVERSITY SO SHE AND I COULD BE TOGETHER. IT SEEMED LIKE THE RIGHT THING.
"BUT IN SEPTEMBER, IN A SPORTS BAR FULL OF BRAYING HOCKEY IDIOTS...
"I REALIZED THAT I HAD GONE MAD WITH LUST AND HAD TO ESCAPE."

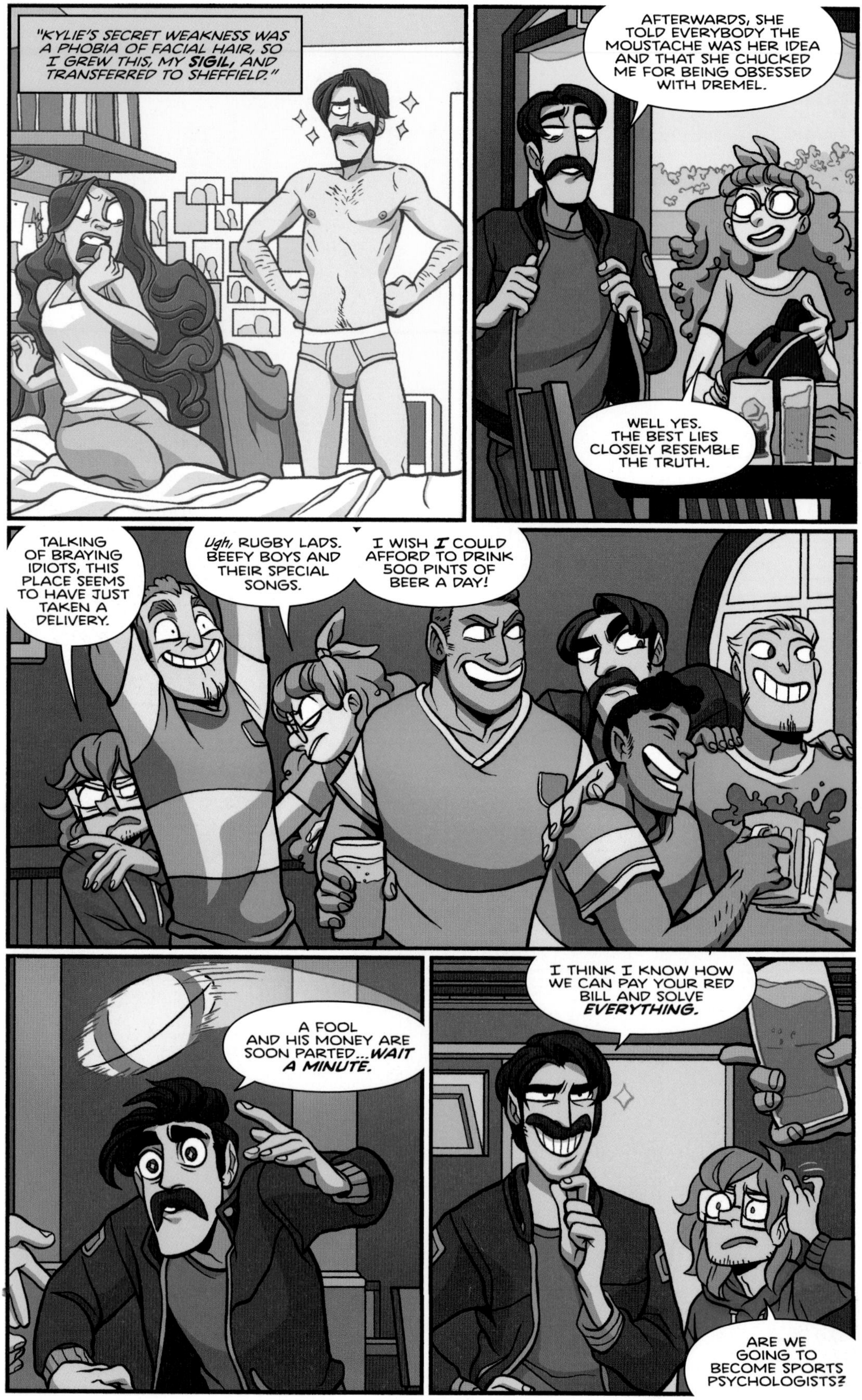
"KYLIE'S SECRET WEAKNESS WAS A PHOBIA OF FACIAL HAIR, SO I GREW THIS, MY SIGIL, AND TRANSFERRED TO SHEFFIELD."
AFTERWARDS, SHE TOLD EVERYBODY THE MOUSTACHE WAS HER IDEA AND THAT SHE CHUCKED ME FOR BEING OBSESSED WITH DREMEL.
WELL YES. THE BEST LIES CLOSELY RESEMBLE THE TRUTH.
TALKING OF BRAYING IDIOTS, THIS PLACE SEEMS TO HAVE JUST TAKEN A DELIVERY.
Ugh, RUGBY LADS. BEEFY BOYS AND THEIR SPECIAL SONGS.
I WISH I COULD AFFORD TO DRINK 500 PINTS OF BEER A DAY!
A FOOL AND HIS MONEY ARE SOON PARTED...WAIT A MINUTE.
I THINK I KNOW HOW WE CAN PAY YOUR RED BILL AND SOLVE EVERYTHING.
ARE WE GOING TO BECOME SPORTS PSYCHOLOGISTS?

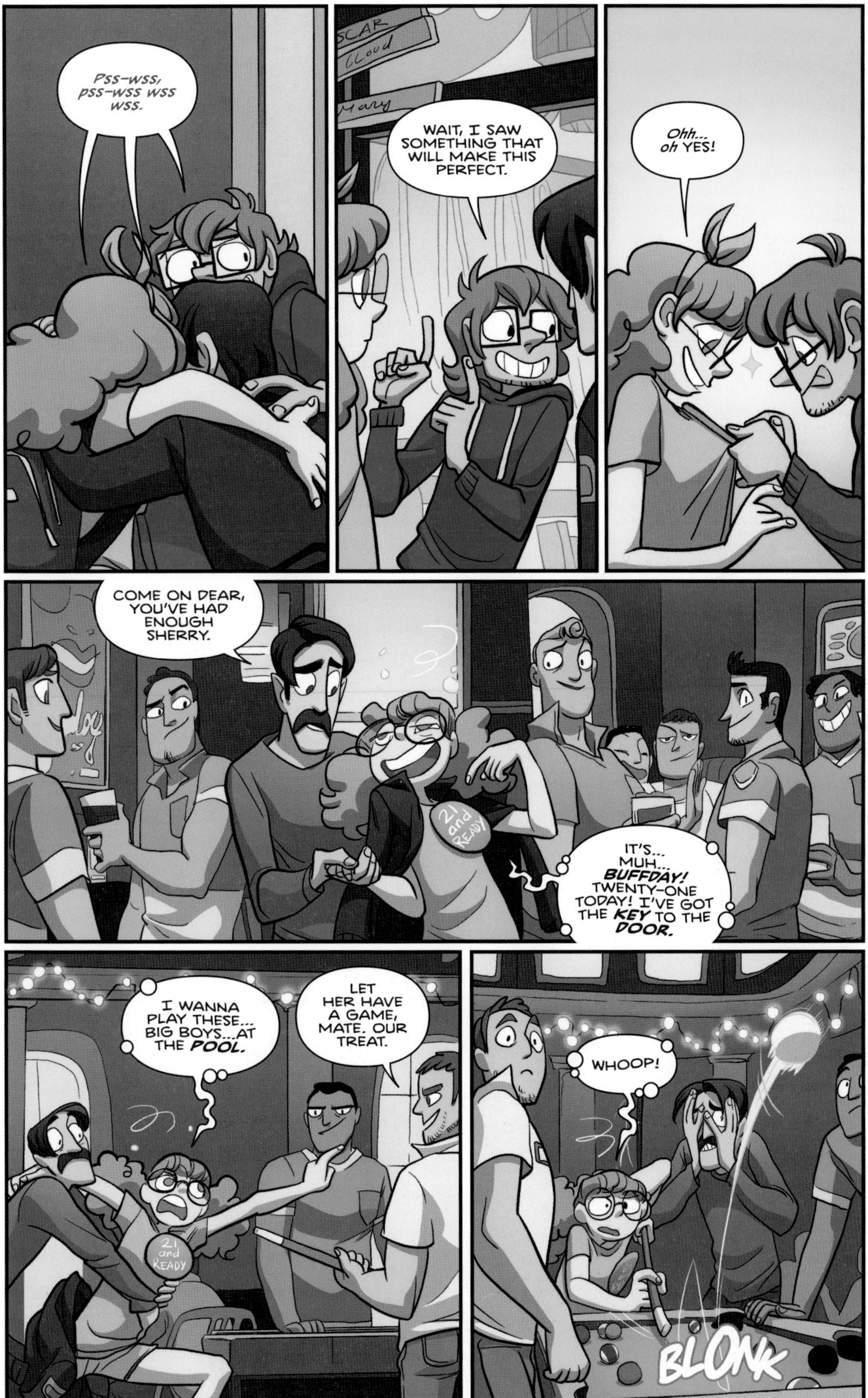
Pss-wss, pss-wss wss wss.
SCAR
Cloud
Mary
WAIT, I SAW SOMETHING THAT WILL MAKE THIS PERFECT.
Ohh... oh YES!
COME ON DEAR, YOU'VE HAD ENOUGH SHERRY.
21 and READY
IT'S... MUH... BUFFDAY! TWENTY-ONE TODAY! I'VE GOT THE KEY TO THE DOOR.
I WANNA PLAY THESE... BIG BOYS... AT THE POOL.
LET HER HAVE A GAME, MATE. OUR TREAT.
21 and READY
WHOOP!
BLONK

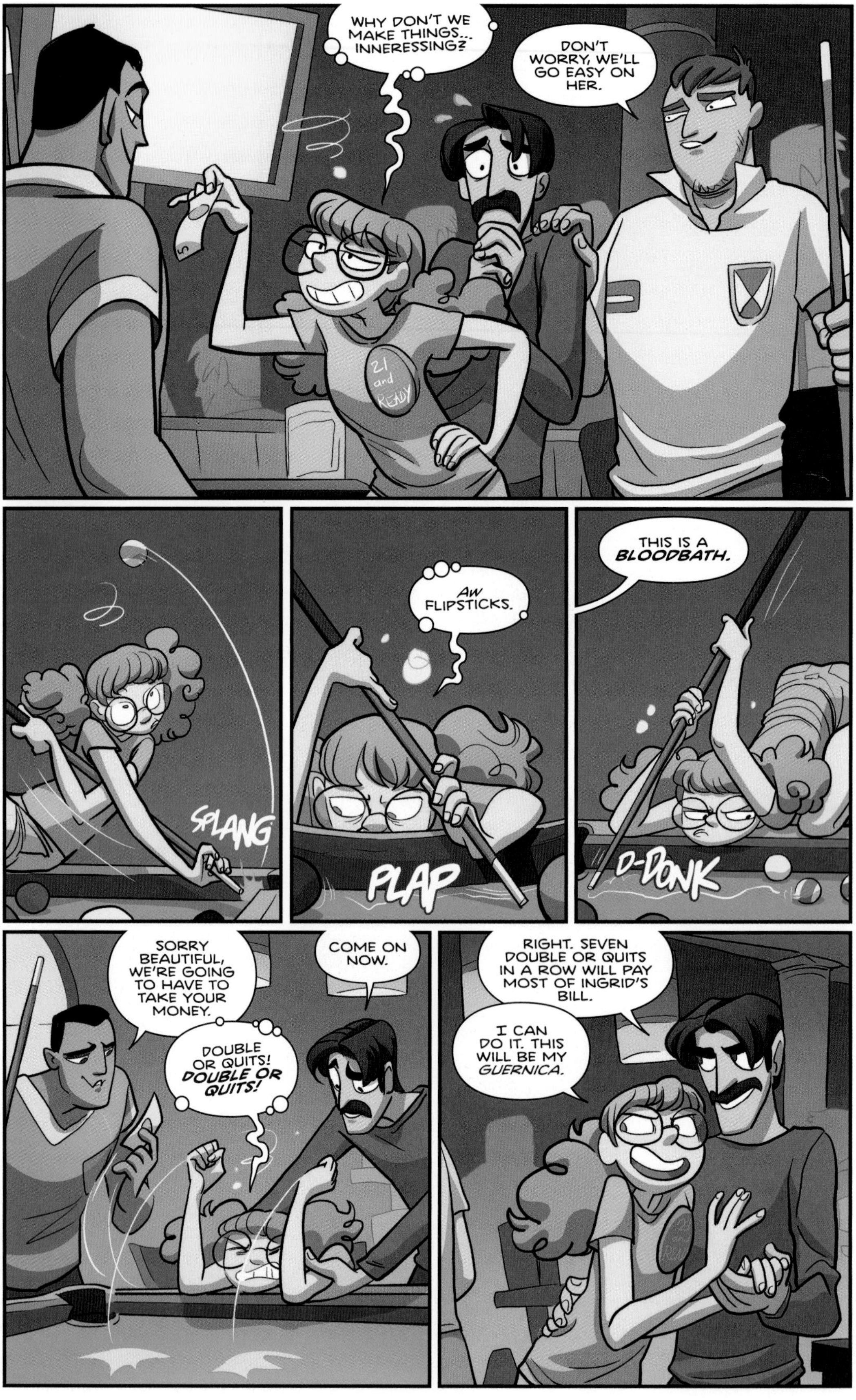
WHY DON'T WE MAKE THINGS... INNERESSING?
DON'T WORRY, WE'LL GO EASY ON HER.
21 and READY
SPLANG
AW FLIPSTICKS.
PLAP
THIS IS A BLOODBATH.
D-DONK
SORRY BEAUTIFUL, WE'RE GOING TO HAVE TO TAKE YOUR MONEY.
COME ON NOW.
DOUBLE OR QUITS! DOUBLE OR QUITS!
RIGHT. SEVEN DOUBLE OR QUITS IN A ROW WILL PAY MOST OF INGRID'S BILL.
I CAN DO IT. THIS WILL BE MY GUERNICA.

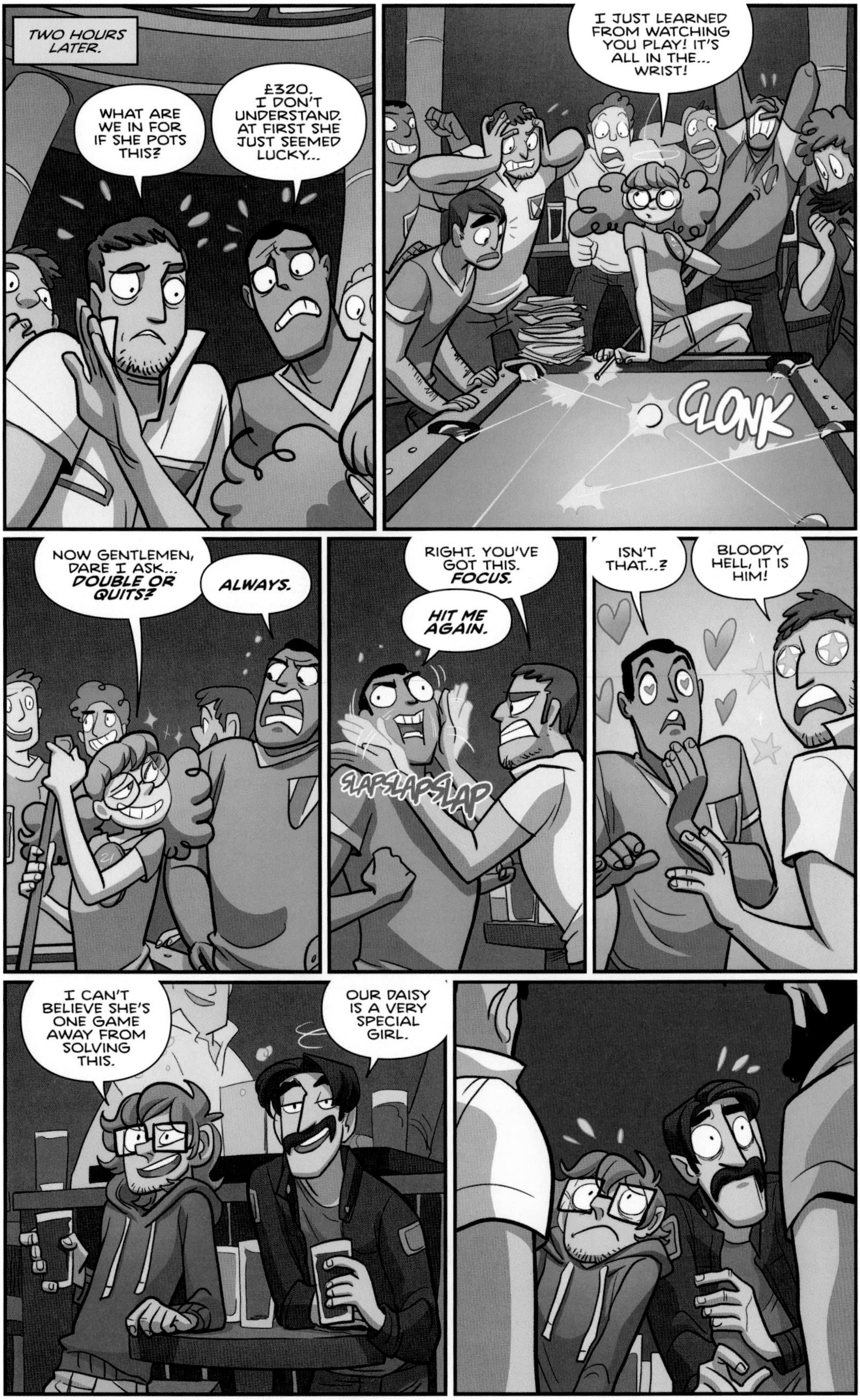
TWO HOURS LATER.
WHAT ARE WE IN FOR IF SHE POTS THIS?
£320. I DON'T UNDERSTAND. AT FIRST SHE JUST SEEMED LUCKY...
I JUST LEARNED FROM WATCHING YOU PLAY! IT'S ALL IN THE... WRIST!
CLONK
NOW GENTLEMEN, DARE I ASK... DOUBLE OR QUITS?
ALWAYS.
RIGHT. YOU'VE GOT THIS. FOCUS.
HIT ME AGAIN.
SLAPSLAPSLAP
ISN'T THAT...?
BLOODY HELL, IT IS HIM!
I CAN'T BELIEVE SHE'S ONE GAME AWAY FROM SOLVING THIS.
OUR DAISY IS A VERY SPECIAL GIRL.

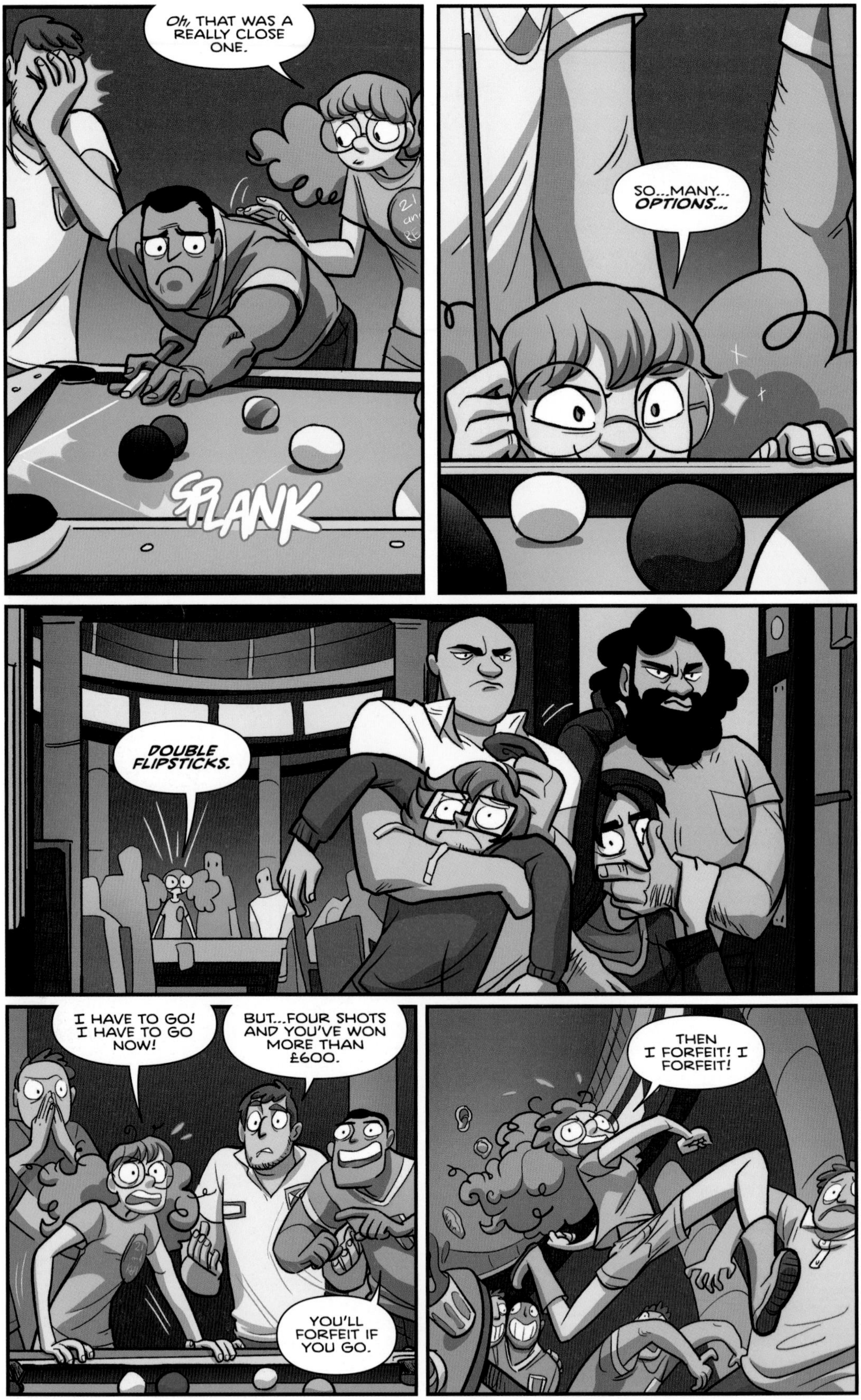

Oh, THAT WAS A REALLY CLOSE ONE.
SPLANK
SO...MANY... OPTIONS...
DOUBLE FLIPSTICKS.
I HAVE TO GO! I HAVE TO GO NOW!
BUT...FOUR SHOTS AND YOU'VE WON MORE THAN £600.
YOU'LL FORFEIT IF YOU GO.
THEN I FORFEIT! I FORFEIT!

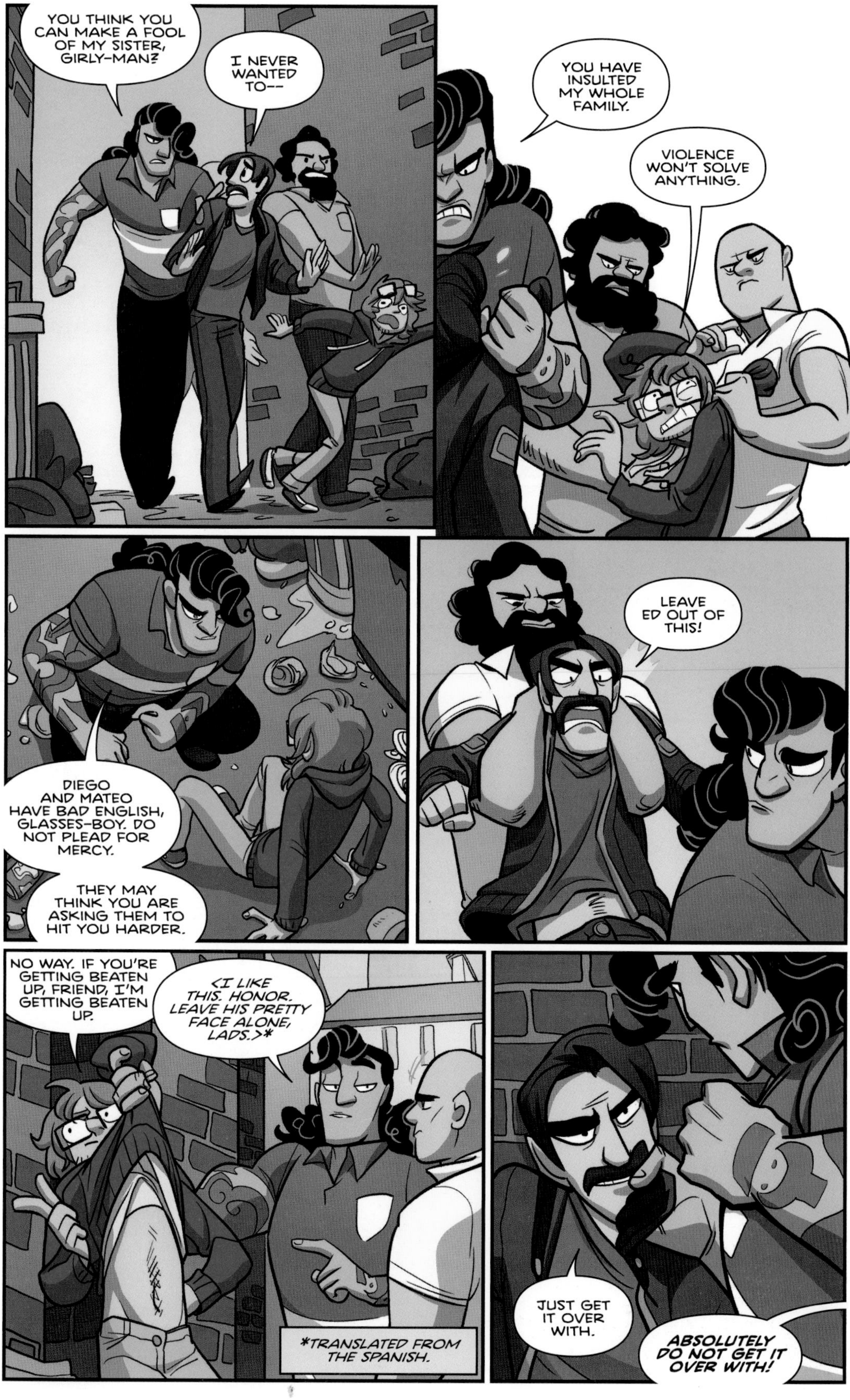
YOU THINK YOU CAN MAKE A FOOL OF MY SISTER, GIRLY-MAN?
I NEVER WANTED TO--
YOU HAVE INSULTED MY WHOLE FAMILY.
VIOLENCE WON'T SOLVE ANYTHING.
DIEGO AND MATEO HAVE BAD ENGLISH, GLASSES-BOY. DO NOT PLEAD FOR MERCY.
THEY MAY THINK YOU ARE ASKING THEM TO HIT YOU HARDER.
LEAVE ED OUT OF THIS!
NO WAY. IF YOU'RE GETTING BEATEN UP, FRIEND, I'M GETTING BEATEN UP.
<I LIKE THIS. HONOR. LEAVE HIS PRETTY FACE ALONE, LADS.>*
*TRANSLATED FROM THE SPANISH.
JUST GET IT OVER WITH.
ABSOLUTELY DO NOT GET IT OVER WITH!

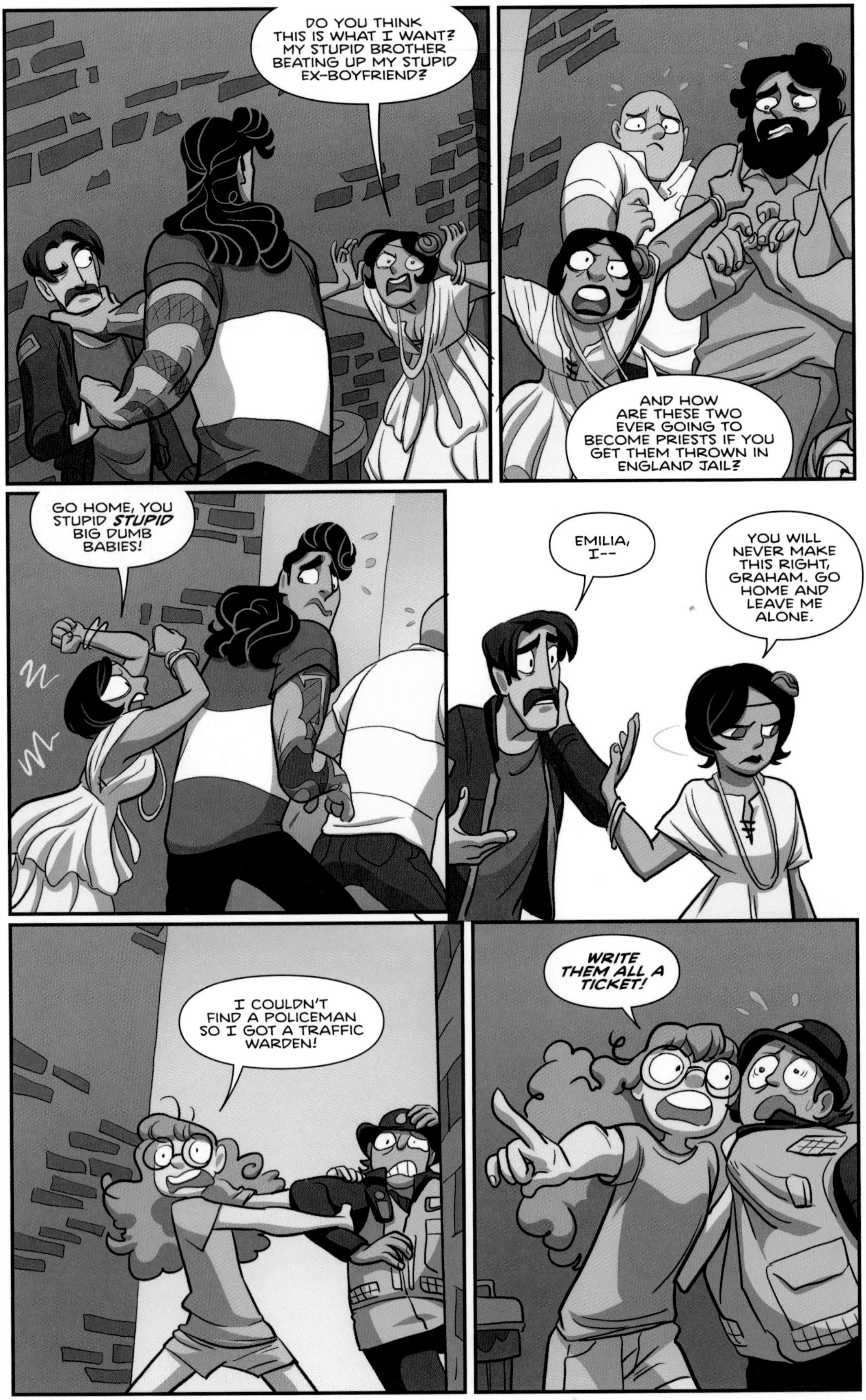
DO YOU THINK THIS IS WHAT I WANT? MY STUPID BROTHER BEATING UP MY STUPID EX-BOYFRIEND?
AND HOW ARE THESE TWO EVER GOING TO BECOME PRIESTS IF YOU GET THEM THROWN IN ENGLAND JAIL?
GO HOME, YOU STUPID *STUPID* BIG DUMB BABIES!
EMILIA, I--
YOU WILL NEVER MAKE THIS RIGHT, GRAHAM. GO HOME AND LEAVE ME ALONE.
I COULDN'T FIND A POLICEMAN SO I GOT A TRAFFIC WARDEN!
WRITE THEM ALL A TICKET!

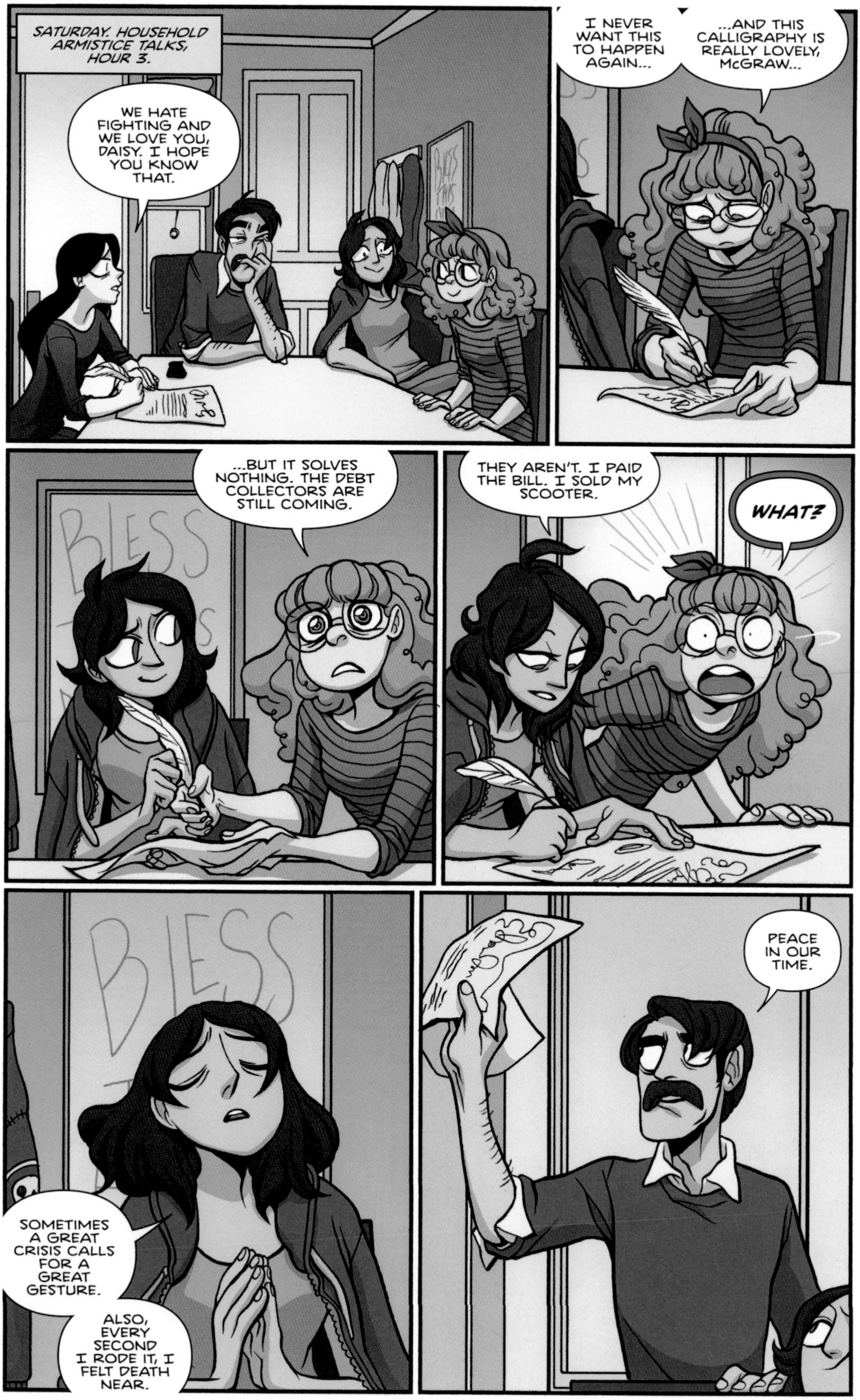
SATURDAY. HOUSEHOLD ARMISTICE TALKS, HOUR 3.
WE HATE FIGHTING AND WE LOVE YOU, DAISY. I HOPE YOU KNOW THAT.
I NEVER WANT THIS TO HAPPEN AGAIN...
...AND THIS CALLIGRAPHY IS REALLY LOVELY, McGRAW...
...BUT IT SOLVES NOTHING. THE DEBT COLLECTORS ARE STILL COMING.
THEY AREN'T. I PAID THE BILL. I SOLD MY SCOOTER.
WHAT?
SOMETIMES A GREAT CRISIS CALLS FOR A GREAT GESTURE.
ALSO, EVERY SECOND I RODE IT, I FELT DEATH NEAR.
PEACE IN OUR TIME.

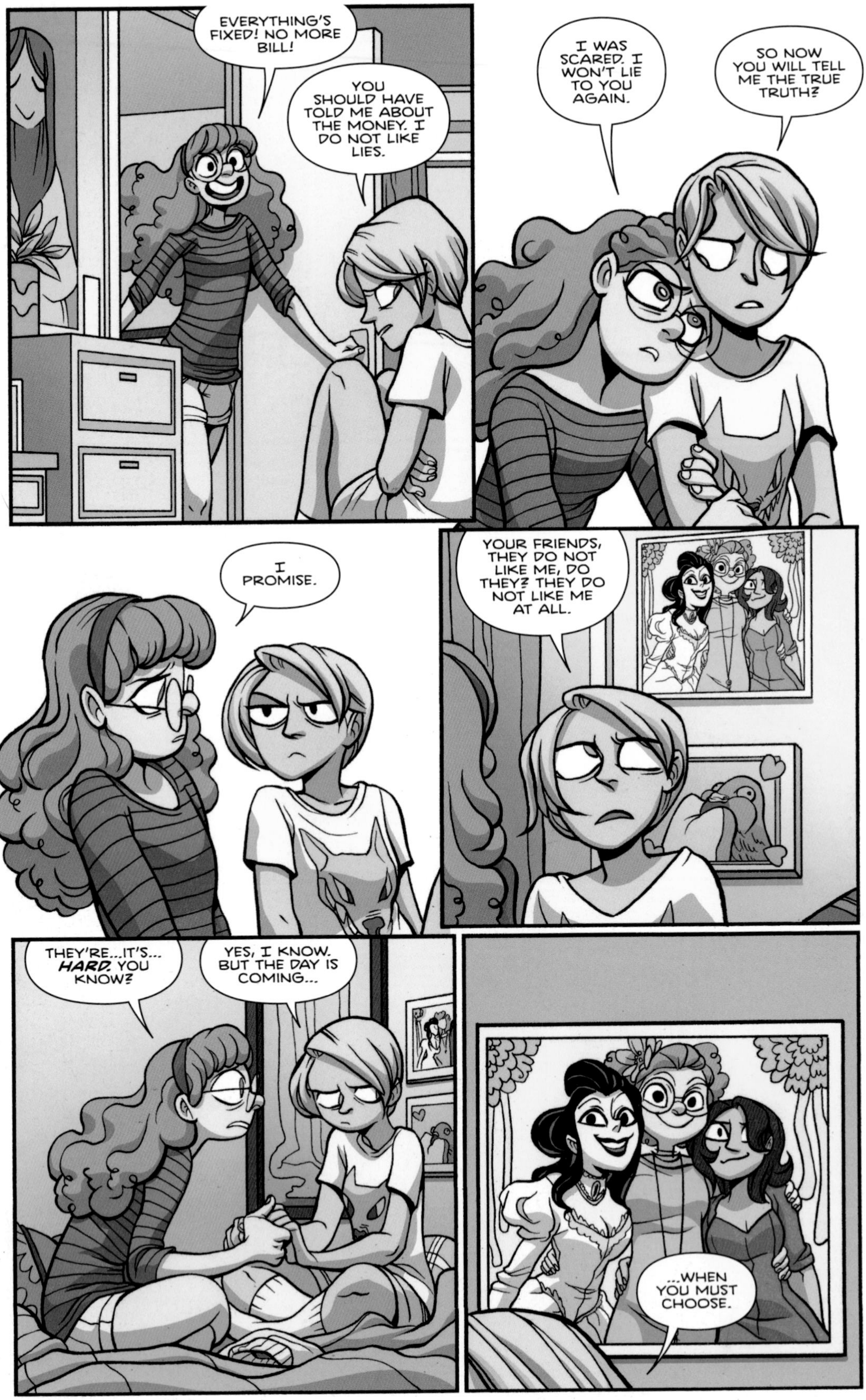
EVERYTHING'S FIXED! NO MORE BILL!
YOU SHOULD HAVE TOLD ME ABOUT THE MONEY. I DO NOT LIKE LIES.
I WAS SCARED. I WON'T LIE TO YOU AGAIN.
SO NOW YOU WILL TELL ME THE TRUE TRUTH?
I PROMISE.
YOUR FRIENDS, THEY DO NOT LIKE ME, DO THEY? THEY DO NOT LIKE ME AT ALL.
THEY'RE...IT'S... *HARD,* YOU KNOW?
YES, I KNOW. BUT THE DAY IS COMING...
...WHEN YOU MUST CHOOSE.

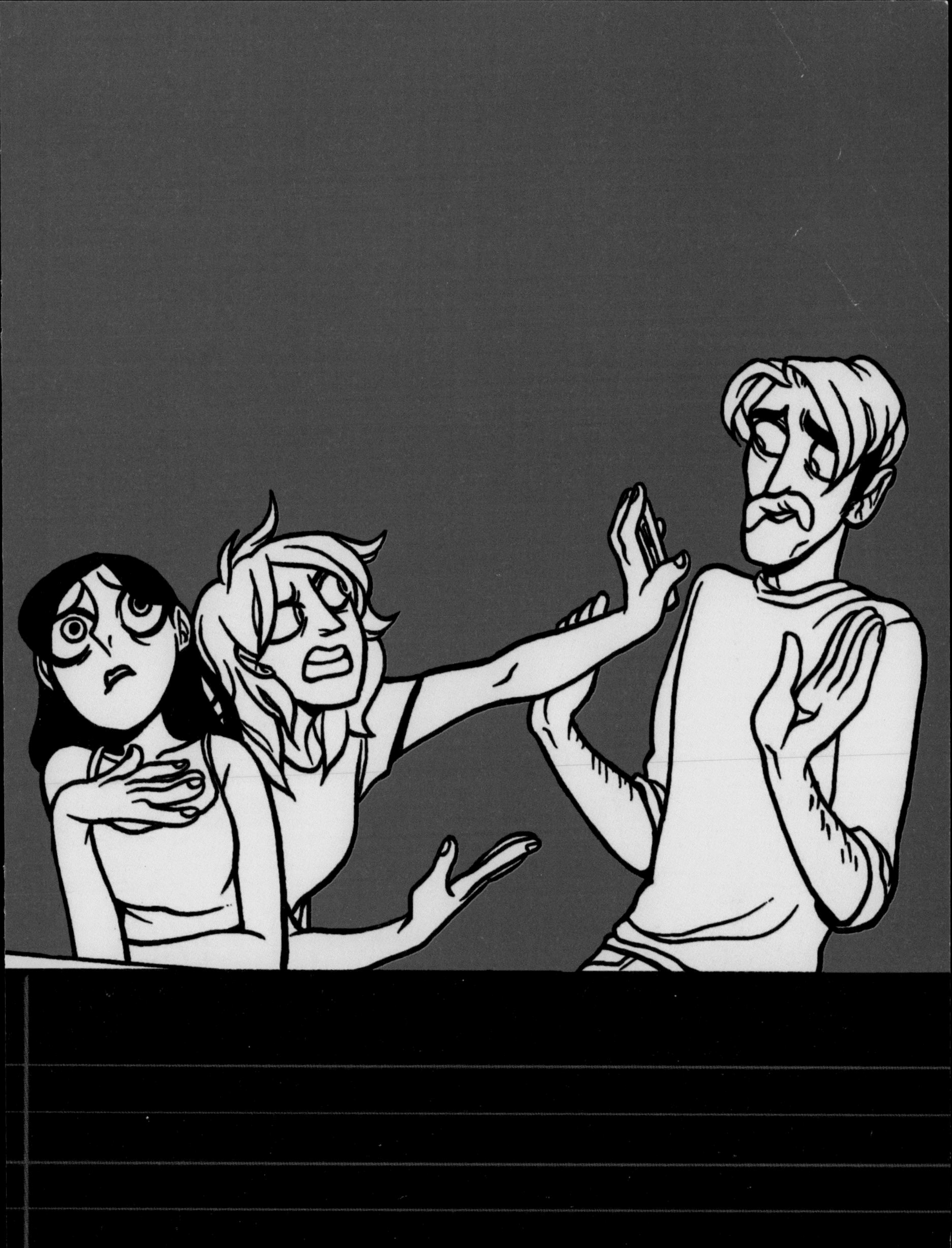

CHAPTER THIRTY-TWO

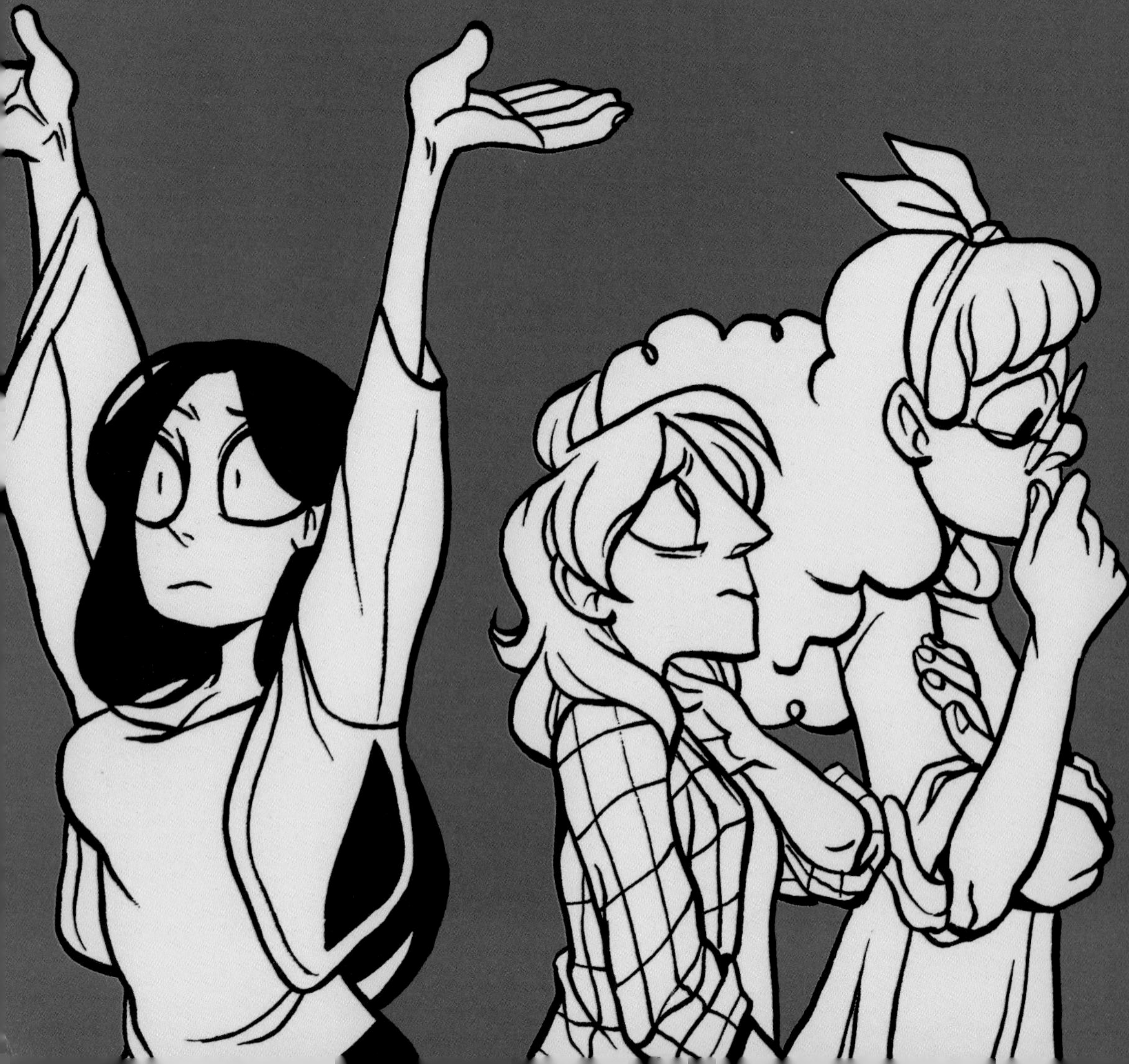

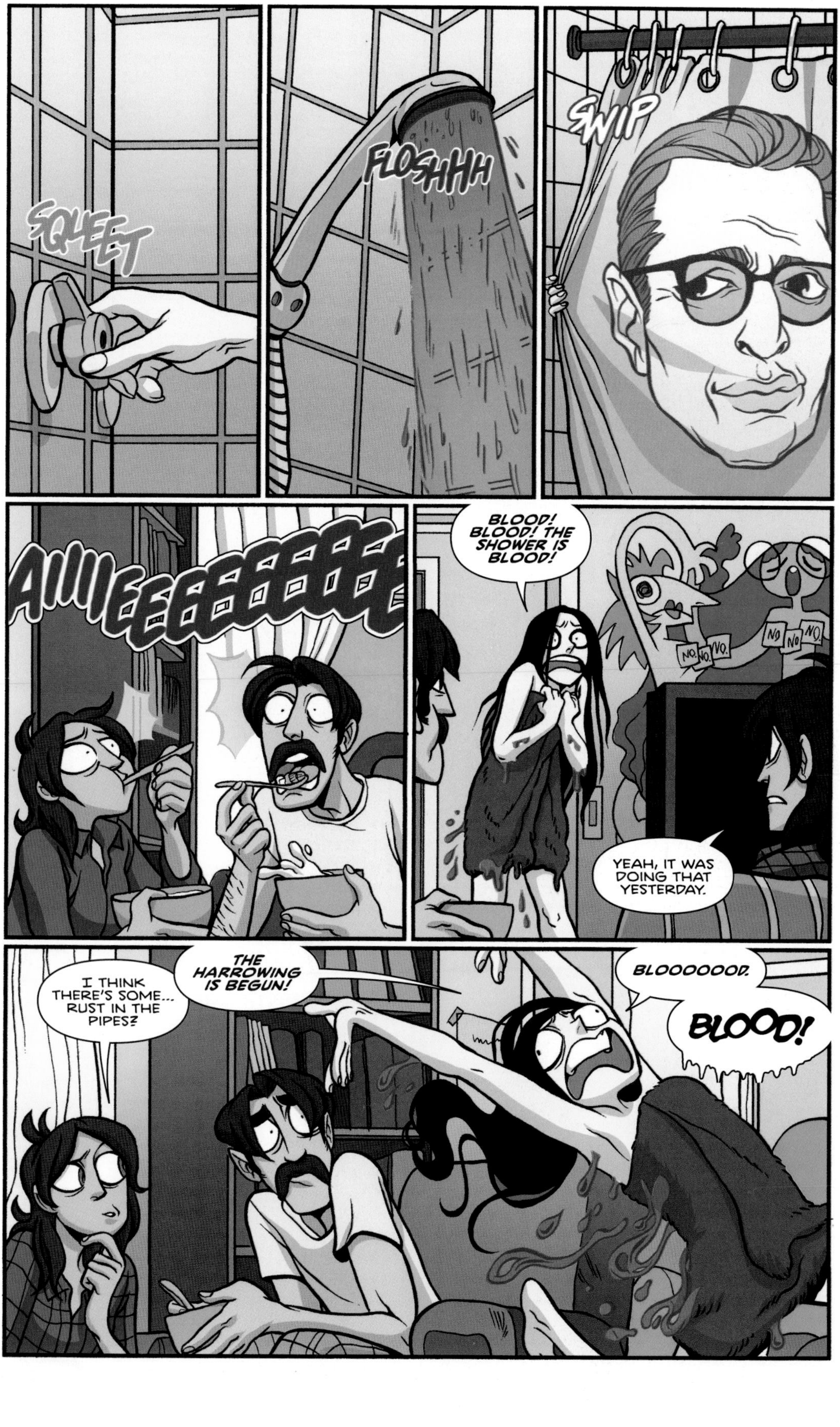
SQUEET
FLOSHHH
SWIP
AIIIEEEEEEEEEEE
BLOOD! BLOOD! THE SHOWER IS BLOOD!
NO. NO. NO.
NO NO NO.
YEAH, IT WAS DOING THAT YESTERDAY.
I THINK THERE'S SOME... RUST IN THE PIPES?
THE HARROWING IS BEGUN!
BLOOOOOOD.
BLOOD!

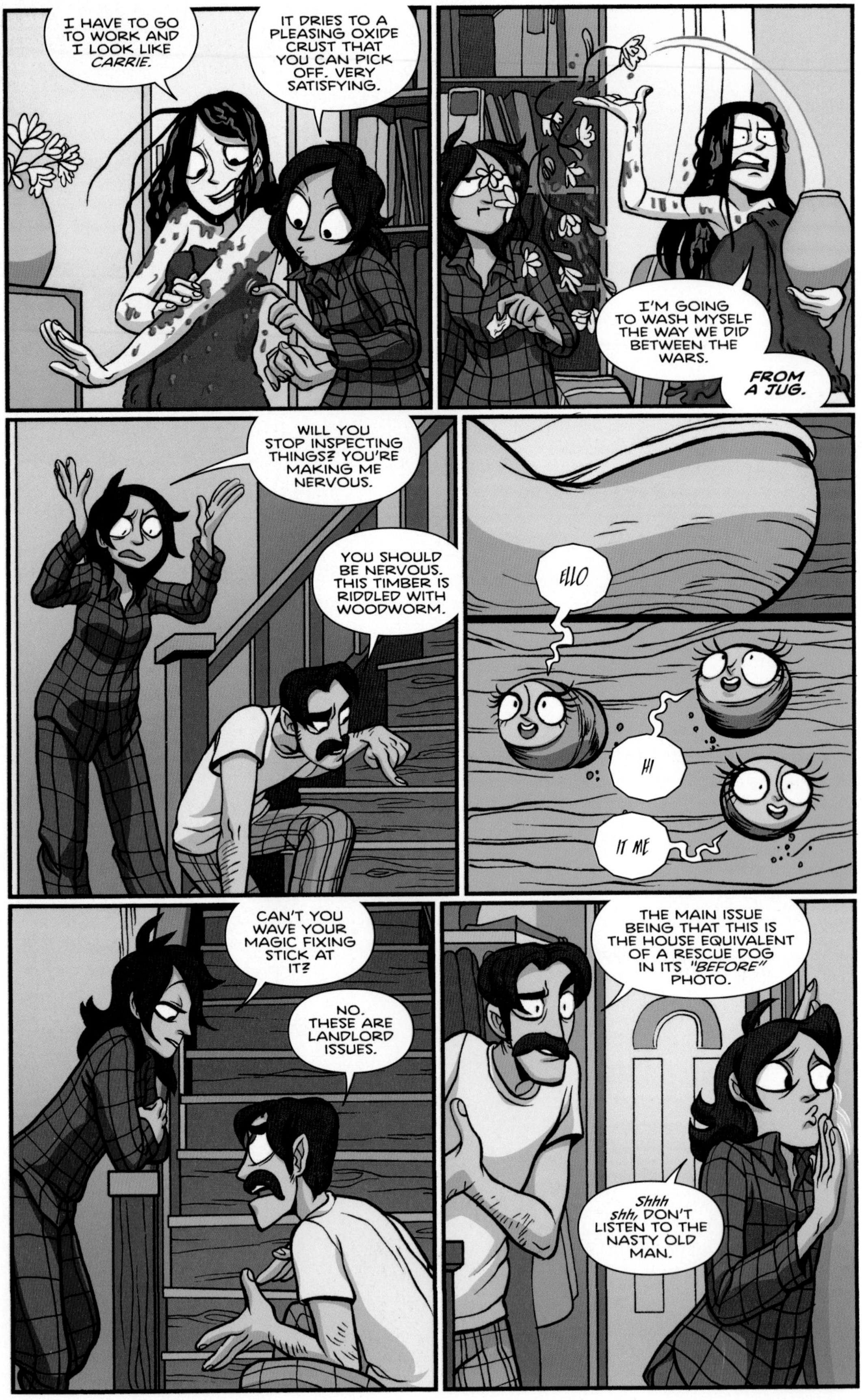
I HAVE TO GO TO WORK AND I LOOK LIKE *CARRIE.*
IT DRIES TO A PLEASING OXIDE CRUST THAT YOU CAN PICK OFF. VERY SATISFYING.
I'M GOING TO WASH MYSELF THE WAY WE DID BETWEEN THE WARS.
FROM A JUG.
WILL YOU STOP INSPECTING THINGS? YOU'RE MAKING ME NERVOUS.
YOU SHOULD BE NERVOUS. THIS TIMBER IS RIDDLED WITH WOODWORM.
ELLO
HI
IT ME
CAN'T YOU WAVE YOUR MAGIC FIXING STICK AT IT?
NO. THESE ARE LANDLORD ISSUES.
THE MAIN ISSUE BEING THAT THIS IS THE HOUSE EQUIVALENT OF A RESCUE DOG IN ITS *"BEFORE"* PHOTO.
Shhh shh, DON'T LISTEN TO THE NASTY OLD MAN.

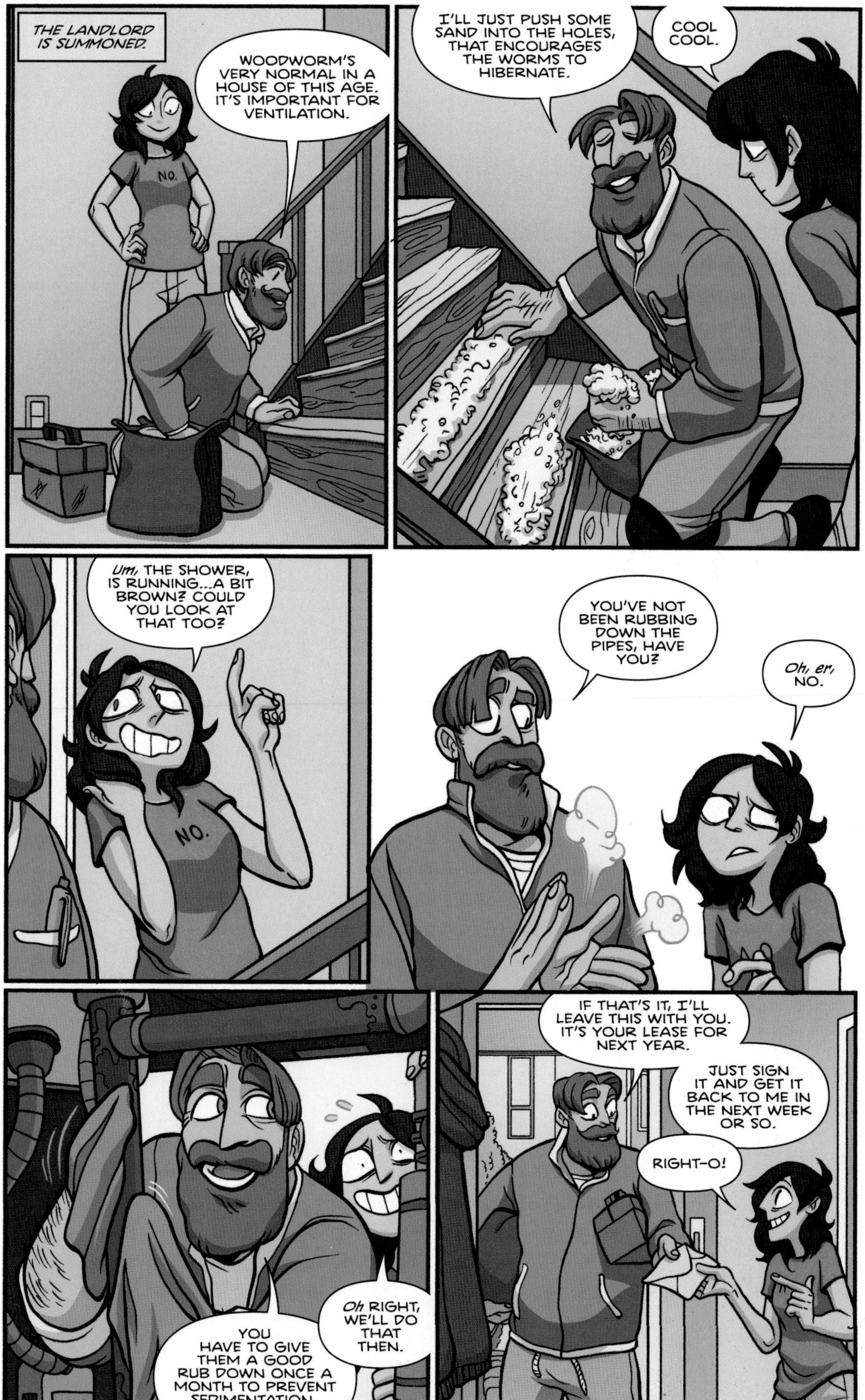
THE LANDLORD IS SUMMONED.
WOODWORM'S VERY NORMAL IN A HOUSE OF THIS AGE. IT'S IMPORTANT FOR VENTILATION.
I'LL JUST PUSH SOME SAND INTO THE HOLES, THAT ENCOURAGES THE WORMS TO HIBERNATE.
COOL COOL.
Um, THE SHOWER, IS RUNNING...A BIT BROWN? COULD YOU LOOK AT THAT TOO?
YOU'VE NOT BEEN RUBBING DOWN THE PIPES, HAVE YOU?
Oh, er, NO.
YOU HAVE TO GIVE THEM A GOOD RUB DOWN ONCE A MONTH TO PREVENT SEDIMENTATION.
Oh RIGHT, WE'LL DO THAT THEN.
IF THAT'S IT, I'LL LEAVE THIS WITH YOU. IT'S YOUR LEASE FOR NEXT YEAR.
JUST SIGN IT AND GET IT BACK TO ME IN THE NEXT WEEK OR SO.
RIGHT-O!

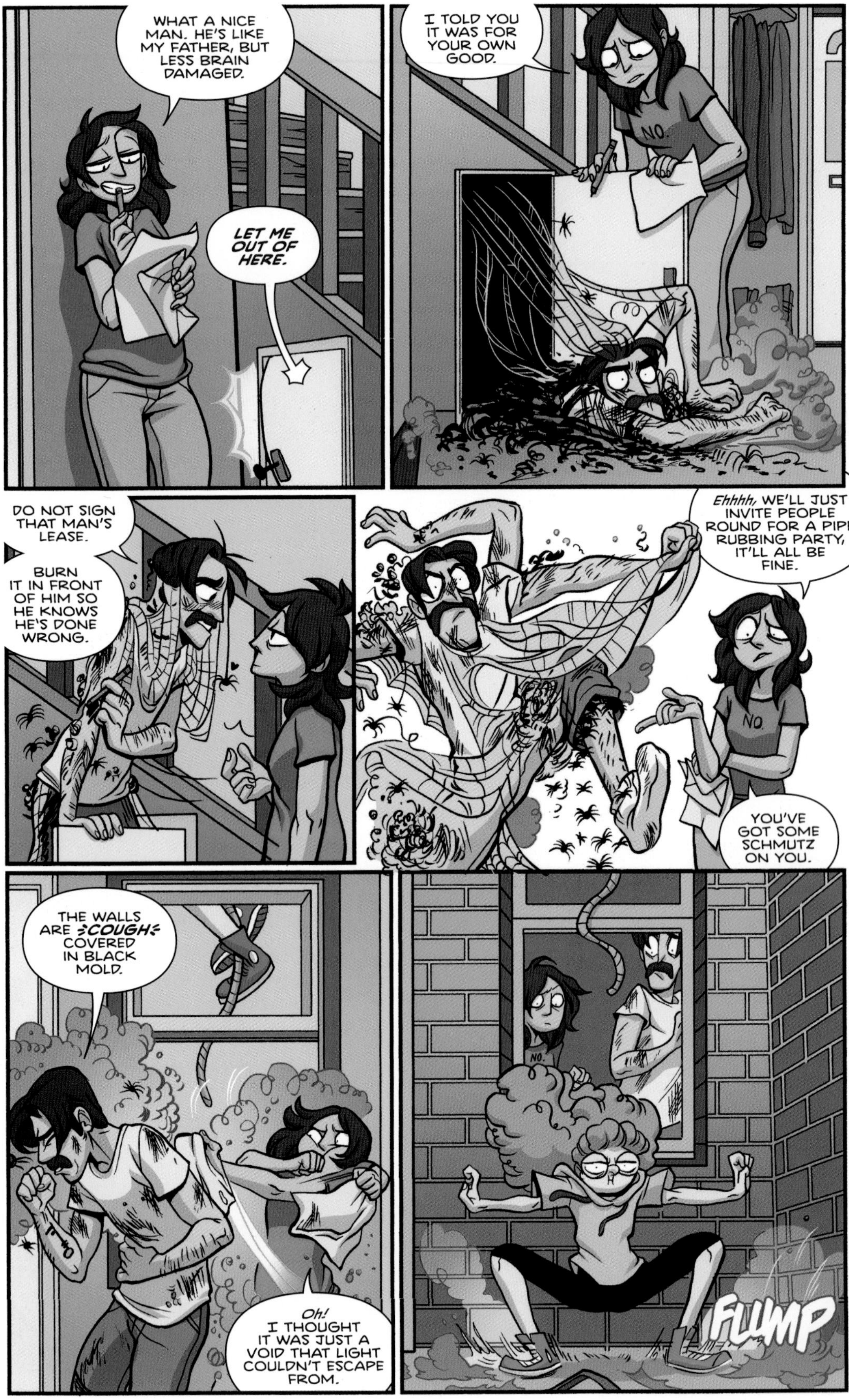

WHAT A NICE MAN. HE'S LIKE MY FATHER, BUT LESS BRAIN DAMAGED.
LET ME OUT OF HERE.
I TOLD YOU IT WAS FOR YOUR OWN GOOD.
NO.
DO NOT SIGN THAT MAN'S LEASE.
BURN IT IN FRONT OF HIM SO HE KNOWS HE'S DONE WRONG.
Ehhhh, WE'LL JUST INVITE PEOPLE ROUND FOR A PIPE RUBBING PARTY, IT'LL ALL BE FINE.
NO.
YOU'VE GOT SOME SCHMUTZ ON YOU.
THE WALLS ARE COUGH COVERED IN BLACK MOLD.
Oh! I THOUGHT IT WAS JUST A VOID THAT LIGHT COULDN'T ESCAPE FROM.
NO.
FLUMP

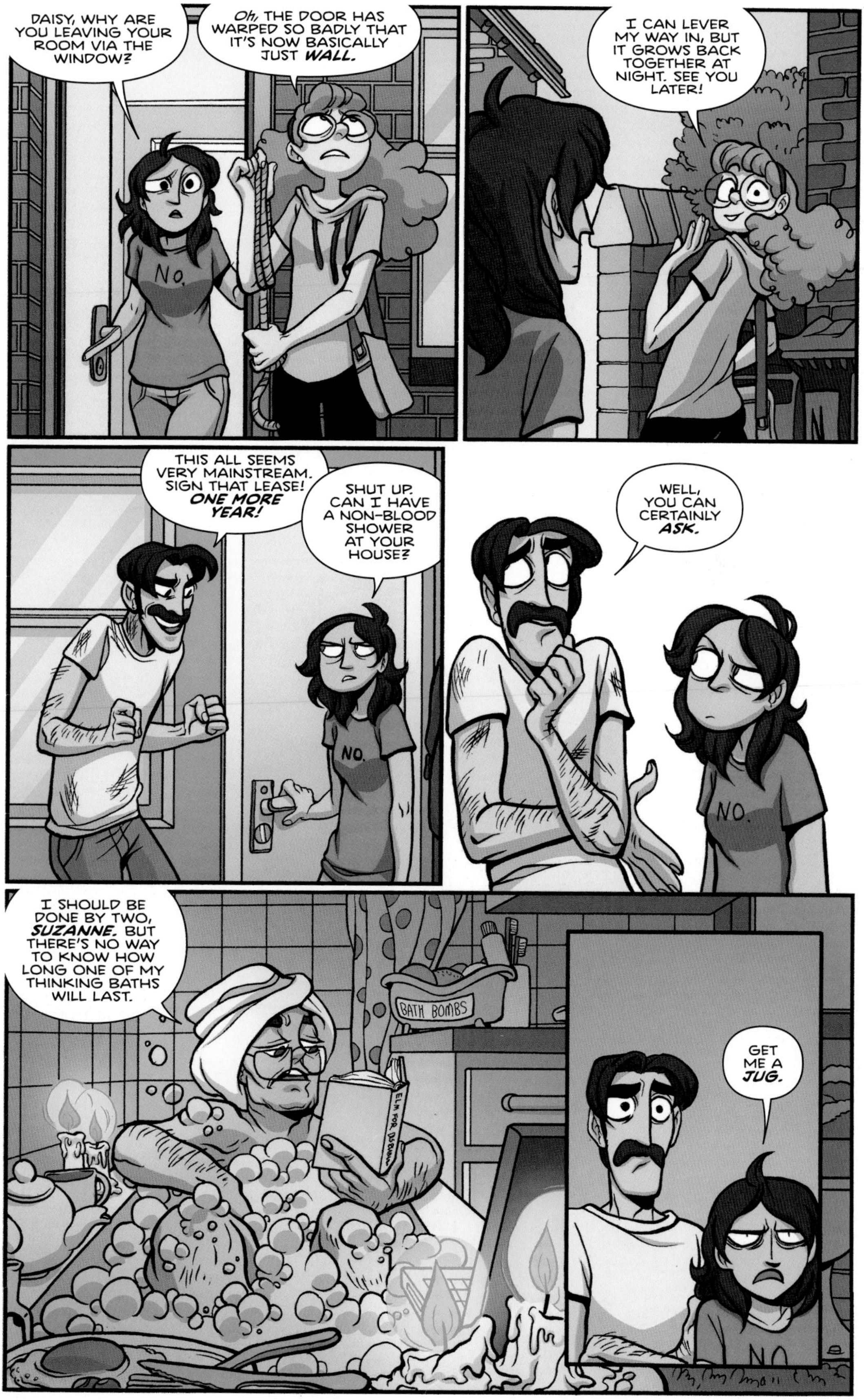
DAISY, WHY ARE YOU LEAVING YOUR ROOM VIA THE WINDOW?
Oh, THE DOOR HAS WARPED SO BADLY THAT IT'S NOW BASICALLY JUST ***WALL.***
NO.
I CAN LEVER MY WAY IN, BUT IT GROWS BACK TOGETHER AT NIGHT. SEE YOU LATER!
THIS ALL SEEMS VERY MAINSTREAM. SIGN THAT LEASE! ***ONE MORE YEAR!***
SHUT UP. CAN I HAVE A NON-BLOOD SHOWER AT YOUR HOUSE?
NO.
WELL, YOU CAN CERTAINLY ***ASK.***
NO.
I SHOULD BE DONE BY TWO, ***SUZANNE.*** BUT THERE'S NO WAY TO KNOW HOW LONG ONE OF MY THINKING BATHS WILL LAST.
BATH BOMBS
GET ME A ***JUG.***
NO

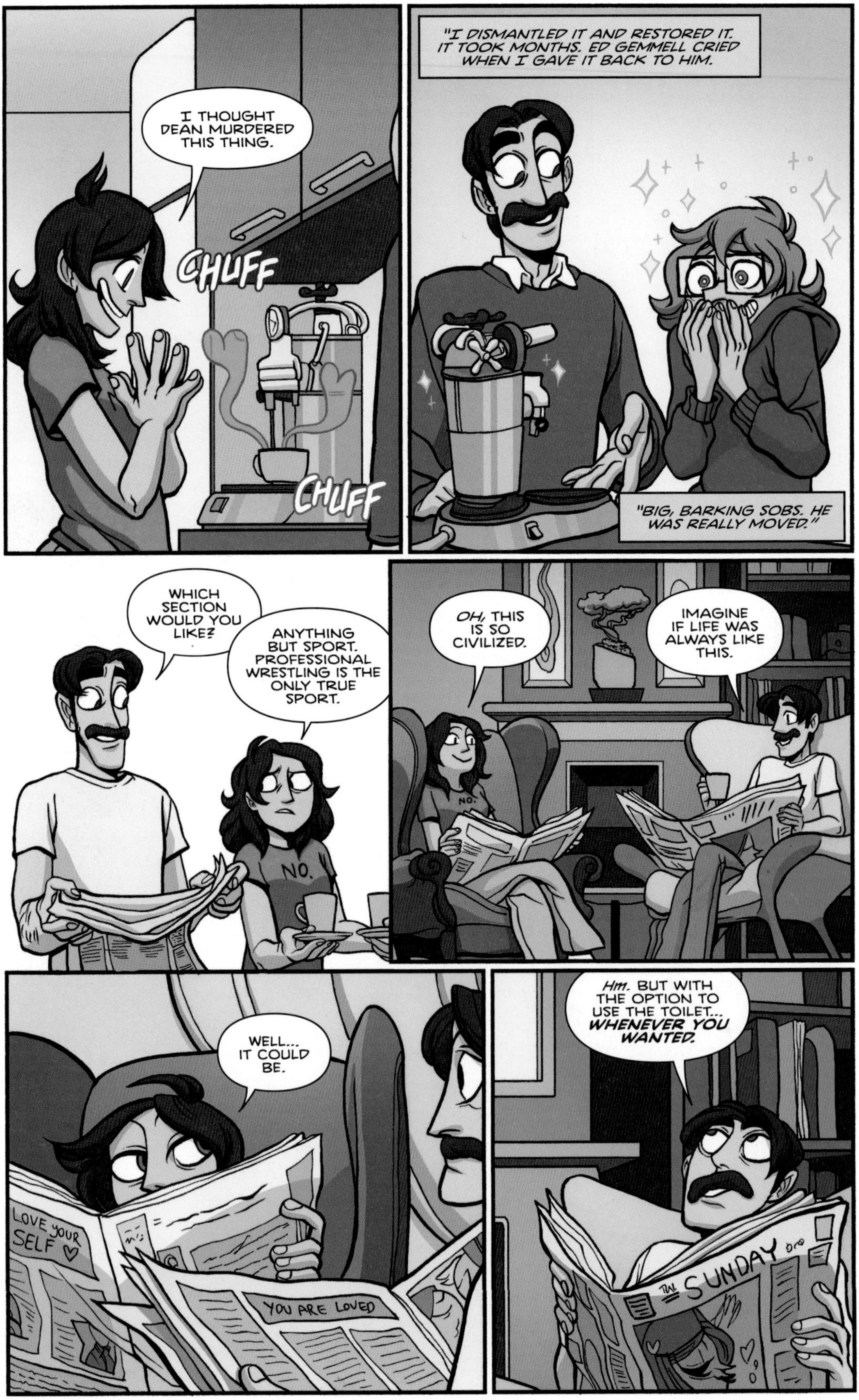
I THOUGHT DEAN MURDERED THIS THING.
CHUFF
CHUFF
"I DISMANTLED IT AND RESTORED IT. IT TOOK MONTHS. ED GEMMELL CRIED WHEN I GAVE IT BACK TO HIM.
"BIG, BARKING SOBS. HE WAS REALLY MOVED."
WHICH SECTION WOULD YOU LIKE?
ANYTHING BUT SPORT. PROFESSIONAL WRESTLING IS THE ONLY TRUE SPORT.
NO.
OH, THIS IS SO CIVILIZED.
IMAGINE IF LIFE WAS ALWAYS LIKE THIS.
WELL... IT COULD BE.
LOVE YOUR SELF
YOU ARE LOVED
HM. BUT WITH THE OPTION TO USE THE TOILET... WHENEVER YOU WANTED.
SUNDAY

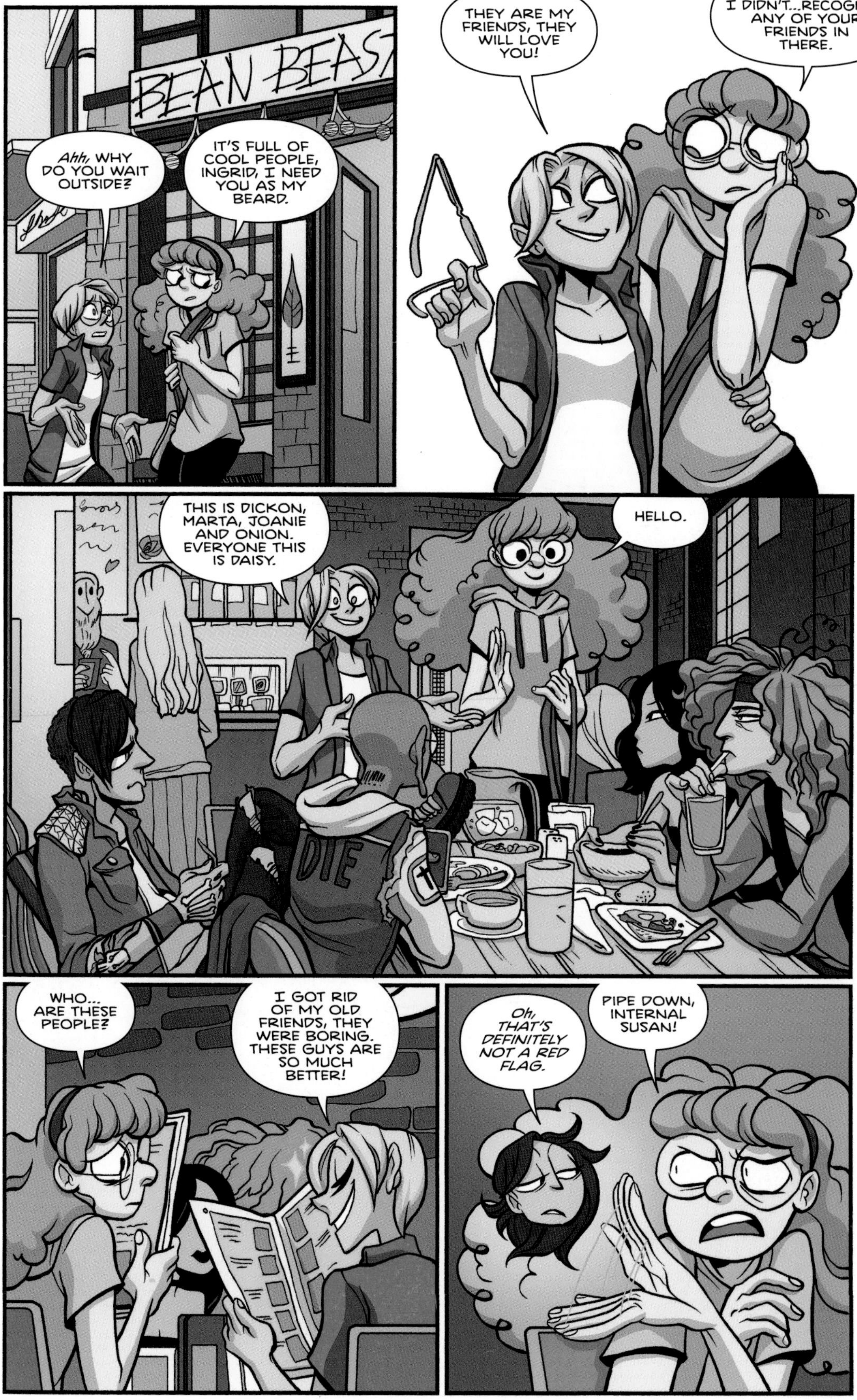
BEAN BEAST
Ahh, WHY DO YOU WAIT OUTSIDE?
IT'S FULL OF COOL PEOPLE, INGRID, I NEED YOU AS MY BEARD.
THEY ARE MY FRIENDS, THEY WILL LOVE YOU!
I LOOKED, I DIDN'T...RECOGNIZE ANY OF YOUR FRIENDS IN THERE.
THIS IS DICKON, MARTA, JOANIE AND ONION. EVERYONE THIS IS DAISY.
HELLO.
DIE
WHO... ARE THESE PEOPLE?
I GOT RID OF MY OLD FRIENDS, THEY WERE BORING. THESE GUYS ARE SO MUCH BETTER!
Oh, THAT'S DEFINITELY NOT A RED FLAG.
PIPE DOWN, INTERNAL SUSAN!

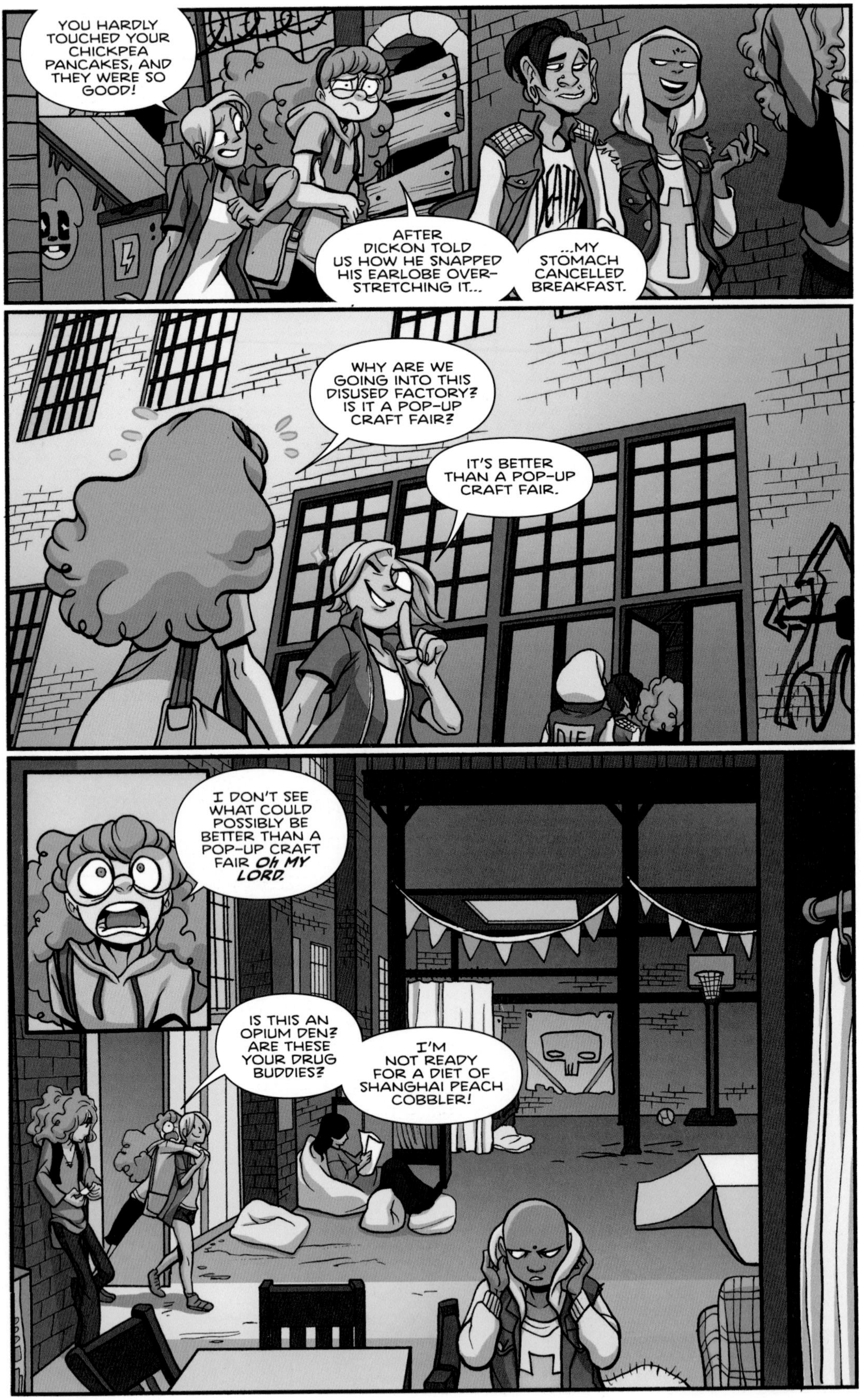
YOU HARDLY TOUCHED YOUR CHICKPEA PANCAKES, AND THEY WERE SO GOOD!
AFTER DICKON TOLD US HOW HE SNAPPED HIS EARLOBE OVER-STRETCHING IT...
...MY STOMACH CANCELLED BREAKFAST.
WHY ARE WE GOING INTO THIS DISUSED FACTORY? IS IT A POP-UP CRAFT FAIR?
IT'S BETTER THAN A POP-UP CRAFT FAIR.
DIE
I DON'T SEE WHAT COULD POSSIBLY BE BETTER THAN A POP-UP CRAFT FAIR *OH MY LORD.*
IS THIS AN OPIUM DEN? ARE THESE YOUR DRUG BUDDIES?
I'M NOT READY FOR A DIET OF SHANGHAI PEACH COBBLER!

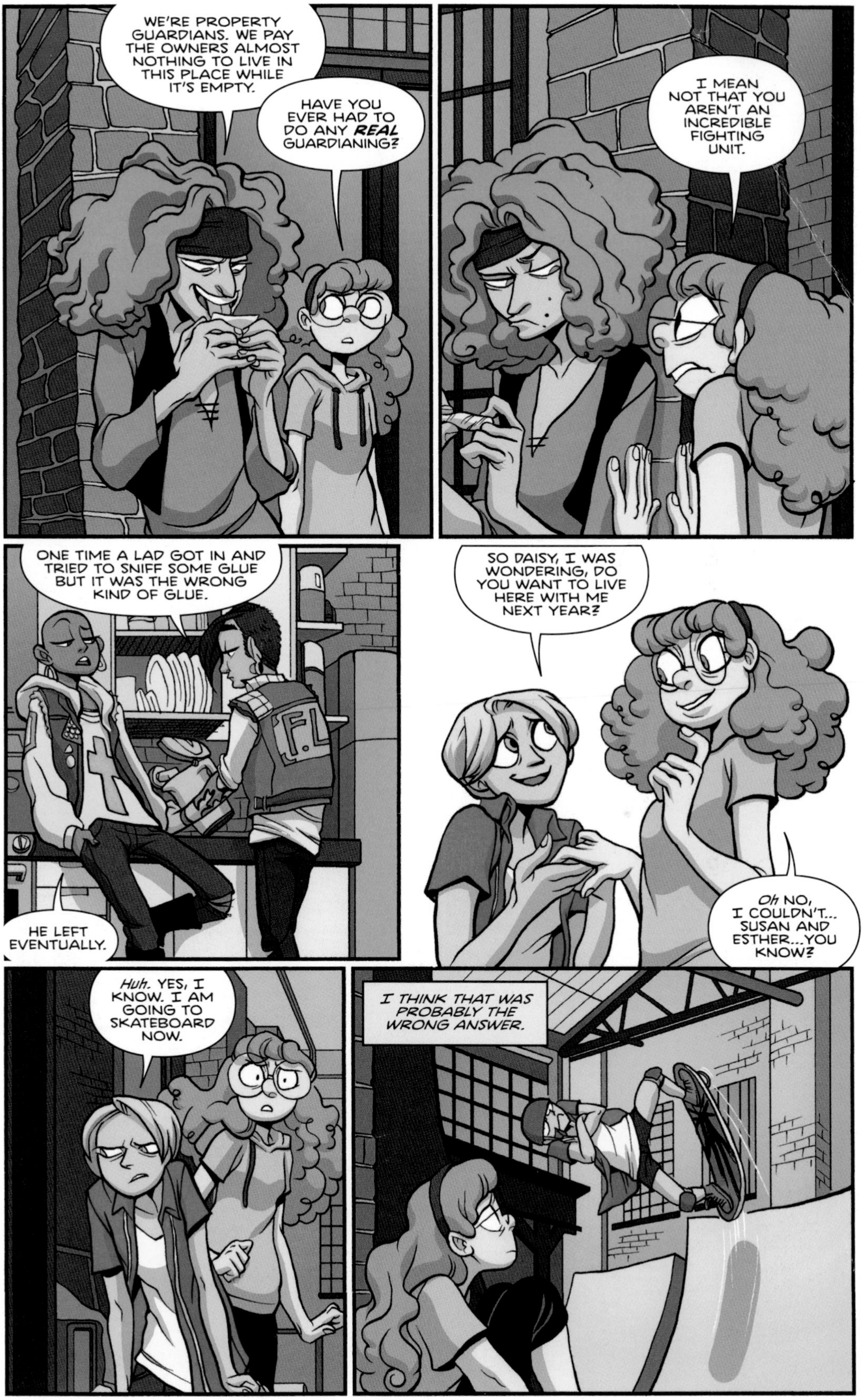
WE'RE PROPERTY GUARDIANS. WE PAY THE OWNERS ALMOST NOTHING TO LIVE IN THIS PLACE WHILE IT'S EMPTY.
HAVE YOU EVER HAD TO DO ANY *REAL* GUARDIANING?
I MEAN NOT THAT YOU AREN'T AN INCREDIBLE FIGHTING UNIT.
ONE TIME A LAD GOT IN AND TRIED TO SNIFF SOME GLUE BUT IT WAS THE WRONG KIND OF GLUE.
HE LEFT EVENTUALLY.
SO DAISY, I WAS WONDERING, DO YOU WANT TO LIVE HERE WITH ME NEXT YEAR?
Oh NO, I COULDN'T... SUSAN AND ESTHER... YOU KNOW?
Huh. YES, I KNOW. I AM GOING TO SKATEBOARD NOW.
I THINK THAT WAS PROBABLY THE WRONG ANSWER.

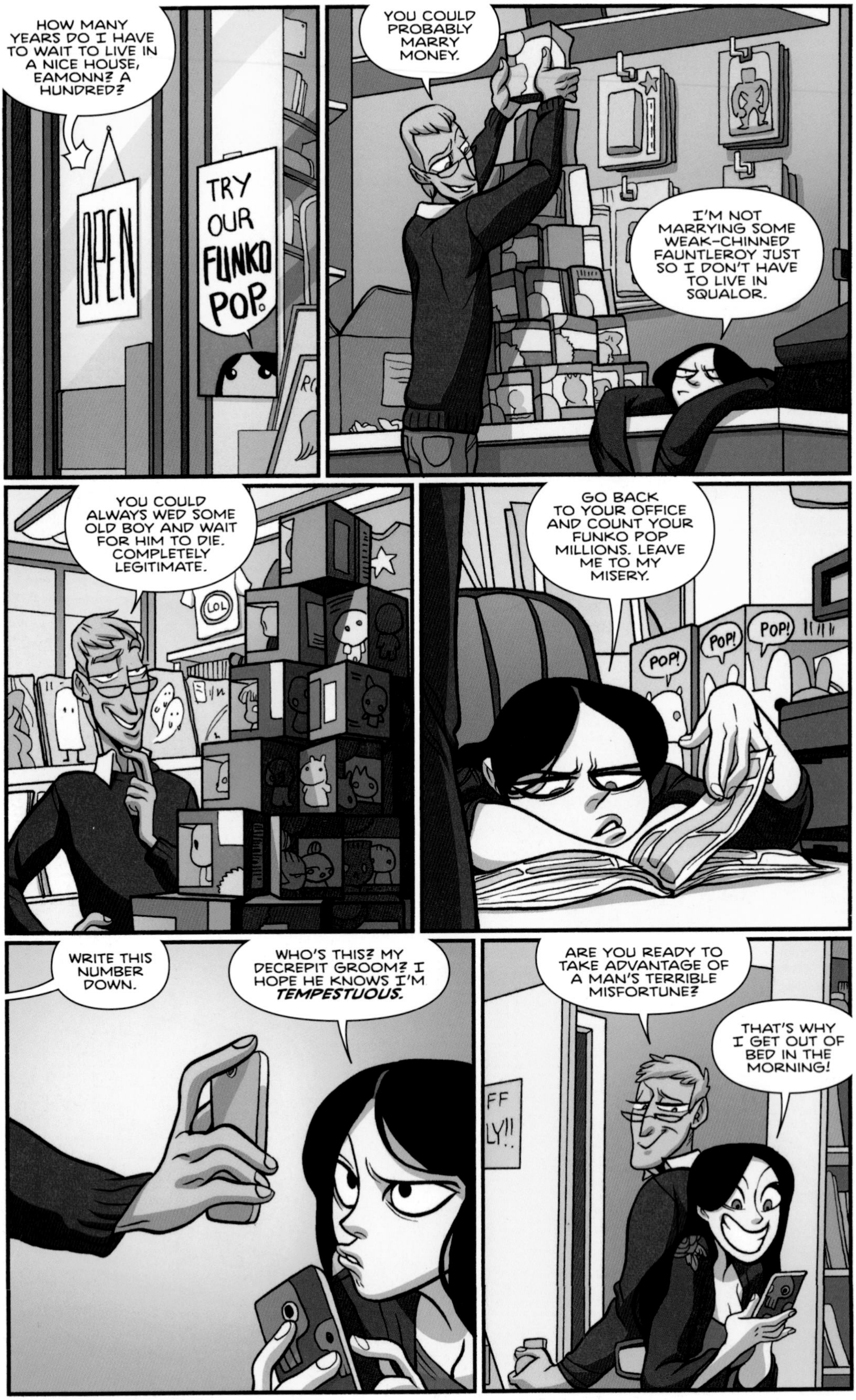
HOW MANY YEARS DO I HAVE TO WAIT TO LIVE IN A NICE HOUSE, EAMONN? A HUNDRED?
OPEN
TRY OUR FUNKO POP.
YOU COULD PROBABLY MARRY MONEY.
I'M NOT MARRYING SOME WEAK-CHINNED FAUNTLEROY JUST SO I DON'T HAVE TO LIVE IN SQUALOR.
YOU COULD ALWAYS WED SOME OLD BOY AND WAIT FOR HIM TO DIE. COMPLETELY LEGITIMATE.
LOL
GO BACK TO YOUR OFFICE AND COUNT YOUR FUNKO POP MILLIONS. LEAVE ME TO MY MISERY.
POP!
POP!
POP!
WRITE THIS NUMBER DOWN.
WHO'S THIS? MY DECREPIT GROOM? I HOPE HE KNOWS I'M ***TEMPESTUOUS.***
ARE YOU READY TO TAKE ADVANTAGE OF A MAN'S TERRIBLE MISFORTUNE?
THAT'S WHY I GET OUT OF BED IN THE MORNING!

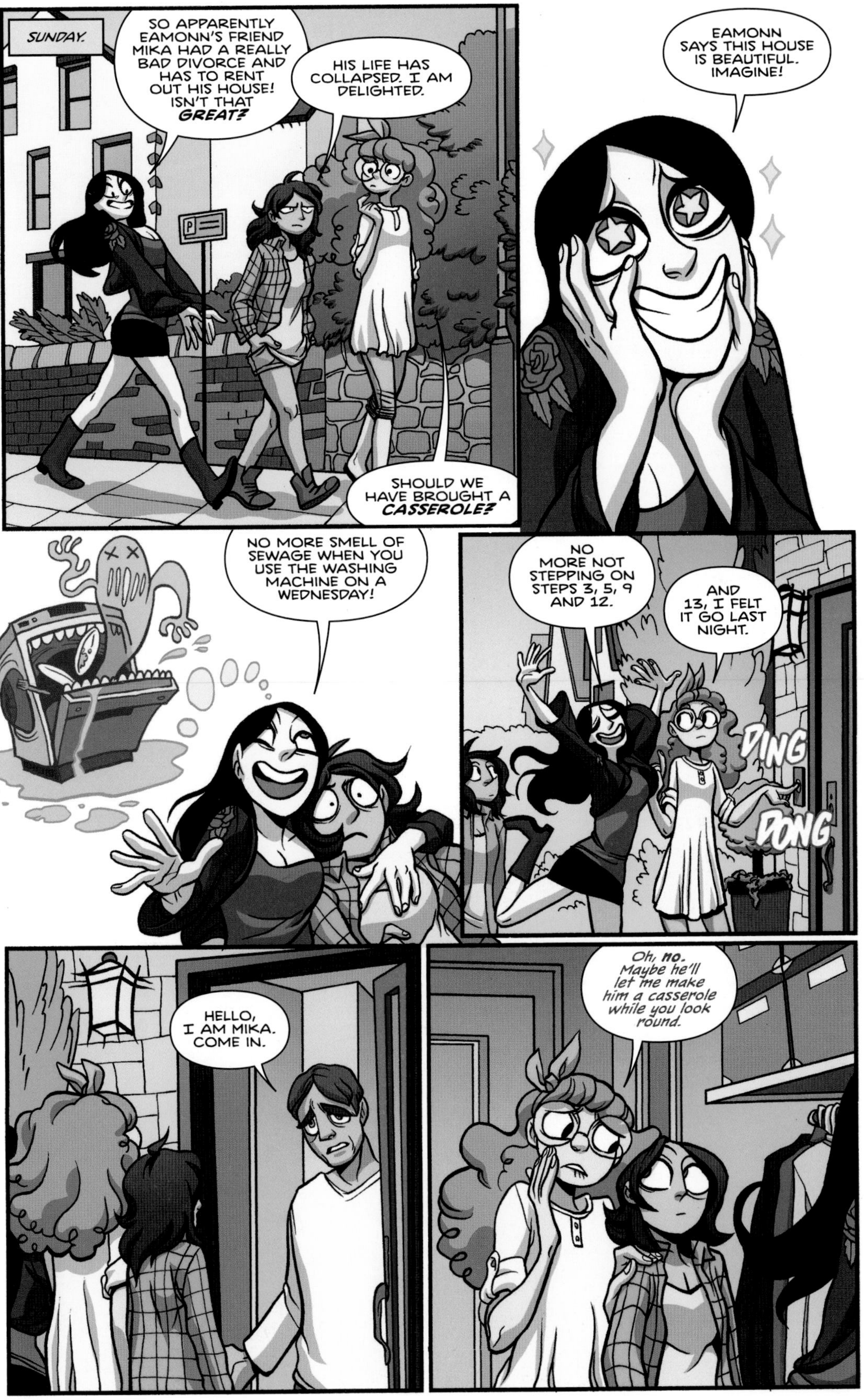
SUNDAY.
SO APPARENTLY EAMONN'S FRIEND MIKA HAD A REALLY BAD DIVORCE AND HAS TO RENT OUT HIS HOUSE! ISN'T THAT *GREAT?*
HIS LIFE HAS COLLAPSED. I AM DELIGHTED.
SHOULD WE HAVE BROUGHT A *CASSEROLE?*
EAMONN SAYS THIS HOUSE IS BEAUTIFUL. IMAGINE!
NO MORE SMELL OF SEWAGE WHEN YOU USE THE WASHING MACHINE ON A WEDNESDAY!
NO MORE NOT STEPPING ON STEPS 3, 5, 9 AND 12.
AND 13, I FELT IT GO LAST NIGHT.
DING
DONG
HELLO, I AM MIKA. COME IN.
*Oh, **no.** Maybe he'll let me make him a casserole while you look round.*

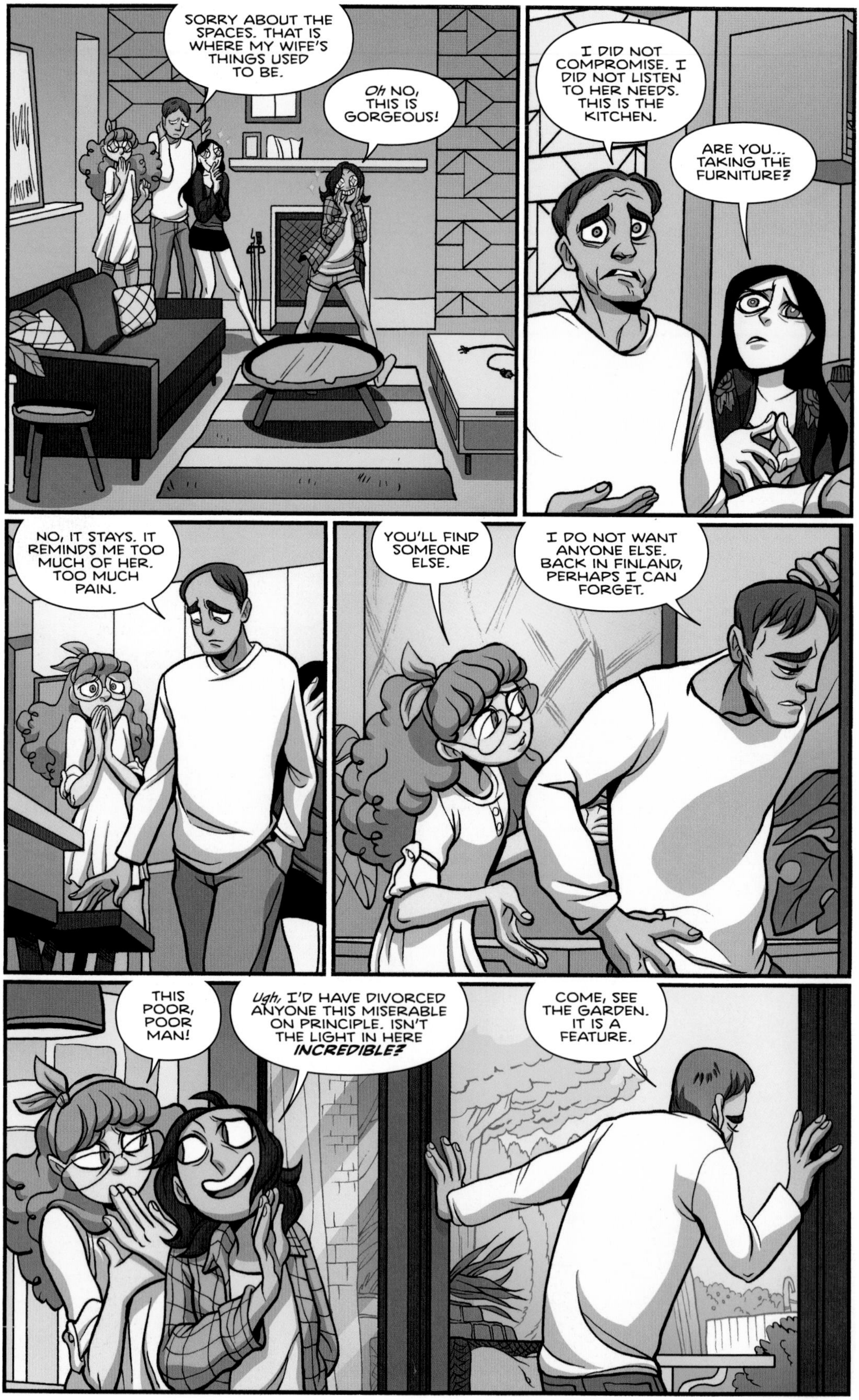
SORRY ABOUT THE SPACES. THAT IS WHERE MY WIFE'S THINGS USED TO BE.
Oh NO, THIS IS GORGEOUS!
I DID NOT COMPROMISE. I DID NOT LISTEN TO HER NEEDS. THIS IS THE KITCHEN.
ARE YOU... TAKING THE FURNITURE?
NO, IT STAYS. IT REMINDS ME TOO MUCH OF HER. TOO MUCH PAIN.
YOU'LL FIND SOMEONE ELSE.
I DO NOT WANT ANYONE ELSE. BACK IN FINLAND, PERHAPS I CAN FORGET.
THIS POOR, POOR MAN!
Ugh, I'D HAVE DIVORCED ANYONE THIS MISERABLE ON PRINCIPLE. ISN'T THE LIGHT IN HERE ***INCREDIBLE?***
COME, SEE THE GARDEN. IT IS A FEATURE.

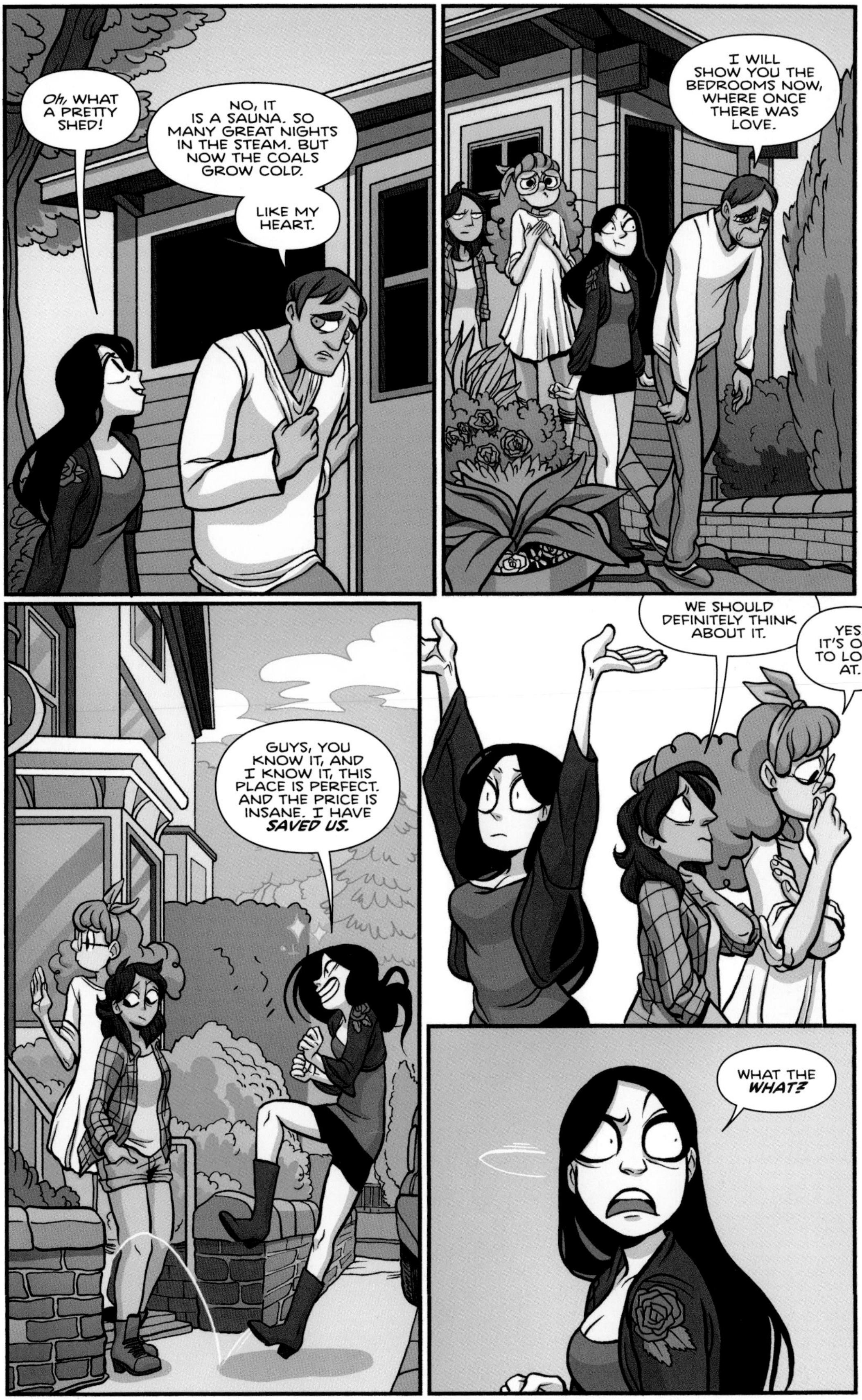
Oh, WHAT A PRETTY SHED!
NO, IT IS A SAUNA. SO MANY GREAT NIGHTS IN THE STEAM. BUT NOW THE COALS GROW COLD.
LIKE MY HEART.
I WILL SHOW YOU THE BEDROOMS NOW, WHERE ONCE THERE WAS LOVE.
GUYS, YOU KNOW IT, AND I KNOW IT, THIS PLACE IS PERFECT. AND THE PRICE IS INSANE. I HAVE SAVED US.
WE SHOULD DEFINITELY THINK ABOUT IT.
YES. IT'S ONE TO LOOK AT.
WHAT THE WHAT?

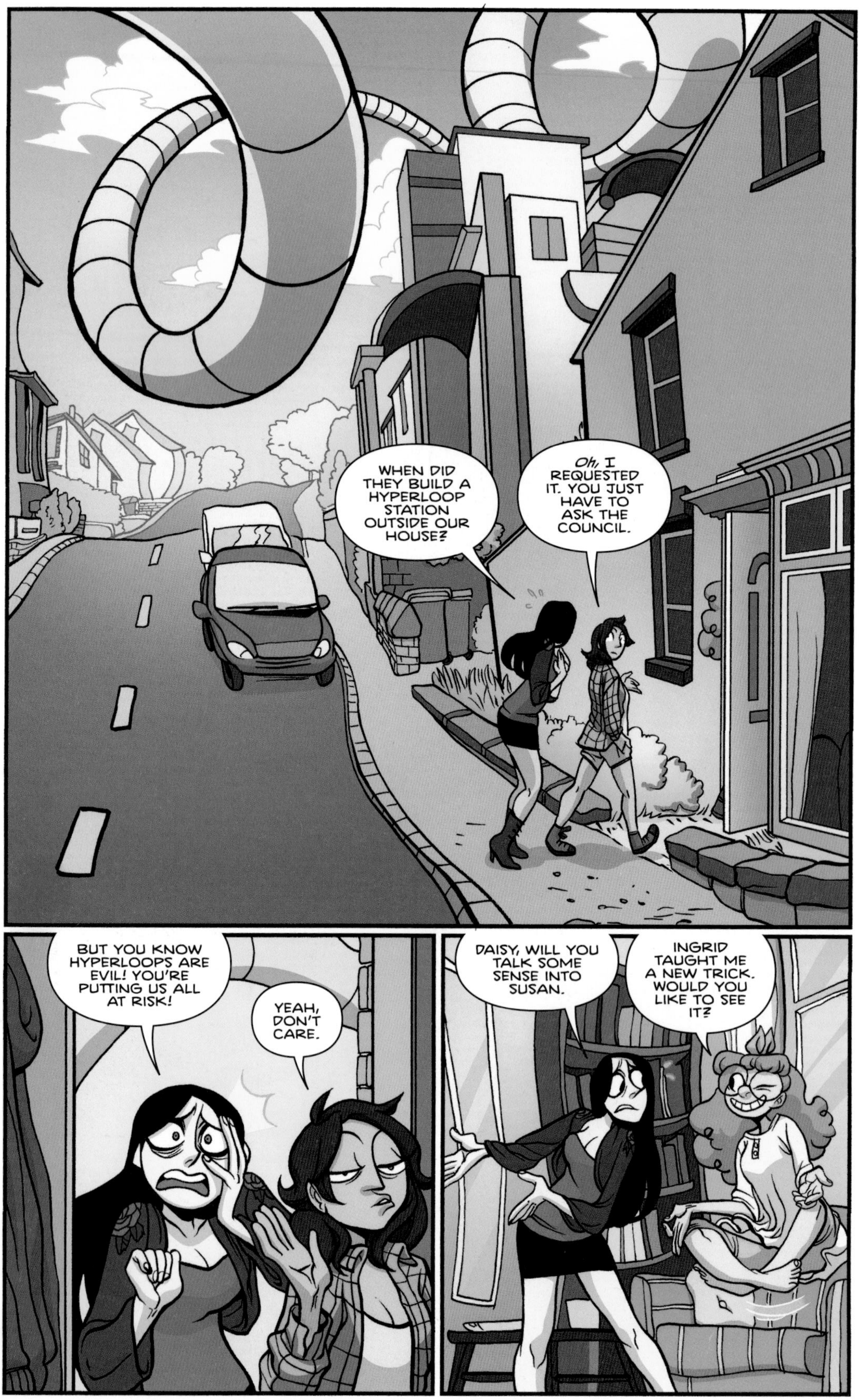
WHEN DID THEY BUILD A HYPERLOOP STATION OUTSIDE OUR HOUSE?
Oh, I REQUESTED IT. YOU JUST HAVE TO ASK THE COUNCIL.
BUT YOU KNOW HYPERLOOPS ARE EVIL! YOU'RE PUTTING US ALL AT RISK!
YEAH, DON'T CARE.
DAISY, WILL YOU TALK SOME SENSE INTO SUSAN.
INGRID TAUGHT ME A NEW TRICK. WOULD YOU LIKE TO SEE IT?

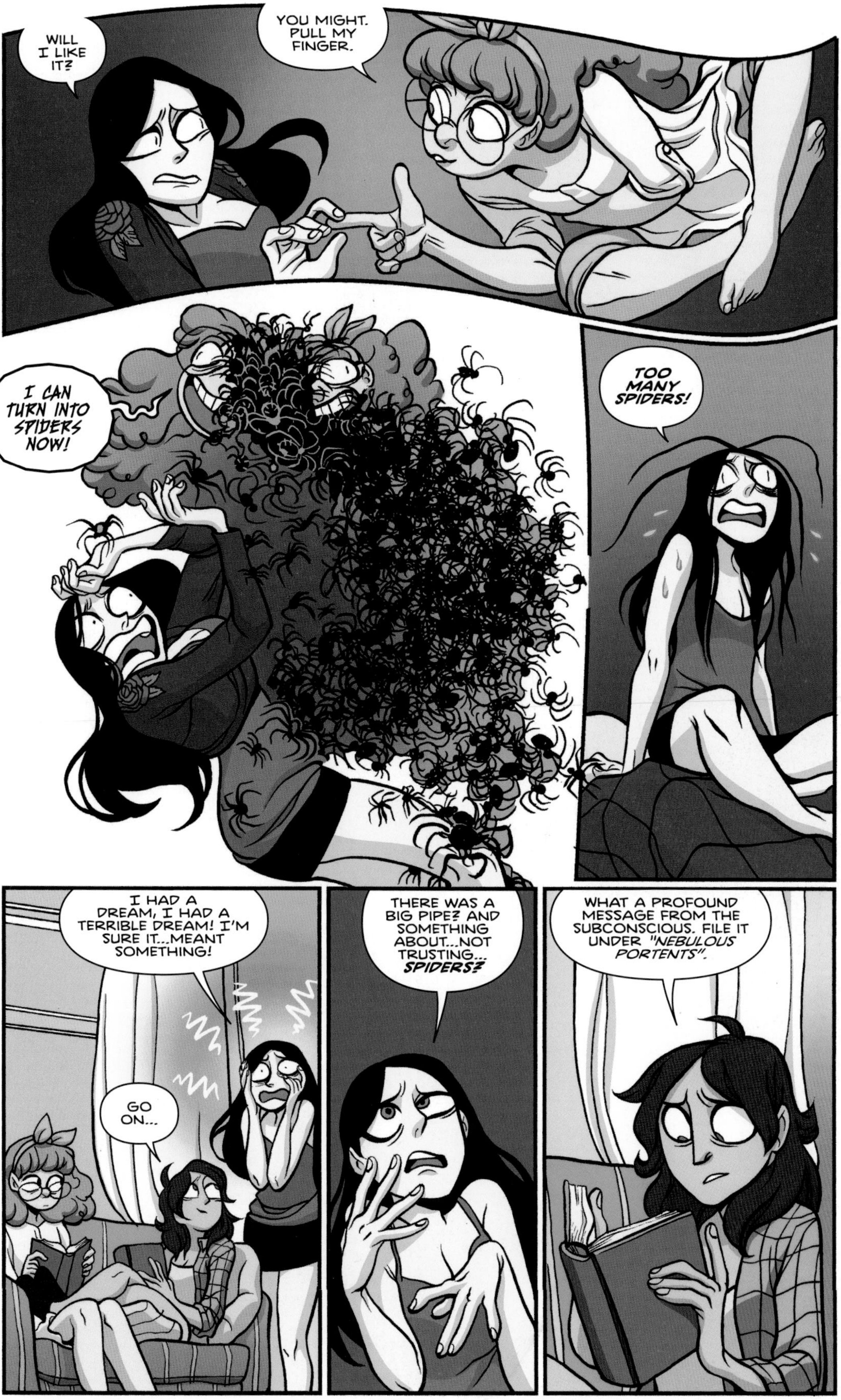

WILL I LIKE IT?
YOU MIGHT. PULL MY FINGER.
I CAN TURN INTO SPIDERS NOW!
TOO MANY SPIDERS!
I HAD A DREAM, I HAD A TERRIBLE DREAM! I'M SURE IT...MEANT SOMETHING!
GO ON...
THERE WAS A BIG PIPE? AND SOMETHING ABOUT...NOT TRUSTING... SPIDERS?
WHAT A PROFOUND MESSAGE FROM THE SUBCONSCIOUS. FILE IT UNDER "NEBULOUS PORTENTS".

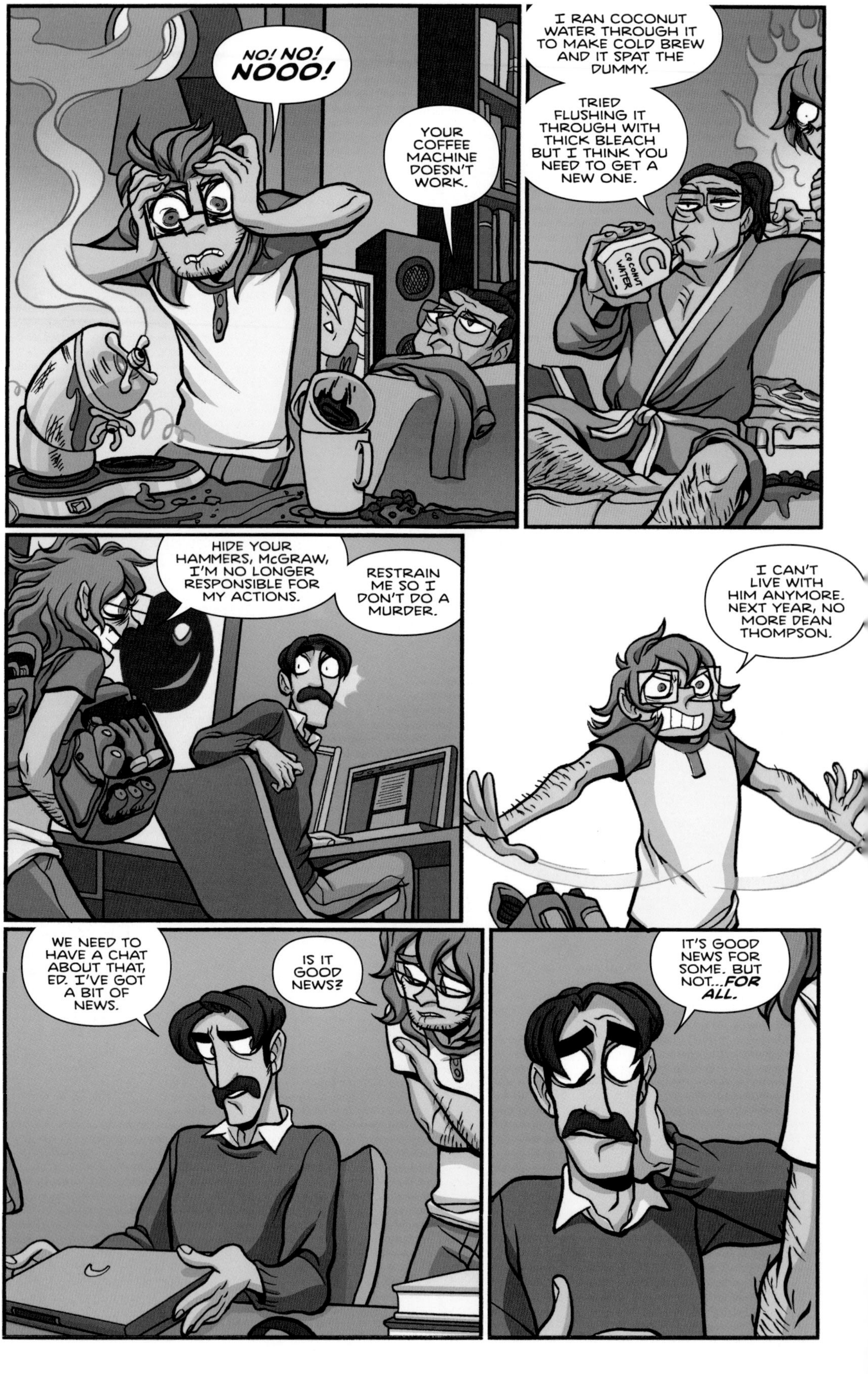
NO! NO! NOOO!
YOUR COFFEE MACHINE DOESN'T WORK.
I RAN COCONUT WATER THROUGH IT TO MAKE COLD BREW AND IT SPAT THE DUMMY.
TRIED FLUSHING IT THROUGH WITH THICK BLEACH BUT I THINK YOU NEED TO GET A NEW ONE.
COCONUT WATER
HIDE YOUR HAMMERS, McGRAW, I'M NO LONGER RESPONSIBLE FOR MY ACTIONS.
RESTRAIN ME SO I DON'T DO A MURDER.
I CAN'T LIVE WITH HIM ANYMORE. NEXT YEAR, NO MORE DEAN THOMPSON.
WE NEED TO HAVE A CHAT ABOUT THAT, ED. I'VE GOT A BIT OF NEWS.
IS IT GOOD NEWS?
IT'S GOOD NEWS FOR SOME. BUT NOT...FOR ALL.

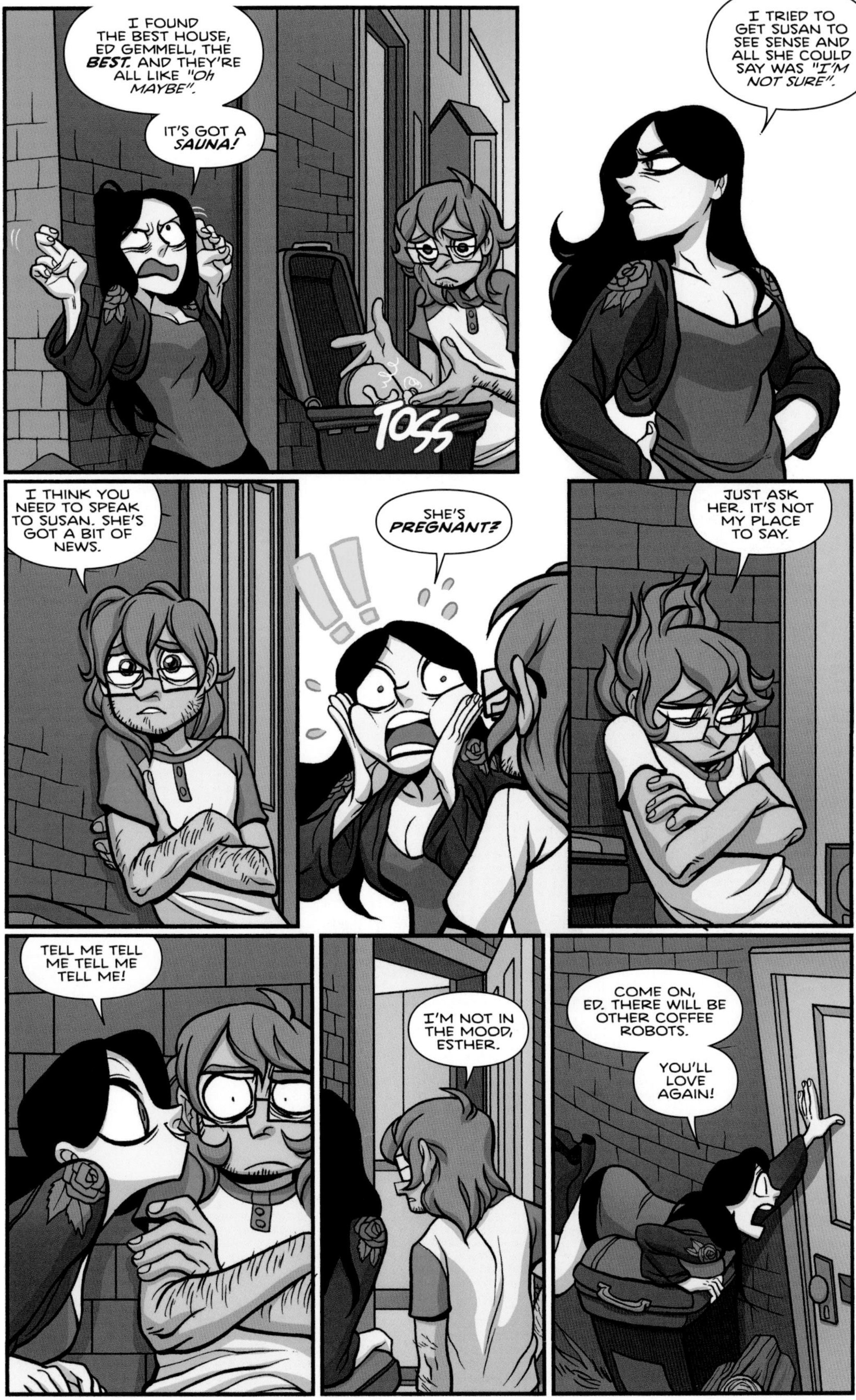
I FOUND THE BEST HOUSE, ED GEMMELL, THE BEST. AND THEY'RE ALL LIKE "Oh MAYBE".
IT'S GOT A SAUNA!
TOSS
I TRIED TO GET SUSAN TO SEE SENSE AND ALL SHE COULD SAY WAS "I'M NOT SURE".
I THINK YOU NEED TO SPEAK TO SUSAN. SHE'S GOT A BIT OF NEWS.
SHE'S PREGNANT?
JUST ASK HER. IT'S NOT MY PLACE TO SAY.
TELL ME TELL ME TELL ME TELL ME!
I'M NOT IN THE MOOD, ESTHER.
COME ON, ED. THERE WILL BE OTHER COFFEE ROBOTS.
YOU'LL LOVE AGAIN!

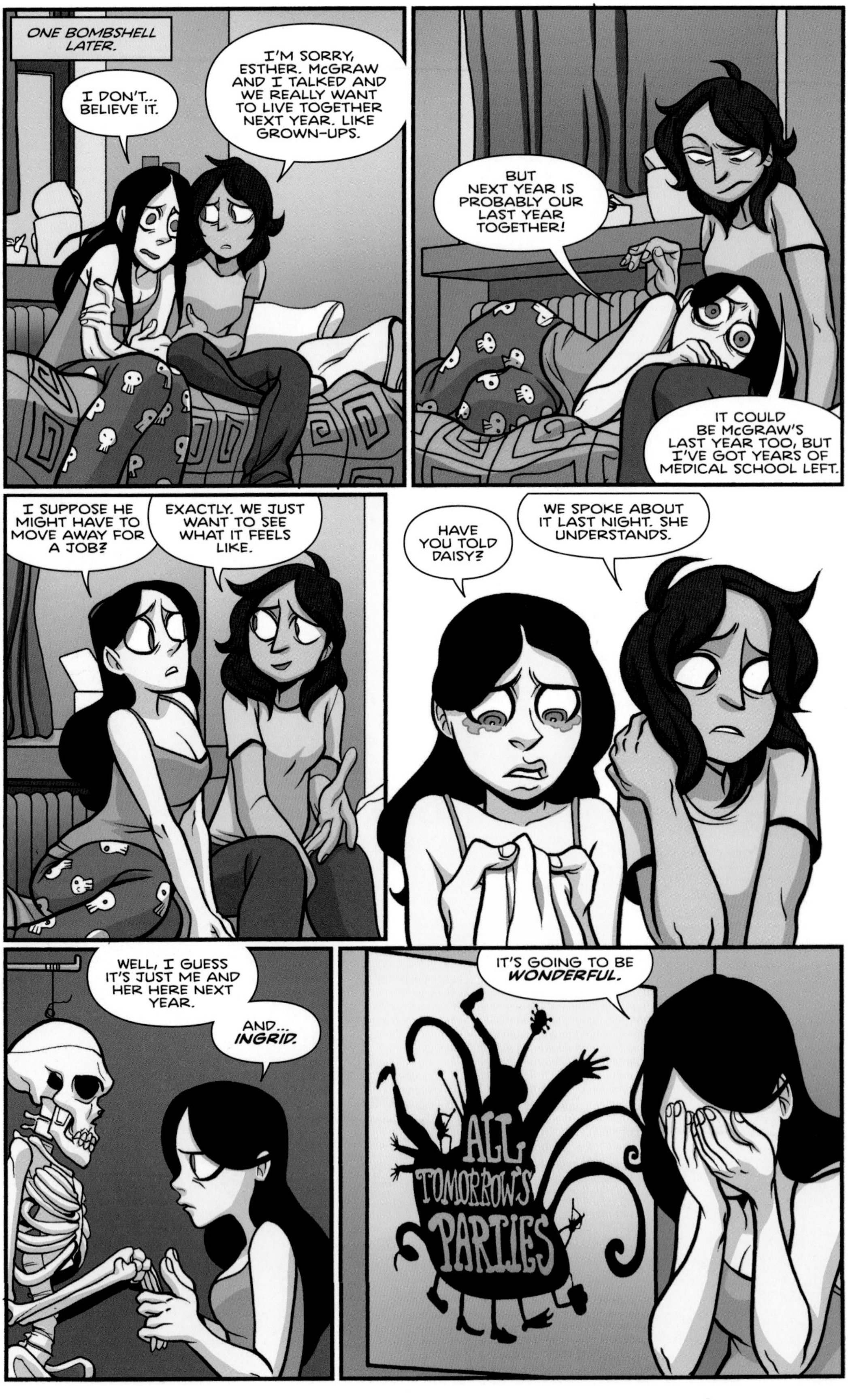

ONE BOMBSHELL LATER.
I DON'T... BELIEVE IT.
I'M SORRY, ESTHER. McGRAW AND I TALKED AND WE REALLY WANT TO LIVE TOGETHER NEXT YEAR. LIKE GROWN-UPS.
BUT NEXT YEAR IS PROBABLY OUR LAST YEAR TOGETHER!
IT COULD BE McGRAW'S LAST YEAR TOO, BUT I'VE GOT YEARS OF MEDICAL SCHOOL LEFT.
I SUPPOSE HE MIGHT HAVE TO MOVE AWAY FOR A JOB?
EXACTLY. WE JUST WANT TO SEE WHAT IT FEELS LIKE.
HAVE YOU TOLD DAISY?
WE SPOKE ABOUT IT LAST NIGHT. SHE UNDERSTANDS.
WELL, I GUESS IT'S JUST ME AND HER HERE NEXT YEAR.
AND... INGRID.
IT'S GOING TO BE WONDERFUL.
ALL TOMORROW'S PARTIES

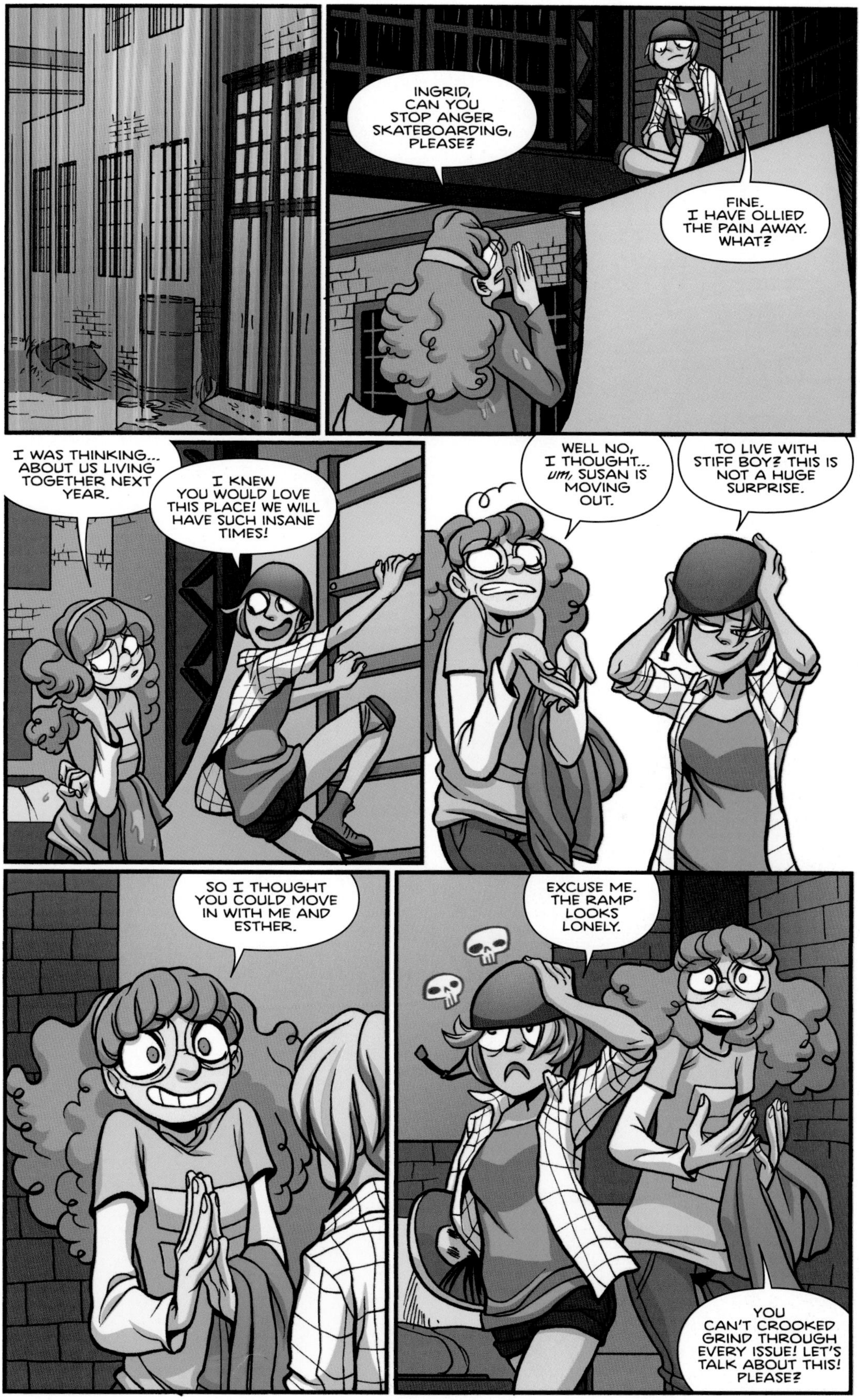
INGRID, CAN YOU STOP ANGER SKATEBOARDING, PLEASE?
FINE. I HAVE OLLIED THE PAIN AWAY. WHAT?
I WAS THINKING... ABOUT US LIVING TOGETHER NEXT YEAR.
I KNEW YOU WOULD LOVE THIS PLACE! WE WILL HAVE SUCH INSANE TIMES!
WELL NO, I THOUGHT... *UM*, SUSAN IS MOVING OUT.
TO LIVE WITH STIFF BOY? THIS IS NOT A HUGE SURPRISE.
SO I THOUGHT YOU COULD MOVE IN WITH ME AND ESTHER.
EXCUSE ME. THE RAMP LOOKS LONELY.
YOU CAN'T CROOKED GRIND THROUGH EVERY ISSUE! LET'S TALK ABOUT THIS! PLEASE?

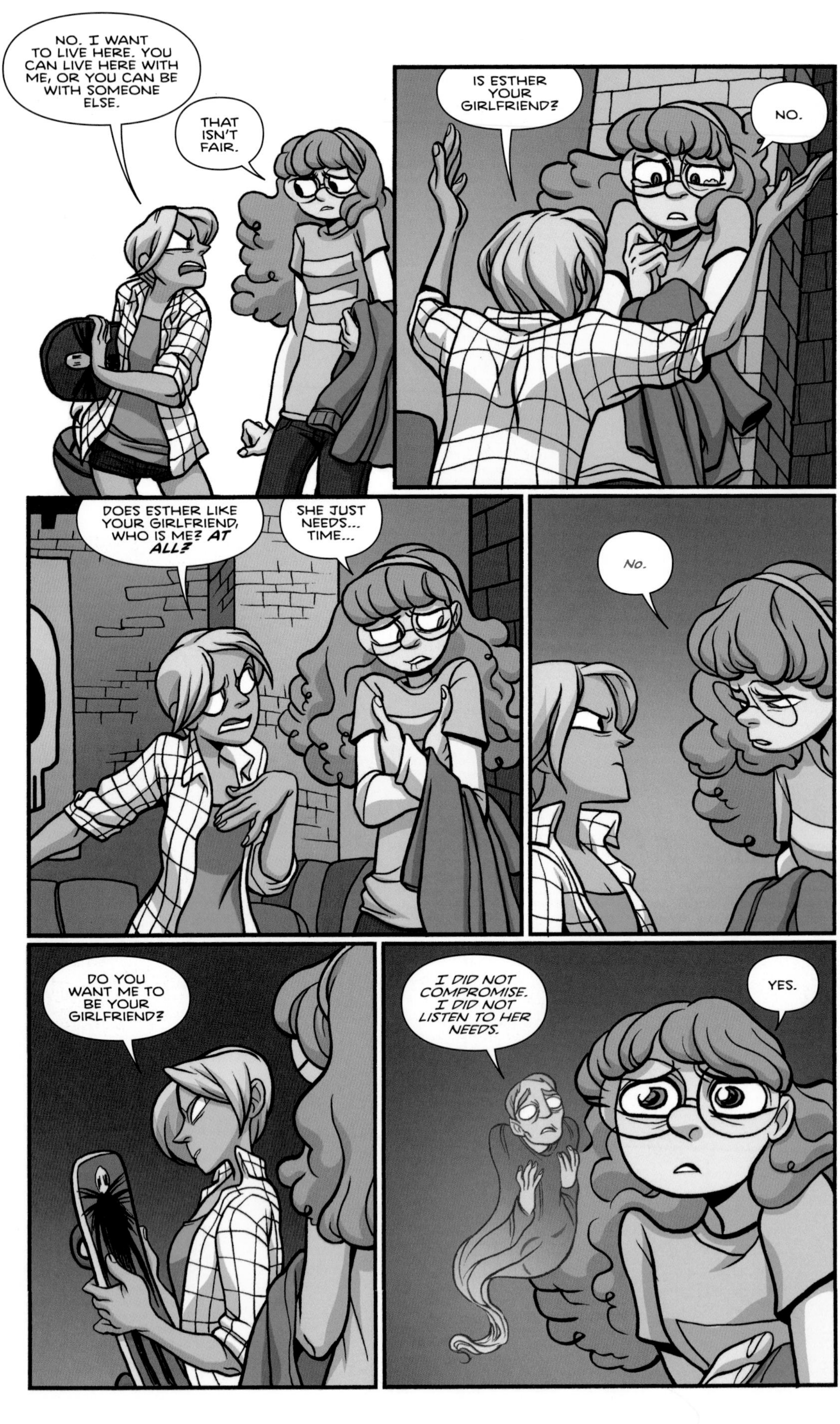
NO. I WANT TO LIVE HERE. YOU CAN LIVE HERE WITH ME, OR YOU CAN BE WITH SOMEONE ELSE.
THAT ISN'T FAIR.
IS ESTHER YOUR GIRLFRIEND?
NO.
DOES ESTHER LIKE YOUR GIRLFRIEND, WHO IS ME? AT ALL?
SHE JUST NEEDS... TIME...
No.
DO YOU WANT ME TO BE YOUR GIRLFRIEND?
I DID NOT COMPROMISE. I DID NOT LISTEN TO HER NEEDS.
YES.

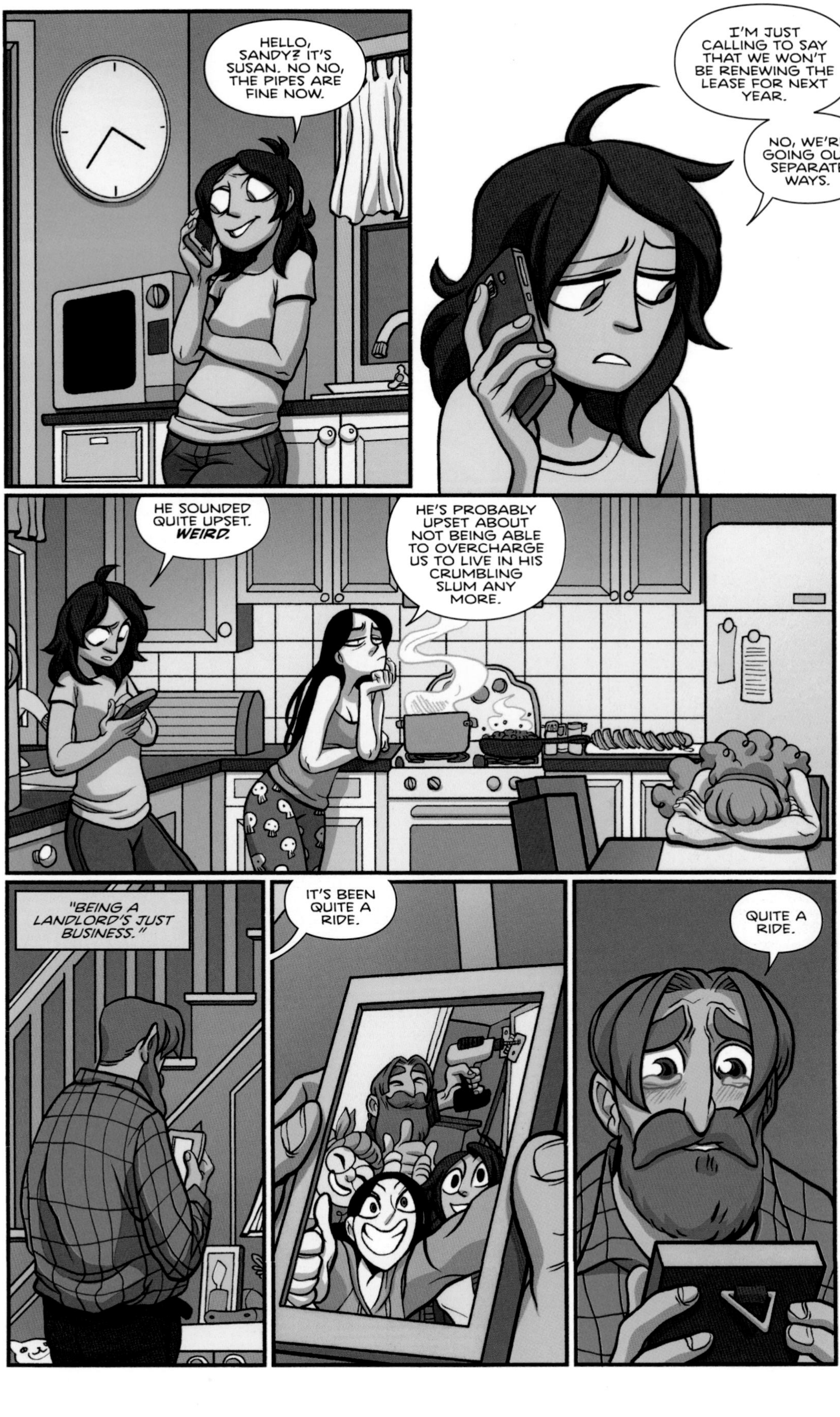
HELLO, SANDY? IT'S SUSAN. NO NO, THE PIPES ARE FINE NOW.
I'M JUST CALLING TO SAY THAT WE WON'T BE RENEWING THE LEASE FOR NEXT YEAR.
NO, WE'RE GOING OUR SEPARATE WAYS.
HE SOUNDED QUITE UPSET. ***WEIRD.***
HE'S PROBABLY UPSET ABOUT NOT BEING ABLE TO OVERCHARGE US TO LIVE IN HIS CRUMBLING SLUM ANY MORE.
"BEING A LANDLORD'S JUST BUSINESS."
IT'S BEEN QUITE A RIDE.
QUITE A RIDE.

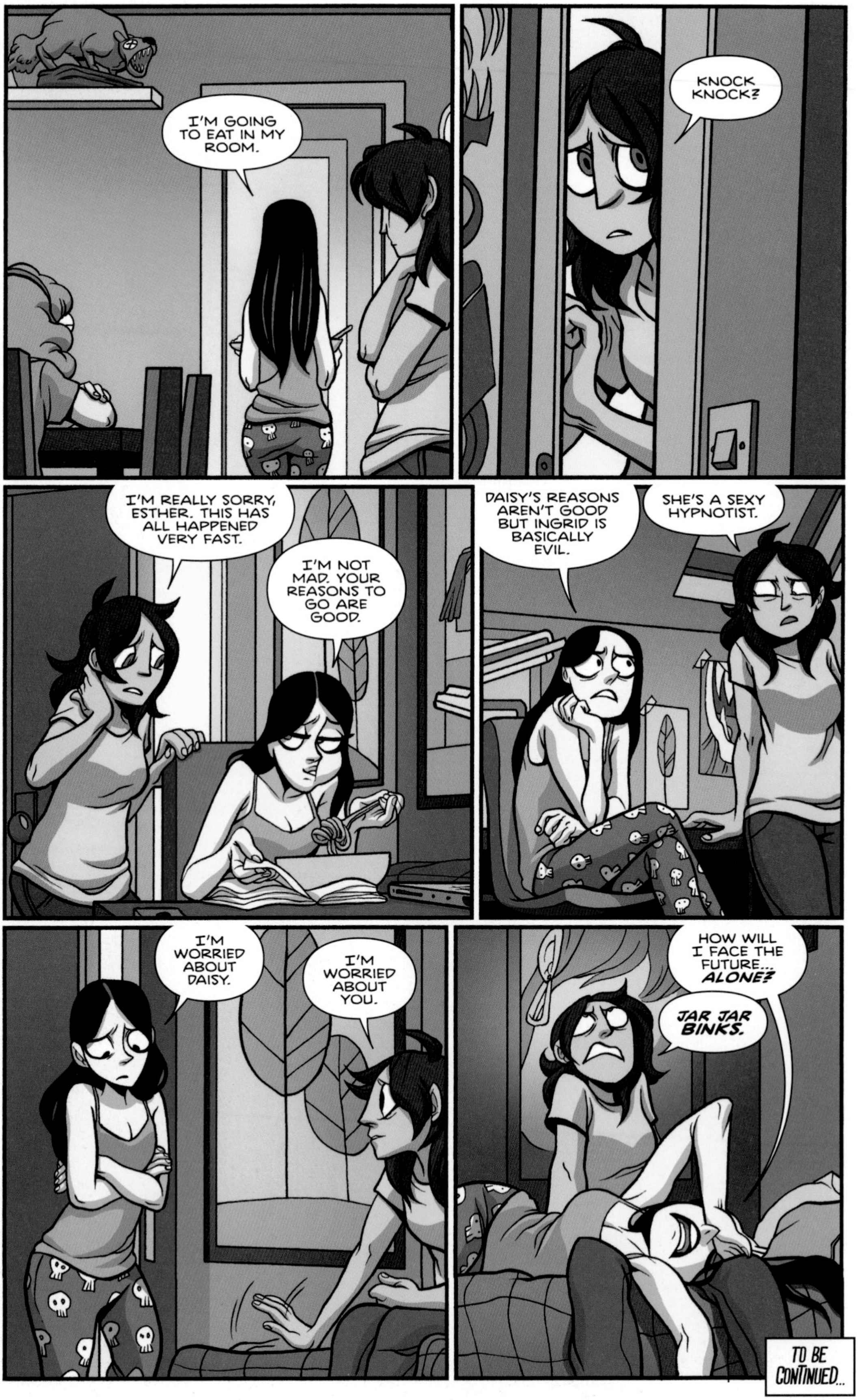
I'M GOING TO EAT IN MY ROOM.
KNOCK KNOCK?
I'M REALLY SORRY, ESTHER. THIS HAS ALL HAPPENED VERY FAST.
I'M NOT MAD. YOUR REASONS TO GO ARE GOOD.
DAISY'S REASONS AREN'T GOOD BUT INGRID IS BASICALLY EVIL.
SHE'S A SEXY HYPNOTIST.
I'M WORRIED ABOUT DAISY.
I'M WORRIED ABOUT YOU.
HOW WILL I FACE THE FUTURE... ***ALONE?***
JAR JAR BINKS.
TO BE CONTINUED...

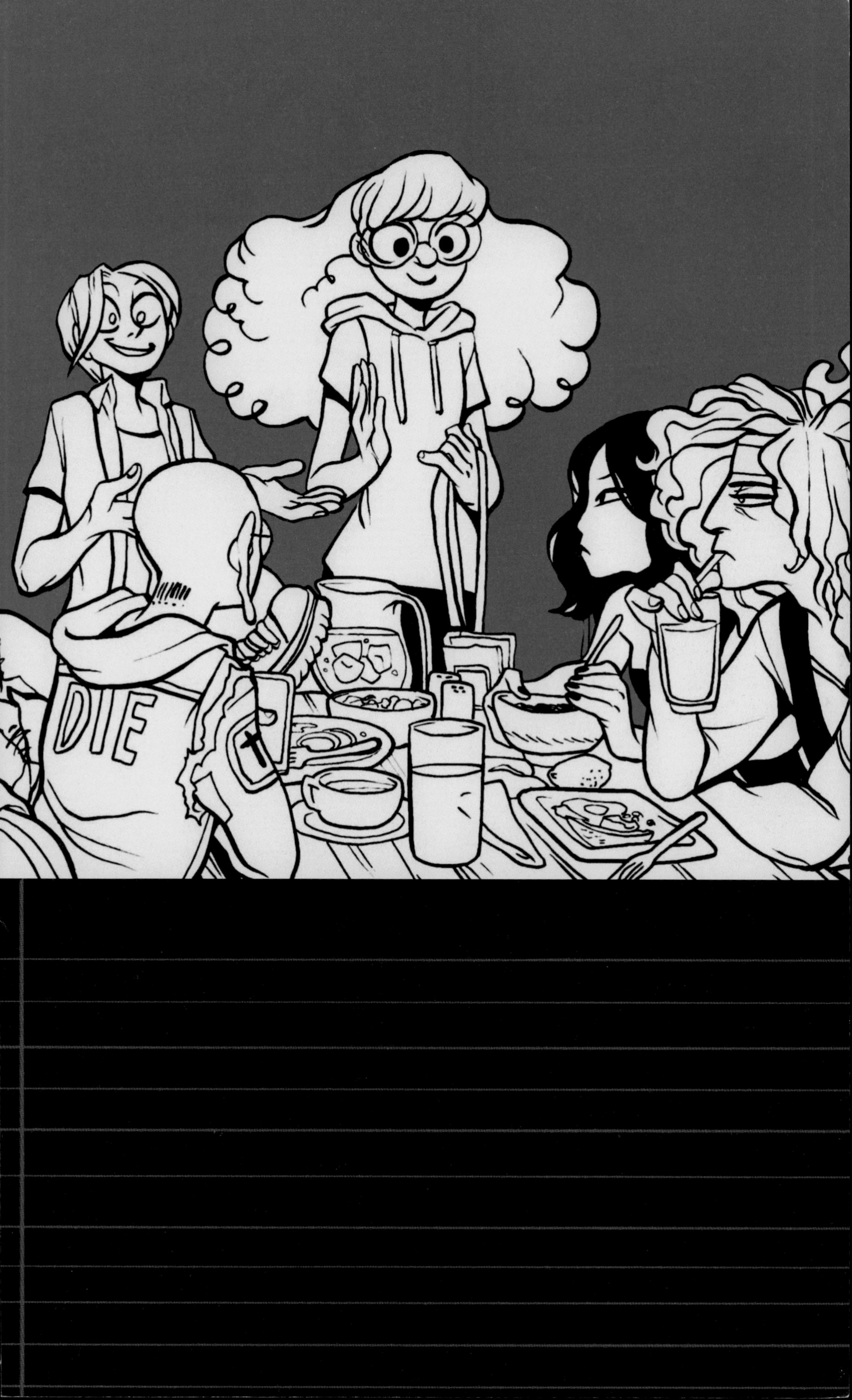
DIE

COVER
GALLERY

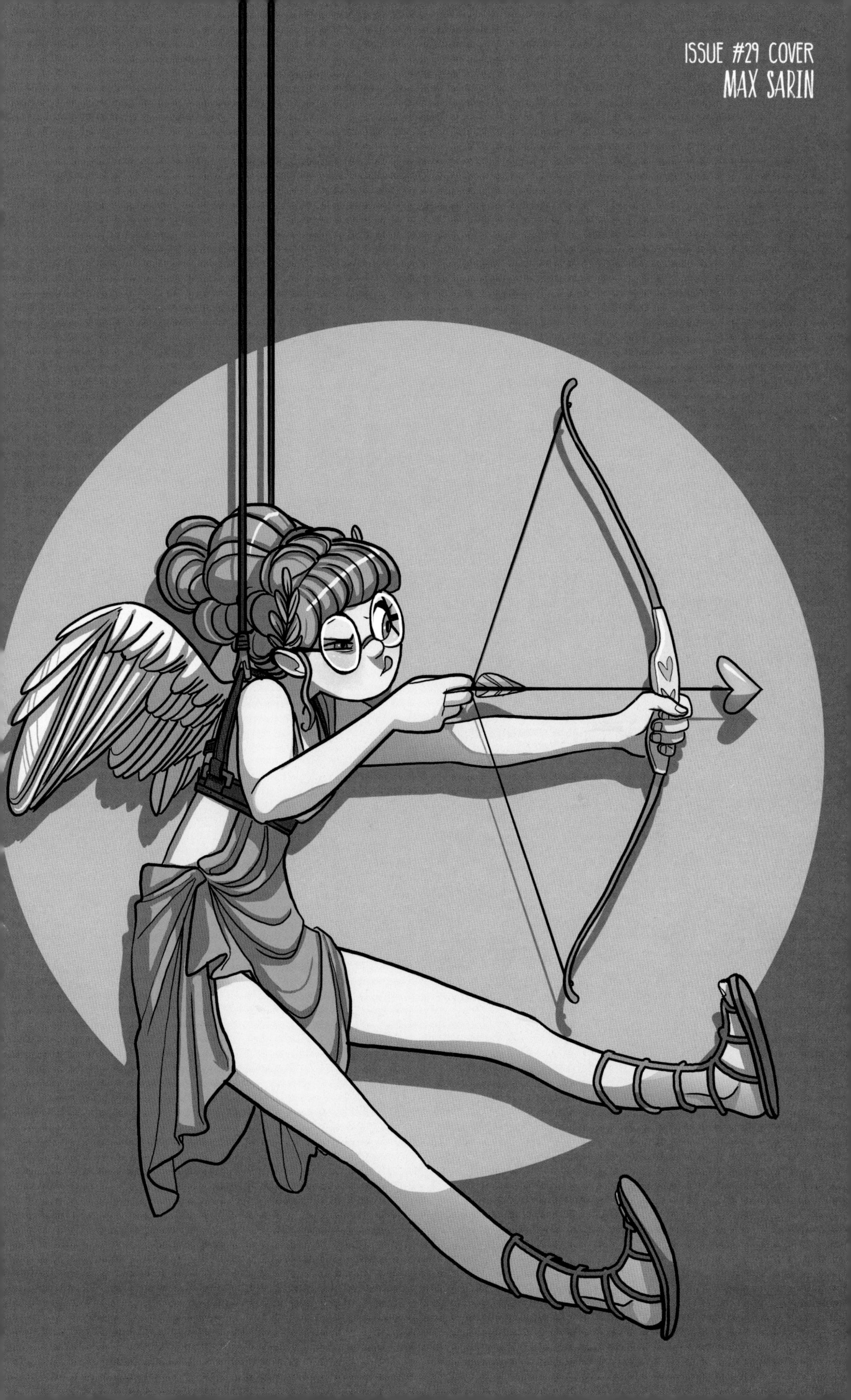

ISSUE #29 COVER
MAX SARIN

ISSUE #30 COVER
MAX SARIN

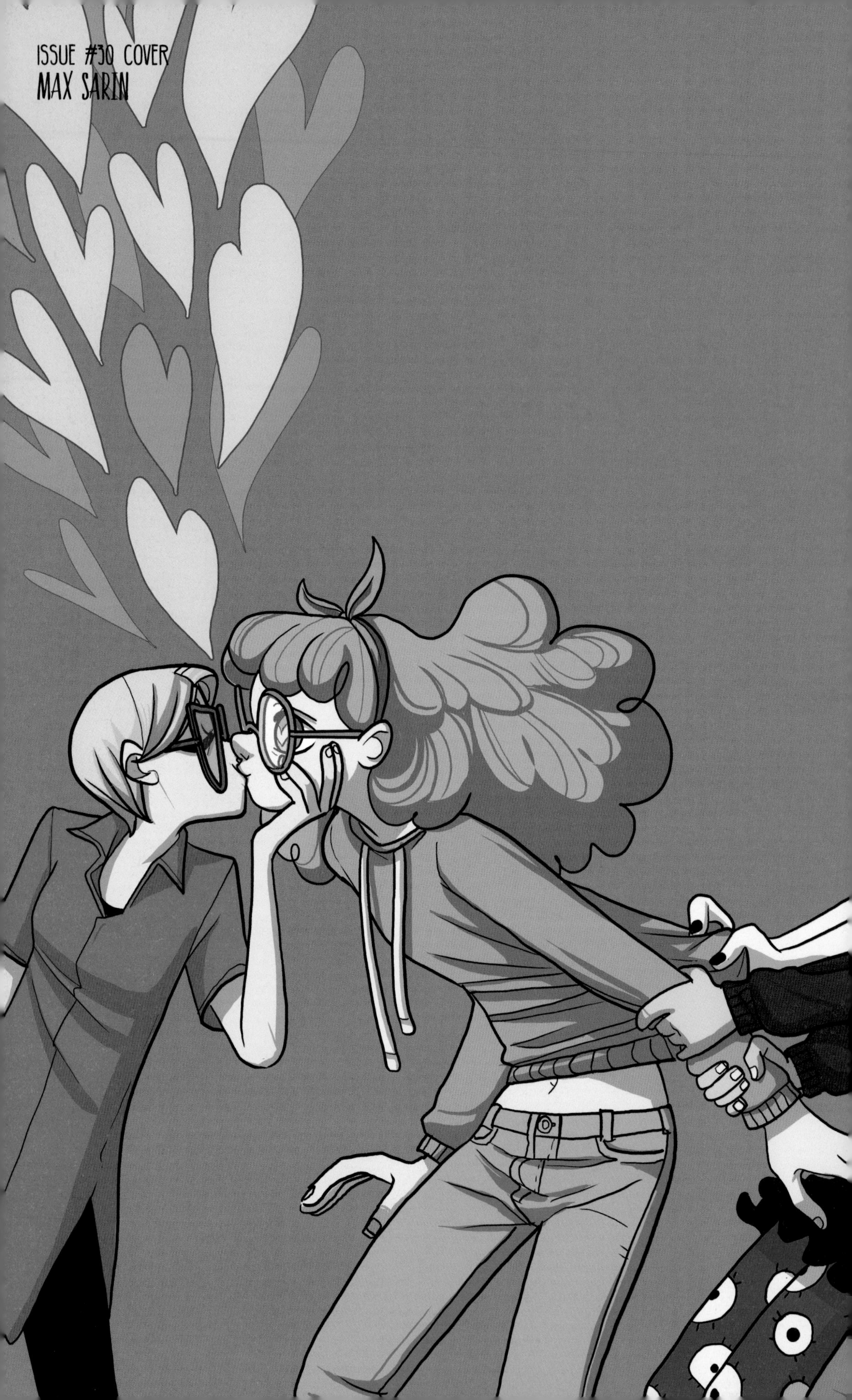

ISSUE #31 COVER
MAX SARIN

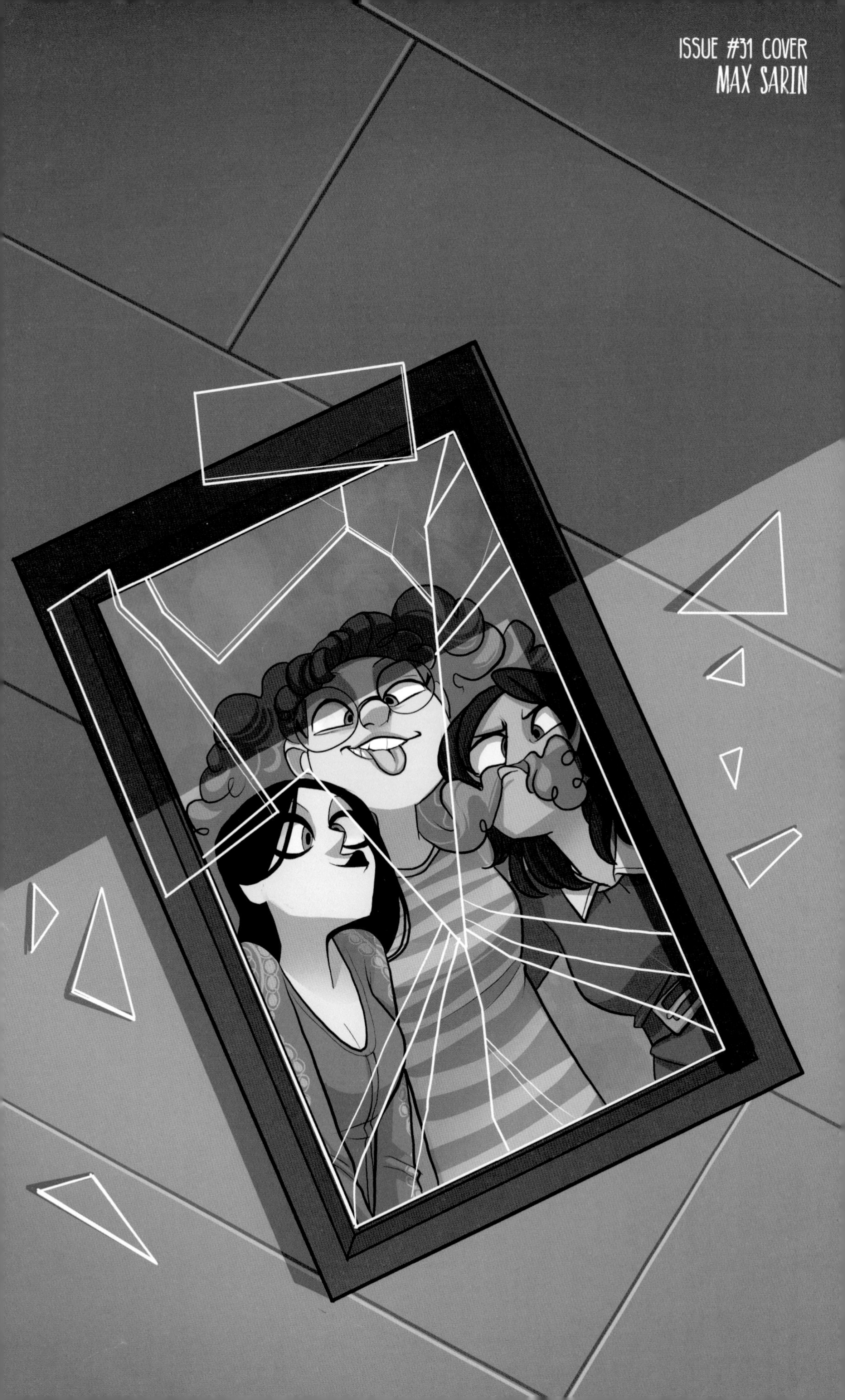

ISSUE #32 COVER
MAX SARIN

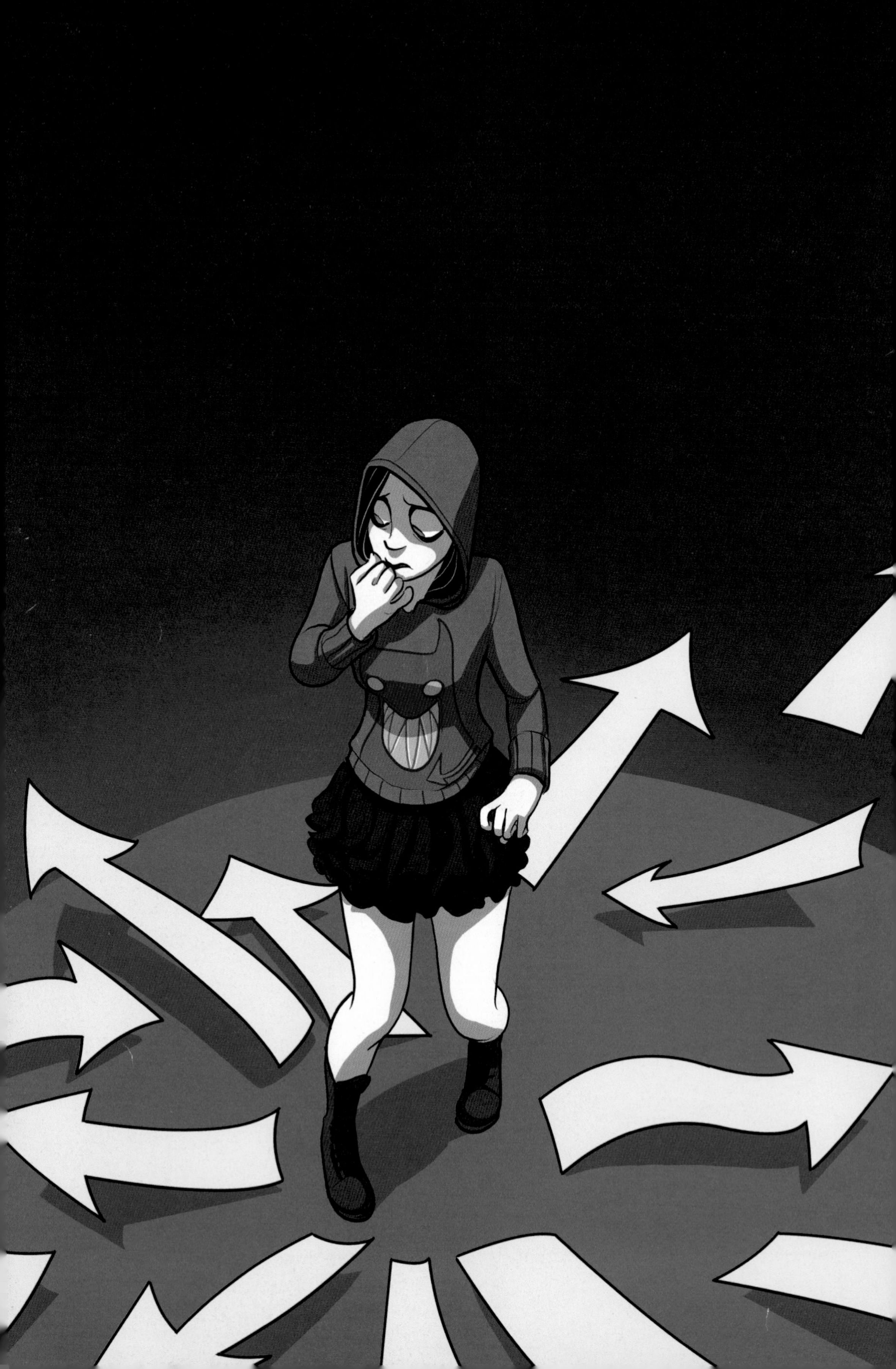

SKETCH GALLERY

SKETCHES BY JOHN ALLISON

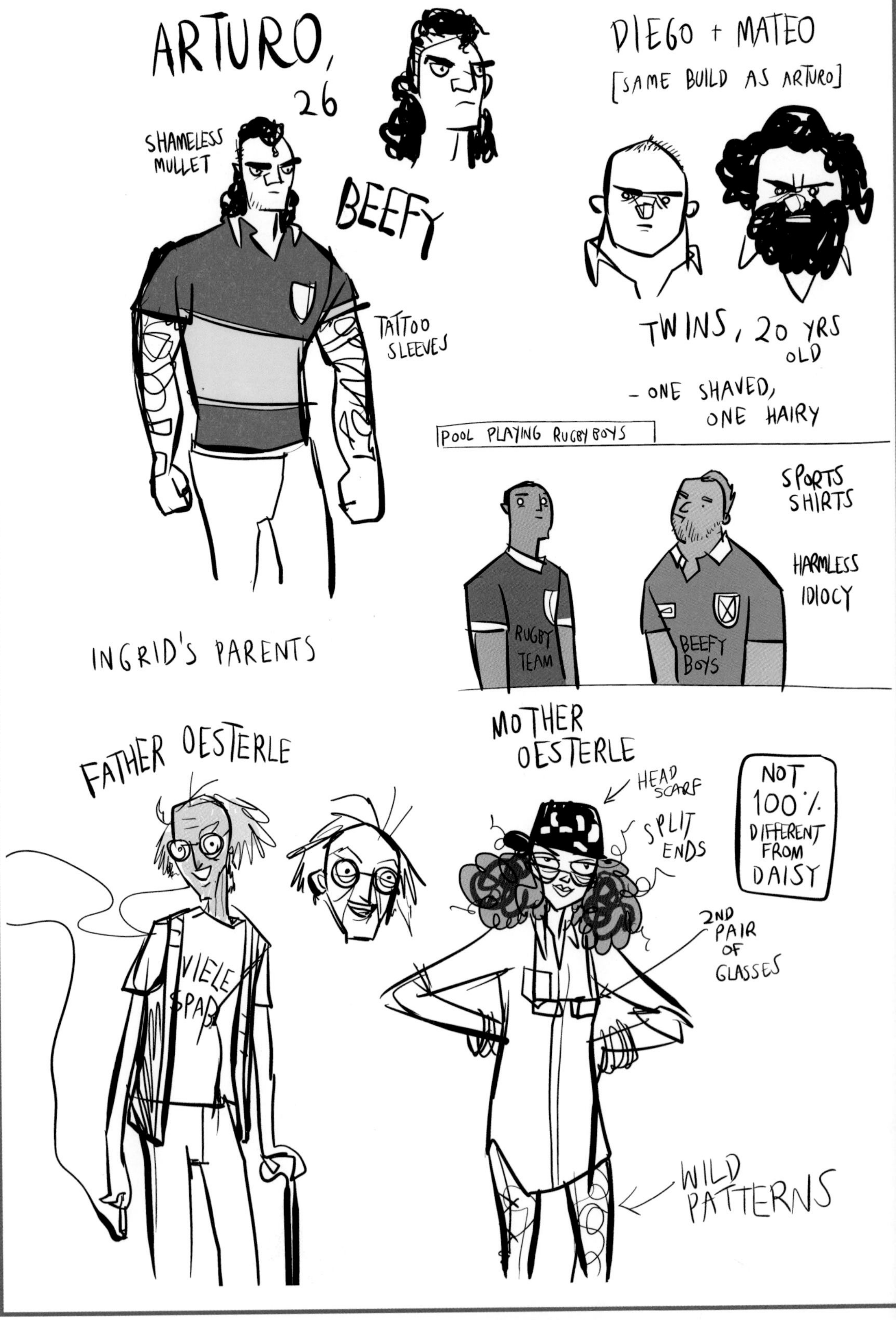
ARTURO, 26
SHAMELESS MULLET
BEEFY
TATTOO SLEEVES
DIEGO + MATEO
[SAME BUILD AS ARTURO]
TWINS, 20 YRS OLD
- ONE SHAVED, ONE HAIRY
POOL PLAYING RUGBY BOYS
SPORTS SHIRTS
HARMLESS IDIOCY
RUGBY TEAM
BEEFY BOYS
INGRID'S PARENTS
FATHER OESTERLE
VIELE SPAß
MOTHER OESTERLE
HEAD SCARF
SPLIT ENDS
NOT 100% DIFFERENT FROM DAISY
2ND PAIR OF GLASSES
WILD PATTERNS

SKETCHES BY JOHN ALLISON

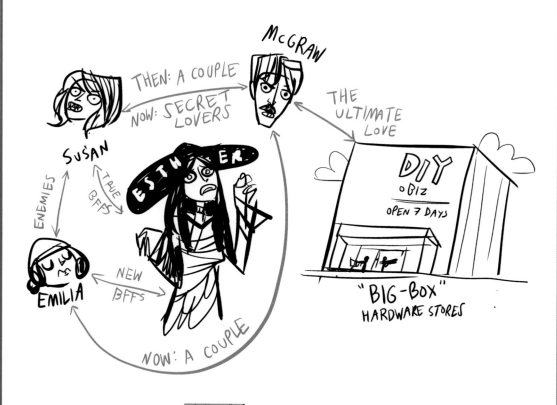

McGRAW
THEN: A COUPLE
NOW: SECRET LOVERS
SUSAN
THE ULTIMATE LOVE
ESTHER
DIY
oBIZ
OPEN 7 DAYS
ENEMIES
TRUE BFFS
EMILIA
NEW BFFS
NOW: A COUPLE
"BIG-BOX"
HARDWARE STORES

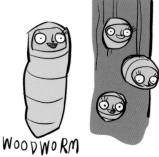

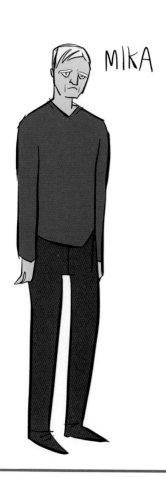

WOODWORM

MIKA

SKETCHES BY MAX SARIN

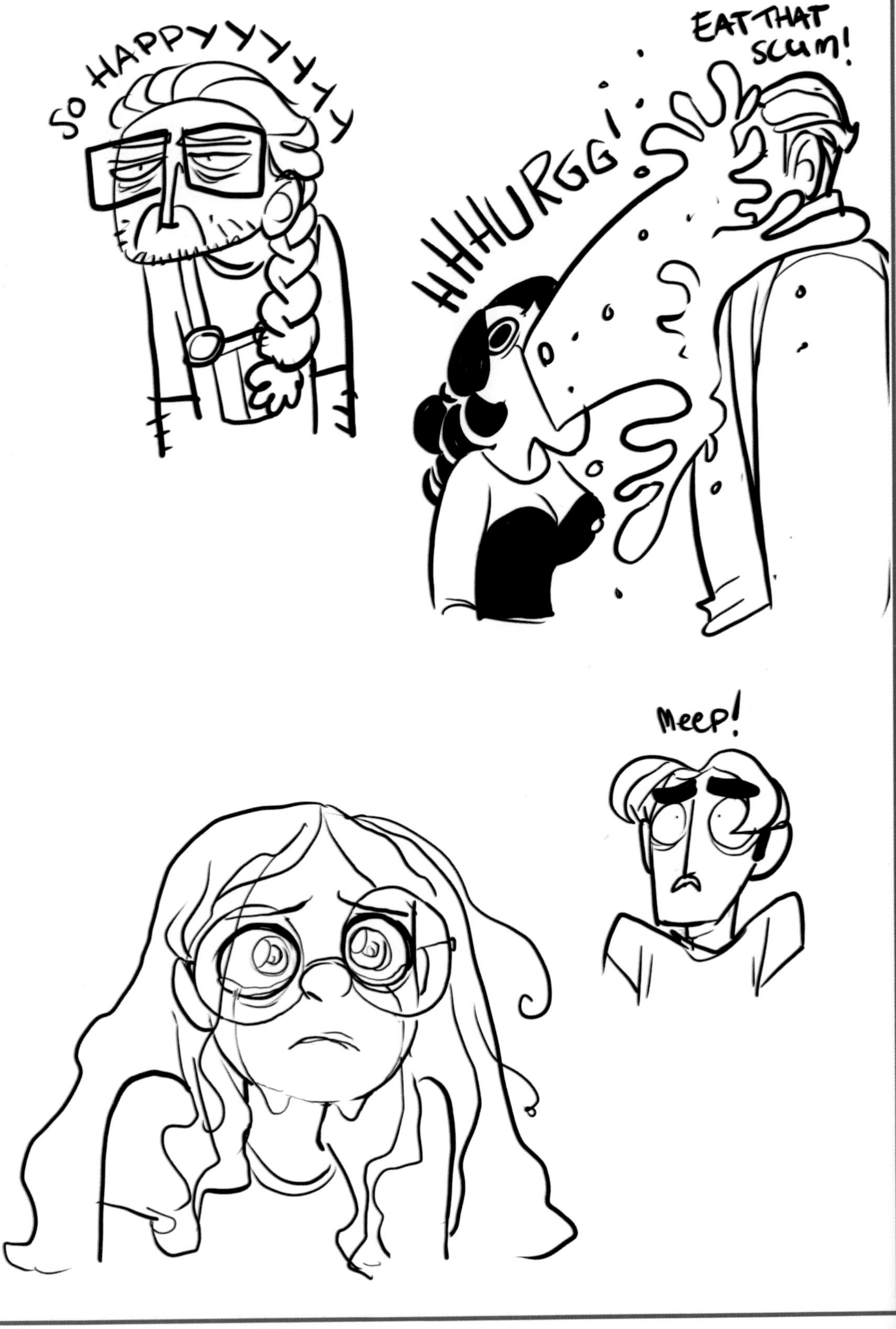
SO HAPPYYYYYY
EAT THAT SCUM!
HHHURGG!
Meep!

SKETCHES BY MAX SARIN

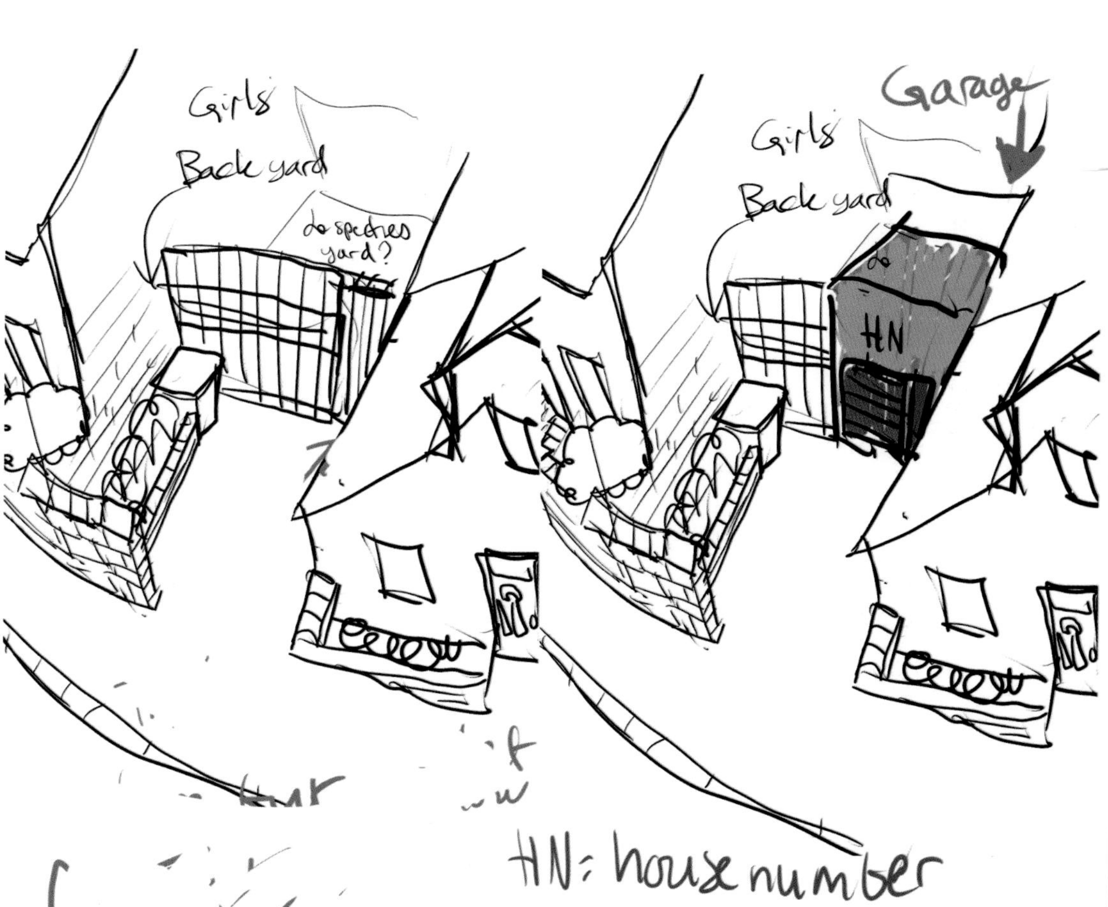
Girls
Back yard
do sketches yard?
Garage
Girls
Back yard
HN
HN: house number

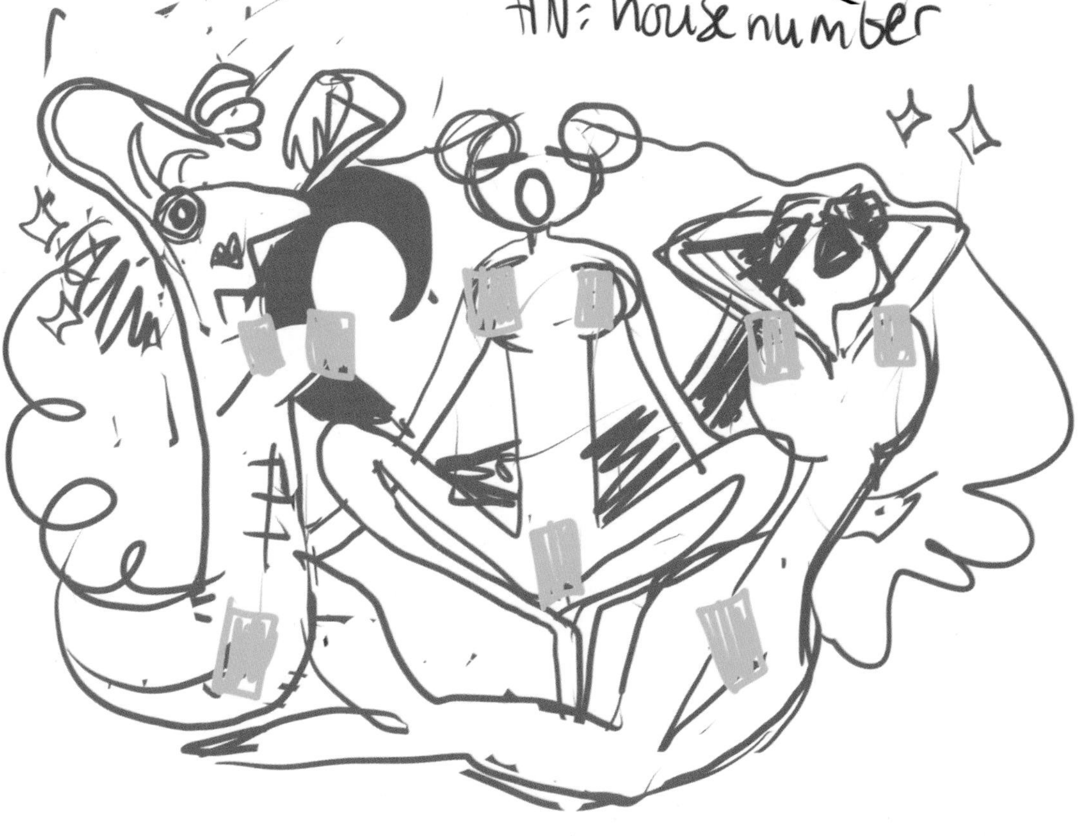

DISCOVER
ALL THE HITS

STEVENSON • ELLIS • WATTERS • ALLEN
LUMBERJANES
BEWARE THE KITTEN HOLY
NEW YORK TIMES BESTSELLING SERIES

Allison + Treiman + Cogar
GIANT DAYS
VOLUME ONE

RIBON • FISH • PEER
SLAM!
VOLUME ONE

Hope Larson • Brittney Williams • Sarah Stern
GOLDIE VANCE
Volume One

THE BACKSTAGERS

TYSON HESSE'S
DIESEL
IGNITION

BOOM! BOX

AVAILABLE AT YOUR LOCAL COMICS SHOP AND BOOKSTORE

To find a comics shop in your area, call 1-888-266-4226

WWW.**BOOM-STUDIOS**.COM

Lumberjanes
Noelle Stevenson, Shannon Watters, Grace Ellis, Brooke Allen, and Others

Volume 1: Beware the Kitten Holy
ISBN: 978-1-60886-687-8 | $14.99 US

Volume 2: Friendship to the Max
ISBN: 978-1-60886-737-0 | $14.99 US

Volume 3: A Terrible Plan
ISBN: 978-1-60886-803-2 | $14.99 US

Volume 4: Out of Time
ISBN: 978-1-60886-860-5 | $14.99 US

Volume 5: Band Together
ISBN: 978-1-60886-919-0 | $14.99 US

Giant Days
John Allison, Lissa Treiman, Max Sarin

Volume 1
ISBN: 978-1-60886-789-9 | $9.99 US

Volume 2
ISBN: 978-1-60886-804-9 | $14.99 US

Volume 3
ISBN: 978-1-60886-851-3 | $14.99 US

Jonesy
Sam Humphries, Caitlin Rose Boyle

Volume 1
ISBN: 978-1-60886-883-4 | $9.99 US

Volume 2
ISBN: 978-1-60886-999-2 | $14.99 US

Slam!
Pamela Ribon, Veronica Fish, Brittany Peer

Volume 1
ISBN: 978-1-68415-004-5 | $14.99 US

Goldie Vance
Hope Larson, Brittney Williams

Volume 1
ISBN: 978-1-60886-898-8 | $9.99 US

Volume 2
ISBN: 978-1-60886-974-9 | $14.99 US

The Backstagers
James Tynion IV, Rian Sygh

Volume 1
ISBN: 978-1-60886-993-0 | $14.99 US

Tyson Hesse's Diesel: Ignition
Tyson Hesse

ISBN: 978-1-60886-907-7 | $14.99 US

Coady & The Creepies
Liz Prince, Amanda Kirk, Hannah Fisher

ISBN: 978-1-68415-029-8 | $14.99 US

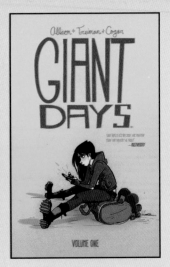

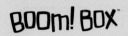